TRICKS
of
FORTUNE

TRICKS
of
FORTUNE

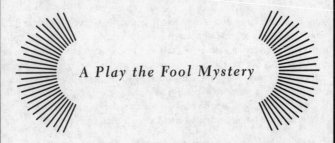

A Play the Fool Mystery

LINA CHERN

BANTAM

NEW YORK

Bantam Books
An imprint of Random House
A division of Penguin Random House LLC
1745 Broadway, New York, NY 10019
randomhousebooks.com
penguinrandomhouse.com

A Bantam Books Trade Paperback Original

ISBN 978-0-593-50068-2
Ebook ISBN 978-0-593-50069-9

Printed in the United States of America on acid-free paper

1st Printing

Production editor: Loren Noveck • Managing editor: Saige Francis
Production manager: Sam Wetzler • Copy editor: Sheryl Rapée-Adams
Proofreaders: Deborah Bader, Catherine Sangermano, and Robin Slutzky

Title-page art: Natalya Nepran/Adobe Stock

Book design by Sara Bereta

The authorized representative in the EU for product safety and compliance is Penguin Random House Ireland, Morrison Chambers, 32 Nassau Street, Dublin D02 YH68, Ireland, https://eu-contact.penguin.ie.

In memory of Vladimir Chern

1946–2022

TRICKS
of
FORTUNE

1

The day Gina was arrested for murder, we were celebrating one year since I had opened my tarot card reading room.

Technically, it wasn't "my" reading room. I was using my sister Jessie's former office at the Lake Terrace Estates outdoor shopping plaza, in return for doing her real-estate ding-dong work.

And it wasn't really a "reading room," since I spent more time stapling pictures of Jessie's face onto other pictures of Jessie's face than I did reading cards.

Also, I hadn't "opened" the business myself. Gina had opened it for me.

But hey, one whole year!

Gina surprised me (scared the shit out of me) that day by leaping through the front door with a bundle of takeout bags from Kabob's Your Uncle, the Mediterranean place next door where everyone was always high.

"Surprise!" The electronic doorbell chimed. Gina struck a saucy pose in the doorway. I dropped a fat black magic marker and splashed a zigzag across one of Jessie's glossy catalog head-shots. She looked like an angry zebra.

I retrieved and capped the marker. "What are you doing here?"

Gina swept off her *Breakfast at Tiffany's* sunglasses and tossed them into a dish that looked like an alien ship. "It's your anniversary! Did you think I'd forget?"

"No? Yes?" I waved her to the low burnished metal coffee table in the reception area. "This is the first time you've been here, so I'm not sure what the right answer is."

"Yeah, you know." Gina sat down and started unloading steaming Styrofoam containers. "I should have come earlier. I just didn't want to show up without warning."

Without warning was the only way Gina ever showed up and sometimes she pretended to feel bad about it. It was fine with me. I was never doing anything more interesting. I last saw her on Christmas, when she had rescued me from the tail end of a bloated family thing by texting me the address of a grungy indoor amusement park on the North Side. It had been shut down to make way for a new Chuck E. Cheese, but Gina knew the security guard. She always knew someone. He opened the place up and we spent the night playing ancient arcade games in the empty jangling hall and riding rickety roller coasters while snow fell outside in thick silence. It was the best Christmas I'd had since I was a kid and actually looked forward to the holiday.

We tore into the meat skewers and baba ghanouj, unwrapping half-moon foil packets of warm pita. Outside, pink and white Valentine hearts had, right on schedule, replaced evergreen wreaths in store windows, and had themselves been supplanted by an invasion of shamrocks and leprechauns. The plaza was a ring of brick storefronts covered with bright, loopy writing like a whimsical crayon scribble, with a central courtyard full of benches painted in optimistic colors perched on bright green turf. An outdoor fireplace was lit every morning in the hopes that someone might enjoy a ten-dollar gourmet hot chocolate in front of it but I never saw anyone out there, although the parking lot was always choked with cars. No one ever walked the quaint cobblestone walks. People drove up, ducked into Whole Foods or Nordstrom Rack, got back in their cars, and left, heads down, no looking around, always moving on to the next thing. The idea was to make people think they lived in a small town where you walked to everything, instead of a flat suburban expanse where everything was a twenty-minute drive from everything else.

"I like this." Gina angled her long legs between the low couch and the floor and looked around the room. She was rocking long raven-black hair, flared jeans, and a T-shirt advertising either a punk band or a physically demanding sex act. She looked like a nineties indie-pop superstar on a reunion tour. Gina frowned at a looming wall cabinet with drawers like metal jaws. "Is that where you crush the Terminators?"

"This is Jessie's old office," I said. The wide, airy room looked like a cross between a fusion restaurant and a factory floor. Slabs of metal covered the walls, pendant lamps clawed their way off the mile-high ceiling, and giant intestine-shaped vases popped out of every corner. The walls offered threatening motivational messages: EAT, SLEEP, SELL, REPEAT and TODAY IS THAT DAY. "I should redecorate. Make it more me."

"I don't know," she said. "I can see you here."

"Is it the stylish professional atmosphere?" I held up a decorative bowl. "Or the potpourri that looks like dried human ears?"

"The plaza is quite fancy, too," Gina said. "If I ever need both recreational cosmetic surgery *and* gourmet dog ice cream, I know where to go."

"Definitely a step up from the Deerpath Shopping Center," I said. Gina and I met a few years ago when we were both working at the old run-down mall across town. She had sort of a slacker goth queen thing going on back then, and I was still getting used to this sleeker, more grown-up Gina, like an actor you only see in bloated superhero epics who pivots suddenly to sensitive indie romcoms. Either way, you never forgot for a second you were watching a movie.

"Well, congrats." Gina crossed her lace-up boots and raised a mint-tea toast. "Sorry I didn't make it out here sooner."

I waved it off. Being friends with Gina was a skill I'd had to learn, like a reverse Morse code composed primarily of pauses and silences. *What do you see in that woman?* Jessie complained. *She's a flake.* It was the worst insult in my sister's extensive dictionary of them. Gina wasn't a flake, not really. Sure, if you did the math, her absences far outnumbered her presences. (*The quality is there*, Jessie would say, *but we need to bring that quantity up.*) When Gina was present, though, she was *present*, like a thunderbolt in a blue sky. It was Gina who had encouraged me to keep reading the cards when my family and everyone else I knew dismissed it as a silly hobby or a mental aberration. As *flakiness*. It was Gina who had told me to quit whining and believe the right thing would come along. And it was Gina who had started the card-reading business behind my back because she had surmised, correctly, that I wouldn't have the balls to do it myself.

"You get a lot of walk-ins here?" Gina said. Jessie had pushed hard to put a BY APPOINTMENT ONLY sign on the front door to make my place look more exclusive, like a life-coaching or therapy center, but I had talked her out of it. I wanted to run a place where you walked in and got help when you needed it. No appointments, no forms to fill out. Just come in and get help. Have a cup of tea while you're at it. Jessie had grumbled but backed off and now the front door read simply OUT OF THE BLUE

CONSULTATIONS in a prissy font you would expect to say *It's Wine O'Clock!*

"If by *walk-in* you mean *drive by at high speed going somewhere else,* then yeah, tons," I said. "A mom and daughter came in this morning." The mom had gushed about mom-and-daughter time and then played with her phone through the entire reading. "Had a bachelorette party last week. Most of my clients come from Jessie, though. She lines up trade shows, art fairs." I dipped a wedge of pita into the hummus. "I did a corporate team-building seminar. They needed to make some stupid point about the dangers of predictive thinking. They were like, see what she's doing? Don't do that."

Gina attacked a piece of dolma. "Corporate waste is the best."

"She's kind of like my business manager," I said. "Turns out the way to stop hating her for trying to control my life is to put her in a position where that's her actual job."

"So she sets up gigs for you and in return you do her shit work?"

"I stuff a mean envelope." I squashed the tiny seedling of complaint breaking through the dirt in my mind. "She keeps hiring these young whippersnappers who soak her for everything she knows and then ditch her for a competitor." I jabbed a couple of thumbs at myself. "She needs an assistant with zero interest in real estate, and even less career motivation."

Gina chewed and nodded. "So, you're happy?"

I shrugged. "I could still be at the other mall, so, could be worse." The job I was working when I met Gina was the latest in a string of shitty jobs I'd either gotten fired from or that had otherwise ended in some spectacular humiliation.

Gina whipped a slice of pita at me, hard. It bounced off my forehead and plopped onto the table, upending a cup of tzatziki.

I picked crumbs out of my eye. "What is your problem?"

Gina laced her fingers and waited for me to arrive at a bullshit-free answer to her question.

I moved a plastic knife slowly through the hummus, making waves. I could slide into this vast hummus ocean, I thought, swim away, and live forever on a hummus island where I never had to answer the deceptively simple question of whether or not I was happy.

"It's good," I said. "It's just, dressing up like Madame von Freakshow so I can tell some drunk VP of sales if he'll score at the hotel bar that night is not what I had in mind. I want to solve a real problem for someone. Something only I can help with. A problem they've taken to everyone, that no one knows what to do with." I felt like an asshole saying this. I wouldn't be here if it weren't for Gina—and for Jessie. At least I could call myself a professional tarot card reader. Wasn't that enough?

"Well." Gina wrapped the leftover pita in a piece of tinfoil. "I need help." She smacked her fist on the table. The tzatziki fell over again. "Finish stuffing your face and then read the cards for me."

"You're just being nice."

"You take that back. You think I don't have problems? My dog died. My husband is cheating on me."

"You don't have a dog and you're not married."

"More problems. Just don't do one of those giant readings where you paper the walls with cards and it takes four hours."

We cleared the table and I slid the cards out of their red velvet bag. I had never read for Gina before. She wasn't a snob about it, and she was all in favor of me doing what I wanted to do, but she was jittery about letting her guard down and cagey about her past. I only saw the flashes she occasionally showed me, and they rarely came together into any cohesive picture. She was either a tarot card reader's best dream or their worst nightmare.

"I could teach you to read," I said, shuffling. Normally I asked the querent to focus on their problem so I could read the clues their body put out while their mind worked. With Gina I had to do the opposite: distract her from anything important so it could sneak out. Chatter, keep things light. "You'd be amazing. You'd be a legend, like that old Puerto Rican dude on TV. People would make you kiss their babies."

"First of all, gross," Gina said. "And second of all, I'd have to smack some fools up. People are too goddamn dumb to see what's right in front of them."

I shuffled one last time, cut the deck, and drew the first card: the Queen of Wands.

Gina splayed out on the blocky couch, trying to squeeze some comfort out of furniture that refused to give it. "Who's this?" she said.

I looked at the queen's pale, angular face. No makeup, no jewelry, no nonsense. Wand at her side, all motivation and organization.

"Someone you worked with," I said. "A leader. Someone with some pull."

"A woman?" I watched Gina's mind whir through the possibilities.

"Not necessarily. It's someone you don't see anymore." Pure speculation. Gina never kept anyone in her life for long. "But someone you still think about."

Gina's eyes went soft. I waited for her mind to settle on a target, then hit her again to keep her from thinking too much. "That's the point, you know."

Gina looked up, glassy. "Of what?"

"You're not meant to see what's right in front of you. You can't read a story from the inside. You need a reader."

Gina grinned. "What if the reader is part of the story?"

"Plot twist." I picked up the deck. "The reader becomes the read . . . ed? The rad?" I slid out the next card. "The Moon."

Gina leaned over the card. "This is a big one. Right? One of the big ones? The Major . . ."

"Major Arcana." The Moon's face was unreadable and wild, like an animal's. "The Moon is about hidden things." A cheap textbook read, no nuance. I was stalling, waiting for a reaction to scroll across her face. "Illusions. Secrets. Hidden danger. Dishonesty."

Gina snorted. "That's just Tuesday for me." Gina did this sort of mercenary informant / detective / PI thing that weaved back and forth over the line of legality and routinely required her to act, lie, pretend, and go after people doing the same, everyone trying to fuck everyone else into slipping up. Licenses? Accreditations? Pshaw. All she had under her belt were a chunk of years as a sworn cop and a slew of contacts in law enforcement who relied on her flexible relationship with the law and her otherworldly talent at impersonating shit balls. Basically, she got hired to do stuff real cops and Feds would get in trouble doing themselves. She never lacked for work.

The creepy-crawlies in the Moon card dragged themselves out of the water, reaching for their cool celestial boss. Emerging secrets. That was it—that's what I was missing. Gina *expected* secrets, lived them . . . but this was different, this was something she wouldn't see coming. Something that would knock her out of orbit.

"Whoever this is"—I pointed at the Queen of Wands—"is hiding something that has to do with you. Something you don't see coming."

"Ooh!" Gina gave a delighted shiver. "Sounds bad!"

"Cards aren't good or bad," I said. "It's all context."

Clouds rolled over the pale sun in the corner of the window and everything went blue. I flipped over the next card:

The Tower. "Oh, shit," I said before I could stop myself.

Gina leaned over the card, its pale prison tower like a thin face with three black eyes, enveloped in flames from a bolt of annihilating fortune. Ruined figures twisted through the black air. "This one looks, how do I say this? Bad."

I peered into the pitch-black wall of the card. Most cards were organized in layers. You could move and move into the background and keep finding something new, secret mountains and lakes, animals, flowers, meaning after meaning. The Tower had no layers, no background, only darkness. *Click-click-click*, the slot machine in my brain rolled up. The story of the three cards fell into place.

"Someone from your past will reappear," I said, "with a secret that destroys you."

Outside, a Lake County Sheriff squad car wheeled, too fast, onto the line between two spaces. A young blond cop in amber aviators hopped out. Two other cops squeezed out of the back.

A flash spiked inside me, like a lightbulb burning out. Even before Sunglasses checked his phone, looked around for my storefront, and tipped the others a nod, I knew they were headed this way.

Here it comes, I wanted to say, *the Tower*. There was a graphic I had seen during the last solar eclipse, a thin blade of shadow slicing the country diagonally from the southwest. I had wondered then if the people in its path could sense the slow creep of darkness moving toward them.

The bell rang and now the cops were inside. The lead swept his sunglasses off. He was watching himself do it. In his mind, he was the star of a show where people were always sweeping sunglasses on and off.

Gina turned to the door. "Sergeant Kaluza." Cool voice, blank face. "What a pleasant surprise."

"It's Commander, actually," Kaluza boomed. His voice was too loud for the room.

"Commander, huh?" Gina raised an eyebrow. "What are you commanding these days?"

"The murder investigation of Lieutenant Matthew Peterson." Kaluza planted his hands on his wide hips. They locked eyes. "You mean, you haven't heard?" Kaluza's lips curled. *Don't bullshit me, sweetheart.* He looked like a guy who missed calling women sweetheart.

Danger lights clicked on, one by one, inside me. I leaped out of my armchair. My thighs made a gluey unsticking noise. "Someone killed Officer Pete?" I said. "Who?"

"That's what we're here to find out." Kaluza stepped toward me with his hand out. Steel handshake, wet cardboard smile. "Commander Dan Kaluza, Lake County Sheriff's Office. How you doing."

"Yeah, okay," I said. "Katie True. Um. Out of the Blue Consultations."

Kaluza was still shaking my hand like it was a wet dog he was trying to towel off before it tracked mud in the house. "Katie True, Katie True." He tilted his head. "Where have I heard that name?"

I extricated myself and snatched up my phone, pulled up a search. There it was, top of the page, a news story. The video was paused on a familiar head of a cop in uniform, thin face with a platform of fuzz on top. I hit play.

"Far-north suburban Sandhill Lake was rocked by tragedy this morning," a grim voiceover said, "when veteran police officer Matthew Peterson was gunned down at the start of what should have been a typical shift."

I stared at the photo. I'd seen the face in hundreds of pictures, videos, websites, and plenty of times in person, but for a second I didn't recognize it. A queasy unfamiliarity stole over everything I looked at, like a blast of reverse déjà vu: the white shining wood of the table, the sand swirl walls, the creeping vine pattern on the back of the cards. Everything swayed and rippled like water that something dark and shapeless was sliding through.

"Peterson was three weeks away from a well-deserved retirement. He began his law enforcement career over thirty years ago," the reporter went on, "and quickly established himself as a fierce and tireless servant of the community he loved."

Here it comes, I thought, and a split second before the next photo cycled onto the screen, I saw it in my mind—every line, every curve—the way you know what you'll see when you step up to a mirror.

In the photo, a lanky young Peterson raced through a wide road choked with cars. It was an off-kilter shot taken by a quick-thinking amateur, one that got picked up by every area newspaper and reprinted hundreds of times. There was motion in it, speed, chaos. You could almost feel the young cop's heartbeat powering the scene like a shaking generator. A plume of icy breath haloed around him. In his arms was a tiny blood-soaked bundle.

"That's it." Kaluza's voice cut through the news audio. He snapped his fingers. "You're the baby."

My insides lurched like they were being sucked through a hole in my center.

"Every time I see that picture I think, gosh, how old is that baby now?" Kaluza watched me but his eyes were glassy, like he was still looking at a picture and not a human being. "How old are you?"

"Twenty-nine." I turned back to the picture on my phone.

You couldn't see the baby in the picture. Only its blood staining the blanket, the seconds of its tiny life ticking away. "I'm twenty-nine."

"Well!" Kaluza said. "I'm in the presence of greatness."

"Gina, what's happening?" I said, but Kaluza was already talking.

"Regina Dio." His voice was higher now, louder. For the cameras. "You're under arrest on suspicion of involvement in the murder of Lieutenant Matthew Peterson, Senior."

Gina unraveled herself from the couch and rose to her feet. She did not look at me. If you get arrested, she always said, shut the hell up. Say nothing, not even I have to go to the bathroom, because it will come back on you. Everything always comes back on you.

Kaluza reached for her elbow but she shook him off. Everyone moved toward the door.

"Katie True," Kaluza said. "Isn't that something." He pulled the door open and the bell chimed again like it was announcing the end of something, or maybe the beginning. "What a blast from the past."

2

You can think of the Major Arcana as a road, my aunt Rosie used to say, a dusty desert highway through life, dotted with signposts that run together to make a story, like the old Burma-Shave ads that used to dot the highways. It's the oldest story in the world, Rosie liked to say, and everybody's favorite because they get to make it about themselves.

"See the little numbers on top? They go in order." Rosie set her bowl of Cheetos on my mom's pristine white couch and picked up the TV remote. The bowl wobbled like a top. Rosie put down the remote and made the bowl wobble again. And then again. I could see she'd taken her afternoon medicine. An array of incompatible snacks littered the low polished-wood coffee table: cheese cubes poking out of a plastic-wrapped tray, an open carton of milk, a can of orange Fanta, and a box of gluten-free crackers nabbed from my mom's DO NOT EAT pantry shelf. I asked Rosie once what the medicine was supposed to cure, and she said, "Closed-mindedness," then snorted and stuffed her face with Reese's Pieces.

I scratched a bare leg against the itchy carpeting of my parents' basement rec room. We were on week two of Rosie's latest impromptu visit. The llama farm where she was working had gone tits up when its owner got hauled in for investment fraud. Rosie's life road consisted almost entirely of detours. Later, when I was in high school, she would split for the West Coast and never come back. These days I still received the occasional postcard from some sunbaked state. The last one cut off in mid-sentence and also seemed perfectly complete.

"So, you put them in a row?" I slid the cards around, pieces of a puzzle where the picture kept changing. Once it had hit me, early on in Rosie's lessons, that the cards meant something different depending on who was looking, their dazzling infinity lit up my mind with a nuclear flash. They felt alive to me, like people or movie stars, but better, because you could make any movie you wanted out of them.

"Three rows." Rosie ran her fingers up and down slowly over the rubber buttons of the remote control. She was a slight, jittery woman partial to wispy embroidered tops and torn jeans, blowy hair cut in a strawberry blond shag. She always ran a little hot, a little out of sync with the world because it didn't move fast enough for her. I adored her visits, although she didn't so much spend time with me as let me accompany her on her haphazard bounce through her days. I liked medicine days the best. She got slow and dreamy then, and it was the best time to ask her about the cards.

"Want to get out of here?" Rosie said. "Let's go get some donuts." She tossed the remote on the coffee table and chewed her lip. "Or some oysters. You got any money?"

"I'm eight," I said. "Anyway, this is supposed to be *educationally focused downtime*." Rosie was always offering to pitch in around the house in return for using us as her personal airstrip any time she crash-landed, but since she tended to wander off and leave a trail of wet laundry and crusty dishes, my mom limited her "pitching in" to the occasional afternoon of spectacularly half-assed babysitting. It was the equivalent of giving a toddler a toy hammer so they can "help" smash up cardboard boxes while you put the cabinet together yourself.

"Ooh!" An old sci-fi movie clicked onto the screen. Jumbly misshapen spaceships drifted through space to booming classical music. "You seen this yet? It's trippy." She stuffed a handful of Cheetos into her mouth and waved vaguely at the movie. "It's science," she mumbled, misting the air with orange dust. On TV, the spaceship was dazzling white inside, and dead silent. Nothing was happening, but it was a slow, hypnotic nothing, joyful and grand.

"Wait a minute." I sat up and scratched my knee. "There's twenty-two cards. They don't go into three rows."

"Ah." Rosie dragged her eyes off the screen. "That's because of the Fool. He's special." She moved the mountain of snacks aside and patted the couch. I scooped up the cards and hopped up next to her. She laid out the rows on the coffee table and placed the Fool over all of them.

"He's part of the road, but he's also outside it." She tapped the card with a midnight blue fingernail, silver grains scattered across it like stars. "He's the zero. He's nothing. Like a baby. But here's the thing." She picked up the Fool and twirled him. He leaped to life like a jerky old film where you could see the trick behind the magic, but it didn't matter, didn't make it any less real. "It's the kind of nothing that's also everything."

She squinted past the Fool at the TV screen. Stars and planets slipped into place behind him, a dark, brilliant knife-blade dance.

"When you're at the beginning," Rosie said, "you can go anywhere."

3

The last thing I saw before I died was the mountain range, like a line of jagged script I couldn't read. A clue I had, as usual, misread until it was too late. The peaks glowed like hot knives.

I lurched awake. The red glow settled into the rooftop neon sign for Chicago Asian Foods. I could see its back edge through my bedroom window.

I kicked off the sweaty sheets and sat up in bed. A dreamlike logic still gripped me: if Officer Pete was there at the beginning of the road for me—at Fool time, Rosie would have said—did that mean I was about to die?

I stumbled out of the bedroom and snapped the kitchen light on; 3:02 A.M. read the microwave clock. I filled the beat-up tea-kettle I'd rescued from Mrs. Ortiz's trash last year and plunked myself onto the lumpy blanket covering the couch. You couldn't see the neon sign from here, only its glow setting the patio cur-tains on fire.

I lived on Route 60 in an east Lake Terrace apartment complex, a bulky, nondescript 1980s-built brown-and-black box. Any passersby probably wondered, before the place disappeared from their mind, what kind of a weirdo would choose to live between the twin sensory assaults of the Metra tracks on one side and the constant retail chaos of Chicago Asian Foods on the other. The answer was me, I was the weirdo. All my neighbors had turned over around me multiple times and at this point I was here only out of sheer laziness.

Officer Pete had been dead for three days. Gina had been who knows where for three days: Jail? Home? I hadn't heard from her since Kaluza and his shadows led her out of my store. The commander had shot me an oily *Have a nice day*, but Gina just glided out. She didn't look at me or say anything. Not *You believe this shit?* Not *Pick me up at the station in an hour.*

And especially not *I didn't do this.*

I shifted on the couch, trying to get the pokey blanket to behave. I had spent the last three days in a stunned wobble from one news report to the next, waiting, like everyone, for answers. By now I could recite the official story by heart: 8 A.M. Tuesday, Sandhill Lake police lieutenant Matthew Peterson, Sr., had radioed that he was checking out an old cement factory out in the northern reaches of town. He called in a suspicious person lurking on the premises and said he was following them into the swampy area behind the industrial complex. He turned down an offer of backup. Minutes later, dispatch radioed him for an update and got only static. When backup got to his location, he was dead.

The news outlets, in the absence of any actual news, churned out an increasingly hysterical slew of tributes to Officer Pete's legacy—tearful interviews with fellow cops, citizens whose lives he'd touched, kids he'd inspired to follow in his footsteps. Every story eventually spun back to its starting point: the thirty-year-old picture of Officer Pete saving the dying baby.

Me.

"And now he's dead," I said aloud. The words sounded mousy and comical, like a tasteless joke.

"Who's dead?" the blanket said.

I bounced to my feet. The blanket sat up and sprouted a face. No wonder I couldn't get comfortable—I'd been perched on the bony protuberances that served my brother, Owen, as feet. He used to sneak into my room when we were kids and fall asleep in the closet or in the toy chest or squeezed under the bed, and the habit had continued unchecked into the half-assed version of functional adulthood he now occupied. He had his own apartment and bed and postgraduate slot in a university genetics research department, but still tended toward jack-in-the-box-like appearances in my apartment.

I shoved Owen's feet out of the way and sat back down. "How long have you been here?"

Owen wrapped himself in a blanket hood, all face and shining marble eyes. He looked like E.T. "Hours," he said. This meant nothing. Owen's sense of time was notoriously unreliable. "You were talking in your sleep."

"I was? Did I say anything interesting?"

Owen squished up his face against the kitchen light. "Also you were making noises. Like a hiccup crossed with a snort." He fished around for his glasses and stuffed them onto his face. "Would you like to hear it?"

"Very kind, but, no, thanks." I got up to check the kettle, which had started whooshing encouragingly.

Owen sat up and I saw a flash of pale skin. "Please tell me you are wearing clothes." Clothes had remained for Owen, since childhood, firmly optional. My mom had to order him "big kid" onesies from a specialty online retailer well into middle school to keep him from stripping down in public. "Please tell me there is fabric between you and that blanket."

"Who's dead?" Owen said. "You said someone was dead."

"Officer Pete."

"The guy from the scrapbook?"

My mom had a clip of the original news story with the snapshot of Peterson racing me on foot toward an ambulance stuck in rush-hour traffic. It played lead in a fat scrapbook full of other news clippings, snapshots, and memorabilia of the incident, which was big news at the time and for years later, kept alive in feel-good, where-are-they-now annual follow-ups until everyone stopped caring.

Everyone except my family. *You almost died. We almost lost you. You wouldn't be here if it weren't for him:* variations on a theme, the endless background track to my family's elevation of the accident to near-magical status. Proof positive that I was Special, meant for Great Things. My childhood was full of their energetic attempts to excavate said specialness by means of piano lessons, art classes, swim team tryouts, Girl Scouts, immersive language retreats . . . an endless search for any proof at all that Fate, having sent Officer Pete into my path, hadn't made a clerical error.

But the classes were always too fast, too loud, too busy, too much. I lost my swim cap (twice). I broke three of the expensive art pencils, ruining the set. I forgot to read the instructions. I didn't practice enough. I just wanted to stay home and doodle or read or lie in bed staring into space (*wasting time*, the worst of all offenses against potential greatness). My parents were at first bewildered and then resigned, and then they were having trouble finding the right meds for Jessie, and then Owen embarked on a highly individualistic path through his developmental milestones, and everyone sort of forgot, thank fuck, that I was supposed to be special.

The accident was swallowed up in family lore, but the scrapbook stayed on the fireplace. It was still there to this day. I never figured out what goal it was supposed to represent, only that I had missed it.

"Yup," I said to Owen. "The guy from the scrapbook."

"He's dead?"

"He died three days ago." I opened the cupboard to see if there were any clean mugs. "It's all over the news. Where have you been?"

"It's midterms," Owen said. "I'm student-teaching undergrad bio and I have to read fifty-three papers comparing and contrasting prokaryotic and eukaryotic cells."

"Yikes," I said. "I'm sorry."

"What are you talking about?" Owen said. "Some of these papers really nail the essential difference between these two equally fascinating evolutionary mechanisms." He rewrapped himself like a burrito. "Who killed him?"

"The entire law enforcement community of Northern Illinois shares your curiosity." There was one normal mug and one hot-pink travel mug labeled THE QUEEN DEMANDETH CAFFEEN. I tossed a tea bag in each. "So far they have squat."

I checked the microwave clock again. Too late to text Jamie? He wouldn't be sleeping either.

Jamie was a Lake Terrace cop. Normally this wouldn't qualify him to work a homicide four towns over, but since Lake County was not exactly a murder hot spot, none of its tiny suburban PDs was staffed to handle anything more complex than shoplifting teens and impatient parents sneaking illegal lefts out of the elementary school parking lot. Whenever anything big went down, an ad hoc homicide team got put together behind closed doors and along countywide whisper networks. Jamie had been a serious homicide detective in his native L.A., and, despite being newish to the area, quickly built a reputation for knowing his shit. Any time there was a murder anywhere in the county, he got pulled off his patrol shift at Lake Terrace to work eighteen-hour days, living on HoHos and shitty police station coffee. I never saw him happier.

This time I hadn't seen him at all. He hadn't been home since the callout three days ago. I was stuck watching the useless news and badgering Jamie for text updates, many of which actually went unanswered. This was unheard of. Jamie told me once it made him physically ill not to answer correspondence, even if he had nothing to say. Things must have been dire indeed.

"They've arrested Gina for it." I watched the tea drift outward, turning the water cloudy and dark. "Or 'in connection' with it, whatever that means. She was at the shop with me, and this asshat with important hair waltzed in and took her away. I haven't heard from her since. She won't answer my calls or texts."

Owen's shiny eyes went wide. He popped up, tossed the blanket aside, and started pacing in front of the couch. As I suspected, he was in his underwear. His skin was so pale it shone. He looked like a deep-sea octopus out for a stroll from under his rock.

"Owen." I rubbed my face. "Underwear does not count as clothes."

Owen rounded the coffee table but did not, thank God, move into the well-lit kitchen. "Has Gina ever killed anyone?"

I was glad he didn't ask the other question: did I think she did it? Not that the one he did ask was any easier to answer. Gina and Jamie said they got that one all the time from *curious civilians* (Jamie) and *cop fuckers* (Gina). They both treated it with an implied eye roll, although I suspected their reasons for chafing at it—like everything else about the two of them—were polar opposites.

"I don't know." I'd never asked Gina because I knew she'd give me the same cheerful fuckery she used to deflect all questions about her former career. She had never mentioned even knowing Officer Pete, although I'd told her the story of my accident countless times. And yet they must have been linked firmly enough that the commander and his minions went to her first, chased her down in the middle of the day like a fugitive.

It hit me again how patchy my knowledge of Gina's past was, though I considered her my best friend. She was like the firebird tattoo on her bicep—an insubstantial whole composed of even more insubstantial elements: fire and shadow. Just when you thought you saw its true shape, it shifted, slipped away, disappeared. I had accepted this as a condition of our friendship.

"Are you going to help her?" Only Owen could get away with this kind of bald-faced directness.

Was I going to help her?

She hadn't said a word to me on the way out to the commander's squad car, but just before she got in, she turned back to the window. I knew she couldn't see me, but a chill tore through me all the same. The look on her face was like a wall painted over so many times you forgot what was underneath. I had seen that look on her face before, and I knew what it meant: *I need help, but I'll die before I ask for it.*

I never thought it would be an actual matter of life and death.

"I *have* to help her." I picked up the cups, stuffed a package of jelly-filled Polish gingerbread cookies in the fold under my chin, and came to the coffee table. Owen sat up as I put his cup in front of him.

"This might sound weird," I said, "but I never pictured him dying."

Owen stuffed an entire cookie into his face. His cheeks ballooned like a beaver's. "Why would you?" he mumbled.

"No, I mean I pictured him *never dying*." Peterson's face in the picture, frozen forever at the moment of his highest glory. "Like he wasn't moving through time like the rest of us."

Owen picked up his cup and the steam rolled over his face like a curtain. He looked like the Wizard of Oz when everyone still thinks he's magical and can make all their problems go away. "The faster you move through space, the slower you move through time, and vice versa," Owen said. "But you're always moving."

He gave me a cookie-filled grin. "No one ever stands still."

4

The cards were on the low mahogany coffee table now, laid out in three rows like Rosie told me. The Fool lorded over the pyramid from his mountaintop, ready to plunge to his doom or take off for the stars.

"So how does it work, this road thing?" I nudged Rosie. "You spend a little time at each card and that's your life?"

Rosie had drifted off, staring at the movie. I thought she was sleeping, but then her eyes blinked slowly, like a lizard's. On the screen, two stone-faced astronauts with old-fashioned slicked-back hair were talking in weird flat voices. Were they robots? They were heading out on some very important exploratory mission in the far reaches of the solar system.

"Sort of." Rosie dragged her attention away from the screen. "But before you take a trip, you have to prepare, right?" She snorted. "Otherwise you run out of food and money by your second day and then all of a sudden you're in Butthole, Alabama, hitching a ride in the back of a refrigerated truck."

I blinked at her.

Rosie sat up and tripped across the cards with her long, smooth fingers. "What do you notice about these two?" She pointed to the Magician, first in the first row, and the High Priestess, next in line.

I leaned in to look. The Magician wore a red robe on a stark yellow background. Flowered vines wreathed him. A staff in his right arm, tall and straight: a candle, or a weapon. A strange twisting symbol floated over his head. On the table in front of him, a coin, a chalice, a staff, and a sword. He was hot, bright, active, alive.

Next to him, in cool blues and grays, the High Priestess wore a robe the color of the horizon, where sky meets water. She sat still between two pillars, one black, one white. Behind her was either a tapestry or a portal into a jungle twisting with mysterious seeded fruit, a tangle of vines you could get lost in and disappear forever. I closed my eyes, one at a time, bouncing back and forth between them. The two cards jumped, mirror images of each other.

"They're opposites?" I said.

"Yes!" Rosie upended the Fanta into her mouth, then crushed the can. She held the cards up for me to see. "Night and day, light and dark. He's standing, she's sitting. He's moving, she's still. They're not really stages on the road, they're a part of you as you move through the road. Make sense?"

"Nope."

Rosie raked her fingers through her bright hair. It stood up like a tiara. "Look at it this way," she said. "You know how some people are always on the go, always moving, always doing something? They've got a plan. They've always thought everything out."

Upstairs, my mom had come home from the office. I could hear her doing her usual circuit of the kitchen, late-afternoon cup of coffee in hand. Stop at the oven, check the roast. Now turn off the coffeepot so it doesn't scorch the coffee and stink up the kitchen. The same routine every day.

"People like that," Rosie said, "have a lot of this guy in them." She picked up the Magician. His enigmatic smile leaped out at me. "Look how he's standing, all upright, he's got his wand raised. He's a doer. He does things. He knows things." She tapped her forehead. "With his brain."

"How else are you going to know things?"

"Keep your pants on, I'm getting to that. Look at these." She pointed to the symbols spread out on the table in front of the Magician. "Recognize them?"

"The four suits," I said. "Of the other cards."

"That's right. Earth, air, fire, water. He's got all the elements under control. He's got everything under control."

I looked up at the screen. The astronaut, tight and square jawed, moved his hands over a console, flipping switches.

"But *doing* only gets you so far. It's only half the story. You get too much of this guy in you . . ."

My mom's voice drifted down the stairs: ". . . if his poop is soft, you're giving him too much cheese. If it's little hard balls then he's not drinking enough water. We've been over this."

"You get too much of this guy in you," Rosie repeated, putting down the handful of cheese cubes she was holding, "and things get lopsided." She side-eyed the cheese, stuffed it into her mouth anyway. "That's where she comes in." She pointed to the High Priestess. "Sometimes *not doing* is just as powerful."

"She does nothing?" I picked up the card. On the TV screen, the astronauts were biding their time, playing chess with the onboard computer, eating boxed food laid out in colorful compartments, sketching the inside of the ship's stark white surfaces. I thought of my mom, standing in the doorway to my room. *Are you just going to lie there doing nothing?* "How is that powerful?"

"Because when you stop moving, you listen and feel. You can know things with more than just your brain." She tapped the card. "The High Priestess understands things in ways that don't make sense to this guy." She pointed back to the Magician.

I understood, in a flash, what she was saying. The way I felt, a second before it happened, that Jessie was about to have one of her epic meltdowns, sending everyone running for cover. The way I knew, when my parents were extra nice to each other at breakfast, that they'd argued the night before. The way those tiny certainties appeared in my mind without having to think about them, like they'd sprung out of nowhere, out of a vast void I didn't know was there because it resisted knowledge, couldn't be arrived at that way.

Something clicked into place in my mind. The High Priestess was the void. And the guide through the void.

"Call them what you want," Rosie said. "Head and heart, sense and nonsense. Conscious, unconscious. Everybody's got a little of both, some people more of one than the other."

She watched the astronauts edge along white circular walls, sideways, upside down, weightless, and free, hurtling onward into deep space.

"You need both if you're going to walk this road. If you're going to *really* understand things."

5

The crime scene was in the white space on the map.

I set the gas pump on hands-free and dug out my phone to check the address Jamie sent me. After Owen went back to snoring on the couch, I had text-badgered Jamie into meeting me for breakfast in Sandhill Lake, close to the crime scene so he could be rid of me and back at work as soon as possible. The location dot swam in a shapeless splotch of white that crowded out the more recognizable forest green and lake blue. No crisscrossing streets, no train tracks, just a white void in the heart of town.

A limp blue helium balloon hovered over the ground next to the gas pump. I stuffed it between the pump and the post but it tumbled back down into its miserable hover, like it couldn't summon the will to plummet that final inch.

"Did you know him?" I asked the cashier in the kiosk as I was paying. We both knew who I was talking about.

"Shit." The cashier was rocking a shapeless beard and a Chicago Wolves tank. A bald eagle glowered in brown ink over his neckline. "Everybody knew him." He was sitting in a crowded cage behind smudged plexiglass. "Came in every morning like clockwork to buy his cigarettes. Then he'd hit Birdie's for breakfast." The cashier nodded toward the rambling gray-slatted diner across the street. "My son played soccer with his boy when they were kids. His son's a cop now, too, God bless him, did you know that?"

"I did." A shiver passed through me. "I do."

"And the wife has coffee over at Birdie's every Sunday," he said. "She's a little different, you know what I'm saying? But she's okay."

"Different" was what my sister and my mom called someone instead of "freak." I was fascinated immediately. Officer Pete's son I knew. Why had I never heard of Officer Pete's wife?

Outside, a truck sped by, blue and silver cans tinkling behind it. BLUE LIVES MATTER, the back window read, like a twisted JUST MARRIED sign. The balloon soared up on a gust of wind, settled again. It looked like a face someone had punched.

"Katie True, huh?" The cashier took off his ball cap and scratched at the bullseye-target bald spot on the back of his head. "That's a name. Where do I know that name from?"

"Yep, it's an unusual name." I grabbed my stuff for a quick exit and ducked at the door. "I get that all the time. Thank you! Have a nice day!"

"No, no. I never forget a name." He slammed his hat back on his head and snapped his fingers at me. "You're the baby. Yep! Officer Pete saved you from the car wreck all those years ago."

He stared at me, smiling, like he was waiting for a prize or a tip. I never knew what to say at this point. The accident story had begun to recirculate, and although not looking like a baby helped a little with anonymity, enough people still recognized my name that I was stopped a few times. They always asked me what I was doing now, and when I told them and they had no idea what to say, they talked some more about Officer Pete. I should have felt elevated by the whole thing but it just kind of made me itch. *Is this it?* people seemed to think once the initial delight and surprise wore off. *Is this how that great story ended?*

"You take care now," the cashier shouted after me as I left. Maybe he was afraid I was susceptible to car accidents.

I drove on through downtown Sandhill Lake. Every tree, every power line and telephone pole wore blue ribbons, bunting, and Mylar balloons. Every house and business, every bait shop, boating supply warehouse, and tiki bar offering Ladies Nite specials was festooned with posters and pictures of Peterson, signs expressing support, grief, disbelief. Revenge. A helicopter pounded through the sky, the third one in ten minutes.

I stopped at the light across from the town's central park. A makeshift shrine of photos, candles, flowers, teddy bears, and blue-line flags ate up the lawn at the entrance. I was surprised to find myself tear-jerked. I didn't think of Officer Pete much anymore, but the idea of him lived in my heart like a childhood lullaby, the kind buried so deep its delicate notes took your breath away when it resurfaced, put you back in the moment you first heard it. The trick Officer Pete had pulled was to make being good seem a little bit bad, a tiny fist punch against a world always trying to trip you up, drag you away from what you knew in your heart to be right. The further down the road I'd moved from that singularity where he and I collided and spun off, the more transparent his trick had seemed, like a cardboard cutout in bright, unrealistic colors. You stepped up, put your face in the hole, took a picture, and walked away to live your life. Your real life.

But . . . doesn't everyone, deep down, want to be good? Whatever "good" means?

Knight of Swords, I thought. The action hero. The rider on the big white horse. That was the story here, written in flowers and hearts and children's toys. And who was Gina in this story? *Knight of Swords, reversed.* The loose cannon, the flunky. Good Cop / Bad Cop.

The GPS nudged me into a turn I would have missed. The white space on the map turned out to be a warren of passages barely identifiable as streets, lined with silent warehouses, unmarked plants, and padlocked, fenced-off factories. A thick mist whited out buildings and cars. Overhead, the pale disk of the sun sat listless in the sky.

I inched along, following the dot, moving deeper into the gloom. Whatever the link was between Officer Pete and Gina, I needed Jamie to help me see it. A few years ago when a dead body had popped up in a dumpster in the mall where I worked, Jamie and I had crossed paths trying to figure out what happened. The case was over, but something about its energy stuck and we found ourselves trying to recapture it at every opportunity. When he was working anything big, we'd spend evenings eating greasy takeout food and pacing around whatever surface he'd strewn with case files and yellow notepads full of his tiny, eerily readable handwriting. I felt bad enabling his round-the-clock workaholism, but I knew he'd be working anyway. We shared a sort of compulsion to tease out the stories of what happened from the stories people told about it—the same thing I did when I read the cards for a stranger. One way or another, Jamie and I would both find a way to do what we did. The part we rarely said out loud was that it was nicer not to do it alone.

A squawking, chattering mess of voices and machinery rose out of the mist: The staging area of the investigation had taken over the parking lot of an abandoned school bus company. Squad cars of every stripe and agency filled the lot, plain-wrapper detective cars, sheriff's units, the Illinois State Patrol. A hulking FBI mobile command center loomed in the corner. Shiny eyes watched me from a K-9 unit—*do not approach*. Cops swarmed the place, big guys made bigger by armor and equipment until they were just eyes and black metal. Guys in suits and beige overcoats, drinking coffee out of Styrofoam cups. The place felt like a giant willful beast that tiny invaders were trying to control from the inside.

I slid in next to Jamie's unmarked Crown Victoria, got out, and slipped through the gate before anyone figured out I had no business there. No one paid me any attention.

At the end of the cracked street, a narrow passage taped off with yellow police tape swirled off into the mist between two empty buildings toward the crime scene, the wet patch of forest where Officer Pete had died. I squeezed my hands into fists, trying to warm them.

Someone was gliding toward me down the path. Jamie? I raised my hand to wave. The shape moved up and my heart took a flying leap into my throat.

It wasn't Jamie. It was Officer Pete. *No one stands still*, Owen said last night, and yet here was Officer Pete, unwounded, untouched by time and death.

The mist moved off. It wasn't Officer Pete. It was his son, Matt. He folded himself in half, slipped under the police tape, and stretched to his full height. I looked up into his face, so similar to his dad's.

"Katie True," Matt said. "It's been a long time."

6

"The first row," Rosie said, "is when you're a kid, just starting out."

It was late afternoon now, and everyone was home upstairs. My mom was working in her home office, now that she was done working in her work office. My dad was in the living room, relaxing with a designer paint catalog. Jessie was in her room reorganizing her stuffed animal collection. Owen was napping.

Rosie and I were still working through the first row of the Road of Life. In the movie, the astronauts were Jupiter-bound. They flipped switches and punched buttons on control panels. The onboard computer glowed and spoke, a soft voice with a big red eye.

"It's the world." Rosie ran her finger across the first row. "Whatever shapes you from the outside in. Like this one." She picked up the Empress, a porcelain-faced lady in a lush garden, sitting on a fire-colored throne. I could almost feel the plush softness of its velvet surfaces. She wore a loose white dress studded with crimson fruit or flowers. On her head she wore a crown of white stars.

"This is Mom," Rosie said. "Kindness, fertility, unconditional love, all that jazz."

I looked at the Empress. Her eyes were kind but I couldn't catch them, like she was watching something sad or disappointing happen off in the distance. I thought of my mom's sleek monochrome suits, her smooth hair. I knew if she caught me wandering the house, she would demand an accounting of what I was doing to fill my time. "That's my mom?"

"More like Mom with a capital M." Rosie bit into a gluten-free cracker and cringed. "The *idea* of Mom." She tossed the bitten-off cracker back into the box. "The cards are symbols, my friend. Ideas. Stories people have told each other since forever, so they tend to be kind of traditional. Reality is more flexible. Like noodles."

A dreamy look crossed her face and I knew she was thinking about noodles. I picked up the card and shook it in her face.

"It can mean someone who acts like a mom," she said. "Or it can mean a mom-type situation. Know what I mean?"

I did. The more time I spent around Rosie, the better I got at untangling the loopy cat's cradle of her thoughts. What's more, the cards had started popping up in my mind unbidden when I tried to make sense of people and what they were doing. It got to be automatic. I didn't think about it anymore, it just happened.

"The Emperor," Rosie said. Red robe, blue armor, snowy-white beard, a rough gray throne studded with the faces of some horned animal, a goat, maybe. The Empress was loose and flowy and soft. The Emperor was stiff and unyielding. He had a scowl on his face and he was joined in that scowl by the goat heads on his throne.

"Dad," Rosie said. "Or the *idea* of Dad. Discipline. Structure. Authority."

My dad was an authority on the difference between cement and concrete. If you needed an expert on mid-twentieth-century adaptations of private eye novels, he was your guy. If, on the other hand, you needed an after-school snack and some help with long division, or someone to resolve an argument over whose turn it was to take the garbage out, you were out of luck. My dad's attention was less demanding than my mom's, but also hazier. Sometimes I joined him in watching an old black-and-white movie where everyone smoked and someone got murdered in some complicated way. He liked to explain what was going on and how the director used the language of film to express it. He wasn't really talking to me, I suspected, I just happened to be there as he talked to himself. Everybody in my family, in one way or another, was always talking to themselves. I wondered if I was in the wrong family, like maybe I took a bad turn somewhere and ended up on someone else's life road.

"Is this guy a priest?" I pointed to the Hierophant. "He's got crosses all over him." The Hierophant looked a lot like the Emperor, red-robed, framed in stiff gray stone, but he had both hands up, like he was ready to deliver a speech or a tongue-lashing.

"Used to be," Rosie said. "These cards were made in Europe back when the church told you what to do and you freaking did it or else. Nowadays, this guy is more like school, the government, cops. The folks who make the rules and make sure you stick to them."

Like Officer Pete, I thought. He and Fireman Tony had just come to school last week to talk about fire safety. I loved it when Officer Pete came to school. I always wondered if he would remember me, and he always did.

"The Lovers." A man and a woman in a garden. Adam and Eve, maybe? There was a snake and an apple tree and a creepy angel with its hair on fire hovering over them. They were naked as all get-out. I giggled. "I know what this card is about."

"Get your mind out of the gutter," Rosie said. "It can be that. But it's also more. It's kind of like puberty, the first level of becoming an adult. When you start to make choices for yourself. Choices are what life is all about."

I was still staring at the two naked people. Last week when Officer Pete had come to the school, Matt came with him. He gave me a rock he and his dad had picked up on Grass Lake, polished to a smooth shine. It was sitting in my room right now, in a little velvet box that some lost piece of jewelry had come in.

Rosie swept her hand across the first row of cards. "You put all those things together and *voila!*" She pointed to the Chariot. "There you are. A nice little cog in the civilization machine. You're young, but you're not a kid. You can control yourself. You can make decisions. You're ready for the world."

The guy in the Chariot was all set to go, holding the reins on a couple of sphinxes, black-and-white mirror images of each other.

"Strap in," Rosie said. "It's time to go."

Officer Pete used to take Matt Jr. with him everywhere. When the news teams were still showing up at our house every year, Peterson always came with Matt, a bony, hyperactive preschooler with a tangled mop of blond ringlets. He would hoist the boy on his shoulders, throw him around until Matt shrieked and sprayed tears of laughter. Peterson was that dad. My dad was the dad who built the elaborate play structure in the backyard as a design exercise, then disappeared into his basement office. The first time I led Matt into our backyard, he went still, just stood there breathing. I was kind of over the playground equipment by then, but the look of greedy wonder on Matt's face made it new again, sharp and unfamiliar as the spires of an alien city. Matt took off, a quicksilver flash. *I did that*, I thought as I raced after him. *I showed him something he liked.*

I don't remember how many times they came over. More than a handful. Matt always had this golden aura around him, like an unruly cherub in an Incredible Hulk T-shirt. Small but strong and slinky, like a weasel or a cat or some sort of intelligent feral liquid. He was always the one to make up the games we played, set mostly in space or somewhere even less hospitable. I took the supporting roles, the damsel in distress, the hyperintelligent villain. The expendable sidekick. Sometimes he wanted to save me and sometimes he wanted to fight me. One time I lay motionless in the sandbox while he read a tearful eulogy over my decomposing body. It was clear he would always be author and lead of whatever we did, which was okay with me. I was just happy to appear, to be seen, however temporarily. I had this wordless certainty that our friendship would not survive past the boundary of the backyard. Matt was the kid who got picked to captain the teams in gym, and therefore to cement the social destinies of the class. I was the kid who did the complex mental math to pinpoint where the ball and therefore other people were least likely to be and go straight there. It was a skill I carried into adulthood, always crawling, like some lazy salt, toward the space with the lowest concentration of responsibility.

By the time the playdates dried up, Officer Pete was traveling the county, doing school presentations on safety and kindness and commonsense stuff kids didn't want to hear from their parents anymore. Matt came along to help out, distribute handouts, hold the microphone. Officer Pete was the coolest dad, I thought, to let Matt skip school.

Everyone loved Officer Pete's visits because they meant we all shoved, squeaky shoed, into the auditorium where Pete, in his spotless black uniform, would shout at us for an hour, making us laugh and telling us how to be kind to each other, telling us we were awesome and we were the future, until we all dissolved in a puddle of hot-faced elementary school delirium.

Every time, I wondered if this was the time Matt would pretend not to know me, if this was the time he would have moved on. But he always caught my eye, always smiled, his face split in a huge gap-toothed grin.

"You know him?" Rachel Berkowitz asked me one time in third grade. I pretended to ignore how she punched the *you*.

By the time I was in high school Officer Pete was popping up somewhere every month, no longer the whip-thin youngster in the scrapbook photo, but still deadly looking and muscular, sun-darkened arms snaked all over in faded blue ink, his trademark buzz cut ceding more and more ground to his forehead. He didn't do much lifesaving anymore; it was mostly feel-good community service–type stuff. Here he was leading a charity Harley ride for wounded veterans, or leading the Cream-a-Cop fundraiser at Lake Terrace Days, outstripping all the other cops because people lined up for his raunchy-yet-still-family-friendly insults. Here he was taking a Taser hit from a giggling rookie at the mall's Law Enforcement Expo, falling down lurching and twitching, to astonished laughter and whoops from the crowd, then hopping to his feet again: *I'm okay!* Here he was with his team of Explorers from the Sandhill Lake PD, a Scout-like group of teen cops in training.

Matt was always there. I looked for him at the mall expos, the torch runs for Special Olympics. He went from Scouts to Explorers, one uniform to another, until I couldn't remember what he'd looked like in shorts and a tee. One summer he went from a gangly cherub to a lean Thor with bright floppy hair, the kind of kid who turns heads. There was a sly wink to our conversations now, an electric charge. Undercurrents.

I saw them both for the last time the summer after my senior year, at this big regional lacrosse tournament they held every year at Sandhill Lake High School. My friends and I had free passes or something, although there wasn't a lick of interest in sports between the four of us. We were just, I figured out later, scared shitless about having to leave home in the fall and would take any excuse to get together and not talk about it.

"I am so going to miss these classic Midwestern displays of competitive patriarchy. You have no idea." Laney, at the wheel, was headed for prelaw at Columbia in the fall, specializing in civil rights. She argued with everyone and was just slightly unpleasant, like every lawyer I had ever seen on TV. We were wedged into her grandma's powder-blue gas-guzzler, one-upping one another with bitchy commentary on how much lacrosse sucked.

"Yeah, because they don't have sports or, you know, the patriarchy in New York," Dipak said.

We inched into the school parking lot through a cloud of sweet-smelling exhaust. "Gangnam Style" blasted out of somebody's open window. Up ahead, Officer Pete waved the line of cars into the lot.

"Ugh," Dipak said. "It's Kindergarten Cop." Dipak watched *A Clockwork Orange* every day after school and made creepy videos of his little brother and sister sleeping, one of which had won him a scholarship to the film school at USC.

I gave Officer Pete a small smile and hoped he would let us roll past without saying anything.

No luck. "Hey, Katie!" Peterson boomed. He was thinner now, older, but his voice was clear and strong as ever. "You excited? I think our Hawks could go all the way this year!"

"Sure could, Officer Pete." I stared at my hands so no one could see my face turn beet red. Everyone waited until we passed him to explode into snorts and guffaws.

"I keep forgetting you know him." Laney had a talent for making the most neutral observation pierce and twist like a blade.

"Hey, isn't that 2.0?" Dipak covered his eyes and peered ahead. "The son? Why does it not surprise me he does that pig-in-training thing?"

Matt wore a powder blue uniform, tall and backlit ahead of us. We locked eyes. Matt, smarter about high school social stuff than his dad, said nothing as we rolled past, but tossed me a quick hint of a smile, a small nod. *There you are.*

A bolt of electricity shook me. I pretended to shake a bug out of my hair so I could turn around. Matt was watching us.

"Hey, kids!" Laney chirped. "Who wants to be a tool of the state?" She played with her tongue ring. "Can you imagine doing exactly what your parents do? I would hang myself."

"I don't know, he's kind of cute." Ezra was the kid who never handed in an assignment all year, then aced all his finals and got straight A's anyway. He'd get ahold of something—music, sports, physics, anything—crack its underlying algorithms, figure out how to excel at it, then get bored and move on. He was taking a gap year in the fall to live on a sheep farm in Scotland while he assistant-directed *Macbeth* at a local private school.

"I'd hit that," Ezra said, looking back at Matt. "I mean, if I had to."

Laney snorted. "You dig that whole Hitler Youth thing, huh?"

"He's the Hitler Youth that finds out at the end of the movie that Jews aren't all bad," Dipak said.

I bubbled inside like someone had set me on a burner. I would ditch my friends and go find Matt. Did he want me to? The look on his face, the sharp, owlish intensity. Yes. Yes, he did. I was leaving in the fall. It was now or never. *Do something,* I shouted at myself. *For once, get off your ass and do something.*

We climbed to the top row of bleachers and spread out. Someone whipped out a bag of Doritos and a six-pack of Cokes. The game had already started. No one was watching. I searched the stands for Matt. There he was in the front row with the rest of the Explorers, parking duty over for now. He turned, swept his eyes over the stands. He was looking for me.

I counted off five jittery minutes, then got to my feet. "I need to hit those gross porta potties," I said. "If I'm not back in an hour, send help."

"Nah. We'll leave without you and forget you ever existed," Laney said without turning around.

I climbed down and swept back behind the bleachers. He was coming through the tunnel that led to the field. We walked toward each other, smiling. My head was stuffed with pink cotton candy clouds, everything too bright, too sweet, the blood pounding too loudly in my ears.

"Come on," he said. "Let's go somewhere we can hear ourselves think." His dad used to say that when the kids at the assemblies got too rowdy: *I can't hear myself think.*

We stumbled through the wet field, fast and jumbly. I ran to keep up with him and the wet grass soaked my shoes. We were both laughing, although I didn't know what was funny. I fell behind and he turned to me, smiled, held out his hand.

I took it and something happened. There was a question I'd asked my mom in middle school after a particularly informative health class. *You'll know it when you feel it* was her answer, but I had no idea she meant I would feel it *everywhere.* I was a lightbulb, a pinball machine. He glanced back at me and I knew he felt it, too.

"I'll show you the old stadium," he said. "It's pretty cool. No one goes there anymore."

The old stadium was dark and there were steps up to the crumbling announcer booth. He helped me over the rough spots. It smelled sweet and wet inside, like old wood and damp leaves. The benches were hard and the wood had split into sharp cracks, but I didn't notice. He had let go of my hand now but I could still feel him, inches away. We could see the game in the new stadium, all lit up, its blue-white glow erasing the surrounding fields, and it felt like we were watching from space, from a slow orbit. When I closed my eyes I could feel us floating through the warm dark.

"Your friends okay with you missing the game?" Matt said.

"They've already forgotten I exist." Laney's joke wasn't really a joke. My weirdo friends and I were a junk drawer, tossed together because none of us fit anywhere else. I felt cloudy and insubstantial around them, like we occupied incompatible states of matter.

Matt didn't ask me to explain. He stared across the dark at the field.

"I guess everything's about to change anyway," I said.

He turned to me. I could see his eyes but not the rest of his face. "What's about to change?"

I had no idea. It was something everyone said. Didn't things change, always? Wasn't that the one thing you could count on?

"I'm going to college, for one thing," I said. "So are all my friends." He was holding my hand again. Now he was rubbing his thumb over mine. My mind slipped sideways into a warm pool. If I didn't keep talking I would melt away. "How about you? Where are you going?"

"I'm not going anywhere," he said. "I'm staying right here." He sounded surprised there would be another option. "I'm on my last year of Explorers, then I'm doing loss prevention at Target this summer, and in the fall I'm doing an internship with Lindenhurst." Police department, I figured. "And then I take the exam."

Not a shred of doubt. I was always awash in doubt, so consumed by what people thought of what I'd just said, it was easier to say nothing.

"I don't know anyone who's going to do the same thing as their parents," I said. "That's kind of cool," I added quickly. I didn't want him to think I was making fun of him, like Laney.

"It is." Matt put his foot down, leaving a dusty footprint on the seatback. He rubbed it off with his sleeve. "What do your folks do?"

"My dad builds stuff," I said.

"Right!" He snapped his fingers. "The playground. That thing was sweet."

"I can't believe you still remember that," I said. "I don't think a career in construction is for me. I Krazy Glued my fingers together helping my dad assemble a cabinet."

Matt laughed. "You're funny."

Sure I was. He didn't need to know I wasn't kidding. "My mom is on the phone a lot." I felt bold now. "But I am actually not sure what she does, so I can't do that either."

He laughed again and I felt warm and deranged, like what I always imagined drinking alcohol might feel like.

"How about after college?" he said. "What are you going to do then?"

"I don't know." I barely knew what I would do *at* college. My friends all had a *thing*, even Ezra, who had multiple *things* but was so freakishly accomplished at all of them no one would ever dare call him flaky or unfocused. When anyone asked what I planned to major in, all I saw in front of me was a colorless blank.

Teachers said I had "potential," when they were feeling generous. When they were not, I had "initiation issues," or a little something called "laziness." I felt like we were all taking an exam and everyone else had a cheat sheet I was missing. Probably because I had showed up late when they were handing them out. As for what I wanted to be when I grew up . . . now that the flurry of childhood ambitions such as astronaut, monster hunter, and George Washington had died down, I didn't have much of an answer. My parents gave up asking. They were happy any time I made it to the school bus on time.

Matt watched me, smiling. How to explain any of this to him, sitting there in a variation of the uniform he knew he would wear for the rest of his life?

"I'll figure it out," I said. "I've got time. I think I'll benefit from a looser, less restrictive environment." That's what my guidance counselor had said, helping me pick out schools. We had settled on this tiny place downstate with fewer kids than my giant suburban high school. My parents took me to visit. The classes had only a handful of kids and they all sat in a circle on the floor and called the professors by their first names. There were grades, and some grades were better than others, I guessed, but you gave them to yourself, and they were all named for colors.

Matt watched my face. I could see him trying to understand.

"Well, what do you *like* to do?" he said. "Have you had any summer jobs or anything?"

"I had one last summer," I said. "I worked at the Renaissance Faire reading tarot cards." It was the bright spot in my year, a riot of sun, colorful clothing, delicious crappy food, fabulous freaks decked out like lusty wenches and scoundrel rogues, trading fake medieval barbs. I thought it would scare me, sitting across from someone, pretending I knew their life, but it turned out I didn't need to. I just said things until they saw their own lives more clearly. The way they looked at me, like I was magic. No one had ever looked at me like that before or since.

Matt waited for me to get to the important part, like I wasn't already there.

"My aunt taught me to read the cards when I was a kid, but I had never read for strangers before." I started talking faster, trying to get it all in before the door closed. I wanted him to see I could love things, too. I could do things, know things. "It was amazing. There was a guy . . ." Matt turned back to the stadium. I was losing him.

"Anyway," I said. "I'd like to do it again sometime." It was the first time I had ever said it out loud.

Matt had let go of me by then, but he took both my hands now. I felt movement inside me again, a rush of sensations that drifted in and out of emotion.

"Whatever you end up doing, it's going to be awesome," he said.

"You seem awful sure," I managed to breathe out.

"Of course I'm sure." He shrugged. "You're a survivor."

A shiver snaked down my neck, like a breath. I knew he was talking about the accident. Everyone talked that way about the accident, as if it were something I did instead of something that happened to me. As if that luck or fortune or whatever it was had rubbed off on me, marked me forever.

"You sound like my parents." I turned away and looked at my hands so I could look at anything but him.

"Hey." Matt reached over and took my face in his hands. His fingers felt cool and warm at the same time, or maybe all my sensations had scrambled by then into one overwhelming sizzle. "It's true. You'll know, all your life, that you got a second chance, and it's going to affect everything you do. You'll see."

A flush fanned out on the back of my neck and I believed,

sitting next to him in the dark, that he was telling the truth. Or that he thought he was. Maybe that was enough.

Matt leaned in and kissed me. The game had stopped for half-time. In the stadium someone had fired a bunch of flare guns and the sparks rose to join the stars.

7

Matt and I shuffled toward each other and stopped. We had shared a tire swing when we could still fit in one together. I had dared him to jump over the creek on his bike. I could still taste him on my lips from the last time we saw each other. And . . . his dad had just died. Did we shake hands? Kiss? High-five? Nothing seemed right.

We settled for a safe-ish hug.

"It's good to see you," he said.

"I'm so sorry, Matt." My voice was muffled by his uniform. BEACH HAVEN PD read the tag on his chest. Beach Haven was a small old town up by the Wisconsin border. There was no beach there, just a bunch of shuttered factories and a greyhound race-track. The town popped up in the news a lot and was the kind of assignment that cops either fought for or avoided like the plague.

We stepped back from each other. "Are you working the case?" I wobbled a little on my feet. The air between us was still warm.

"No, I just . . ." He looked back down the path. "I'm not even supposed to be here. I just don't know where else to go." He ran his hands through his hair. Up close, he looked like his dad only in flashes and twists, like one of those shifting holographic stickers. Officer Pete's face had a chipped hardness to it, like stone. Matt's was softer, kinder. It was the eyes. Always, since we were kids, I knew by his eyes what he was thinking.

Now his eyes looked dead. Something swam in them, like driftwood from a shipwreck. "I have to keep moving," he said. "If I stop moving, I'll start thinking, and that's never a good idea."

He shook off whatever was on his mind. "So," he said. "How long has it been?"

"Ten years?" I followed his subject change since that's what he seemed to need. "Eleven? Ever since the . . ."

"Lacrosse tournament," he said. "I remember."

I felt the warmth of the old stadium around me, the sweet vegetation smells. I'd had a lot of ideas back then about how things would turn out. Very few of them came to pass.

"I didn't know you were in town," Matt said. "You went to college and I figured you'd never be back."

"That was the plan," I said. "And you know what they say about plans." I couldn't remember exactly what they said, but plans got fucked up was the gist. I didn't feel the need to fill Matt in on the embarrassing sequence of failures unspooling behind me since the night at the stadium, starting with me dropping out of college after a year of somehow not being able to "find myself" in a place specifically designed for that purpose, and continuing on through a series of mediocre jobs that I did with mediocrity and lost in various mediocre ways.

"I had no idea." Matt smiled for the first time since coming off the path. *I did that*, I thought. *I made him smile*. "I would have looked you up."

"I wanted to look you up, too . . ." *But I was embarrassed about coming back to town so I avoided everyone I used to know*, was what I was about to say, but I opted not to sound like an asshole. Matt was always going to stay in town. He didn't see it as something to be ashamed of.

"What are you doing with yourself these days?" he said.

"Oh." I felt a sudden embarrassing itchiness. "I, um, have an office in Lake Terrace Estates."

"Wow." The prestige location impressed everyone, until I told them what I did there. "Doing what?"

"Reading tarot cards." Fuck it. Wasn't I proud? I was. Most of the time. Except all the times I wasn't. "I've had my own place for a year now." He didn't need to know every nuance of the words "own" or "place."

"Wow." His smile was spray-glossed in place. "Isn't that something."

"How's your mom handling things?" I blurted out, partly to keep from scratching myself raw and partly because I was still puzzled by the mom-ex-machina thing the eagle-tattoo guy had said at the gas station. Why had I never met Matt's mom, or even heard him mention her, when we were growing up? She never showed up at the community events. I didn't even know her name until it started popping up in the news this week: June. Who was June?

Matt looked up to watch a pair of cranes flap past on huge lazy wings. "My mom," he said. "Yeah. It's complicated." He tossed me an eye roll. "Don't you hate it when people say that? It's lazy. Like they don't want to think about the real answer."

"Hmm," I said. Everything he was saying was true and also he was stalling. I knew it and he knew I knew it. I wished we were in my office and I were reading the cards for him. The Two of Swords swam up in my mind, the blindfolded figure by the rocky shore balancing two heavy swords. Two choices, both crappy.

"They were basically divorced," Matt said. "They were just too lazy to fill out the paperwork. She was never all that supportive of his career. We don't talk much."

What was it like, I wondered, to share a private life with someone who was public property? It couldn't be easy.

"You know, my dad had that picture framed on his desk," Matt said. "You know the one."

"I know it." I felt very warm in my puffy jacket. "My mom made a whole scrapbook of newspaper clippings and pictures and stuff, about the accident." I kicked a small rock. It skittered into a crack in the concrete and stayed there. "She still has it."

"You were important to him," Matt said. My chest went tight and a sweet disorientation hit me, as if a bubble had swirled out of the past and trapped us in its golden halo. "I wanted to be like him for as long as I can remember," he said. "And now that he's gone I'm not sure that . . ."

A tear sneaked down his face and he gave it a sharp swipe with his sleeve.

"I know exactly what you mean," I said. "All my life, everyone's told me I was supposed to be somebody, because of what your dad did for me." Matt looked off to the side but I could see how intently he was listening. I wondered if he remembered he was one of the people I was talking about. "And I don't feel like I've gotten there yet." The words felt thin but sharp and true. "But maybe that's just part of being human. Having doubts."

"My dad never had doubts." He looked grave and a little disappointed, like I was not quite getting what he was saying but he appreciated the effort.

"Your dad was your dad," I said. "Did you see the park back there? In town? All the stuff people put up for him?" I pointed behind me, toward the real world outside this misty bubble. "I think people need someone like him. Even when he's not here. You know what I mean?"

His face changed, stiffened. "I do." He enfolded me in a sudden desperate hug. It felt like he wanted to swallow me, absorb me. "Thanks, Katie," he whispered. "I'm so glad I saw you today." He seemed almost sad about it.

There was a polite cough behind us. Matt let me go. I tripped over a rock.

"Hi." Jamie was standing there. I hadn't heard him come out of the mist. "Sorry I'm late," he told me, then turned to Matt. He glanced back and forth between the two of us. "Do you know each other?"

"We go back a long time," Matt said.

Something small and sharp flickered over Jamie's face and disappeared, like a pebble sinking into water. Where Matt's face was an open book, Jamie's was a secret volume in a dusty library, lost in the stacks. I was one of the privileged few he let close enough to learn his oblique system of codes and signifiers, but sometimes even I struggled.

"I've got to get back to work," Matt said. "Jamie"—he held out a hand—"great to meet you." They shook hands. "Thanks for letting me get in your way."

"Not at all," Jamie said. "I wish we had more for you. Keep in touch."

Matt gave me a final look and headed off toward his car. I had walked past his Beach Haven squad car without knowing it was his. We watched him drive off.

"I'll drive," Jamie said simply, and turned to walk back down the street toward the staging area. I hurried to catch up.

We didn't speak again until we were in his car, driving out of the white space on the map. The Metra train rumbled by and the overwhelming blue of downtown flashed all around us again. When we passed the gas station, I saw that the balloon was still there, bouncing in the wind.

"I've known Matt since I was a kid," I said. "It's kind of a long story." I stole a glance at Jamie, trying to read his face. Jamie did not want his face read; the book was closed.

"Peterson stories," Jamie said, glancing at a huge poster of Peterson's face. I looked up at the bitter curl in his voice but his face was smooth and placid as always. "Everyone's got one."

8

The bird of the day at Birdie's Dockside Diner was the indigo bunting, a brilliant puffball the color of dark sky. It was chalked in eerily realistic detail on a daily specials board where you would expect to see cheerful endorsements of French onion soup.

"Why is your hair wet?" I asked Jamie.

"Just got out of the swamp for the third time." Jamie dipped a tea bag mechanically into his mug and stared out the window. Beyond a deck full of stacked plastic furniture, Sandhill Lake shivered and roared. My parents had taken us up here once for a day of outdoor fun that I had spent barfing over the side of a pontoon boat. "Still no murder weapon."

Jamie looked like crap, although Jamie's *like crap* was most people's Insta-worthy *woke up like this!* His blue oxford was wrinkled, both elbows splotched with ink. Working nonstop usually gave him a jangly, energetic shine, like a machine edging into its optimal gear, but today he looked spiky and pale. I was dying to grill him about Gina, but I could tell he needed a moment.

At six in the morning, Birdie's was empty save for a Chicago PD cop staring out the window in front of a long-dead cup of coffee and three guys hunched over half-eaten plates in a booth across the room. They were wearing dark suits that probably looked sharp three days ago. A solid guy I took for the owner slouched in a booth by the kitchen, scowling at a mountain of paperwork.

"When was the last time you ate?" I asked Jamie.

"Vending machine ran out of peanuts . . . yesterday?" The tea bag continued to rise and fall, unsupervised. "Day before?"

"Do I need to come up here every day and make you eat?" I grabbed the tea bag away from him and tossed it on a saucer before his tea went nuclear.

"Great idea," he said. "Just toss some food into the swamp. I live there now."

Tiny spritzes of polite veiled shade were the closest Jamie ever got to complaining. His mug had a small yellow bird painted on the side. AMERICAN GOLDFINCH read the scrolled label. Mine was the prairie warbler, a pissed-off yellow borb with a tiny, sharp beak. The inside of Birdie's looked like someone had scooped out your typical wood-slatted thirty-two-ounce-marg-slinging Chain O' Lakes good-time shack and pastry-squirted into it the guts of a natural history museum. Birds occupied every inch of free space: chattering blue jays, sharp-beaked grackles, purple finches, chimney swifts, and dark-eyed juncos like little gray ghosts. The section of wall behind the cash register boasted a framed *Lake County Today* cover featuring the owner brandishing a camera: "Local amateur photographer Ismayil Asadov captures the natural beauty of the Chain O' Lakes." Next to it, the owner with a hawk-nosed nature-show host I recognized from PBS. The owner with a plastic-faced local politician whose campaign rallies were usually titled with the word "freedom." Picture after picture of the owner with Officer Pete, smiling, eating. Holding children, trophies, food.

"You guys got enough people on this case?" I cut my eyes at the exhausted suits across the room. "I can call my mom's Sip 'n' Sleuth Book Club."

"I get why the FBI and the Marshals are here." Jamie propped his chin on his palm and watched a mom and her bundled-up toddler chase each other through the waterfront park. "But the Secret Service?" He turned to me. "Did *you* know the Secret Service is authorized to work local homicides? I didn't. Everyone wants a piece of this." His voice rose with fake cheer. "Everyone just wants to *help*."

"You mean they want the credit," I said.

Jamie tipped me a knowing nod and sipped his polluted tea. He grimaced and put the mug down.

"Officer Pete was kind of a big deal around here," I said.

"I understand that," Jamie said with a little irritation. "But it feels like this isn't about him." He glanced at the suits and lowered his voice. "Maybe you've noticed, but cops are in a bit of a PR slump these days. I think a lot of people were itching for something like this to happen. Everyone loves a martyr."

In the park, someone had spray-painted a mural of Officer Pete nailed to a cross. It was creepily detailed, like whoever painted it had taken a lot of care to make the blood look realistic.

"At least the Feds have been helpful in organizing and disseminating the leads." He studied the American goldfinch. "Of which there are hundreds, by the way."

"That sounds promising." I checked the menu, a formidable plastic-coated monolith covered with tiny food-related hieroglyphics. It was full of the usual diner favorites but colored up with intriguing guest appearances from spiced lamb, eggplant, stewed plums, and pomegranate sauce.

"The leads are mostly garbage." Jamie shook his head. "And guess who gets to follow up on them." He hooked a thumb at himself. "The local pissants."

He picked up his mug and pierced me with a wry look. "They let her go."

I gripped my coffee mug hard. I was a pro by now at the art of looking casual while dying of curiosity, but my Jedi mind tricks didn't work on Jamie. His eyes glittered over the mug's silver rim. He knew exactly why I was here.

"So she didn't do it." I slumped against the back of the booth. Relief flooded me, followed immediately by irritation. Why the fuck hadn't she called me, then?

"I didn't say she didn't do it," Jamie said. "I said they let her go." He scrolled on his phone for a picture, then slid it across the table. "Here."

I leaned in. It was a ladies' pin, a gold dragonfly with little white jewels studding its pale rose wings.

"They found it at the crime scene," Jamie said. "Gina confirmed it was hers, but she said she lost it years ago."

You'd find a dozen like this pin on a spinny rack at Walmart. One of the wing stones was missing, the empty space gaping like a wound. It didn't look like something Gina would wear, but it did look old and loved. Who gave it to her? What did it mean? The more I stared at the photograph the realer it seemed, like I could reach in through the glossy membrane and touch it. The outline of a story was trying to emerge but it was clouded by panic.

"How did they know the pin was Gina's to begin with?" I handed Jamie's phone back to him. "Fingerprints?"

"Dan recognized it," Jamie said. "He and Gina used to work together. They all did. Peterson, too." He saw my stunned face. "She didn't tell you that?"

I looked down at the menu. The tiny letters swirled in my eyes. "No, she didn't."

"They all worked at Sandhill Lake years ago," he said. "Although I'm not sure I'd qualify anything that goes on there as work." He put his phone away. "And I thought Lake Terrace PD was bad."

I was still seeing the dragonfly every time I blinked, a white-gold afterimage burned into my eyelids. The panic had settled into a molten-metal curiosity. I recognized this feeling.

"Does Gina have an alibi for that morning?" I said.

"Nothing we can back up," Jamie said. "Also nothing else that puts her at the scene. We can't charge her with anything, but at this point it's the most solid lead we have." Jamie rubbed his face and yawned. "And Dan is not about to let it go."

I grunted. Dan Kaluza was all over the news now. He moved fast and talked loud, forever vaulting over things to get to the podium and assure TV reporters in his foghorn voice that the task force was *leaving no stone unturned* and *grabbing the bull by the horns*. He talked to the camera a lot. Gina had told me once there were two types of cops: the kind who did the job and the kind who wanted to be seen doing the job. I had zero doubts about which category Dan fell into.

"He wanted an arrest before the big funeral tomorrow, which is obviously not happening," Jamie said. I had driven past the church, where barricades and traffic cones were going up. They were expecting so many people to come, they had to limit attendance to family and close friends only. "Dan's running for sheriff in the next election and he needs points."

Jamie rubbed the back of his neck and came away holding

some sort of horror movie goo. He grunted and went off to the men's. The suits eyed him listlessly as he passed. The owner got up to meet him and they shook hands, exchanged words. The owner clapped Jamie on the shoulder, then headed over to me. He was a squat, wide guy in old-fashioned horn-rimmed glasses that made him look like a Nobel Prize winner or an important composer of screechy, atonal classical music. Gray streaks silvered his cap of tight jet-black curls. He walked slowly, like he was determined to give every move the consideration it deserved.

"Every day he does this." He shook his head at Jamie's cold tea and replaced it with a fresh cup, filling it from a bubble-shaped carafe of hot water. "He doesn't eat enough. Do you cook for him?" He put a fresh tea bag on the table and refilled my coffee.

"I like him too much for that." I sipped my coffee. It was good, hot and fresh, with a hint of something herby and warm I couldn't identify, cardamom, maybe, or cloves.

"He likes the breakfast qutab. I'll bring you two of those. You'll love it." I was really pleased to have the choice made for me. "How long you're together?"

"Oh." I tapped my fingernail in a jerky rhythm on the table. "It's not like that."

I got variations of this question a lot, though rarely this straight up. More often, it came in the form of giggles and winks and meaningful stares. I had no good answer. Jamie was this sort of slick hard candy shell of togetherness and organization with a gooey marshmallow center of loneliness and dysfunction that I found fascinating and irresistible. He had an oddball sense of deadpan humor, once you learned what to look for. He always answered my texts unless he was wading through a swamp. For knowing each other only a year-plus, we shared an instinctive mutual understanding that bordered on the creepy. We weren't *similar*, exactly, but *complementary*, like two puzzle pieces so oddly shaped they fit only with each other. It worked well as long as we didn't think about it too deeply. It also worked too well to risk fucking it up. I got the feeling we both understood this, and so there was a sort of force field we both agreed not to breach lest it cause some sort of matter/antimatter explosion. The answer to the question was, I had everything from Jamie that I needed. He was like all the good parts of having a boyfriend without all the crazy.

I scoped around for a subject change. "Did you draw the bird?" I said. "It's amazing."

He slipped into Jamie's spot and set the carafe of hot water on a napkin. "Do you want to know a secret?" he said.

"About birds?" I leaned in. "Always."

"That bird is not really blue. The indigo bunting."

"It's not?"

"They have no blue pigment in their bodies. It's just the way their feathers catch the light."

"You mean like the sky," I said. "The sky isn't really blue."

He clapped his hands and pointed at me. "Exactly like that!" This was a pretty great bird secret. "I'm Izzy." He held his hand out and we shook. "Hello."

"Nice to meet you, Izzy. I'm Katie True."

"They don't live where I come from," he said. "But I saw them in Cuba years ago. I went for work."

"Were you an artist?"

"I was a petroleum engineer," he said. "In Azerbaijan. They sent us to Cuba for the People's Symposium on Equitable Redistribution of Natural Resources." He pursed his lips. "It was like a reward. My team overfulfilled the production plan that year. I even got to meet Brezhnev." He dug out a tattered old photo of himself, much younger but with the same recognizable Elvis

Costello glasses, standing next to a droopy-jowled old guy in a brass-choked military uniform. Behind them was a dismal desert landscape dotted with nodding-donkey oil derricks.

"Look at that old goat," Izzy said. "I think he was asleep when they took this."

"Wow," I said. "That sounds like a really impressive job."

"Yes, it does! I hated it!" The photo disappeared into a hidden pocket. "I wanted to be a biologist. I like birds very much. And to cook. I like birds and to cook." He stared at me. "Katie True. Do I know you?"

Oh, shit.

"Yes!" He hopped to his feet and pointed to the jumble of photographs on the wall. Sure enough, there we were, jammed between a picture of Officer Pete with Richard Daley and another of him with Mr. T. "There you are!"

"There I am."

"I need a picture of you." He hopped out of the booth and whipped out his phone.

"No, I really don't think—" I flailed at him. *Snap!* "Okay." Now I would forever grace the walls of Birdie's looking like I was leaving rehab.

"So." Izzy sat back down. "What do you do, accident girl?"

"I read tarot cards." WTF, who cared at this point. "But I think Accident Girl reads better on a business card."

"I had a great-aunt who read the cards," Izzy said. "She also *played* cards, she had a terrible gambling addiction! And she drank. A lot." He looked impressed, dreamy. "She won so much money gambling, she used to go drinking and then hire a brass band to follow her home."

"Now, that is a woman who knew her own worth," I said.

Jamie appeared, freshly groomed and much happier. His hair was already drying.

"You take care of this one, okay?" Izzy switched places with Jamie. "He's one of the good ones." He collected his water carafe and disappeared.

Outside, a cold drizzle had started. Jamie watched the mom and the kid take shelter in a picnic pavilion. "Something's not right here," he said.

"What do you mean?"

"I have never worked a high-profile case like this that didn't shake loose in two days, tops." Steam curled around his long fingers. "But we've got no solid suspects, no decent leads, and the crime scene makes no sense. Something's wrong."

Jamie was a pathological overachiever and it bugged him when things didn't fall into neat categories.

"You know what your problem is?" I said. "You are inexperienced with failure."

Jamie's eyes sparkled over the rim of his mug. "I had mono during my advanced failure seminar."

"When something throws you for a loop, you automatically go to stuff that's worked for you before." I placed my hand grandly on my chest. "Whereas I can draw on a whole storehouse of terrible solutions that didn't work in the slightest."

Jamie scratched his temple and gave me a lopsided grin. I didn't realize how much I depended on the bloom of warmth on his face until it went missing. "I am struggling to follow this logic right now."

"That's the spirit," I said. "Allow me to be your failure guide. Tell me what you know so far and I'll suggest something that makes no sense. How about the crime scene? Let's start there."

Jamie reached for the condiment caddy and started moving things out. He pointed to a set of blue jay–head salt and pepper shakers. "Here's his baton and pepper spray. Also his smashed-up glasses and radio. This is where he gets shot the first time." He tapped his chest. "In the vest pocket. He gets shot, he runs." Present tense, like he was watching it happen. He moved to the ketchup bottle a few inches away. "Here's where he drops his Taser. And here"—he pointed to a pile of mustard packets—"signs of struggle. He gets shot again. For the second and last time." He picked up a packet and contemplated it. "You couldn't have a more textbook demonstration of the use-of-force continuum."

"He was shot with his own gun?" I said.

"Presumably. The gun is still AWOL." The news had shown pictures of a small, dim clearing next to a puddle that barely qualified as a pond. Tall grass, cattails, yellow police tape.

"Did he have a body cam?"

"Normally he would have, but Sandhill Lake is switching over to a new system, so no one's had body cams for a month."

Convenient, I thought. *Would someone know this?*

Izzy swept in and deposited two steaming plates in front of us. Golden-brown semicircles of stuffed flatbread garnished with some sort of sweet-smelling green herb. It could have pulled the cover of a foodie mag.

Jamie stared at his plate, then moved it aside and picked up the death mustard again. "Imagine you're a regular person."

"I'll give it a shot," I mumbled. The flatbread was stuffed with a savory mix of egg, spiced meat, cilantro, and onions. It was so goddamn good I wanted eight more of them.

"You get into a tussle with a cop, his gun goes off, now you've accidentally shot him. What do you do?"

"Wet my pants and run?"

He waved the mustard packet. "Exactly." I loved it when I got one of his questions right. "An amateur wouldn't follow him and finish the job." He tossed the mustard back on the table. "I think we're looking for guys with felony records. Which makes it even weirder that we haven't found them yet."

"Wouldn't guys like that be better at hiding?"

Jamie shrugged. "Criminals are friends with other criminals. They'd all sell each other out in a heartbeat. We've talked to every banger, every biker, every dealer in the county, and no one knows anything? Not even with fifty grand on the line?" The county was offering a fat bag of cash for information leading to an arrest. "I don't buy it. Someone should be singing by now."

Over the lake, a huge white bird, like a stealth airplane, slid along the horizon. Jamie watched it glide around the bend in the lake and disappear. "There ought to be a trail a mile wide, but there's nothing."

I pretended to study the condiments, but I was watching Jamie stare out the window. We did the same job—he as a cop and I as a reader. We untangled the invisible ropes of fear and greed and jealousy that tied the story into place. Jamie dealt in facts and I dealt in the hazy halo around the facts. We filled each other out, iron filings lined up on opposite sides of the same force field. Sense and nonsense. Action and stillness. Reason and intuition. He kept me doing things and I kept him feeling things.

"And here's the really weird part. There's all this struggle"—he waved the mustard again—"but only one set of footprints."

I paused stuffing my face. "You mean Officer Pete's and another set?"

"No," Jamie said. "Just his."

A train whistle warbled through the heavy air. This part hadn't made it into the news reports. "Could it be a suicide?"

Jamie twitched an eyebrow. "Not unless he chased himself around the clearing. Plus he would have dropped the gun. And the kill shot trajectory is wrong." He turned his cup to see the whole goldfinch. "He was shot in the chest, from above, behind his vest. Who kills themselves that way?"

It made sense, but the image of Officer Pete alone in the

clearing wouldn't leave me, the blank-faced killer hovering over him like a vengeful ghost. I had come here for answers, but there weren't any. Only questions, tumbling after each other.

"So, what's next?" I said.

"We have to do a victimology." Jamie picked up his qutab and took an absent-minded bite.

"What's that?"

"A full workup of the victim's life. A complete biographical study. Lifestyle, bank records, habits. Digital activity, phone records, social media, known associates, personnel files, everything. Family interviews. Anything that might help explain why someone wanted him dead. It's standard. At least, when a homicide doesn't clear right away.

"Family gets hit the hardest during these things," Jamie said. "Especially the spouse. The spouse is the gold mine. Even if they didn't do it, even if they don't know who did it, they always know something. They always point the way."

There she was again, June the Mysterious.

Jamie started eating with a little more interest. "Everyone was hoping to avoid the victimology."

"Why?"

"It's a lot more work, first of all. We're talking months, not weeks, to go through all that stuff. Longer, if everyone's fighting over the juicy bits.

"Plus." He looked uncomfortable. "You start looking that closely at anyone, even a guy everybody loved, and you start seeing things you don't want to see. It's making everyone jumpy. Especially Dan. Those two go way back, which puts Dan between a rock and a hard place. He needs to solve this case, but he doesn't want to seem like he's attacking the guy's reputation."

Jamie fell silent, watched the mom and kid climb up a slide shaped like a friendly octopus. "Everyone has a story about him.

Everyone has a connection." His voice was low and flat with some emotion I couldn't identify. He was an outsider, a transplant. Whatever history we all shared with Peterson, Jamie was locked out of it. "It makes it hard to separate the truth from the stories. And we owe people the truth." He nodded at Izzy. "Even if the answers don't fit the stories."

I felt an odd sparkly tug from my end of the force field that bound me to Jamie. The nonsense end, the no-logic end, the intuitive, secret, silent-knowing end. We were entering my world now, the world where things didn't make sense, unless it was the kind of crooked, nonlinear sense that was beyond Jamie.

"You've got the best story of all." Jamie put down his mug.

"Oh." I felt like someone was tugging at strings tied deep inside me. "I guess you've heard."

"Of course I've heard," he said. "That's the one they always start with." He looked gentle and sad, like he was remembering something long gone. "His origin story. Do you remember it?"

"No, I was just four months old. But I've heard the story a million times." *I couldn't have avoided it if I tried,* I didn't add. "My mom was picking me up from daycare. It was icy and the car slipped and went into oncoming traffic. A truck hit her." I traced the rim of my coffee mug, a silver circle going round and round. "There was something heavy in the car, I don't know what it was, but it hit me, and I guess it fractured my skull."

Outside, the lanky white heron was back, balancing on the post at the far end of the dock.

"Officer Pete showed up and there was an ambulance coming but, you know, it was rush hour on Route 83, so it wasn't coming fast enough. He grabbed me and ran to the ambulance. If he'd gotten there a minute later, I'd be dead. So, long story short, I owe him my life." I traced a crack in the smooth tabletop. "Maybe more."

"Well, I don't know." Jamie smiled, and a dazzling shiver passed through me. Jamie rarely smiled. Each one counted. "You created 'Officer Pete.' I think *he* owes *you*."

"It feels like we made an agreement that day," I said. "We signed a contract." I whooshed out a breath. "I, Katie True, do solemnly swear to kick ass. And I haven't held up my end." The feeling that had hovered over me all my life was stepping forward, taking center stage now that Officer Pete was gone.

"What constitutes a kicked ass?" Jamie said. The fog had cleared from his face. Maybe he had just needed to eat. "Who designates an ass as having been adequately kicked?"

"I don't know," I said. "But everyone sure has opinions about it."

"What's your opinion?"

My eyes drifted to Izzy's wall of fame, found the picture of me and Officer Pete. When I was a kid I liked to slip the yellow clipping out of its plastic sleeve in the scrapbook and flip it over, peer into the world behind the picture. There was nothing on the other side but faded pre-internet newsprint. The facts behind the story were gone, subsumed and flattened into the only version of the truth that survived time and imagination. In its place was an opaque brilliance like the curved face of a gazing globe. Stare all you want, all you'd see staring back at you was your own squished face.

"I'm going to figure out what happened here," I told Jamie. Gina's dragonfly flickered past me and I knew if I didn't reach out and catch it, it would fly away forever. "The truth, not just the stories."

9

The front door chime went off and kept going off.

I hopped up to greet whatever army of visitors needed urgent tarot readings, but it was just Jessie, wedged in the doorframe with a gigantic leather briefcase. She looked like a stork that had landed a fish bigger than its own head and was too stubborn to let it go. The doorbell was stuck in the on position, chiming its mournful two-tone melody like a haywire carousel.

Together we popped Jessie free. She stumbled inside, dumped the case on the coffee table, and struggled out of her tailored wool coat.

"They've got Route 12 blocked off up by the Chain O' Lakes," she gasped, plopping into the slim, curvy armchair across from the couch. "It took me an hour to get down here." She closed her eyes and whooshed out a big yoga breath.

I sat down across from her. "They had to increase the search perimeter from two miles to five."

Jessie opened an eye. "How do you know that?" She was at the same time uninterested in details and jealous that someone would have more of them than she did.

"I saw Jamie this morning." I reached over and flipped the sheet of paper I'd been writing on facedown. I'd been buzzing ever since I left Jamie. He didn't have much to say about my grand pronouncement that I was going to get involved because that would have been tacit acknowledgment that my involvement was not a shockingly bad idea. Still, I could see it made him feel less alone. He was, of course, no help with what I should do next, so I was on my own for now, brainstorming ideas for where to look for answers. So far all I had was a list of names and a bunch of questions about each one.

"Jamie filled me in on the case details."

"Well, tell Jamie to wrap it up." Jessie waved her arms to erase what she'd just said. "Not that I'm complaining!" She put her hands over her heart. "Those boys are doing their best and God bless 'em."

Boys? I thought. *God?* What the hell had gotten into her? Jessie, like most people who never had anything bad happen to them, had no opinion on cops aside from an unspoken snob-adjacent hunch that anyone so familiar with crime is part criminal themselves. Like if she let a cop sneeze on her she might catch crime. She had always been grumpy about all the attention the accident had netted me, almost like she wished she'd been in the car, too. Nothing like a brush with death to make people admire you, I guess. I had tried to explain to her the nuances of this sort of fame but gave up quickly. Nuances were not Jessie's jam.

"Since when are you such a back-the-blue gal?" I said.

"You know, Katie." Jessie laced her hands together. Oh, God. This opening always preceded something that belonged in a clip art–infested PowerPoint at a corporate retreat. "Sometimes, you come across an opportunity that requires you to pivot. To be flexible. Even if it means leaving your comfort zone."

I blinked. "You walked out of a Bakers Square once because they had switched from peppermint pie to spearmint pie."

"You need to recognize these opportunities when they come up, or they'll pass you by."

"I'm sorry, did you actually hear me, or were you too busy pivoting and being flexible? Do I even want to know what this so-called opportunity is?"

Jessie smoothed her hair. "The Petersons approached me last month to help them upgrade their living space." She rummaged in her purse for a shiny, bullet-shaped lipstick tube and a compact. She sighed and stared wistfully into space. "I had just found them the *per*fect little lake getaway, too. On Baines Hill."

"My condolences for your loss." I snorted. So that's where this trumpet blast of pro-cop sentiment was coming from. Houses on Baines Hill, on the ritzy south shore of Sandhill Lake, ran into the million-plus range. The commission alone would allow Jessie to pave her driveway with Land Rovers, but that wasn't the real prize. The real prize was the in she would get to the elusive upper echelon of northeastern Illinois's public servants — mayors, judges, police top brass, and the like — a scene she had thus far been unable to crack because it was composed entirely of cranky old dudes and their equally cranky wives who had been doing things the same way for decades and had all their own people for everything. A superstar like Officer Pete — or his estate, if the man himself was so inconveniently unavailable — was her ticket.

"Don't worry, all is not lost." Jessie dropped into a meaningful sotto voce. "June is still going forward with the sale." She did a gross fist pump. "It's happening, baby."

"What is wrong with you?" I flicked one of her own business

cards at her. It lodged in her upswept hair and bounced off. For a second a tiny Jessie face perched on top of Jessie's real face. "You are a monster."

"Now, hold on a second. Check this out." She whipped out a glossy catalog and smoothed it out on the table in front of me.

A great squatting beast of a house stared up at me from the crisp pages. A toothy bay window ran its length, the photo snapped from across the lake to fit the whole house. There were inside shots, too, of a living room big enough for a state dinner, bedrooms with skylights, roller rink–size spaces with no discernible purpose. The house was all windows and glass, empty and forbidding. A fortress.

"Do they need something this big?" I said. "It's just the two of them. Just one of them, now."

"That's the best part." Jessie popped open the lipstick and applied a pale purple that made her look dead. "You know how Officer Pete ran that youth-cop group? The . . . the"—she snapped her fingers—"the Discoverers? The Adventurers?"

"The Explorers."

"Whatever. He wanted the house to be an unofficial community center for them." Jessie clicked the lipstick shut. She was powdering her face now, peeking at me over the lip of the compact. "A lot of them are like, poor or abused and don't have access to nature and fresh air and stuff, so it's a paying-it-forward sort of thing. See? I'm not the monster you think I am." Jessie pressed the powder into her face, sharp and machinelike. "I'm helping Officer Pete continue his legacy after his tragic and untimely death."

"Come closer," I said. "I need to vomit on your shoes." Writing real estate copy had permanently warped Jessie's brain, like in that story about the nice scientist lady who develops superpowers after learning an alien language. Sadly, the only superpower

Jessie's real estate–speak gave her was the uncanny ability to believe her own bullshit.

I picked up the catalog. A strip of glare sliced the house photo in two.

Jessie shrugged. "She's a supportive wife who wants to carry on her husband's dream. Which I am helping her do." Jessie put the catalog back in her briefcase. "This will make me look *so good*. I am *killing* it."

"Word choice, Jessie." At the word *supportive* all my alarm bells went haywire. Matt had used the same word about June to mean exactly the opposite. My fingers itched to make a note on my page of questions.

Jessie pointed at me. "You could stand to be more supportive, too. Here." She produced a small cardboard box full of tiny blue-line flag lapel pins and handed me one. She was already wearing one, small but noticeable, on her blazer.

"When did you have time to get these?" I imagined a box in Jessie's pathologically organized garage labeled IN CASE OF GRUE-SOME MURDER OF PROMINENT LAW ENFORCEMENT OFFICIAL.

"I know, right? I'm freaking amazing. Especially with all the running back and forth up to that . . ." *Say it*, I begged her in my mind. *Swamp. Shithole. Glorified trailer park.* Sandhill Lake was a tough, tattooed bruiser of a town where Al Capone used to dump bodies, Chicago to the core, a summer boating haven for generations of cops and firemen coming up from the far South Side after retirement to buy up lake houses. The top brass settled on Baines Hill and the rest were beneath Jessie's sight lines.

". . . to Sandhill Lake," Jessie finished. Her face smoothed out. "Let no one say I don't go the extra mile for my clients. Or the extra ten, even with gas prices the way they are these days."

She produced a brick of flyers and a box of business cards and thunked them on the table. "Anyway, I just came to drop these off for you to collate. It's a double batch because Darcy quit on me to like, build houses for whales in the Amazon rainforest. So I guess I'll be handling the funeral all by myself tomorrow, thank you very much."

"Wait." I looked up. "*The* funeral? Officer Pete's funeral? The one no one can get into? I thought that wasn't open to the public. You're going to be there?"

"I'm handling the flowers," she said. "Orchids. Classy, simple, eternal. But get this: they're blue! With little blue ribbons threaded through them." She gave me a shark's smile. "*Courtesy of True Real Estate* written on each wreath."

A neon sign buzzed to life in my mind. "And Officer Pete's family will be there?"

"They're actually thinking of skipping it?" Jessie said. "Because they haven't finished *Real Housewives of Salt Lake City* yet." She zipped the briefcase back up. "Of course they're going to be there, you dolt. Matt, June, everybody." She pointed at me. "You'll like June. She's one of your people."

I was too excited to identify the flavor of insult Jessie had just lobbed at me. I eyed my facedown list. "You know what, Jess, I'm free tomorrow. Screw Darcy and her whales. I'll help you with the flowers."

Jessie swirled her coat onto her shoulders and side-eyed me. "You?"

"Just trying to be supportive." I picked up the blue-line flag pin. "And also I love . . . those flowers. That you just mentioned."

"Orchids," Jessie said.

"Right." My eye twitched and I glanced at my sheet of paper. "Orchids. My favorite."

"What's that?" Jessie said.

"I was doodling. It says *I heart real estate* all over the page." I picked the paper up. "Want to see?"

Jessie snapped up her briefcase. "I'll pick you up at eight sharp. Wear black, but none of your lacy Wednesday Addams crap. Do you even own a pair of pantyhose?"

"I'm not going to dignify that with an answer," I said.

After she left I flipped the sheet of paper over and circled *June Peterson* over and over. Questions, questions, questions, all stretching out ahead of me like paving stones in a bright road.

This was the best part.

10

There was fuck all in my closet that would pass Jessie's appropriateness filter. The parts of my wardrobe that were not jeans, T-shirts, and stretch pants fell into two categories so wildly divergent they rounded the bend and bled into each other. I looked like I was on my way either to play canasta with a geriatric relative or to an art installation where a dude lifted cinder blocks with his balls.

When the doorbell rang, I was in the middle of a costume change that left me in lace-trim bike shorts and a cape. It was dinnertime, so I figured Owen was hungry and had discovered once again that groceries do not buy themselves. Maybe I could squeeze him for takeout.

"I'm out of those little sausages that look like dog treats," I said, opening the door. "So we'll have to—"

I stopped short. The visitor was not Owen. The visitor was Gina.

She looked me up and down. "Am I interrupting the raven's feeding time?"

I gaped at her. When it became clear my speech faculties were not going to accommodate an invitation to come inside, she glided past me into the living room and sat down in the old nursing chair I'd inherited from Jessie. I watched her discover with a mild shock that both the chair and the footstool rocked. When she'd gotten her sea legs, she crossed her feet and leaned back, rocking a little.

I found my voice. Sort of. "What the— Where have you— What the hell do you think you're—"

Gina waited for me to exhaust my store of indignant sentence fragments. From a hidden pocket she produced a pint of ice cream and set it on the coffee table. "Here. For you."

"Un-fucking-believable." I put my hands on my hips. The ice cream was my favorite, this off-brand rocky road they carried only at the gas station down the street. Gina knew I loved it for its faint but unmistakable whiff of bacon. Was this her way of showing actual remorse, or was it business-as-usual Gina, punching through life unaware of the human toll? I wasn't sure which option pissed me off more. "Ice cream makes all of this okay?"

"If you don't want it . . ." Gina shrugged and reached for the ice cream.

"I'm pissed off, I'm not crazy." I tossed the pint into the freezer and slammed the door shut. "Do you mind telling me what the fuck is going on?"

Gina crossed her legs. "I got arrested," she said. "For Pete's murder."

"I'm aware of that, thank you." I dropped into a kitchen chair. "I also know you worked with him. For years. You didn't feel the need to mention this? Any of the dozen times I told you how he pulled me out of that wreck when I was a kid?"

Gina shrugged and crossed both feet on the footstool. She was dressed aggressively neutral, in colorless slacks (I never used the word slacks unless there was no alternative), a quote-unquote blouse designed to disappear under other clothes, and canvas shoes pointier than sneakers, not so pointy as to make a statement on anything in particular. Everything was some color I forgot immediately. Everything repelled the eye, deflected attention. Which was exactly what drew my attention to it. She was hiding. Stress dressing.

"All that stuff is in the past," she said.

"Yeah, well, the past has a way of popping up when you least expect it." A memory fluttered past me: the cards, the day Pete had died. *Someone from your past will reappear with a secret that destroys you.*

I got up and started banging around the kitchen because I was hungry and also because I wanted to twitch angrily in private. "You could have at least let me know you were safe."

The word hung in the air like a thick fog. I caught the tail end of a scrunched look on Gina's face. We were thinking the same thing: she was not safe.

"I just figured you'd have the whole story from Jamie by now," she said.

"That's beside the point and you know it," I grumbled. "You want something to eat?"

"I'm good." She checked her fingernails. They were lacquered the color of curdled milk. "Have you?" she said. "Talked to Jamie?"

She wanted to know what I knew but didn't want to ask. Playing it cool but overdoing it. People acted bigger when they were freaking out—louder, faster, jerkier. They tugged their hair, messed with their clothes, shuffled their feet. Gina went the other way. She drew inward, went still, like a desert lizard conserving energy in an inhospitable environment. I watched her drag her fingertips over the armrests. To anyone else, she'd look like she didn't give a shit. To me, she looked like she was barely keeping it together.

"I had breakfast with Jamie this morning." I examined a slice of bread for mold. "He forgets to eat when he's working."

"Did you wipe his chin?" Gina said. "They're such messy eaters at that age."

"Shut up."

"Really, it's kind of sweet. You two have skipped boyfriend-girlfriend and gone straight to third post-widowhood marriage."

I unscrewed the peanut butter jar and stabbed its insides with a butter knife. Gina was looking around my tiny living room–kitchen combo like she'd never been here before. The walls hadn't been repainted since before I'd moved in and had settled into a sort of cream or egg color, tastier names for "dirty." What little stuff I had had come my way by accident: cast-off furniture from Jessie, art left behind by friends I didn't see anymore. A couple of smashed-up souvenir trivets from my parents' trip to Barcelona, a mismatched set of beach glass jars. For a tiny space, it was weirdly empty. I'd been working on it this year, trying to make it my own. After ten years, I had to admit the place was no longer temporary.

"This is new, right?" Gina rapped a knuckle on the scuffed wood of the coffee table.

"Newish." I shot her a weird face. I'd bought the coffee table at a resale shop last month to replace the milk crates I'd been using for years. We'd had a whole-ass conversation about how proud I was about owning a piece of grown-up furniture. Other people forgot details; Gina didn't. She was acting like someone had just handed her the script for the dropping-in-on-a-friend scene and she hadn't learned the lines yet.

"What else did Jamie say?" Gina said.

"He said the case is a clusterfuck." I dropped the knife and left a peanut butter glob on the floor. It looked like a dopey face with two mismatched eyes. "The crime scene is weird, there's a bazillion leads but they're all garbage, and everybody's fighting over who gets to do what." I mopped up the peanut butter face with a napkin. "They're going to do a victimology, but Dan's dragging his feet."

"Of course he's dragging his feet." Gina leaned forward. "Dan was Pete's boy. He could barely tie his shoes without Pete's say-so. They'd get shit-faced together, then clean up each other's puke at work the next day." She tossed herself back in the chair and it rocked wildly. "Those guys start sniffing around Peterson's life, it's going to make Kaluza look like the asshole he is."

"If Dan was so close to Pete, why would they let him lead the investigation?" I glued my sandwich together and poured a glass of milk. "Isn't that a conflict of interest?"

Gina gave a low, mean cackle. "Who's *they*?" Her eyes glittered. "Everyone's on the same big happy merry-go-round."

"Jamie told me they found your pin at the crime scene." I stuffed my sandwich into my face to avoid shouting at her all the questions my brain was currently shouting at me. Chief among them: *did you do it?* "Your dragonfly pin."

Gina's lips went tight. "My mom gave me that pin when I graduated high school. It was part of a set. One had pink wings and the other had green ones. The symbolism was not lost on me: fly the fuck away while you can, and don't look back. You can see how well that worked out."

"Welcome to the wounded dragonfly club," I mumbled around a mouthful of sandwich.

"I loved those pins. I wore them all the time," Gina said. "Until they *mysteriously disappeared* at work one day."

"What do you mean, mysteriously disappeared?" I shoved what was left of the sandwich in my mouth. "What happened to them?"

"Elves." She stared me dead in the eyes, tilted her chin. "Real problem with elves that year. Playing tricks. Stealing stuff. Fixing people's shoes at night."

"You know what?" I tossed my plate and cup into the sink and turned to her. "*You* came *here*. Do you want to talk about this or don't you? Because I do." I folded my arms. "Your turn."

Gina didn't move, but her knuckles went white on the armrest. "Remember when you said you wanted a problem to solve?" she said. "A real one?" Her face was porcelain white. Ice-chip eyes. "I've got a problem. And I need your help."

The temperature in the room dropped ten degrees, or shot up ten degrees. I was sweating, and I didn't know why. I had the urge to close my eyes, as if I needed to hear better.

"Peterson and I were not exactly besties when we worked together. And pretty much every cop in the county knows it." Gina's hands uncurled. She looked like she was counting to ten. "That was one reason I didn't tell you I knew him. I didn't want to break your sweet little heart."

"I'm not a toddler, okay?" I was leaning against the counter. I could feel its sharp corner digging into my back. "Did you kill him?"

"No." Gina's expression didn't change.

"Would you tell me if you did?"

"Of course not." She smirked. "Would you?"

"Well, I don't know," I said. "Am I you or me in this scenario?"

Gina untangled herself from the chair and went to the patio door. She moved the blinds and looked outside. "Dan is not going to let this go, and I need to get him off my ass."

"Why?" I said. "If you didn't kill him, you've got nothing to hide, right?"

Gina gave me a *really?* look. "Trust me when I say it's not that simple." She turned back to the window. There was an orange-ish blinking out there, some sort of emergency. "There's stuff I don't need coming out when all of this is over."

What stuff? I was about to say, but Gina kept talking. "I need to figure out who really did this," she said, "so Dan can move on and leave me alone." She looked like the words were stuck in her mouth. "And I need your help to do it."

"Can't you do it yourself?" I said, but my voice sounded far away, my mind racing ahead. Sandhill Lake floated in front of me, flashes of sun off its gray surface, a bright, curvy miniature world in a soap bubble with rainbow skin. A pleasant fire kindled in my fingertips, same as earlier today when I listened to Jamie list the case details. Same as I felt in front of a card spread, clos-ing off one set of senses and opening another secret set. I felt like I was walking into a darkness I couldn't see into but knew I had the tools to navigate. "You were a cop," I said. "You know this scene inside and out. You just want someone to do your dirty work."

"When have I ever had a problem with dirty work?" Gina scoffed. "But I need to keep a low profile." Something sharp sur-faced and sank on her face. "If I start poking around, I'll attract even more attention."

What the hell did that mean? My thoughts cartwheeled through Gina's Greek-oracle nonsense, finding nowhere to land.

"Besides, no official investigation is going to do this right," she said. "Especially not if it's headed by that nimrod Kaluza. Jamie's good, but Dan has him on a choke chain. We need an outsider. Not a cop. Just someone who's smart and fair and can see through all the bullshit around this thing."

Bullshit you yourself are a part of, I wanted to say. Gina folded her arms and sat back. My hands burned and burned. A circle closed inside me, as if the winding path I was walking had come back to its starting point. The place was the same, but I was different.

"I'm way ahead of you." I was grinning like an idiot. "I'm going to Officer Pete's funeral tomorrow." My voice came out bubbly and high, like I'd just taken a big snort off a helium balloon. "And I'm going to find out as much as I can."

Gina's smile spread slowly across her face. For the first time since she'd walked through the door she looked like herself, half human and dangerous. Fire and shadow.

"I should have known," she said.

Joy raced through me like a wildfire. I'd been hearing that phrase and all its tiny, sharp-toothed variations all my life, with all its sidecar sighs and eye rolls and disappointments. Coming from Gina, like everything that came from Gina, it took on a meaning outrageously opposite. It meant what I wanted it to mean.

Now we were both laughing. She unfolded herself from the chair and stood up. "Get dressed, P. T. Barnum. This calls for a drink." She shouldered her purse and moved toward the door.

"It most certainly does not." I was still standing in the kitchen in my bike shorts, hands smeared in peanut butter. "Jessie's picking me up at fucking early o'clock tomorrow. I can't be hungover."

"Peterson won't mind." She jingled her car keys. "Come on. I'll drive."

Of course she would. I wiped my hands and went to the bedroom to change. "You don't happen to have a pair of pantyhose in your car, do you?"

Gina strode out the door, not looking back. "Sheer, black, or fishnet?"

11

The Olde Prairie Inn was a repurposed nineteenth-century house with a plaque near the cornerstone designating it Historically Important. Blue shutters, window baskets, neon signs advertising Pabst. It was cheery and well-kept but radiated a standoffish vibe, like a beautiful magic house that only the purest and most dedicated drunks could enter. The lot was half full, mostly American-made trucks in various shades of black.

"What are we doing up here?" I said. We had driven for over thirty minutes to Round Lake Beach past farms, forest preserves, and looming white pharmaceutical manufacturing campuses. "We couldn't get hammered in Lake Terrace?"

"Why? So you can play Skee-Ball while you get hammered?" Gina got out of the car and took a drag on her cigarette. It was her third. In the car, she had lit up one after another.

"I thought you were quitting," I said.

"When I was a kid, I swore I would never smoke." She flicked the stub and ground it into the pavement. "Never smoke and never drink coffee. My mom and dad smoked like chimneys and drank coffee by the gallon. I came out of my room in the morning and it would hit me, this mix of cigarette smoke and coffee, *bam*, like a brick wall in the face." Gina never talked about her past unless she was drunk or distracted by something even worse. She patted her pockets, then caught herself. "Guess we all turn into our parents eventually."

Gina's dad was a career kleptomaniac and her mom was a sweet train wreck who never got her shit together after he went off to prison and never came back. I could tell Gina needed badly for me to disagree with her.

"That's horseshit," I said. "My parents are rich and pathologically organized. There's no way I'm turning into them."

Gina snorted. I waited for her to move but she stood there, staring at the bar with her eyes shielded, even though it was nighttime.

The place was dark and noisy inside, a wooden man cave with rafters in the ceiling and slow fans slicing the thick air. It was all odd little alcoves that were probably convenient for whatever telegraph office or tuberculosis hospital the place used to be, but now resembled the insides of a giant unhappy beast. Old-timey pictures covered the walls and string lights crisscrossed the bar. Amber stained-glass lamps made every booth look like a surgery theater. The jukebox played something nasal and folky that longed aggressively for *better days*.

Gina moved inward. The photographs on the walls, I saw as we passed them, were full of uniforms. Cops roughhousing with German shepherds and lining up for a shaving cream pie in the face. Group shots, one after another, of area squads from Libertyville, Mundelein, Grayslake. Black-and-white vintage photos of old cars with fins and gumball lights. Awards, plaques, trophies. A small foldout table bulged with candles and knickknacks, a framed service portrait of Peterson in the center. LIEUTENANT MATTHEW PETERSON, a printed banner read. END OF WATCH— MARCH 4, 2025. Next to it: the Picture. Peterson and me.

I looked around. Everyone in the bar was either a cop or played one on TV. "You brought me to a cop bar?"

Gina shrugged. "Never know who we might bump into."

Someone we could grill about Peterson's death, in other words. I couldn't believe I was dumb enough to think we were just going for drinks. Eyes followed Gina, conversations slowed and stopped. One squat old dude stared openly, like a kid who hadn't learned yet that it was rude. Others looked away as if from a car crash. Gina glided forward, dreamlike: Moses parting the Sea of Cop, a cold wake fanning out behind her.

I caught up with her. "Is this you lying low?" I whispered. "Staying out of it?"

"What are you talking about?" Gina didn't bother lowering her voice. "*You're* asking the questions. This is your baby." My baby, my ass. She just couldn't keep her hands off anything she wanted to do herself.

We came to a booth with two guys and a woman around a table crowded with empty beer pints, rocks glasses, and wadded-up cocktail napkins. The guys looked like photos of the same guy twenty years apart—thick and thicker-set, both bald as eggs. The woman was squat and solid, with a freckled face and wild red hair tamed and cropped. She was anywhere between her late forties and early sixties. I could see her on a ride-on lawnmower with a cigarette dangling from her mouth, shouting at a gaggle of rowdy grandkids in the backyard of a Lombard bungalow while "Old Time Rock and Roll" played in the background. The guys wore matching golf-wear with the Sandhill Lake PD logo on the breast, and the woman rocked a beige pantsuit a size too snug.

Much ass had been kicked by her over the years. She sported a magnificent black eye and a ladder of cuts on her forehead like a triumphant warning: *Try it.*

"Two old-fashioneds for the road." Gina planted herself in front of the table, hands on hips. "You are a creature of habit, Maureen."

The woman named Maureen regarded Gina and something passed between them, a complicated shape on a taut, invisible thread. Bump into, yeah right. Gina knew all along where we were going and who we would meet. Who was this leather strap of a woman?

"Gina," Maureen said. "What a nice surprise." She was not in the least surprised. I got the feeling very little surprised her.

"Ron, Bill." Gina nodded to each of the guys. They stared at her with goat eyes. "Such a shitty liar," Gina said to Maureen. "I don't know how you made it so long as a cop."

The guys slid each other a dark glance. Maureen smiled. "Good thing I'm not a cop anymore."

"So I've heard," Gina said. "Hope the retirement party was a banger. My invitation must've gotten lost in the mail."

"Come on now, Gina." Maureen's smile firmed up. "You know you wouldn't have come." Total flex, being the first to break the nice-nice barrier. Maureen had just deployed some heavy artillery in whatever silent battle of wills was going on here.

"We would've called you," the younger guy cop said. "But we didn't need any rent-a-cops to work security that day." The older cop snickered.

Gina nodded pleasantly. "Could have used some for that one Halloween party, remember? The one where I caught you bobbing for apples in Pam Sterling's panties?"

Bald Sr. hooted like a dopey owl. He was rewarded with an icy look from Bald Jr. and buried his large face in his large beer.

"What are you doing here, Gina?" Maureen's eyes shone. These two had worked together, and they knew each other inside and out. I remembered a woman boss Gina had talked about with a smidge less bitchery than usual, but she'd seemed so airy and closed off about her, I assumed the woman was dead. Gina talked about everyone in her past that way.

"I came for clothing tips," Gina said. "I'm interviewing for Assistant Vice Douchebag at the National Association of Bureaucratic Asswipes and I don't have a thing to wear. That's a really nice suit, by the way."

Maureen picked up her drink. Gina clenched and reclenched her fists. I waited for Good Cop to step in before realizing that was me. "You worked with Officer Pete?" I asked Maureen.

"I did." Maureen swirled her golden-brown drink. "For years."

"I'd love to hear about him," I said. "Mind if we join you?"

Maureen looked at Gina. "Is this one of your bullshit games, Gina? Are you trying to make me look like an idiot?"

"In that suit?" Gina said. "I think you've got it covered."

"I'm not free right now," Maureen said, eyeing Gina even though she was talking to me. "You're welcome to make an appointment at the village office."

Bald Jr. smirked and flicked Gina a silent toast.

"Are you sure?" I stepped forward. "I knew Officer Pete, too." I searched the room, found what I needed, and pointed. "There we are. The two of us. I'm Katie True."

Three heads swiveled. The air went still, like a tornado had torn through and moved off. Bald Sr.'s face clouded over.

"I'm the baby." My fingertips crackled. I could have raised my hands and blasted these idiots with a bolt of righteous chaos. "I'm Accident Girl."

Out of the corner of my eye I saw Gina turn to me. *That's right,* I thought. *You're not the only one at this poker table.*

"Guys," Maureen said, staring at Gina, "give us a minute, will you?"

"What the hell happened to your face?" Gina said. "Somebody finally try to take a whack at you?"

"They should have tried harder." Maureen was drinking the unorthodox third old-fashioned, and Gina was pounding whiskey sours and throwing back tequila shots in between, no salt or lime. I was nursing a dangerously strong vodka tonic with a fat lime garnish. "Just some idiot in a Public Works truck taking the curve too fast up on Route 59 by the bridge. Damn near ran me off the road. Car's in the shop."

"Gina told me you were dead," I told Maureen.

Maureen fished her maraschino cherry out of her glass. "If wishes were horses."

Gina threw back another tequila shot and slammed the glass on the table, glaring at Maureen like they were in a drinking contest over the viscount's daughter's hand in marriage. I was still trying to work out what I was doing here and why, a question that came up often when Gina was driving the bus. I took my vodka in tiny, careful sips, feeling outclassed in every way by these two hard-drinking broads.

"So. Maureen Loeffler, village manager. Has a nice ring to it." Gina grimaced like she'd tasted poison. "When did that happen?"

"Last October."

"Sounds like a hoot," Gina said. "What are you working on these days? Termite control in Veterans Park? Upgrading toilets at the PD?" Gina had been baiting Maureen all night, like a teen who gets a bad dye job to spite her mom. When did she ever give this much of a shit what someone thought of her?

Maureen laughed. Anything Gina tossed her way she deflected

with a chuckle or a grin, leaning into the blow like a champ. It pissed Gina off even more. "Even better. I just started a financial audit of all village departments, including the PD. Doing a full inventory, down to the last pencil." Maureen shrugged. "Someone's got to make sure one and one add up to two."

"You sure anyone on your staff can count that high?" Gina tossed back another shot. If I drank that much that fast, I would be dead. Do not pass drunk, go straight to dead.

I lunged into the pause. "Can you tell us about—"

"Who killed him, Mo?" Gina burst in.

Subtle. The booze had both sharpened and loosened Gina. There was a halo around her, something black and wavy with tentacles.

Maureen dunked her cherry, then set it on a fresh cocktail napkin. "Honestly, Geen? I kind of thought you did." She looked around. "And I'm not the only one."

So Gina wasn't just being paranoid. All the more balls on her, to walk in here like a queen, knowing everyone suspected her of murder. I felt creepy-crawly, like we were spotlit on a stage, surrounded by darkness and staring eyes. How did Gina end up the villain in this play?

"Come on, Mo, give me a little credit," Gina said. "If I'd killed him, they'd never have found his body." She looked sweaty and crazy, all glittery eyes and teeth. If I were, say, trying to convince people of my innocence, I'd avoid murder jokes, but that was just me.

Unless she's hiding in plain sight. The thought swam up in my mind like a bubble and burst in a sparkly pop.

"What are you doing here, Gina?" Maureen leaned in and dropped her voice. "Why are you getting this nice girl all mixed up in your petty little obsessions? Does she need this? She's just an ordinary . . ." Maureen scanned me for clues about my role in all this and came up with nothing. "I'm sorry, what do you do, exactly?"

"I read tarot cards," I said.

I watched the inevitable marquee scroll across Maureen's face: *Huh. So that's what she's doing these days.* She turned to Gina, like this level of nonsense needed to be taken straight to Mom. "Wow," she said. "This is beyond the pale even for you, Geen. You're consulting psychics now?"

I swallowed a tart, fizzy mouthful and sat up. This was it: my shot to push these two out of the exclusive arena of their history and into my arena, where they weren't so smugly sure of themselves. "You ever had your cards read before?" I said.

Maureen sat back. "Honey, I stopped believing in magic around the time I gave up candy cigarettes."

"Candy . . . *cigarettes*?" I looked at Gina, who shrugged. "Do you smoke them or eat them?"

"Oh, to be young." Maureen tossed back her drink.

"Why don't we ask the cards who killed Officer Pete?" I put a whisper of mystical fuckery into my voice just in case.

"Aren't you always saying the cards aren't some Q and A vending machine?" Gina said.

I hauled off to kick her under the table.

"No, hold on, Gina, hold on." Maureen plucked the cherry off her napkin. "Let the young lady do her thing." Now Maureen was the one being contrary. "Didn't I always say you should use every tool at your disposal?" She tossed the cherry into her mouth and grinned at Gina while she chewed. Gina looked like she was ready to leap across the table and strangle her.

I set my kicking leg down. Maybe Gina was a necessary part of this, like the irritating speck of sand the oyster tries to sneeze out in the process of making a pearl. Whatever had happened between these two—and Peterson—it was still alive, still fertile.

Sometimes the cards were better at showing the right questions than they were at giving answers. Gina and Maureen, horns locked, would point the way.

I took out the deck, cleared the table. Maureen watched me shuffle. "All right!" She snapped her fingers in a jazzy pattern. "Let's do this! Show me . . . the killer!" She looked to see if anyone was laughing. "*Family Feud*," she told me. "Are you too young for that, too?"

I closed my eyes, took a breath, and flipped over the first card.

Seven of Pentacles. Dude leaning on a hoe next to his garden of flourishing pentacles, pleased as fuck to have his time and patience rewarded.

"This card is about roots. About things that take care and patience, and grow over time." I was straining a bit to push this in the direction I needed it to go. "Like a career. You worked with Officer Pete for a long time, didn't you?" I said to Maureen.

"Going on twenty-five years." Maureen sucked a drop off her hand and squinted. "He came to Sandhill Lake in the early aughts and he was still there when I retired last year."

I squeezed the lime into my drink. Bubbles hissed and rose to the top. "Was he a good cop?"

"He was a *great* cop," Maureen said.

Gina made a wet retching noise.

"What made him a great cop?" Start easy with the question Maureen *wanted* to answer.

"He was a team player. Always ready to help." She drew a wiry finger along the rim of her glass. Her voice had shifted into a more official register. "He was one of those guys who was always late for everything, and half the time it was because he was helping someone."

Gina opened her mouth, slammed it shut. Her fingers did an arrhythmic dance on the table, like an overexcited heart. "The other half was because he was a self-absorbed bastard who didn't see anyone else's time as valuable," she added.

"Three of Cups," I said. Three ladies dancing in a circle, cups upraised. "Collaboration. Sociability. How did he get along with people?" I glanced at Gina. "Any conflicts with anyone?"

"Oh, he was very sociable." Maureen tossed Gina a look. "Funny as hell." She laughed a little. "It was a party every day, working with him." *She's protecting him*, I thought. *Why? From what?*

"A party with a lot of booze." Gina picked up a quarter and flicked it off her thumb. "He totaled not one but two squad cars because he liked to start the party at work. Dan Kaluza once found him passed out in a ditch in his truck and had to tow his ass home." Her black hair shone blue in the dim bar light. The accountant clothing looked loose and wrinkled on her, like a skin she was about to unzip and step out of. She looked feral.

Seven of Wands. "Challenges, problems," I said. "Was there anything he *didn't* do well?" Easing Maureen into giving up the dirt.

"Well, he thought big. He was an idea guy." Maureen frowned and shifted in her chair. "And sometimes that meant he wasn't great with details."

"Gee, you think?" Gina growled. The quarter spun across the table in a silver orb. "He couldn't string two words together on a report. Or follow basic procedure. How about the time he whipped out his gun and started cleaning it right in the middle of the telecommuting room, with all these civilians around? That's just like, basic gun safety, Mo."

I turned to Maureen. "Was his behavior ever . . . corrected?" *Mirror their language.*

Gina folded her arms and turned to Maureen with a vicious mock curiosity on her face.

"Of course it was corrected." Maureen ran a hand over the back of her neck. "Any infractions are always—"

"You lying twat." Gina upended her rocks glass and crushed the ice in her teeth. "Dan taking Pete to Chasers to talk about his problem drinking is not discipline. The gun-cleaning thing?" She slammed her hand on the table and the quarter bounced off in a silver swirl. "Automatic one-month suspension. Did he get that? Did he get *anything*? He did whatever the fuck he wanted, Maureen, and you know it."

Maureen blinked. "When you have an employee who excels in certain areas, you play to their strengths. Compromise a bit." She had lowered her voice to defuse Gina's imminent explosion. Straight out of the manager manual. "Do you know what compromise is, Gina? Let's do a little vocabulary lesson." She must have skipped the page about avoiding sarcasm in volatile employee situations.

"Oh, I know your definition of compromise." Gina crossed her arms. "I know how you spell it, too. K-i-s-s-a-s-s."

"Strengths! Okay!" Things were spiraling a bit. I tried to rein them in. "Let's talk about his strengths. What were they?"

"He was great with high-profile community initiatives," Maureen said. "Like the Explorers. He headed our Explorer post for years. It was his baby. He'd just ordered them new uniforms, got them into the top five at the state competition last year. The kids loved him. And he really loved shaping the minds of young law enforcement."

"Oh, Christ, are you kidding me?" Gina roared. She hopped to her feet, dipped her fingers in her glass, and sprayed Maureen in the face.

"You know what," I said, "let's all just . . ." I drew another card and didn't even look at it. "This is a card of peace. And of sitting down and talking quietly."

Maureen rose to her feet slowly. Neither she nor Gina was looking at me. Perhaps my attempts to pit them against each other had worked too well.

"Oh sure, he loved to *shape the minds of young law enforcement*," Gina mocked. "Especially if those minds had young nubile breasts attached to them."

"Enough, Gina." Maureen wiped her face with a soggy cock-tail napkin. "He's dead. It's over."

"Are you going to sit there and tell me he wasn't a perv?" Gina's voice rose. People were looking around. "If it moved, he'd fuck it. I don't remember a time when he *wasn't* fucking around on June. She just stopped caring."

My ears stood up like antennae. Officer Pete was cheating on June? This gave their relationship an intriguing push from "distant" to "hostile." I tried to avoid judging stuff between two people who were not me, but everything I was hearing this evening cut across the grain of Officer Pete's white-knight-with-a-badge exterior. The Officer Pete emerging here—a low-key drunk, a selfish dope, a vain, arrogant deadbeat, and now a habitual sleazeball—was not the one I had grown up with.

"Sit down, dummy," Maureen hissed. "You're making an ass of yourself."

"I'm surprised he never tried to slip it to you." Gina talked right over her. "But then, you were a bit old for him, being, you know, able to vote and drink."

Maureen, who'd been staring at Gina, flickered away for an instant, glanced at her drink.

"Did he?" Gina lowered her voice. "Try to get with you? Oh my God. He did, didn't he?" Her face cracked with rage. "What did he make you do?"

I froze. This was it. We had come to something very important.

I didn't relish the thought of anyone else getting killed, but I needed to let this play out.

Maureen picked up her drink and swirled it. Then she put it down and stared at Gina. "He didn't make me do anything."

Gina made a low, throaty noise. Her face was flat and twisted. She picked up a cocktail napkin and tore it in half, over and over and over. She didn't seem to know she was doing it. "Were you . . . and he . . ." Gina stepped toward Maureen, very slowly. "Were you fucking him, Maureen?"

I shrank back in my chair and started shoving the cards willy-nilly into their bag. This was bad, very bad. Needless to say, the reading was over.

"Everything makes sense now." Gina's eyes went black. "Was this going on when—"

"Yep, there it is." Maureen exploded. "Five seconds. That's how long it took you to make this about you. You know what, God forbid you should grow the hell up and take a little responsibility for your own actions instead of blaming everything on everybody else."

"Oh no. No, no, no, no. You did *not* just say that what that motherfucker did was my fault." People were watching now.

"I am just saying there are times to push and times to step back and—"

Gina roared and dove for Maureen. The music got very loud. Gina and Maureen grappled and twisted and I snatched my drink up from the table before they crashed down on it. The table creaked and toppled over, raining glassware. I cowered in the corner holding my cards in one hand and my drink in the other. Here came Bald and Balder to pull the two women apart. Gina elbowed the younger one off and clawed at Maureen again like a wild animal, punching and tearing. Maureen was stronger and faster. She twisted Gina's arm and pinned her to a nearby pillar. Gina struggled and huffed, but Maureen held her fast and eventually she calmed.

Maureen leaned down and spoke into her ear. "You listen, Gina, and listen good. Back. The hell. Off. I'm saying this for your own good. They're already looking at you, so stop making things worse for yourself. Let it go." She released Gina and stepped back.

Gina swayed and shook herself back into her jacket. A trickle of blood crawled down her forehead and she swiped at it with her sleeve. "Sure. Let it go." She swept her hand through the air along an imaginary neon marquee. "That ought to be on the official seal of the Sandhill Lake PD. 'Let it go.' Right up there with 'Look the other way.'"

"I'm telling you this as a friend," Maureen said.

"Oh yeah," Gina said bitterly. "You always have my back."

Maureen's face went still. She went to the wreckage of the table and picked out her purse. "Katie, it was nice to meet you." She did not look at Gina. "Best of luck. And be careful who you trust."

"You"—the bartender, a thick woman with a bleached shag and an apron reading DAY DRINKING! in a trippy flower-child font was pointing to Gina, tapping her heel—"and you"—she swiveled over to me. "Out."

12

"In and out like ghosts," I said. "No one even knew we were there."

Gina shot me a crabby look over her plate. On the way back from the Olde Prairie Inn, she had declared a hankering for "real" New York pizza. We ended up driving an hour into the city to a bare-bones section of Elston Avenue lined by towering warehouses and empty lots of cracked concrete behind chain-link fencing.

"You ever have a friend you *didn't* try to kill?" I said.

Gina liberated a string of cheese from her hair and popped it into her mouth. "You're alive, aren't you?" Whatever current had electrified her into a clawed death machine was off, but I couldn't stop seeing her twisted face lunging at Maureen. The two of them had been friends, and yet Gina had almost jabbed her eyes out. How long before I did something that turned that blank-eyed rage on me?

"I can't believe that horny old bat," Gina said. I assumed she was talking about Maureen, although it was a milder, tired sort of obligatory swearing, almost affectionate.

I licked grease off my thumb. "Was she already sleeping with him when you all worked together?"

"I don't know," Gina said. "It sure would explain why she was always sticking up for him. Why she let everything slide."

Gina's clothes were filthy and rumpled. She looked like a cartoon drunk. "There's a certain amount of shit you need to eat if you're going to be a woman cop. I get that." She shrugged. "Maureen was always a lot better at it than I was." Gina smirked. "And the results speak for themselves!" You couldn't tell with her sometimes if she was proud or sorry.

"Do you think Maureen could have killed him?" I said.

"I'd put money on June before Maureen. Maureen could send his ass home at the end of the day." Gina shuddered. "June actually had to live with him."

"Did you know her?"

"Met her a couple of times. Kind of an odd bird. A little crunchy. Free spirit, earth mother type. Definitely not your typical cop's wife. I kind of liked her."

The June-labeled absence in my mind was starting to fill in, just a pencil sketch for now, a sky, sun, horizon, an outline of a person. A shape looking for its suit and number.

Dimo's Real New York Pizza was a grimy Edison Park takeout joint wedged between a currency exchange and a fenced-off empty lot. When we walked in, the old Bulgarian dude who ran the place came out from the kitchen and kissed Gina on both cheeks. We took the window table, one of three in the whole place. There was no menu. Gina and Dimo exchanged some kind of impenetrable code, and he shuffled off to the kitchen. The pizza he served us was studded with a fragrant spiced sausage and some starchy vegetable that smelled of faraway woods. It was the best goddamn pizza I had ever had in my life.

"It's good, right?" Gina folded her slice in half. "Told you it was worth the drive."

"When you said *real*, I was afraid we were looking at a nine-hour drive to New York."

"I love Chicago, but I am solidly in the New York camp on the pizza issue." Gina drank from a sweating brown plastic tumbler of ice-cold soda. "Also, New York is a *real* melting pot. Chicago is like a pantry organized by one of those neat freaks who doesn't like different foods touching."

"Small-town intolerance, big-city belligerence," I said. "We got it all."

Gina had gone to New York on a theater scholarship after high school—her brief shot at achieving escape velocity. When it turned out talent and ass busting didn't get you as far as money and connections, she ended up back in the northern Chicago burbs in the tiny welfare apartment her mom and two younger sibs had shared ever since her dad went to prison. How she went from acting to the shifty weeds of law enforcement, I had no idea. In between was a whole lot of snaky dot connecting with no clearly discernible picture to show for it.

"Was your mom glad to have you back from New York?" I wondered if I could get a few more dots to connect tonight, if I was casual about it.

"Oh yeah, she was stoked." Gina flicked her eyebrows. "First thing she said when I dropped my bags was 'We need milk.'" She looked out the window. It was showcase night at the ballroom dance studio across the street and people kept clacking past the overflowing garbage cans in their dance shoes and sequined ball finery.

"She'd just been fired from Walmart. My brother and sister were still at home." She shrugged. "Business as usual. I had to bring in some cash, fast." She cupped a swirl-patterned shaker of Parmesan cheese in her hands. "Luckily, there's plenty of cash to be had in Lake Forest, if you know where to look."

I inhaled a stealth chunk of pepper and gave a hacking circus-seal bark. Year after year, Lake Forest sat comfortably atop the list of highest-income towns in the entire state of Illinois. "You lived in Lake Forest?" I wheezed.

"Yup. Right next door to Michael Jordan." She made a face. "Get real. I lived in Pinewood. Lake Forest's shitty unincorporated neighbor. They share a school district, which means I went to Lake Forest High School, with all these overprivileged little shits and their parents. I knew that scene inside and out. I went to Goodwill, got myself some of their castoffs, and started hanging out wherever they did. The gym, the yoga studio, the coffee shop, the juice bar at Whole Foods. Wherever. All I had to do was figure out what they wanted and sell it to them." She blinked. "At a significant markup."

"What did they want?" I said.

Gina watched lights sparkle on the pavement outside. "They wanted to go backward," she said slowly. "There was nothing left for them to win, so they obsessed over what they'd lost. The women all wanted to be young and hot, and the men wanted their dicks to stay hard. Or some version of that."

A couple swept by, the woman in a wide maroon poodle dress, the man in a matching zoot suit. For a second I thought I was staring into the past.

"I worked out some characters. I had this sporty chick named Sandy." Gina sat up, spread her shoulders. "What's up, ladies!" she screeched. I checked Dimo but his attention was absorbed by an ancient tube TV blaring a PBS documentary about black holes. "You want nutrition *and* performance but you *don't* want to take a thousand pills, amirite?" Gina clapped her hands and finger-gunned me. "I got you, girl!" She picked up the Parmesan jar and tapped it with a nail. "DermaShred! One pill? Done!"

She dropped back into her regular low, smoky voice. "Baby laxatives from Dollar General. Put them in cute little bottles, sold them for ten." Sandy popped out of her again, high and bright. "It does not get any better than that, ladies!"

I dropped my pizza. My head spun. Gina dropped into a dreamy breathy voice, a mom singing a lullaby. "Brianna worked the yoga studios. Sold healing stones from the mountains of Nepal, guaranteed to balance your chakras and increase mind-fulness." She was talking in the third person, like these were actual people instead of pieces of herself run through a blender and weaponized. Gina's sharp, deadly sparkle shone through again. "Picked up the rocks up at Lake Bluff Beach. Those fuck-ers couldn't find Nepal on a map." She bowed her head and folded her palms. "Namaste.

"I had a whole crew of ringers," Gina went on. "So if some old turtle didn't want to shell out a hundred for a bottle of Alpine sheep-stomach face cream that was actually Jergens, I'd have one of my people come in and vouch for it." She took a deep breath of thick oregano-scented air. "I had a whole actors' studio. Taught them everything I'd learned in New York." She flicked an eye-brow at me. "Anyone who says you can't make money acting isn't doing it right."

I stared out the window at the orange city sky, a light spot where the moon was supposed to be. *Edge*, said the breathless voiceover from the documentary. I could only catch every other word. *Void. Limit. Nothing.* I remembered the fun, bubbly, edgy Gina I'd met at the old mall. So like this Gina, and also not like her at all.

"Did anyone ever want their money back?" I said.

"Not. A fucking. One." Gina bounced her cup on the table with each syllable, making the ice cubes jingle. "They were so used to throwing money at problems, with a crap hit ratio, they just wrote it off and moved on." Her eyes flashed. "I thought I would show them how to appreciate what they had. Teach them a lesson." Lines of red light from the neon sign slashed her face into angry stripes. "Not one of them ever learned it."

It wasn't the money that turned her on, I realized, it was the game. It was getting people to line up and dance to her tune. It was all the power she didn't have as a kid.

"I can't believe you never got caught," I said.

"I didn't say I never got caught," she said. "I just said no one asked for their money back." Gina took a bite. "I got cocky. I started slipping up." She shrugged. "That's when that salty old bat busted me."

"Maureen?"

Gina nodded. "I'd never met a woman cop before. All the cops I knew in the city were these doughy old Italian guys that looked like basset hounds. I tried the sympathy card on her at first. Gave her my best sob story." She waved it off. "That was a bust. She was mean as a snake. Lump of coal for a heart."

A dreamy look passed over Gina's face. She communicated almost entirely in a language of negativity in all its forms, conjugations, and declensions. I'd become skilled at parsing the nuances of her constant barbs, sarcastic asides, side-eye, and backhanded compliments. Coming from Gina, a chain of creative insults this long was a flat-out declaration of love.

"She said, oh, you had it tough? You and every other fuckup that comes through here." Gina rolled her eyes. "That part I'd heard before. But then she asked me for help."

"Help?"

"Well, *asked* is a generous term. More like, gave me no choice if I wanted the charges dropped. But just the fact that she thought I could do it . . ." Gina shrugged and looked outside into the dark. I felt a tapping in my heart, an echo of something familiar. I understood Gina and Maureen's relationship a lot more clearly now.

I chugged my soda, streaming peppery tears. "What did she need help with?"

"There was this pastor who was dealing pills to his congregation. Big megachurch up on Green Bay Road. This motherfucker." She crushed a napkin. "My dad never set foot in a church in his life, but this guy was just like him. Rules were for chumps. Didn't apply to him." She traced a shiny bead of water across the oilcloth and watched the trail it left, beads of water splitting and re-forming. "The second I saw him, I knew I had to bring him down."

"So what did you do?"

"Put on my mom's old church clothes and went to church!" she howled in a wavery old-woman voice. "I was saved! Praise the Lord!" She slipped back into Gina. "Watched him. Chatted him up. Had dinner with his family. Took pictures." She upended her soda into her mouth and crunched the ice. "Put him away for thirty counts of possession with intent to distribute *and* five counts of disbursing charitable funds without authority and for personal benefit. Because of course he had his fingers in the till, too." There was an avaricious glow to her face. "That was it. I was hooked. A year later I was a rookie at Sandhill Lake and Maureen was my boss."

A happy ending, I guessed, if that was where you stopped the story. I wanted to ask her why she quit, but I sensed hidden rocks in the water.

"You must have really liked it," I said carefully.

Gina picked up her cup. "Turned out it wasn't for me." She gave me a cold stare. "Just a bunch of paperwork and office politics. I might as well have been an accountant or some shit."

She was lying. Gina looked at you straight on when she lied, because you expected the opposite. She flicked a glob of cheese into her mouth and I knew we were done. The doors were closed again.

I imagined a younger, wilder, fiercer Gina. The pleasure on her face when she described stealing, manipulating people. She had enforced the law for a while, or some version of it, when the law coincided with what she wanted. Was it inertia that kept her on this side of it, gravity and habit, like one of Dimo's planets, autopiloting around the sun until something knocked it off course?

"So you became a cop by accident," I said.

"If by 'accident' you mean 'getting arrested,' then yes. It's common. Half the guys I worked with had juvie sheets a mile long."

I gaped at her and she sprayed a quick laugh. "What, you think all cops are like Jamie?" Her voice got syrupy and bright. "Little Boy Scouts who lie awake at night and dream of helping people?" She shrugged. "Scratch that selfless hero bullshit hard enough, and you'll always come up with some weirdo personal grudge," Gina said. "Most cops are just regular dudes who need an excuse to go around punching people in the face."

"I think Jamie really does want to help people." I knew kids like Jamie in high school. They carried color-coded folders for every subject, kept their lockers clean enough to eat out of, and read ahead every night *just to stay on top of things.* Jamie had had a free pass to do whatever he wanted in life. Why his compass settled on police work instead of the doctor-lawyering his parents had probably envisioned for him, I did not know.

"Maybe he does." Gina stared out the window at the cold

streetlight, streaks on the wet pavement reflecting the streetlight-orange sky. "Some cops do." She picked up her straw, let a glittering stream of soda roll into her mouth. "And some only think they do."

She turned to me and her eyes flashed. "Those are the ones you have to watch out for."

A man in a tuxedo waltzed by outside, whirling a laughing preteen girl in a tiny sequined gown and platform dance shoes. Gina followed them with her eyes. "Is Jamie going to the funeral tomorrow?"

"Dan's making them all go. So they can smile and shake hands and look like they're doing something. Why?"

"I need you to help me find something," Gina said. "Before Dan does."

"What is it?"

"A voice recording," Gina said. "I have a pretty good idea where to look, but I'll need Jamie."

"Sure, I can talk to him tomorrow," I said. "What do you need?"

"Well, that's the thing." Gina turned from the window and looked at me. "I don't want you to talk to him. I'll need you to keep this between us."

13

"Bloom blast!"

I turned to see if a gruff but lovable pirate wanted to teach me about the letter B, but it was Jessie, testing for drafts from the ceiling vents, waving her hands over the massive orchid displays we'd just dragged into the church sanctuary.

"It's too dry in here," Jessie said. "The blooms are drooping. See how the blooms are drooping? They're going to fall off any second."

"That would definitely be the biggest tragedy at this funeral," I said. "Will you relax? No one's even looking at the flowers."

Jessie spun toward me, lips flared.

"I just mean," I added, "people aren't sweating the tiny details right now." It was always a risk, reminding Jessie of her place in the solar system.

"It's *all* tiny details, Katie." Jessie snapped. "*Life* is tiny details." She'd been creating teaching moments for me all morning and I wanted to stuff her face into the nearest orchid spray. I was sweating in the hideous True Realty blazer she made me wear, I ached all over from dragging around heavy ceramic planters, I was sick of hiking up Gina's borrowed pantyhose, and my eyes kept threatening to slide shut because I had lain awake all night, turning over in my mind, like a dark kaleidoscope, the events of last night. I finally rolled into a black sleep around sunrise.

Jessie stormed off to complain about the heat before her flowers exploded or whatever. I sank into an empty pew. Our Lady of the Lake was a breezy glass cavern festooned with blond wood and impressionistic stained glass riffs on the saints.

I searched the small pre-ceremony crowd of insiders for anyone who might have been June. She'd been a ghostly presence in the newscasts, coloring every flowery expression of grief—*survived by his loving family*—but it was always Matt who handled the onscreen interviews. Who was she? What did she look like? A younger Maureen, tough and slick, a former cop? A sleek prairie Kardashian, from the looks of some of the other cop wives in here? All I knew about June Peterson was that she was "different."

Izzy and his mighty battalion of a family had absorbed three pews and counting. I came over to say hello and was sucked into a vortex of handshakes, back pats, shoulder squeezes, and cheek smacks, spinning out blinking on the other side. I didn't know exactly how to ask, without being rude, how Izzy had scored an invite to this very exclusive shindig.

"Officer Pete is practically family," Izzy said, as if reading my mind. He patted the shoulder of a tiny multi-great-grandpa in a dashing gray suit sitting on the edge of the pew. "Uncle Emil has a bad heart. Terrible. Officer Pete's been over how many times now with the ambulance, three?"

Uncle Emil whipped out a razor-thin phone, flashed some peace, and took a selfie.

"Three." Izzy pocketed the old man's phone. "If it weren't for

Officer Pete you'd have sneaked away from us by now." I kind of loved that he thought of death less like a permanent departure and more like a post-curfew trip to the club.

"I want to be an ambulance driver when I grow up," said a skinny ten-year-old mashing buttons on a handheld game console.

"You could be a doctor," Izzy said. "Or own the ambulance company."

"People need ambulances, and ambulances need drivers," the kid said. His game let out a fiery belch and a scream. "I can be anything I want. You said."

"Exactly, so why be an ambulance driver?"

Maureen watched me from inside a cluster of suits, her black eye covered with makeup. No evidence of having smashed someone's face into a table the night before. What happens at the Olde Prairie Inn, et cetera. All the other suits—Dan Kaluza, the mayor of Sandhill Lake, a couple of gray-haired twins from the state's attorney's office—were flashing Jessie's flag pins on their lapels. How many of them knew about Peterson and Maureen? How many cared?

Maureen shot me a hard, even look, then nodded curtly and turned away. I wondered if she knew Gina was here, too, skulking on the edge of the chaos outside the church. Jessie had nudged the rented van through a thick crowd, young moms putting kids on their shoulders to watch the procession of squad cars from all over the state, old men standing at attention, groups of beefy young guys passing beers back and forth and holding signs: BLUE LIVES MATTER, COP KILLERS BEWARE, standing on top of trucks with Punisher skull decals in their back windows. There was a high-voltage crackle in the air, like a party but a grim, vengeful one, full of rage that bled over into glee. *See?* it seemed to say. *We told you.* A stone-faced cop had waved us around to the back of

END

the church to unload, and that was when I'd glimpsed Gina in the crowd, gray sweatshirt hood over her scowl. Jessie said something to me and by the time I looked back out the window, Gina was gone.

She had wanted, last night, access to an old computer at the Sandhill Lake PD, and she wanted Jamie's help, but she didn't want him to know what he was doing. She was asking me to use him, and the idea of it was making me sick. When I asked her what was on the recording, all she said was *trust me*. I was hearing that a lot from her. *Trust me.*

"Nice blazer." Jamie had appeared beside me, making me jump. He had come over from a huddle of guys in identical dark gray suits and with plastic badges around their necks. Jamie wore a suit like a second skin. The rest of the guys looked like the suit was wearing them.

I flipped him a cheerful bird, which earned me a whack on the head from Jessie, passing behind me with a bouquet. "You're lucky I made it out of my pajamas this morning." I filled him in on the previous evening's adventures.

"I can't believe this," Jamie said. "We've been banging away for a week and have nothing. You get in one bar fight and come out with a suspect with a credible motive. Did Gina ever mention Maureen before?"

I felt an uncontrollable itchiness. "Not specifically."

Jamie gave me his slow blink. "She didn't tell you about Maureen, she didn't tell you she knew Peterson, and she didn't tell you she worked at Sandhill Lake?"

"I knew she was a cop," I offered. When I thought about trying to explain Gina's complicated, gap-filled history, my tongue went numb. "She's not one to dwell on the past." I was making excuses for her. *Trust me . . .* "Are you going to interview Maureen? That ought to be a fun one."

"Not for me," Jamie said acidly. "The victimology interviews are going to some FBI lox who's never left his desk in his life. Dan needs to look like he's playing ball. Also, this way he can say he didn't investigate Peterson himself, should anything bad come out."

Dan Kaluza materialized next to Jamie like Oscar the Grouch popping out of a garbage can. "I heard my name. All good things, I hope?" He looked me over. "Miss True, good to see you again." An avaricious gleam flickered through his face. The accident had made me interesting, useful.

"I wonder if we could have that chat soon," Jamie said. "About the victimology interviews. I have some thoughts about—"

Dan gave me a quick get-a-load-of-this guy side-eye. I gave him a blank stare. "Jamie, Jamie." Dan clapped Jamie on the shoulder. "It's a funeral, huh? Today is about the family."

"Of course," Jamie said.

"I mean, I'm struggling myself." He wiped his forehead from the effort. "Man, that morning, when I got the call about what happened? I about rear-ended the car ahead of me in the drop-off lane at the middle school."

Jamie went still. "Your son plays soccer, right?"

"Center forward!" Dan bellowed. "Scored three goals this month alone."

"Very impressive." He gave Dan a chilly look that could not have been less impressed.

"Listen, Jamie, about the interviews," Dan said. "Love the enthusiasm, but as commander, it's my job to make sure things get organized and delegated in the most efficient way possible." Dan glanced at me. This was at least partially for my benefit. "And to be honest," Dan continued, "I think it would make the family more comfortable if the interviews were handled by someone with a bit more connection to the community. Someone local. Someone who grew up here. You understand."

"I do," Jamie said. "Which is why I'm confused about why this detail is being assigned to the Feds. Who are not local."

Dan's jaw looked wired shut. A snort bubbled out of me, and he turned to me sharply. *You're on the list now*, his flat blue eyes seemed to say.

"We'll talk later," Dan said. More shoulder clapping for Jamie, another handshake for me, and then he was gone.

"I want to punch him," I said. "Can I punch him?"

"He's my boss," Jamie said.

"That's a no?"

Jamie was still watching Dan walk away. "Hey." I snapped my fingers in his face. "Are you a middle school soccer fan now? What was that all about?"

"He said he was at the middle school the morning Peterson was killed. But I ran into his wife a few days ago, and she said *she* was dropping their son off that day." Jamie put his hands in his pockets. "He's lying."

Jessie appeared next to us. "Here they come," she singsonged. "Showtime." Jamie tossed me a nod and went back to his row. Jessie grabbed me by the elbow and shoved me next to her in front of the largest and gaudiest of the orchid sprays, just inside the door. "Smile!" she hissed.

A flood of dark cloth poured in from the vestibule. I craned my neck, watching for anyone I recognized. Matt appeared in the doorway in his dress uniform, all black and gold. He looked so much like his young dad I thought if I reached out a fingertip he would ring like glass, smooth and unreal as a photograph. He shot me a quick smile and moved on toward the front row. Out of the corner of my eye, I watched Jamie watch us.

When everyone was settled, Jessie and I slipped into the last remaining aisle seats in a middle row. A big bald guy whose uniform made him look more like a bandleader than a cop started in on the introductory remarks. Between the piano-scored video montages, the soft mumbly speeches, the orchid-killing heat, and no sleep the night before, I began to nod off. Jessie poked me in the ribs, but I sank deeper and deeper into a warm pool.

The vestibule door banged open. Everyone turned toward the asshole who had interrupted the funeral sermon, which was nice because it meant no one except Jamie, smirking at me from the back row, saw me flail awake.

A woman walked out of the wall of light, a solid honey blonde in her fifties, with a thick fringe of bangs, wearing a black bell-sleeve minidress exploding with beaded yellow sunflowers. She blinked and looked around like she'd just strolled by the church and thought hey, cool, a funeral.

Heads turned, hands shielded eyes against the knifelike vestibule light.

"June's here," Jessie snorted in my ear. "Finally." I could hear the gears grinding in her head, pitting her innate judginess against June's status as her client. "Wearing a rather festive funeral dress."

The door clapped shut and June set off down the aisle. The sunflowers glittered and raced, her black thigh-high slouch boots clacking through the silence. She carried a large beaded purse studded with the same bright sunflowers as her dress. Jasmine and clove twined in her wake as she passed me, and I heard a tinkle of silver and stones.

I watched her float past, unable to move. This was Officer Pete's wife? Matt's mom? She didn't just seem alien in the tough, solid Peterson family, she seemed like an alien on earth. She reminded me of someone, but when I tried to see who, they slipped away, like they were holding my hand but walking a few steps ahead so I couldn't see their face.

In the front row, Matt turned. His eyes went flat. June landed

a row ahead of me across the aisle, shifting from foot to foot—
pardon me, sorry, excuse me, thank you so much—while people
grumbled to their feet to move over for her. Like a final twirl of
icing on the lopsided cake of her arrival, her giant beaded purse
flopped open and spilled its contents all over the floor. A bright
stream flooded the aisle—coin bracelets, flowered handker-
chiefs, bits of embroidered silk, beaded jewelry.

Something green glittered on the floor, feet away. My heart
flash-froze.

It was a dragonfly. A brass pin with large colored wings set with
tiny white jewels. The same in every way as the one in Jamie's
photograph, but with green wings, not pink.

The other pin in Gina's missing set.

People crawled around the aisle, helping a hand-wringing
June reassemble her purse. When I looked up to see if Matt was
watching, his seat was empty. The door to the vestibule had
clicked shut again.

I got up, ignoring Jessie's glare, and followed Matt out.

I found Matt in a side room off the vestibule, sitting on the floor
in the middle of a semicircle of tiny desks. Posters covered the
walls: rainbows and stylized hearts, cursive messages of acceptance, love. A chain of tiny handprints spelled out the word
COMMUNITY.

There was a crayon storage thing on the teacher's desk, a wheel
with a million holes in it, crayons arranged tips up in a graduated
spectrum of color. It looked like a space flower come to earth to
eat us all. I picked it up and sat on the floor across from Matt, my
back against the teacher's desk. The funeral seeped through the
walls, traces of sound, slow voices, pretty, mournful chords.

"He would have loved this." Matt looked up at a roll of distant laughter. He looked like he was savoring the smell of someone cooking his favorite meal. "The speeches, the music, the flowers."

Someone actually noticed the flowers? Jessie could die happy.

"All except the hair." He held a wrinkled scrap of paper in his hands. "They combed his hair all wrong. He looked like an accountant. Like he died in his sleep." He gave me a grin. "Every cop's worst nightmare. A cop wants to go down fighting." He looked down. "At least he got what he wanted."

I pressed my hand into the crayon tips, their baby needles like puppy teeth digging into my skin. Did Matt know his mom had Gina's dragonfly in her purse? My hands itched for my cards but I'd left them in the van because Jessie's blazer had only those stupid fake decorative pockets, like pockets were so awesome to look at. There was so much I wanted to ask him, and this was exactly the wrong time to be doing that.

"What do you have there?" I asked him.

Matt gave me an unreadable look. Then he crooked a finger at me. *Come here.* I felt at the same time warm and tingly but also tight and springy. I crawled over and squeezed in next to him on the floor between the desks. There wasn't much room. We sat close, our bodies touching.

He handed me the scrap of paper solemnly, like it was a document of authenticity.

In the picture, Officer Pete, young, shirtless, muscular, eyes behind glasses, pushing the sun out of his eyes, stood next to little Matt, maybe five or six years old, right around the time I met him, his white-gold hair flopping in his face, the two of them laughing. They were standing in front of a sleek shark-nosed boat, deep cherry red like a secret fruit in a magic garden or a treasure in an underground cavern filled with gold and rubies. Dream colored, fantasy colored. I wanted to eat the boat. Cursive lettering leaped along the boat's bow, interrupted by Matt's and Pete's bodies: AMER . . . US. Their arms were around each other. The photo had been scanned in, taken before everyone had a camera on their phone. It was crooked, charmingly off-kilter, like something that flew in from another world, another time.

"That was the day he got it," Matt said. "It's a thirty-five-foot Chris-Craft Launch with the full teak package. It was his baby." He held the phone in both hands, like a slippery fish about to escape. "He called it the *American Lotus*, for the lake flower." He stared into the air like he was seeing it in front of him, a summer's day, white sun flashing on the water, cicadas screeching in the wet air.

"We used to go out on Grass Lake together, just the two of us. He said the lotus beds used to cover the whole lake, and they made up this story about how it was this rare Egyptian lotus, to drum up tourist business. They'd take them out there in these huge boats to look at it. The boats tore up the lotus beds and now they're mostly gone. But every once in a while you can see a few flowers here and there. They have these bright yellow blooms that stand up from the pads, and they only flower for a few days, in August, so you have to catch them at just the right time, and they're just . . ." He trailed off and turned away.

When he spoke again his voice was thicker. "He would say, *That's us, Matty! You see those little flowers? See how they rise above all that green? Some people are like that. Exceptional. You and me, we're like that. It's a lot of work, but it's worth it, huh?*"

I took his hand and he squeezed it.

I geared myself up and took my shot. "I saw your mom out there." Matt's hand stiffened in mine, then softened again. "You came separately." And also you shot eye daggers at her when you saw her, but I didn't say that part. "You two aren't close. Why?"

Matt looked at me like we'd been sailing over the lake in a glorious bubble, and I had just popped it. He took the photograph from me and folded it into a uniform pocket.

"Are you and Jamie close?" he said.

I went red but he wasn't looking at me. He was looking behind me, as if talking to someone hovering over my shoulder. *His dad.* I shivered and fought the urge to turn around.

"We haven't known each other long," I said. "But yeah, you could say we're close."

Matt nodded like I had answered correctly. I watched myself come into focus in his eyes. "Then you know cops," he said. "You know how they are."

Did I? I'd grown up with the usual rosy glow around the idea of cophood that you get handed with a basic elementary education, boosted by my experience with Officer Pete. Nurses, firemen, cops: *community helpers!* A cardboard cutout of a smiling cop with his hand raised, ready to help.

Jamie and Gina gave me a glimpse behind the cutout, of the struts and wires holding the thing together. Or keeping people from looking too closely. What was back there? A collage of bright reflective surfaces, low whispers behind bright smiles. Competition masquerading as friendship. Conflict as language, selective listening. An exteriority I found alien but fascinating, like a museum diorama of a distinct human species whose specimens still walked the earth in tiny, zealously tribal clusters. Like us but not like us at all.

Subdue, pacify, cover, smooth over: that was the job. Magician stuff: act, reason, do. Solve the problem, don't think about the cause. Causes got passed to the next person up the chain. Thinking, feeling, listening—High Priestess stuff—was not in the job description. Maybe I clicked with Jamie and Gina precisely *because* they were outliers in all that bright exteriority, like flashes of negative space. Jamie the brainy introvert, and Gina, unhinged even by cop standards. Both moved comfortably through the environment but had just enough High Priestess in them, enough reflection and quiet that we saw eye to eye.

COMMUNITY, the rainbow-colored handprints shouted.

Did I know cops? Matt watched me, waiting for an answer. Was I on board? Could I be trusted?

"Yeah," I said. "I guess I know cops." I wasn't sure we were agreeing to the same thing.

"You accept certain things," Matt said, "if you're going to be with a cop. They're not all good things, but you accept them or you leave and marry an accountant."

Accountants were getting a walloping in this conversation. "They don't seem like they had very much in common."

"Too bad they didn't figure that out until after they got married. They met out west, where she grew up. On an organic farm or something." He dismissed it with a wave. "They should have known it would never work, but I guess they weren't thinking.

"My dad wasn't perfect," Matt said, "but he was my dad."

A chill wound through me. He didn't say it in an *I love my dad no matter what* sort of way. He said it like he had no choice, like Maureen had said it last night, the way she stuck up for Pete's rule bending in favor of what he did for the *community*. Dan, too, the way he was tiptoeing around the investigation. Matt knew his dad better than anyone but saw him the least clearly, because he was too close. He was a mirror, a closed door. I wasn't going to get anything from him.

The only one not pulling their punches on this thing was Gina. Gina and Jamie. The outliers, the freaks.

And me.

"I'm going to help you, Matt," I said.

"With what?" He looked genuinely puzzled.

I steeled myself. "People loved your dad," I said. "He was a huge part of this community, which is wonderful, but it's also working against him. It's making everyone jumpy. Too eager for justice. We owe it to him to slow down and figure out the truth, no matter where we find it."

Matt looked like he was searching for a polite way to ask where the hell this was going. "And you're going to help, how, exactly?"

I was running my fingers faster and faster around the crayons, and I forced myself to stop and put them down. "Remember how I told you I read tarot cards? Well, I also help Jamie with his cases. I kind of use one to help the other. That's how Jamie and I met—we solved a murder together last year." I licked my lips and continued. "It sounds weird, but trying to solve a problem with tarot cards is a lot like doing an investigation. Jamie and I just use different sides of the same skill.

"It helps to look at things from the outside, you know?" I smiled at him and he smiled back. "No one expects me to be paying attention, but I am."

"So you're on board, huh?" He gave me a mock-evaluating look, the smile still peeking through. "We've retained your services?"

"I am," I said. "You have. I'm going to figure this out."

"Well, then." He got to his feet, walked over, and helped me to my feet. "I guess you'd better get to it."

He held my hands a long second before letting go. "I never know what you're going to say next."

That's because we don't know each other, I almost said. Either I'd just done something great or I'd broken everything beyond repair. Sometimes it was hard to tell the difference.

14

"This is where things get interesting," Rosie said. We were finished with the first row of the Major Arcana and moving on to the second.

Rosie licked her fingers and wiped them on her top. "I hate to break it to you, kiddo," she said in a mock-secretive whisper, "but half the stuff you learn up here, when you're a kid"—she swept a fingertip over the first row—"is crap. It doesn't work when you get older. The second row is your real self coming out from under all the crap."

The door at the top of the stairs opened and a shaft of yellow light spilled in from the kitchen. "Are my crackers down there?" my mom shouted down. "The gluten-free ones?"

Rosie picked up and shook the empty cracker box. "No crackers here," she shouted back.

There was a suspicious pause. The door shut with a grumpy squeak.

"Anyway," Rosie went on, "this is the real you." She picked up Strength, the garlanded lady with her pale hands around the maw of a ringleted lion. "You could turn out totally different than you expected to. Or different than you were expected to." She tapped the self-important Chariot. "Maybe the things you thought were weaknesses were actually strengths."

This excited me tremendously. I pictured myself accepting an award for never finishing a meal before getting distracted and wandering off. A commendation for staying in the shower so long my skin turned to stewed prunes. First prize in a staring-into-space contest. The list went on.

"Now that you know who you are and what you need to do, do you have the balls to get started? Even when everyone says you shouldn't?" Rosie picked up the card again. The garlanded lady looked like she was taking no nonsense from this lion.

"This card says yes," Rosie said. "Yes, you do."

The crowd outside the church thinned, slow pockets of people and cars moving off into a heavy, overcast midafternoon. I looked for Gina, but she was either gone or hiding. My head buzzed, a hive of fuzzy bits wiggling around, trying to fuse into a whole.

"That was interesting." Jessie, lips in a white bow, squeezed the ten and two on the steering wheel. She was pissed no one had complimented her flowers, and even more pissed that she couldn't openly complain about it.

We zipped south on Route 59, an empty stretch of road with no visible beginning or end. Jessie opened up to a careful five above the speed limit. "Did you and Matt have a nice chat?" She had a cheese grater smile on her face, not at all furious that I clocked in more conversation minutes with a Peterson—any Peterson—than she did.

"He *loved* the flowers." Better to keep Jessie in a good mood. It had occurred to me that June Peterson might be less enthusiastic about buying a giant mansion tied to her husband's career now that he was gone, considering their edgy relationship. But I didn't know how to broach the topic with Jessie, or if I even should.

"Really?" Jessie turned to me. "He said that?"

"He said Officer Pete would have loved them, too."

Jesse drummed a cheery rhythm on the steering wheel. We were heading back into familiar territory, the empty landscape filling with strip malls, sprawling supermarkets, and crowded subdivisions of identical houses. Jessie was like a deep-sea fish that needed a certain density of surroundings so she didn't implode.

We passed an outdoor mall with an REI. Jessie stared at it dreamily. "I wonder if I should get Mike another set of compression tights for CrossFit. The crotches wear out really fast."

I did not know what to do with this information so I let it slide past. "When you were showing the Petersons the house," I said, "were they, you know, friendly? With each other? Did they get along?" I couldn't get June out of my mind, her air of celestial sadness. The dragonfly pin hiding in her purse, a sparkly fragment of something much larger, something as yet invisible.

"Oh my God, they were adorable." She did a weird thing that I thought was supposed to be a kissy face. "Couple goals."

I tossed her a side glance. Jessie's inability to read the room was legendary. Her assessment of the Petersons' demeanor was either a complete wash or the best evidence yet that they hated each other.

There was a weak lightening in the clouds where the sun was supposed to be. I got bold and pushed my luck. "So, is June still going forward with the sale? Even though Officer Pete is . . . ?"

"What's with the questions?" Jessie narrowed her eyes. "You're not helping Jamie investigate this, are you?" She said *investigate* the way I once heard a shaggy street preacher say *fornicate*.

"I'm just curious." I put on my best weepy bereaved-person-being-interviewed-on-*Dateline* voice. "You know how *special* Officer Pete was to me."

Jessie groaned. "Yes, please tell us one more time how he saved your life, because we haven't heard about it in all of five minutes."

Mission accomplished. Jessie's buttons were large and shamefully satisfying to push.

Her irritation irked me, though. "Is it really so bad for me to wonder what happened to him? Maybe try to help Jamie?" I said. "Jamie and I do the same thing, just in different ways."

Jessie groaned. "You're joking, right? Has Jamie ever, in the course of doing his job, been arrested for destroying an entire building?"

"I was not arrested, first of all, I was *detained*, there's a difference. And I didn't destroy this so-called building, which was just a garden shed. I just, you know, made everything inside it fall down. And break."

"Has Jamie ever called me in the middle of the night because he had lost my car and when we drove to Hammond, Indiana, to get it, it smelled like a pack of hyenas had been living in it?"

My previous investigative involvements had had some rough spots for Jessie that time had not yet smoothed over.

"Listen, Katie." Jessie's voice was high and delicate. She was choosing her words with care. "You have a life goal now. And that's great. I love that for you. It's what you've been missing, right?" She nodded her coercive nod.

"Yeah . . . ?" She was starting slow with things I couldn't possibly disagree with, and before I knew it I would be signing over my firstborn child.

"It's not the goal I would have picked, but that doesn't matter anymore, we're past that." She patted her chest, pleased with her own flexibility. "I'm just happy to help you succeed. For example . . ." She took a deep breath, quivering with barely concealed excitement. "I was going to wait to tell you, but what the heck!"

Uh-oh. This level of excitement in Jessie never boded well for me.

"You'll be reading cards at the grand opening event for Riviera Heights this coming Wednesday." She stared at me like she had just told me I'd won the lottery.

"Oh, wow," I said, racking my brain for what the hell Riviera Heights was supposed to be. I could tell from Jessie's face that I had been told this. Possibly more than once.

Jessie groaned. "Remember how I told you last week Future Builders approached me to be the exclusive listing agent for their Riviera Heights development?"

I kept my face still. I knew Jessie was saying words and I even knew what each one meant, but together they made an indecipherable wobble of noise I had probably let slide past me the first time she had mentioned it.

"The Petersons' house is the first sale in the development, and the sales office isn't even officially open yet. I had to do a little arm-twisting." Jessie wiggled in her seat. "To be honest, tarot cards don't correspond one-to-one with their project messaging." Translation: GTFO of here with your trashy carnival sideshow. "But I told them you were very professional and very entertaining and, I mean, Future? Fortune? Fortune-*telling*? Hello?" She smacked her forehead. "It's a no-brainer!"

Then she told me how much they were going to pay me for the privilege of profaning their shindig and I almost leaped out of my skin. It was more than I made in two months at my old job at the mall.

"Wow." Something collapsed slowly inside me, like a skyscraper being demolished. I thought of the idiot at the management consulting convention last month asking me if there was a fourth Long Island iced tea in his future. I could expect more of the same at this grand opening event.

Jessie bounced in her seat with the joy of landing me this sweet gig that I was mentally tearing apart. I wanted to die of shame. "Thank you, Jessie. I appreciate this. I appreciate all your help."

"That's right!" She looked at me. "We're doing it, right? It's happening for you."

"It sure is," I said.

"So you've got to focus on your goal." Jessie waved her hands. "This other stuff, running around playing cops and robbers? It's a distraction. Don't get in your own way."

We passed through the light and Jessie's face went dark. "You're not Jamie. You're not trained for this. And when you do things you're not trained to do, bad things happen. Not just to you, but to everyone around you." She gave me an intense look. "This house sale is huge, okay? Please, I'm begging you, stay out of this Peterson stuff. Don't mess this up for me."

Jessie turned on her blinker and slipped into the left-turn lane at Route 60. Tick tock, tick tock. I watched the light blink, light up Jessie's face. What would she do with this sale, with the money, the prestige? What possible goal was she working toward that she hadn't already accomplished? A closetful of compression pants to keep Mike's crotch healthy and safe? Another after-school activity for her daughter, maybe tae kwon do, or medieval lute classes, that the girl could get tired of and drop after three weeks? It didn't matter. Jessie had her reasons, just like I had mine. I had asked her to trust me, to help me, and she did, even though my reasons, to her, had been opaque. Now she was asking the same of me. I didn't need to understand why.

Jessie was watching me, searching my face. I stared at the road. I was trying very hard not to see faces in front of me: Pete,

June, Matt, Dan, Maureen, Gina. For no reason at all I thought of hooks, barbs, jagged edges, tangled wires. I could feel them all over me, gripping me in place for whatever came next.

My silenced phone flashed white on the seat next to me. It was Gina: **Did you talk to Jamie?? Call me.**

Jessie turned onto 60. The back of the supermarket approached, neon blinking red, red, red, red. *It would be so easy*, I thought, *to walk away*. To do what I was told, play nice at the event, drum up business, show Jessie I could be a straight A student. Do the easy thing, the smart thing, the safe thing . . .

. . . and tell Jamie and Matt and Gina and myself—everyone who was counting on me—that I was giving up.

Which one was supposed to be the easy thing?

No. I squeezed my fingers shut, imagined I was digging them into the soft mane of a lion. I wasn't giving up.

"Okay, Jess," I said. "I promise I won't mess this up for you."

15

Metallica Hour was in full swing when I got home from the funeral.

Owen was perched in the dark on the couch armrest, hunched over his laptop like a large overeducated vampire bat. He was chewing furiously on a plastic drink straw. The rest of the couch was littered with notebooks and loose paperwork.

"How long have you been here?" I eyed the empty kitchen table, a place to work that was unlikely to result in a head injury. Owen needed to put his body in mild physical danger so his brain could mind its own business and not bother him while he worked.

"He's played it four times." He pointed up, to the strains of Metallica's "One" drifting into the hall from my next-door neighbor's. "It's the album version, which is seven minutes and twenty-seven seconds long, so . . ." His freckled face scrunched into a math grimace. "I've been here twenty-nine minutes and forty-eight seconds. And counting."

"New neighbor." I tossed my keys somewhere I forgot about

immediately and snapped the kitchen lights on. "It's strictly Norteño in the morning, all these cheery accordion songs about drinking and screwing. And then after work it's the soldier who gets his limbs blown off and begs for death. On repeat." Metallica had wandered through the languid hopelessness section of the song and was launching into the pounding abject horror section. "I don't know where my dude goes during the day, but it must be a dark, dark place."

Owen hopped off the couch and stretched. He was wearing khakis and a shiny button-down shirt over his skinny frame, probably pressed and cleaned for him by my mom. If you kind of squinted and didn't allow him to talk, he could pass for a totally typical graduate student.

He gave me a suspicious once-over. "Why do you look nice?"

I went into the bedroom to peel off my scratchy blouse, the stupid ruffly skirt, and Gina's pantyhose like an old snakeskin. The True Realty blazer was, mercifully, back in Jessie's possession. She had snatched it back from me, appalled, when I told her I didn't use gluten-free laundry detergent. "I just came from Officer Pete's funeral," I shouted back at Owen.

Slamming and banging emanated from the kitchen. Owen was sniffing around for snacks like a bespectacled bear. All he would find was a jar of grape jelly that had congealed into a solid lump at the bottom and a bag of stale dried banana chips. I hoped he would have the common sense to choose the more edible of the two.

I stuffed my hair into a ponytail and came back out into the kitchen.

"So?" Owen was holding the grape jelly. "Who killed him?"

"I don't know." I took the grape jelly away from him and handed him the banana chips. "But everyone's lying. Everyone's hiding something."

"Excellent." He stuffed a handful of banana chips into his mouth and chewed. "Who's lying? About what?"

In the fridge, I found a bag of baby carrots that had sprouted a white sheen like a network of tiny spiderwebs. They smelled okay so I crunched one and did not die immediately.

"One: Maureen Loeffler, that's Officer Pete and Gina's old boss, was sleeping with Pete." Owen and I followed each other around the table, trading the chips and carrots back and forth. I held up fingers, tracking the lies. "Two: Dan Kaluza, the head honcho of the investigation, is lying about where he was when Pete was murdered. Three: June Peterson, the wife . . ."

I stopped and Owen ran into me. How to describe the unbridgeable gulf between June and everyone around her? No one knew who she was. "She had something in her purse. A pin. It was Gina's. Part of a pair." I started moving again, inching carefully over the dark splits between the floor tiles. "They found the other one at the crime scene. That's why Gina was arrested."

Owen took a carrot and stared at the jelly. I could tell he was thinking of dipping one into the other. "Gina is Number Four, then?"

"Gina is Number Four," I repeated hollowly. Had I turned the lights on? Everything looked dim and incomplete, like an alien ship had settled over the kitchen. I went to the patio door and drew open the blinds. "She had some beef with Peterson that she doesn't want to talk about." My stomach did a painful flip when I remembered the jagged text bubble sitting unanswered on my phone. I was not about to explain to Owen that Gina had asked me to use Jamie for access to a secret computer at the Sandhill Lake PD, where she might find a video or recording or something that she didn't want anyone to see.

I'm not going to lie to Jamie, I had told her.

You wouldn't be lying, she had countered, sitting across from me in the pizza parlor with a streak of red light slashing her face. She suggested instructions, explanations, workarounds. Exactly how it wasn't lying, I couldn't remember, only that she was innocent and this thing, whatever it was, would make her look guilty. The details were fuzzy.

Outside, the sliver of visible sky was darkening. If I craned my neck just right I could see into the Chicago Asian Foods parking lot, traffic picking up with folks running in after work for last-minute errands, or to grab a bowl of soup at the ramen bar. A white Public Works truck sat at the close end of the lot. The driver's arm hung out the window. It reminded me of Maureen and her near miss.

"Hey, Owen." I was not sure exactly what I wanted to ask him. "You remember how Officer Pete used to do those assemblies at school? Was he still doing that when you were a kid?"

"There was a health and safety one," Owen said, "but I got Mom to write a note because I was afraid of pictures of feet. Why?"

"I'm finding out all this stuff about him that people don't know. Or maybe just don't care about."

"Like what?"

"Drinking too much, messing up at work, putting people in danger, skeezing on teenage girls. I don't think he was this great cop everyone thinks he was. And maybe not such a great person either." Outside, the white truck started up and rumbled off. I couldn't hear it behind the glass but I could see it shaking. "It doesn't line up for me with the guy who talked to a bunch of third graders about kindness and sharing and stuff. You should see Sandhill Lake, it looks like a hospital gift shop exploded. The funeral today, the crowd." I shivered. "It borders on creepy."

"It's my estimation that every man ever got a statue made of him was one kind of sommbitch or another," Owen said in a sudden honky-tonk voice.

"What?"

"*Firefly*, season one, episode seven. 'Jaynestown.' A classic episode. Jayne is disappointed that everyone sees him as a hero when in reality—"

"Yeah, no, I get it. Nobody's perfect. Not even cops." Gina, eyes bright as ice chips: *You think all cops are like Jamie?*

"That's four," Owen said in the sudden silence. "Four liars. Any more?"

"There's Matt," I said. "I'm not sure he's lying so much as not seeing things clearly. I didn't get much from him except that his parents hated each other. Which takes us back to June."

Owen picked a chip out of the bag, sniffed it, put it back, and selected a more suitable one. "Didn't you and Matt have a thing?"

"That was years ago," I said. "And not a whole thing. Not all the things. Just a few things." I thought back to the lacrosse tournament, remembering the things. They were really nice things. "How is this relevant?"

"Do you and Jamie have a thing?"

"No. I don't know." I snatched the chips back from him and stuck him with the carrots. "That is even less relevant."

"Well." Owen clapped chip fragments off his hands and hauled his laptop to the kitchen table. Apparently whatever he was about to do was absorbing enough that he didn't need to risk falling off the couch in order to do it. "Have you checked out the Petersons' social media yet?" He sat down and started tapping away. It made perfect sense to the little weirdo that I would of course toss my shabby little hat into the massive ring of investigative firepower aimed at Officer Pete's murder.

"A little." I'd been clicking through the Petersons' accounts all day, pretending to be watching cat videos whenever Jessie got suspicious. "All it did was confuse me. There's like, a thousand accounts." I plopped down across from Owen. "Pete's personal accounts, his work accounts, which include the department accounts, the Explorer accounts, and then all the same ones for Matt, who's even more online. June I haven't even touched yet." My head was pounding just talking about it.

"I need a system. For that, I need the brain that thinks. My Magician brain." I lifted my hands like I was holding a brain in each. "But if I want to really understand anything, I need the brain that just kind of sees and feels. My High Priestess brain. I can't use both at the same time. I'll burn my brains out."

"You have a binary brain." Owen sat down and opened his laptop. "It's either at zero or one. You need a quantum brain. A brain that can be in multiple states at once."

My eye twitched. "Where can I get one of those?"

"I'll be Brain One." He was already typing. "I'll search up and list everyone's accounts." His fingers flew over the keys. "You go through them one at a time with Brain Zero." He looked up. "Do we need a pivot table?"

I blinked at him.

"No pivot table." Owen sounded disappointed. He typed for a few minutes, then turned his laptop to me. On the screen was a neat chart crisscrossing each family member's social media presence, all decked out in neat columns and highlighted bands. It was like looking inside Owen's brain.

"Okay." I sat down and cracked my knuckles. "Here we go." I blanked my mind, opened the ancient hand-me-down laptop Owen gave me last year, and delved into the Petersons' lives. Or those parts they wanted people to see.

Officer Pete's social media was all bright pictures of domestic tomfoolery, backyard picnics, bocce ball and Baggo on the lawn, a yellow Lab curving through the air with a Frisbee in its jaws. Pete and a bunch of teenagers dressed for either paintball or a covert raid on a small but well-armed dictatorship.

"Lots of Explorer stuff here," I told Owen. Official competitions, events around town, group shots in uniform. Matt drifted through all of them, just one of the guys. COULDN'T HAVE DONE IT WITHOUT YOU, LT! under a pic of a raucous victory party, the group lifting Officer Pete onto their shoulders. "Boy, they really are kind of like his kids." I could see where Jessie's big-ass house would fit into things.

Owen clackity-clacked in his nerd chart. I clicked through photo after photo, looking for some clue of how June fit into this story of the Petersons' lives. She appeared in brief, confusing flashes, and never in shots of her and Pete. Only in group shots with friends who were, by and large, the same small family of cops: Dan, Maureen, other faces I recognized from the funeral. ALOHA FROM MAUI: a set of photos of blue water and green palm trees like a kid's crayon drawing. Officer Pete shirtless and oily, knowing he still looked good for an older dude. June in round white sunglasses and a vintage high-waisted bathing suit, like a model in a 1960s washing machine ad. Toasting the flaming sunset behind them with drinks that were mostly fruit salad. A sweaty group shot with snorkeling gear. Pete with his arms around June and Maureen, the big red *American Lotus* like a jewel in the background. MY GIRLS!

Ugh. Did June know what that really meant? I searched her clear, round face and found nothing. Who was she? I could see who Pete and Matt were: it was all out there. June was invisible.

"Wow," I said. "They closed down Soldier Field for Pete's fiftieth birthday a few years back."

"Soldier Field like, where the Bears play?" Owen said.

"The same." I flipped through flash-blurred shots of Peterson and his red-faced friends against the enormous hollow background of the stadium. Rows of empty seats, emerald turf. I knew suburban cops made bank around here, especially a veteran like Officer

Pete, but Jesus, how much would something like that cost? I flipped through more expensive-looking events, more vacations, shots of designer cocktails in plush downtown lounges, all with the same group of people. June's sweet-sad face made an occasional appearance, but not often.

"How about June?" Owen asked, checking his chart. "We don't have much on her so far."

"No kidding. You said she just has the one Insta account, right?" The profile pic was not of June's face, but of a silvery tree of life. The few posts there were mostly pics of bright jewelry and mosaics. There was a link in the bio to an Etsy shop called June's Treasures.

I clicked on the link and had to take a breath. JUNE'S TREASURES, the site read. BEAUTIFUL THINGS FROM EARTH AND BEYOND.

It was a whole universe of strange, beautiful artwork, jewelry, decorations, and clothing. A lot of it was desert themed, pieces of a brilliant, bejeweled, barren alien landscape totally unlike the Midwest: smiling suns with flaming arms, emerald lizards, fiery phoenixes and peacocks, date palms throwing their bedazzled arms to the blue sky, tiny jeweled desert birds, mosaic coyotes howling at the moon. It was at the same time realistic and stylized, a metaphor made real. Each piece was a portal to somewhere else. There was a starkness to them, a loneliness, but also warmth, and a quick, lively imagination.

"Did you find her?" Owen said.

"I found her." I held my breath and watched a tiny clipper ship with lapis lazuli sails float through a sea of stars. "I found the real June."

16

"I went to that place in the new mall." Owen was walking back in the door with an armload of crinkly white takeout bags. He plunked the food on the counter. "The Stick-up."

I closed the laptop and rubbed the sting out of my eyes. A thick silence had settled over the apartment. Metallica Hour had blown past and I hadn't even noticed. I'd been poring over June's Treasures, flipping through image after bright image, trying to decipher in each the code to their invisible creator. I needed to meet her myself, in person, one-on-one. With my cards.

I creaked to my feet and stretched. Outside, streetlights were turning on, Route 60 snaking with traffic. Owen and I set up shop on the coffee table and tore open the takeout bags reading COMFORT FAVORITES . . . STUCK UP! They were full of Midwestern potluck food "reimagined" with incompatible ingredients and inedible garnishes, rolled into balls and stuck on skewers. Meat-loaf chunks, pizza bites, fried tuna casserole balls. It was messy and hard to eat, which I think was supposed to be the "fun" part? Jamie was absolutely going to hate it.

Owen had a tomato sauce–drenched meatball halfway to his mouth when his phone dinged. "One of my students," he said. The meatball dripped a glob of sauce on his pants. "They told me undergrads would be lazy and unmotivated, but so far they've been very enthusiastic. Lindsey, for example, sends me pictures of herself studying. Here." He passed the phone across the table.

In the selfie, a plushy brunette in cat's eye glasses lounged on a dorm-sized bed in a heart-studded pj set. The walls behind her were covered in anime posters full of big-eyed girls in thigh-high boots. She was making a kissy face and flashing a peace sign. **Getting my study on, yo!** A book was artfully arranged in front of her: *The Genetic Elegance of the Drosophila Fruit Fly.*

Owen put his phone down and reclaimed the meatball. "She has a real thirst for knowledge."

"I'll give you the 'thirst' part." This was new territory for everyone involved, except maybe Lindsey. I wanted to grab my phone and scour this Lindsey's social media for any evidence that I might eventually need to track her down and suffocate her with her adorable jammies for mistreating my brother. "You realize this girl is trying to get with you, right?"

Owen snatched his phone back. "Where does she say that?"

I dropped onto the couch next to him. "Skimpy romance-themed clothing: check. Provocative hip angle: check. Infantilized room decor: check."

Owen put down the phone. "She sends me a lot of texts late at night with questions I know she already knows the answers to."

"Uh-huh."

"And she invited me to a study group at the pub." He scratched his head. "No one else showed up."

"You need to be careful with this," I said.

"Why?"

The doorbell rang, thank fuck. "I would love to explain." I sprang up to answer the door. "But I'm not going to. Ask Jamie."

"Jamie!" Owen tossed the meatball onto the table and grabbed his phone. The meatball plopped off the table and rolled under the couch, where it would probably live forever. Owen danced up to Jamie and shoved his phone at him. "This young woman is sexually attracted to me."

"We're trying out some new greetings today," I told Jamie.

"Hello, Jamie," Owen tried again. "This young woman is sexually attracted to me."

"Wow, that's . . ." Jamie took the phone. "That's a nice bedspread."

"Indeed it is." I turned to Owen. "See?"

Jamie was still in his funeral suit, lanyard off, tie crooked. I could always tell what time of day it was by his hair, a thick chestnut brown mass he attempted to tame every morning with gel. It moved through a sort of astronomical clock of derangement as the day wore on. Right now the clock was at "stylishly disheveled." Jamie strode over to the couch and in one fluid motion folded himself lightly next to Owen. He looked like he was moving on springs. Now, *this* was Jamie at work.

"Aren't you sprightly this evening," I said. "Did someone give you a stack of serial killer interviews to transcribe?"

"Even better." Jamie picked up a Rice-A-Roni ball skewer and studied it, then put it down. "I talked to some folks, asked around about Dan and Pete. How they got along. Or didn't." He separated a Rice-A-Roni ball from its skewer and popped it into his mouth with an impressive minimum of rice loss.

"Got the usual stuff at first. Brothers in arms. Take a bullet for each other. Ride or die." He chewed thoughtfully, then went back in for more. "But they had kind of a falling-out at Peterson's big annual Christmas party a few months ago."

"About what?"

"Peterson got tired of Dan talking about running for sheriff—can't imagine why—and joked that he was going to post some old funniest-cop-videos montage thing he had made years ago, just to mess with Dan's chances. Dan flipped out, which of course egged Peterson on, and things escalated. Sounds like they almost came to blows."

Jamie dispatched his Rice-A-Roni skewer and moved on to the fried Hamburger Helper bites. "Apparently they argued all the time. Arguing was their love language, I'm told." He grimaced. "I could live happily the rest of my life without ever hearing that phrase. But this was unusual. Everyone noticed."

"Ugh." Dan and Pete's friendship rolled to life in front of me like frames from an old-fashioned filmstrip, a grainy sunlit montage of backslapping, competitive binge drinking, tattoo one-upmanship, friendly lawn games taken way too seriously until the wives were shouting from the patio to quit being children already and come inside. A lot of dick-length metaphors.

"I wonder what was on Pete's video." I picked up a deviled egg skewer and eyed it for an entry point. "Bribery? Strippers? Coke?"

Owen looked up from his project of trying to transfer a meatball from one skewer to another without using his fingers. "Improper use of workplace equipment?"

"I'd love to find out, if I could do it quietly," Jamie said. "Peterson used to post copies of the videos on the internal department servers, but those get cleaned out every few years. I know he had his own copies, but I wouldn't even know where to start looking for those."

I froze. The corn dog I was holding dropped its tiny hot dog, leaving me holding the corny outside. The edge of an idea surfaced in my mind. I might be able to help both Gina and Jamie and not have to lie to anyone.

"I know where you can start looking." I stared into the corn dog tunnel so I wouldn't have to look at Jamie. "Gina said something about a computer where Peterson kept stuff." *It's not lying*, my brain screamed. *It's the truth*. "She could tell us about it."

"What's wrong with your face?" Owen said. "Are you getting that thing again where you have to hold your eye to keep it from twitching?"

"Eat your chili dog rolls," I said.

"Sounds like a plan." Jamie leaned back on the couch. "How about you? Find out anything interesting at the funeral?"

"Me? Oh. Yeah. June had a dragonfly pin in her purse." I was still mentally wandering through the shivery logistics of hiding things from Jamie. "Just like the one at the crime scene. Gina had two, and June has the other one."

Jamie blinked at me. He looked suspiciously at the fried meatloaf ball he was about to eat, then put it down.

"But your Dan thing is good, too," I added.

Jamie wiped his hands and leaned back on the couch. "I have this dream," he said. "That I, too, might someday be able to work this case. I hope you don't think I'm overreaching."

"Don't give up, Jamie." Owen launched himself at Jamie in a marinara-stained approximation of a hug. "I believe in you." Owen was still working on recognizing sarcasm, although his empathy was coming along nicely. Jamie patted Owen's back like a hyperactive cocker spaniel's.

"You should hurry up and eat so we can have dessert." Owen held up some kind of shrink-wrapped kits. "They're s'mores! Each one has a different theme. There's Conversation Hearts, Animal Crackers, and Candy Corn." He turned to me. "You still have Jessie's old firepit on the patio, don't you?"

"It's thirty degrees outside." I got up to use the bathroom. "Talk some sense into him."

When I came back, Jamie and Owen had their heads together over Owen's phone. They were whispering. When they saw me they sprang apart. Jamie looked guilty.

Owen looked up. "Jamie recommended I wait until my class is over to pursue an extra-pedagogical relationship with Lindsey. It would eliminate any ethical ambiguity in the situation, as well as the possibility that she may only be attracted to me because I am in a position of power." He put his phone away. "Which Jamie knows about from his extensive experience with the 'badge bunny' phenomenon."

"How extensive are we talking?" I raised my eyebrows.

Jamie looked like he wanted to launch a fried meatball at me, or at Owen, or both.

"Holster honeys," Owen said. "Beat babes."

Jamie was this sort of sweet-looking, unpretentious brand of hot that netted him stares when we were out in public, and one time, a cheeky whistle. I teased him mercilessly about it for weeks afterward. I had also seen him, on a dime, turn steely and sharp, dangerous as a blade. It was . . . impressive, and I could imagine the spell it might cast. Who didn't want to feel safe, after all? I knew he had had girlfriends, but he rarely talked about them, and even though I saw so many things about him clearly, this was something I could only imagine in flashes, mysterious fragments. What did he like? What did it take to send shivers down his spine, make his eyes slip shut?

He caught me staring at him and smiled. I looked down, too fast.

"S'mores!" Owen said, standing up and waving the dessert kits.

By the time Jamie and I had managed to light Jessie's firepit and drag the pile of snooty s'mores kits out onto the patio, Owen had lost interest and was watching a documentary about tree frogs.

"He set us up," I said. "Look at him." Owen was shoving kernel after kernel of totally manageable, non-themed popcorn into his gob while Jamie and I struggled to get the goddamn s'mores kits open.

Jamie had opted for the Valentine's Day kit. The skewers were bright pink and the cookies were larger versions of those gross toothpastey Conversation Hearts offering grammatically repugnant messages like LOVE AF and YOU AND ME AND MAYBE. I went for the animal cracker one. Everything was gooey and sticky and covered with candy sprinkles.

"What happens if you mix the kits?" Jamie looked like he wanted to lick his fingers but was too civilized. "What if I want to put my heart on your rhino?"

"They won't s'more. You'll have to turn Bluetooth on and off."

I put my hands out to the fire. It was too warm for coats, so I was wearing the cape that Gina had ridiculed last night during my impromptu fashion show. A passing car on Route 60 tossed light over Jamie's face.

I dreamed of Jamie sometimes, always the same vivid, luminous dream. He was so clear in it, the gleam of his dark hair, the shine of his eyes. We were playing a mirror game, hands up, copying each other's movements. First it was funny and then it was serious, like our lives depended on doing the same thing at the same time. And I didn't know—if I reached across the barrier, broke the pattern, would he reach back, or would he turn away? I couldn't take the chance—even though I knew he was thinking the same thing. So we did nothing. Just stayed there in that mirror world, separated by an invisible barrier.

Every time, I woke up with a shock, flooded by the stone-cold certainty that somewhere across town in his gloomy rented farmhouse, Jamie was dreaming the same dream.

Shapes leaped out of the fire, tall figures reaching for each other and dancing away. I was still stewing about my Gina problem, just on the verge of figuring out how we could all get what we wanted, but . . . should we? I watched Jamie's breath plume in the air. We always solved problems together. And now he was part of the problem and I so badly wanted to ask his advice but I couldn't. And there was no one else to ask.

"Jamie." I wasn't sure I had spoken out loud. Even after he turned to me I wasn't sure. Was he hearing my thoughts? Were we dreaming?

"Your friend," I said. "Tyler." In Los Angeles, years ago, Jamie had had a close, prickly, complicated friend. Their relationship had spun out of control like a wayward backyard firework and guttered out in the worst possible way. "Did he ever do anything you weren't sure . . . weren't sure was a good . . . sure why . . ."

Sure, sure, sure. The word flowered in my mind in bright clones, barely language anymore, all breath and motion. What was I asking? Have you ever not been sure if your friend was a killer or not? If she was lying to you or not? If she was your friend or not?

An airplane blinked across the sky in a bright ellipsis. "You mean was I ever not sure if he was being honest with me?" I nodded. "All the time," Jamie said. "It was like a chess game with him, all the time."

"That sounds exhausting," I said.

"I could always figure him out. I would try to remember if he'd done anything like this before. Look for parallels in the situations. Figure out some reasons for what he was doing. Eliminate the impossible ones, pick the most probable one." Jamie shrugged. "Usually, though, it just came down to a feeling." He turned to me and his eyes were large and clear in the firelight. "Do you trust her?"

A river rushed through me, at the same time fast and

motionless. I turned back to the fire. Did I trust her? How many times had I had to answer this question? I never later regretted answering yes.

Tomorrow was Sunday. June would be at Birdie's, like the gas station guy had said. If I could talk to her, if I could pencil in more of this story, I would be that much closer to helping Gina put this in the past, where she seemed so badly to want it.

"Your zebra is burning," Jamie said.

He was moving before I could leap from my chair, snatching the flaming skewer out of the pit. By then, his skewer was on fire, too. A flood of sparks rose into the sky. Jamie doused the pit with a bucket of snowmelt. It exploded with steam. With a deft flick of his wrist, Jamie covered the remaining fire with dirt from a defunct flowerpot.

I staggered out of my chair. Jamie, wreathed in smoke, held his skewer like a wand over the wreckage: Fire. Water. Air. Earth.

He smiled at me. "You look like some kind of priest in that cape," he said. "Priestess. High Priestess Katie."

17

"Now that you know who you are and what to do"—Rosie pointed to Strength—"you need a guide." She moved on to the next card. "The Hermit."

We were starting the second row of the Major Arcana.

"What's a hermit?" To me, he looked like a hunched-over old man with a staff and a lantern.

"It's an old dude who lives by himself on a mountaintop and wears clothes made of tree bark."

"Why?"

"To get away from the world and all its noise!" Rosie pounded her head. She looked like an old man trying to get a bunch of unruly teenagers to quiet down. "You ever feel like there's just too much *noise*?"

When did I *not* feel like that? My head was constantly abuzz and aflame with noise and lights and motion, like an arcade game but less fun. No one else seemed to have an arcade in their head. I'd look around the gym when Officer Pete came to talk to us and think, watching everyone stare at him, *How are they sitting so still?* There was always noise in my head that my body was either trying to follow or get away from, like a flock of intriguing but overexcitable bees. My dad told me once that all the atoms we're made of, all the atoms in the universe, are always vibrating. How was I supposed to keep still when even the tiniest parts of me were always moving?

"When you get away from everything and keep quiet, you can finally hear that little voice that talks to you from the inside." She tapped her apparently newly quiet brain. "That's wisdom."

Was it? Either the little voice inside my head was not wisdom, or the wisdom of doing things like emptying the entire Elmer's Glue container to see how much was inside (not as much as you'd think) was too profound for me to understand at this time.

"It can also be someone who helps you find that wisdom. Your guide."

"Is it always a man?" I peered at the cranky old guy on the card. He looked a little judgy.

"It can be anyone who's got something real to say to you," Rosie said. "Even if everyone else thinks they're a freak." She pointed back to Strength. "Takes a lot of Strength to let your freak flag fly."

"How am I supposed to find this person?"

"Oh, you'll know them when you see them," she said. "Your freak flags will be the same color."

It had snowed the night before, a typical Chicago early-spring freak cold snap. Everything froze. Through the window of Birdie's, clear white sun flashed off the lake.

I was watching for June but my eyes kept sliding from the door, losing focus. The bird of the day was an unfinished mourning dove, a ghostly outline waiting for Izzy to navigate the dregs of the Sunday breakfast crowd. The gas station guy had said June came here every Sunday but didn't say how early. Eight o'clock was the best I could do. I wondered if I had already missed her.

Izzy came over with a coffee refill. A blueberry scone dusted with sugar crystals sat untouched in front of me. "Is Jamie coming?"

"Nope, he's back at work today." My eyes skated across the black surface of the coffee. Jamie didn't know I was here. I hadn't told him.

"You must be very close with the police," Izzy said. "You have police in your family?"

"No, I just kind of collect them by accident," I said. "I'm not the superfan you are, though." I nodded to the altar of Officer Pete.

"Me?" Izzy made a face and fake spat on the floor. "I hate police." He rolled up the sleeve of his T-shirt. There was a scar in the thick muscle of his upper arm, old and white and deep. It ran the length of his bicep.

"Police gave me this." He scrunched up his sleeve in his fist and moved closer to show me. I backed away. "When I was at Institute. With a razor. His friend held me down. I had a bootleg Beatles record and he took it away."

My throat closed up. "Because American music was illegal?"

"Pft." Izzy tossed his head. "Sure, it was illegal. That's not why he took it away. He took it away because he wanted it for himself." He laughed. "You know what the song was? 'I Me Mine.' I don't even like that song!"

His smile turned sharp, all teeth and eyes. "You know what we call cops over there? *Musor.* Trash." He slid into the booth across from me and set the coffee carefully on the table. "And you think

they're better here?" He shrugged. "Look on the news. They're
either beating people over the head just like Soviet cops or they're
sitting on their ass collecting the government paycheck."

The coffee cup felt like lava. I let go and squeezed my hands
to get the sting out. "How about Officer Pete?"

"Now, Officer Pete was different," Izzy said. "Officer Pete is
the reason I'm here. The reason all of this is here." He waved
around the restaurant. "When I bought this place I had no business. No one came in. I was in the red for a whole year." I could
see how a brainy, bird-obsessed former Soviet with ambitious
ideas about breakfast food might take this time-honored local
Palace of Drunk outside Sandhill Lake's comfort zone.

"And then one day, Officer Pete came in on his break," Izzy
said. "He ordered a double-chocolate donut, black coffee. I still
remember. 'You bake this yourself?' he said. 'It's the best donut I
ever had and I've been a cop for a lot of years.'" He paused.
"Because cops like donuts here."

"So I've heard."

"He took a dozen donuts back to the station with him, and that
was it." Izzy snapped his fingers. "Where the cops go, people follow. Here I am, twenty-five years later. Just paid the place off. It's
mine. All because of a donut."

"He did like to support community businesses." The words felt
gooey in my mouth but I felt like there was nothing else to say
here.

"Community, shmommunity," Izzy said. "That is Soviet bullshit, if you excuse me. The man wanted a donut. I just happened
to want the same thing." His eyes slid to the window. The playground on the shore was crusted with bright ice swept into fan-
tastical shapes. It looked like an ice castle some gloomy, lonely
monarch had built to suit and abandoned. "I came here so I
could do what I wanted, what I loved. Without getting beat up or

having to bribe a police just so I could walk down the street in peace." He'd forgotten to roll down his sleeve and I could still see the scar, shiny and old and angry. It would never go away.

"And if what I do helps other people, if it feeds them or shows them how beautiful their world is . . ." He motioned around. "This is how it works, yes? This is the only way. We all do what we want, we follow the rules, and everybody wins. Your Officer Pete was no different." *My* Officer Pete? "He did what he loved, he did it honestly and well, and it helped everyone. This is why we loved him. This is why he was good. He was a good police."

"Sounds pretty good." *In theory*, I didn't add.

Izzy stood and collected his carafe. "You tell Jamie I said hello." I watched him sit down in front of the mourning dove. He picked a stick of chalk from the rainbow in the box next to him and began sketching in hard, confident strokes.

When I looked away from him, June Peterson was watching me from a booth across the diner.

How had she slipped past me? Her coat was folded beside her on the chair and a mug of coffee (blue-gray gnatcatcher) steamed in front of her next to a cheerfully misshapen blueberry muffin. She watched me with an open, curious gaze, steady and unruffled as a child's. She had clearly been there a long time.

My face flushed. I figured I'd know what to do when the moment came, but now that the moment had been tossed into my lap I was in danger of letting it shatter on the floor. June was getting up now. She was picking up her purse and coat and cup and walking over. She was coming to stay.

One by one, the purse and coat and cup came down across from me. The purse was a shining beaded boat, green shifting into blue, a wonderland of marine flowers. It wasn't the same purse she had at the funeral. I wondered if Gina's dragonfly was still in that one, waiting in the dark. For what?

"I know you." Not *do I know you* or *have we met.* Her voice was soft and high, a little breathy, like she'd been running lightly down a forest path and plunged into sunlight. "Yes," June said, a confirmation from some silent internal committee. "I do. I know you from somewhere." She sat down.

This I had been prepared for. "I was at the funeral yesterday," I said. "My sister and I did the flowers. The orchids."

"Ah!" She took a deep breath and let it out. "Blue orchids. Like the song. Do you know it?"

"No, I don't think—"

She started singing in a low, unexpectedly rich voice, a melody of complicated dips and soars. Izzy, by the bird board, looked up like he was watching the notes float away.

"*I dreamed of two blue orchids, two beautiful blue orchids last night, while in my lonely room.* They don't come that way, you know, the orchids." She stopped singing as suddenly as she had started. "Blue? No. Nature doesn't do a lot of blue. They put dye in the water and the flowers—*slurp!*—suck it right up. They're fake." She gave a high trilling laugh. "Isn't that just perfect."

Later, this conversation would play to me like abject lunacy, the way she flickered from subject to subject like an impatient hummingbird. At the time she merely seemed to be watching everything at once, like a mythical guardian someone had set watch over eternity.

"I'm sorry for your loss." I always felt stupid saying this, like the person would reject it, even though I knew that wouldn't happen.

"No," she said firmly.

"Oh," I said. "I'm sorry. I didn't mean to—"

"That's not where I know you from." She reached over the table and cradled my hand in both of hers. It was like putting my hand in a cloud. She held me for a few seconds, then laid my hand back down with a small pat, like she was tucking a child in for the night. "You're the baby." A sudden smile opened on her face. "The baby from the accident." She gave me an apologetic little shrug. "I see things sometimes when I touch people."

Time slowed and stopped. "I am," I said. "I am the baby."

Her voice dipped. A strange, bitter note entered it. "That was when it all began."

"When what began?"

She wasn't listening. She was looking at my cards. "Ah! You're a reader." She looked the way my mom did in her monthly accounting of which of her friends' kids had ascended to the vice presidency of Fartface Pharmaceuticals or some investment firm dedicated to making rich people richer. I didn't know what I would need to accomplish for my mom to look at me that way.

"Where do you read?" June said.

"I have a place," I said. "In Lake Terrace."

"But it's not really yours, is it?" June said. "Or it doesn't feel that way."

She watched me evenly but instead of creeping me out it made me feel warm, comforted. I put the cards down and moved them around on the table in slow circles.

June gave me a wide smile. "Well?" she said. "Are you going to read them for me?" Like she had known all along I would be here and why and was waiting for me to catch up. Again, that feeling of timelessness circled through me, as if June had lived this scene countless times, even though it was only my first.

"I will," I said. "Yes. Read for you." Too firm, too loud, scrambling for my footing. I gathered up the cards and shuffled, my thoughts racing. *Did you kill him? Why? Why do you have Gina's pin? Why are you and your son not speaking? Why? Why? Why?*

I drew a card: Page of Wands. "Creativity," I said. "Inspiration. You're a creator."

"Oh, how nice!" She sipped her coffee. "Yes, I am."

"I've seen your work," I said. "It's beautiful. *From earth and beyond*—that's exactly how it feels. It reminds me of the desert. Is that where you're from?"

"Funny, isn't it?" June picked up her cup and stared out the window. "You can live somewhere for a long time, and still feel like you're from somewhere else."

"I feel that way every day," I said. "And I was born here."

"I'm from New Mexico," she said. "A tiny little town. Population 250, you'd blow right past it on the interstate and never even know. The town sits on a hot springs. My family owned a little spa there. I did massages, treatments."

"That's where you met your husband, wasn't it?" I said. Matt had called it an organic commune.

June traced the bird on her cup with a fingernail. "I was . . . very young. They were passing through town, he and his friends. Taking a road trip. Celebrating graduation from the academy. His friends were pretty much what you'd expect." She wrinkled her nose. "But he was different. He was . . . honest. Pure. He made me feel safe. And I think he liked that.

"When I touched him, I saw a little boy. I didn't know if I was seeing him or the son he would have. 'Do you want kids?' I asked him. 'Because if you don't, you should be careful. There's a little boy trying to get through.' I thought he would laugh at me, the way his friends did, but do you know what he said? He said, 'Let him come. He'll be welcome.'

"A week later we were married and on our way back to Chicago." She smiled. "We had Matt later that year. And all the while when he was growing up I wasn't sure whose face I was seeing, his or his dad's. It was the same face."

Her artwork made sense to me now. Lost landscapes, open and still but full of life. The mother, the artist, the creator. The Empress.

"I saw something in your purse." I didn't even draw another card. "At the funeral. Your purse slipped and fell open."

"Ugh!" she groaned. "My purse is a mess. I go to craft fairs. Flea markets. I look for materials, you know, for my art. I buy things and then I forget they're there until everything comes spilling out." She studied me. "What was it?"

"A dragonfly," I said. "Brass, with green wings." I didn't know what to say next. It belonged to my friend and I think you were trying to frame her for murder? "It looked familiar."

She was already digging through her purse. "Dragonfly, drag-onfly." Soft embarrassed murmurs, *forget my head if it wasn't attached.*

"Aha! Was it this?" She pulled out a hot pink beveled glass butterfly. It tossed the light in cheerful shards on the table between us, making the Page of Wands blush.

"No, that wasn't it." My throat burned. I knew what I saw. It was a dragonfly, and it was Gina's. I needed to pull the reading back to Gina, to Pete, but didn't know how. I felt lost. I drew another card but the cards were stubborn and confused, like my mind.

Three of Swords, a bright red broken heart in the rain.

"Grief," I said. "Sorrow."

"I miss him." She stared out the window at the white horizon. When she looked at the card, we both knew she wasn't talking about Pete. "Matt loved his dad," she said. "Loved him so much it scared me. It was like they were one person in two bodies. Talked the same, thought the same, looked the same. They wore the same clothes, for God's sake. Same size clothes, same size shoes ever since Matt was a teen." She took a sip of her coffee. "I always knew one day Matt would discover his dad was not per-fect, and it would destroy him.

"It was always them against me. I was always the bad guy, the outsider," she said. "I couldn't say or do anything right." Wet stars glistened in her eyes. "And now it's too late."

She turned to me and I could see Matt in her round open face. "Did you really come to the funeral for the flowers?" she said gently.

"No," I said. There was no point in lying. She would know. "I came to the funeral because I want to help. I want to figure out what happened."

June laughed a beautiful tinkling laugh, like chimes stirring in a summer backyard. "Well, those are two different things, now, aren't they?" she said. "Who do you want to help?"

"Matt. You. Officer Pete." I didn't mention Gina. "He saved my life." The words tumbled out like wooden blocks. "I don't want it to be for nothing. I owe him." It felt like the simplest thing to say, simpler than the truth.

June's face froze for an instant, like ice had swirled through her and moved on. "He was never the same after that," she said. "Something turned on inside him. He was . . . supercharged. More excited about his job than ever. But it was different. I felt like he was always looking around after that, seeing if anyone was watching."

You created Officer Pete, Jamie had said. At the time I felt proud, but now I felt an odd stab of guilt.

I drew another card: Six of Pentacles, a rich guy tossing coins at adoring beggars. "Charity," I said. "Generosity. Selflessness." I thought of the rainbow handprints at the church: COMMUNITY! "You don't think he did what he did to help people? To help others?"

The cards were spiky and disjointed. They weren't hanging together in a story or pattern; they were just showing me flashes, hopping from one thing to the next.

June watched me with a little smile. "Do you think it's possible, truly, to do something for others? For someone other than yourself?"

"I think so," I said. "If you're risking to lose more than you get out of it."

"Ah, but that's tricky, isn't it?" June said. "What if the risk is the point? Generosity can be a very powerful drug for some people."

"I . . . I'm not sure what you mean." Except I did. I'd had this conversation before. With Jamie, with Gina, with Owen. I had just had it with Izzy.

The radio, tuned to the local Lake County station, paused for a newsbreak. "No leads yet in the murder investigation of Sandhill Lake police lieutenant Matt Peterson. The case has confounded authorities for nearly a week."

We turned to the voice at the same time. It wasn't saying anything we didn't know. June's eyes wandered back to the window, pulled to the still iciness outside, the gray lake, the empty sky.

"Police are exploring every possibility," the radio said. "But at this time, the answers are still out of reach."

"They have no idea." June's eyes filled again. One shining tear rolled down her cheek, white on shining white. I was about to agree that the cops were nowhere, but then she turned to me. Her eyes were black.

"They have no idea," she said, "what they're getting into."

18

"I have news," Jamie said over the phone.

"Where are you?" I leaned back and tried to put my feet up on the desk but the desk was too high. I ended up bent double like I'd been stuffed into a broom closet. Jessie's stiff, judgmental furniture was fiercely inconducive to slacking.

"I'm back at Lake Terrace for a few days, catching up on paperwork," he said. "I never thought I'd miss this place. It's Windsor Palace compared to Sandhill Lake."

It was pouring outside my office. Sopping-wet people ran around in search of lunch.

"I have news, too." I attacked a fingernail with my teeth. Jamie was about to straight-up hate my coffee date with June, I just didn't know exactly why. I scooped him? I didn't warn him ahead of time? The exact flavor of bollocking headed toward me was a mystery, but I could hear it whining and growling and gathering speed like a mildly annoyed thunderstorm. "You go first," I said.

"I've set up an interview with June," Jamie said. "Wednesday afternoon."

"Dan saw the light, huh?" My own sharp disappointment surprised me. Suddenly, I didn't want to press June any further, although yesterday I had wanted nothing more than to solidify her as a suspect and knock Gina out of the top slot. Gina was still the only one with any hard evidence linking her to the murder, and every second that ticked by made everyone more trigger-happy. I could feel the vicious charge in the air intensifying, the tone of the news more keening and hysterical, background infighting between the agencies reaching a fever pitch. Even Jamie and his sharp, eager tone on the phone just now depressed me.

And yet . . . I felt weirdly protective of June. She was the kind of eccentric other people tended to dismiss, unless they were eccentric in exactly the same way. Like me. I realized who June reminded me of: Aunt Rosie, waving at me from the far edges of the U.S. map. It made me suddenly and inexplicably lonely.

"I should go talk to her myself," Gina had said last night on the phone, her voice hoarse.

"The last time you went to 'talk' to someone, you ended up punching her in the face," I said. "Just sit tight. You're going to make this worse."

"Sit tight? Dan called me three times yesterday. He all but asked me for a stool sample. I swear, he's going to start manufacturing evidence soon." There was an edgy silence on the phone. "What if I just follow her?"

"Gina."

"Why does she have my pin, Katie?" I could hear her smoking furiously in the background. "Why is she lying about it?"

I wished, sitting there in my office, that I had never seen the damn thing fall out of June's purse. What if June wasn't lying about it at all? What if I had just seen what I wanted to see? It wouldn't be the first time.

"That's great that you'll finally get to interview June," I said to Jamie through my teeth.

"Your turn," Jamie said. Someone burst into scratchy, nasal laughter behind him. "What's your news?"

I squeezed my eyes shut. "I, um, I may have run into June at Birdie's. We had coffee yesterday morning."

The silence on the other end of the phone felt like soft, deadly quicksand. "Yesterday morning," Jamie said. "What time?"

"Eight."

"Eight A.M. Sunday. Let me get this straight." Christ, did I hate it when he did this. "At eight on a Sunday morning, when your default activity, if you're even conscious, is unspackling your face from your pillow, you instead put on clothes—I hope—got in your car, and drove, without hitting anyone, the fifteen miles to Sandhill Lake to *run into* June Peterson?"

I licked my lips. "Eight . . . ish?"

"How did you even know she would be there?"

"The guy with the eagle told me."

The silence on the other end was so profound I figured Jamie had either hung up or fallen into a well. "Are you talking to this man with the eagle right now?"

"Oh, fuck off. It was the guy at the gas station across from Birdie's. He said she's there every Sunday morning. Do I at least get points for paying attention?"

"All right." Deep sigh. "Let's hear it."

I unrolled my conversation with June beat by beat, but the deeper I sank into it, the fluffier and more amorphous it seemed, like fighting my way through sticky-sweet Marshmallow Fluff. I felt like I was trying to explain to Jamie this great idea I'd had when I was high. The more details I added to convince him I'd learned something useful, the less I believed it myself.

When I was finished there was silence on the phone. "Did you ask her about the dragonfly?"

I stifled a groan. "She denied having it." I felt like a screwup, a toddler. What had made me think I could handle this?

"But you saw it, right?" Jamie said. "You're sure you saw it?" Gina had asked me the same thing last night on the phone.

"I'm sure," I said sharply. "Look, I really wanted there to be a big glaring sign over her head reading KILLER, but I just feel like we're barking up the wrong tree with her."

"Is that so?"

"She's a little strange, sure." I had left out of the parts of our conversation where June had burst into song, and also the parts where she claimed to read people through touch. "But she's gentle. And sad. She sees things other people don't. Not like, in a goofy psychic way, but . . . Well, maybe in a goofy psychic way, but I just . . . She's not a killer, Jamie. I don't see it."

Jamie didn't answer. I heard the gears turning in his head, compressing the mush I'd fed him into something hard, clear, unassailable from any side.

"They were barely keeping it together, marriage-wise," Jamie mused. "She blames him for her estrangement from her son. She has a definite, if somewhat mystifying, link to the crime scene." This was by far the most generous thing he could say about my half-assed clue. "And she clearly knows more than she's saying. What was it she said? 'They don't know what they're doing'?"

"What they're *getting into*." This is what Jamie did; he made sense of my impressions, filled them out. Why did it feel so weird this time, so wrong? "You're not seriously suggesting this fifty-plus-year-old woman wrestled her muscle-head husband's gun away from him, chased him around a swamp, overpowered him, and shot him twice?"

A careful silence. "I'm suggesting that nothing I've heard so far has eliminated her as a suspect."

I snorted. "This is the part where you always ask me, Do I have any facts, or just vibes?" Even though I myself had just used vibes as the basis of my argument. I tried to imitate Jamie's voice back to him but I'm a crap mimic and just sounded like I was fighting a respiratory infection.

"Facts? Fine. I did some prep work on her for the interview. Checked out her alibi. She told us she was at home when she got the call about Pete. Now I have two neighbors confirming she left the house in a rush early Tuesday morning, right before Pete died. The old lady two doors down said it was during *Good Morning Lake County*, which puts it between seven and eight o'clock, and God bless people who still watch live TV. The other neighbor was vaguer on the time, but they both noticed it was unusually early. Apparently she never leaves the house before ten on weekdays."

I felt like he had slugged me. June was lying . . . again? Why?

"She gave us a false alibi," Jamie said.

"Yeah, I got it, thanks." A spike of anger lit me up head to toe and sparked out. I wanted to punch a hole in what he had said, but I couldn't. "It still doesn't mean anything."

"It doesn't mean she murdered him, no. You're right about that."

I balled up a scrap of paper and tossed it at the trash, just to toss something. He was treating me like a kid. *Handling* me.

"I think you felt a connection with her," Jamie said carefully. He was trying to defuse whatever conversational bomb he sensed was about to go off. "That doesn't happen to you often. And I don't think you want to believe that someone who is so like you could be capable of murder." There was a pulsating neon pause. "I think you might be losing objectivity."

"Oh, I see." I swung my feet off the desk and the hollow *whump* bounced off the walls, around the room. "This is about me now?"

I wanted to take it back the second it was out. Jamie said nothing. He didn't have to. His answer hung in the air: *Isn't it always?*

The doorbell loosed its flurry of electronic flutes and a burst of frosty wind tore through the room. Matt stood inside the door, wiping his feet, shaking the rain off his uniform.

"I have to go," I told Jamie. "Someone just walked in."

Matt gave me a huge, bright smile. He was always surprising me. I'd forgotten what it was like to be surprised.

19

"This is the best meal I've had in days," Matt said.

The fifteen-dollar hot dogs he'd gotten from the artisan fast-food place were pretty fab, I had to admit. We devoured them in the midst of a pile of crinkly paper and tinfoil diapers littering the too-low coffee table. He was in the area, he'd said, dropping off evidence at the county crime lab. He offered to run out and get us lunch.

I was working extra hard not to make a mess, either of my person or conversationally. Matt didn't seem to be struggling at all. He was comfortable everywhere, even on Jessie's torture device of a couch.

Outside, the rain had let up and the skies drifted open, the parking lot settling into an early afternoon lull. Matt's squad car was parked outside.

"This is fun," Matt said, and immediately looked like he regretted it. "I feel bad having fun." He balled up his napkin and set it at the corner of the table. "I feel like if I do anything but grieve, I'm doing it wrong. I'm letting him down."

His face was creased and tired above the smile. Even when we were kids he'd always said whatever was on his mind, unworried that it might make him sound like a wimp. I'd envied not just that kind of openness but the clarity behind it. Not just to express what you feel but to even know it? It felt like a superpower.

"I'll try to keep the fun to a minimum," I said. "Would you like to look at some of my sister's real estate brochures?"

Matt laughed and held my eyes too long. *Oh my God*, I thought. *Is this a date?* I slapped at my face with a napkin just in case.

"Your dad wouldn't want you sitting around. He'd want you to have a little fun." I pushed my soda straw in and out of my cup, making it squeak. "What was his favorite thing to do for fun?"

"Oh, no question—being on his boat," Matt said. "He'd wanted a boat since he was little. He grew up in the city and every once in a while they'd come up here and rent one." I thought of my barfy day on the water but said nothing. "He said he never felt as free as he did then.

"He said a lot of the Explorers kids reminded him of himself. Not much money, tough family situations. I didn't have brothers or sisters, and the Explorers were kind of like my family. They were always around. That's why he wanted that house he was going to buy from your sister. For those kids. So they could come over and feel like they were just as good as the kids who had everything."

Outside, ladders of light climbed into the sky. A candle-like glow settled over the parking lot and seeped through the windows, the shining metal furniture throwing off sparks. I thought of June. The house was Pete's dream, not hers. I wanted to read for Matt, and this was the best opportunity I would get. He was too close to his dad to see clearly, and the cards would help him. And me.

"Sorry," Matt said. "I'm rambling." He sat up and stretched. "Tell me about this place! I like it. Very professional."

"That's what I'm afraid of," I said. "Professional is not exactly the vibe I'm going for."

"What vibe are you going for?" He leaned in to put his drink on the table, watching me.

"More *chat-with-a-friend* and less *get-impaled-on-a-fake-decorative-birch.*" I picked up the cards and started shuffling.

"You said you and Jamie are a team now, huh?" Matt raised his chin and motioned to the lunch graveyard on the table. "Is this going to be okay with your teammate?"

"That we're eating hot dogs?" I kept my voice cool but my heart was rabbiting. "Yeah, don't mention hot dogs around Jamie. He goes crazy. Ever since the war."

Another perfect golden laugh from Matt. "Fair enough."

I felt a door open, either in him or in me. Either way, I decided to walk through it.

"Jamie says when a cop interviews someone, most of the time they don't know what they're looking for, right?" I stuffed the garbage into one of the takeout bags. "Some questions stick, some don't. You go with the ones that do and eventually you see a pattern. A story. The cards are like that, too."

"Aw," he said. "I was hoping you might read my mind."

"The point is not to read your mind," I said. "The point is to help you make sense of what's already there. Especially if you can't see it yourself." I shuffled and cut. The slap of the cards against my hands cut through my post-food blurriness, pulled me together.

"So," I said. "Are we going to do this?"

"Do you say an incantation or something?" Matt said. "Burn some candles? Am I going to get excommunicated?"

"Don't be silly," I said. "All I need is a tiny pinprick of your blood." Matt paused a little too long. "Kidding. There's no magic here. Sorry to disappoint."

"No magic?" He tilted his head and gave me another nuclear

smile. "That *is* disappointing." It bordered on cheese, what he was doing, but he was so earnest about it, it was actually kind of sweet. I was so fucked.

The cards took over and a familiar greedy curiosity stole over me. Questions whirled through my mind, but I held them off. Too early. I closed off the Magician frequency, opened the High Priestess: *Listen. Be silent.*

The first card was the Nine of Swords.

Oh boy. Talk about getting tossed into the deep end. The weeping insomniac beset by a battalion of ghostly nighttime swords was a little on the nose.

"Grief. Haunting. Regrets. I mean . . ." I shrugged.

Matt gave me an astonished grin. "You sure there's no mind reading going on here?"

"Everyone always says that." I picked up the deck and shuffled. "I promise, even if you weren't grieving, you'd find something in your life this card could point to. Our brains are wired to look for patterns. You get a bunch of random images, your brain is automatically going to make a story out of it. It's why the cards work. It's not magic, but it's real."

I gathered the deck to shuffle again. "Two of Cups." A pair of lovers joined hands around two golden chalices. Locked together, for better or for worse. "A partnership," I said. "A relationship."

"I like the sound of that," he slid in smoothly.

"Hold your horses," I said. "It's reversed."

"Is that bad?"

"Not necessarily. It can mean the opposite, or it can mean another dimension of the same thing. Like another room in the same house." I didn't tell him I flat-out ignored the reversals when they didn't ring true. This time it leaped up at me like certainty itself. Take your pick of which fucked-up relationship it referred to: Matt and June? Pete and June? I watched Matt study the Two of Cups. Matt and Pete, even? Who got along with their dad as well as he did? It was uncanny, and June had hinted as much. I wasn't sure I was ready to open that door yet.

"This relationship looks happy on the surface," I said, "but isn't, underneath."

"Oh dear." He leaned over the table for a closer look. "Who's the unhappy couple?"

I chewed my lip. I was, quite possibly, about to bring this reading to a screeching halt. "It's your parents," I said. "Your parents are—were—the unhappy couple."

Matt pursed his lips. "No argument there."

I took a breath. "I talked to your mom the other day."

Matt's smile dissolved into sharp angles. "You talked to my mom. Why? Is she a suspect?"

"Well, only in the way that everyone is until they're not, right?" I forced a smile but Matt's face didn't change. "I just wanted to find out more about her. About her life with your dad. Just like they do during the victimology. Jamie has his official interview with her on Wednesday. I thought I'd get the other side."

"Okay." He sat very still. "Did she say anything that actually made any sense?"

Not much, I had to admit. "Just that she loves you and misses you. She's worried about how you're taking your dad's death."

Matt scoffed. "Is she even the least bit upset that he's gone? Don't answer that. I don't want to know."

I went all in. "Listen, Matt, you keep talking about how badly they got along. I have to ask . . ." On the Two of Cups, a winged lion's head hovered over the couple, lips pulled back in a snarl. "Is there any chance your mom was involved in your dad's death? Or knows something she's not saying?"

Matt raised his eyes to me. A sharp laugh burst out of him. "You're joking, right?"

"I've heard some things that don't add up."

"What things?"

"You remember Gina Dio's dragonfly pin that they found at the scene?" Matt waited for me to continue. "Your mom had one just like it in her purse at the funeral. The same one in a different color."

"What does that prove?"

"Not everyone knows this, but Gina had a set of two. A pink one and a green one. They both disappeared years ago. One showed up at the crime scene, and the other one was in your mom's purse."

"You saw it in my mom's purse?"

I nodded.

Matt sat back on the couch and rubbed his forehead like he had a headache. "Okay. Okay. I forgot you're friends with Gina Dio." He scoffed. "Honestly, I didn't realize she had friends."

He clasped his hands together in front of him. "My mom buys stuff for her art. She's got all kinds of things in her purse all the time. Beads, pins, what have you. It could have been anything."

June had said the same thing, but I knew what I saw. Didn't I?

"Katie, I think you're missing something really crucial here." He moved toward me and took my hand. His eyes shone with a sort of dark fascination.

"If you really are friends with Gina, you know that she is an accomplished liar. I've heard all about her work, and I know she's very good at what she does. Which is lie, and hide, and manipulate people to get what she wants." He bent to meet my eyes. "You know this."

I did.

"And you also know she's a loner. She does not make friends easily or often, and she rarely does it accidentally."

"What are you saying, Matt?"

"I think she sought out your friendship in particular because she needs something. You have some role in whatever she's planning. And my guess is she's already driving wedges between you and the people you're close to. That's what she does. That's how she gets what she wants. She's manipulating you."

There was an odd ripple in the air. I thought of Gina asking me to use Jamie.

"You have an incredible opportunity here, Katie. You're in a unique position to find out things from her that no one else can. Dan's been doing his best, and he's got nothing. And will continue to have nothing. Because she knows what she's doing. Honestly, I'm shocked she was sloppy enough to leave that dragonfly at the scene. But you're smarter than that. You see things. It's like you said." He shrugged and gave me a cheeky grin. "Sometimes the person no one expects is the best person for the job."

I felt hollow and cold. What was the job here? To prove Gina was a killer?

"Don't talk to my mom." I snapped my head up at the edge in his voice, but his face was smooth. When he spoke, the edge was gone. "She's a dead end. I know she's part of the victimology, but honestly, if there's anyone who knows *less* about my dad—the real him—I don't know who it is."

I moved my head up and down but I had no idea what I was agreeing to. Everything had gone sharp and bright. The candlelight was gone.

"My dad is lucky to have you in his corner, Katie." Matt moved in close to me and took my face in his hands. "And so am I."

When he kissed me I felt like I was made of light, air. I felt like I was disappearing.

20

"It would be much easier if I could just grab these videos off the server when I'm at Sandhill Lake." Jamie riffled through a file rack, distastefully picking up a set of plastic green beads studded with twinkling shamrocks. His normally spotless desk had broken out in a dollar-store pestilence of shamrocks, bowler hats, and signs with "Mc" pasted inappropriately in front of every word. "I'm heading over there in a few minutes. Are you sure they don't have a backup server somewhere?"

"Backup server!" Gina was parked in a rolling office chair, boots on Jamie's desk. "You're lucky they have toilet paper. Dan hasn't worked at Sandhill Lake in years, so anything from his era is long gone."

Jamie sat down. His chairback sported an insert with a green bowler hat that, when lined up just right, flew over his head the message IRISH YOU A HAPPY SAINT PATRICK'S DAY. It looked like a festive holiday mugshot.

"Who did this to you?" Gina said.

"Bailey," Jamie said absently. "They're fixing the fluorescents over his desk so he's borrowing mine while I'm on the callout."

"What a shame." Gina rolled across the desk and hit the wall, feet splayed out like a kid on a coasting bike. "I thought maybe you went to Hobby Lobby and picked up a sense of humor."

I perched glumly on a squeaky chair in the cramped area around Jamie's desk at the LTPD, where he was catching up on email before he went back up north to rejoin the investigation. I tossed the occasional mooing noise into the conversation to distract everyone from the emotional shitstorm raging inside me.

Gina had coolly volunteered to help us locate copies of Peterson's annual gag reels so we could judge for ourselves whether or not they were worth the hassle of murder. I should have been thrilled for another shot to prove Gina's innocence, but I couldn't stop watching her sit there, still as a snake, dishing out the right snarky joke here, the right insult there, just enough to be recognizable as herself. Jamie had no idea she was using him—with my help—to get at this mysterious recording that would either prove or disprove her guilt. I didn't even know which it was supposed to be.

And then what? I had asked her last night. *What will you do with it? How will it help?*

One thing at a time, she said, sending smoke into the flat sunset sky over the park. She smoked all the time now, one cigarette appearing in her long fingers after another. Every time we met, my clothes reeked afterward of the smell of her worry, her secrets coating me head to toe. Secondhand guilt. I hadn't chosen it, but I stunk anyway.

Except I *had* chosen it, hadn't I? I watched Jamie make careful circles with his mouse, and a fist squeezed my heart. *She's manipulating you,* Matt whispered in my head, *driving wedges.* Nothing

Matt had said was false. I felt like a feather, something weightless and inert tossed about on air currents.

"I'm not crazy about investigating my own boss," Jamie said. "I'm not crazy about any of this, to be honest."

"Really?" Gina said. "Funny, I thought this was your happy look. It's so different from all your other looks."

"I'm guessing you have some way to access these files that I'm no doubt going to hate?" Jamie checked his watch. He still wore a watch.

"Peterson had this prehistoric laptop on his desk, an old beat-up Dell." Gina moved her boots. "You come across anything like that?"

"Yeah, I remember it," Jamie said. "It's dead. It's in a box of junk on the desk Dan is using."

"It's not dead," Gina said. "Not if you know how to start it up. It's the best security system ever. You can only boot it up if you know how. Pete used it for anything he didn't want anyone to know about. He had quite the collection of porn on there involving cheerleaders." She rubbed at a scuff mark on the chair. "And horses."

Jamie looked like he'd eaten rotten fruit. "How do you know the files are still on there?"

"I know he used that laptop to put together the reels. He showed me once. Plus he was a terrible pack rat and never threw anything away. Especially not something like this." She twisted her face into an imbecilic grin. "Ooh, Pete, these are soooo funny," she drawled. "Ooh, Pete, thank you for inventing humor." She dropped into her own steely voice. "Anything that made him the center of attention."

"How do we know Dan hasn't looked at the laptop already?"

"We don't, but it's worth a shot, right?" Gina turned to me. "I meant to ask, did Matt say anything about Dan yesterday?"

Jamie looked at me. "Matt?"

My face blazed. I hadn't told Jamie about yesterday's lunch with Matt. I kept looking for an opening in the conversation and the longer I waited, the more awkward the revelation would be, and then it just didn't happen. "He stopped by my place for lunch yesterday," I mumbled. "I asked him some stuff about June."

Jamie's face went still, but not before something small and naked flashed through it. Gina flicked her eyes between us but kept her mouth wisely shut. She was the only one who didn't seem confused by the Schrödinger's relationship I was having with Jamie. She had warned me away from dating cops, not in a coy sexy-bad-boy kind of way but in a seeing-how-the-sausage-is-made kind of way. She and Jamie treated each other with grudging respect, despite some serious disagreements about methodology. Namely, Gina thought Jamie had a stick up his ass and Jamie was horrified by Gina's loosey-goosey interpretation of the law, even though they were supposedly on the same side of it. They were usually traveling to the same place but didn't like sharing the road.

"What did he say?" Jamie pulled up to the desk and flipped through a set of folders. "Anything significant?" All business.

"He didn't think she was worth talking to," I said. "He was actually kind of weird about it."

"He's protecting her," Gina chimed in. She spun her chair to face Jamie. "Hey, 3PO. What are the numbers these days on intimate-partner homicide?"

"One in five," Jamie said.

"One in five." Gina finger-gunned me. "If I were the betting type I'd—"

"Burn down another casino?" Jamie said.

"Statistics are fireproof, my metal friend," she said. "I'm just saying I don't think we should give up on her quite yet."

Jamie and I glanced at each other. Our earlier conversation

about June had left me with an oily aftertaste, and I could see he felt the same way.

"All right." He sighed and pulled up a notepad. "Why don't you tell me how to start that computer up?"

Gina laughed. "Yeah, no. I have to do it myself."

Of course she did. I was morbidly curious to see how she was going to convince Jamie that this was a good idea.

Jamie gave her his slow blink. "I've turned on a computer before."

"Okey dokey." Gina blew her hair out of her face. "You turn it on. Wait exactly three and a half minutes. No more, no less. Then hit Control-Alt-Delete." Jamie wrote diligently in his neat, backward-sloping hand. "It won't look like it's doing anything, so you have to wait another three minutes. Then you get a blue screen. If it makes a noise like a panicky horse, you blew it. Turn it off, start over. But wait two minutes for it to cool down first, or you'll have to start again."

Jamie's pen went still.

"If, on the other hand, it makes a sound like a plane taking off, then you're in. All you need to do then is hit Control-Alt-Delete again, and this time you should get a DOS prompt." She gave him an innocent glance. "You do know how to start up Windows from a DOS command prompt, right?"

Either she had just rattled off the most convincing tech bullshit I had ever heard, or I was exactly the kind of gullible boob it was meant to razzle-dazzle. I watched Jamie to find out which it was.

Jamie put down his pen. Gina folded her hands neatly and sat back in her chair. "Or you could just grab it for me and I could do it myself."

"I am not going to *just grab it* for you," Jamie said. "Poking around Peterson's old computer can reasonably be explained. Removing it from the premises cannot."

"So sneak it out."

Jamie looked offended. "I do not sneak."

"Okay." Gina steepled her fingers and stared at the grimy tiled ceiling. "I can pose as the vending machine guy," she mused.

"Oh, for God's sake," Jamie said.

"You got a better idea? You can't boot it up yourself, and you're afraid to—"

"Just give me a few days. Let me watch Dan for a bit, figure out when he comes and goes, and when he—"

Gina groaned. "By the time you even finish this sentence, we could've been in and out of there."

"What's your rush?" Jamie said tartly. "Peterson's still dead."

"My rush is to not go to prison for something I didn't do. If we can prove that Dan—"

"I could do it," I said.

Gina and Jamie turned to look at me like they had forgotten I was there. "I'm not sneaking you in," Jamie said.

"You won't have to," I said. "You're both overthinking this. Jamie, I'll come visit one night when you're there. I'll, I don't know, bring donuts."

"Are you *trying* to attract attention?" Gina cackled. "You bring food, they'll swarm you like cockroaches."

"Fine, no food. You let me in, totally legitimately, right before your evening roundtable, and while everyone is at the meeting, I'll get in there, grab the computer, and take off."

"What if you get caught?" Jamie said.

I shrugged. "I got lost. I was curious. I have cataracts and I thought this was the bathroom."

Jamie gave me his slow blink. "You were taking the computer to the bathroom?"

"It wouldn't be the first time," I said. "Look, I can make something up. You guys don't have that luxury. I can play dumb. You guys can't."

"Do you really think this won't come back on me?" Jamie said. "I can't believe I'm even discussing this." He stood up and gathered his stuff. "I have to be at Sandhill Lake in thirty minutes. We can talk about it later."

"I'm going to bounce, too," Gina said. She slid out of the chair, shoved it aside, watched it crash satisfyingly into the wall, and gave me a fist bump. "Later."

I had to run to catch up with Jamie on his way out to the parking lot. His body was tight and focused, like an arrow.

"You know," Jamie said, not looking at me, "at least when she was a real cop she would have had a supervisor to tell her when she was over the line." He was pissed, and I doubted it was entirely at Gina.

"Peterson was her supervisor for a while," I said. "Look how that turned out for him."

The barest sliver of a smile crossed Jamie's face. He pushed open the door into the parking lot and a blast of wind slammed into us. I followed Jamie to his car.

"I'm only about eighty percent serious," he said, unlocking the car, "but did she kill him?"

"I can say with total and complete eighty percent confidence that she did not," I said.

Jamie tossed his briefcase into the passenger seat and let the door close. He turned to me and leaned against the car, folded his arms. "Has she told you yet about what happened between her and Peterson?"

"Whenever I ask, she puts me off. Or changes the subject." I could hear how shaky it sounded, that my own best friend was hiding something this big from me, and that I hadn't bothered to chase her down for it. It made both Gina and me look bad.

I turned away. In the decrepit little gas station across the street, a Public Works truck idled next to the banged-up air dispenser.

After meeting Maureen, I was seeing Public Works trucks every-where. One of those weird brain glitches where once you're aware of something, it seems to follow you around.

"I was hoping Gina would tell you herself," Jamie said. "But just so you know, I've seen all the paperwork. The files, the reports."

"What paperwork?" I said. "There are files? Reports? Tell me."

Jamie sighed. "She filed a complaint against him and it didn't go the way she wanted. Things got out of hand."

"Define out of hand."

"She broke two of his ribs and shattered his nose. Put him in the hospital."

The wind rose again and I curled up against it. No wonder everyone hated her at the bar that night. No wonder she wanted to lie low. Slow anger at Pete crept over me: what did he do to her? And anger at Gina—how did she expect me to help if she wouldn't talk to me?

Fine. There were reasons. I just didn't know them yet. But I would, with Gina's help or without. I would tear this thing apart.

"Look, I think we know by now that your Peterson"—my Peter-son again—"was no angel. But that's a moot point. The more important question is, was Gina angry enough to kill him? Because right now she has the best motive of anyone." Jamie paused. "Do you remember what we talked about the other night?"

Did I trust her, he had asked me. I was exhausted of answering this question. All anyone saw were the gaps between Gina and me, the shortcomings. No one saw what I saw, how the fierceness she showed the world was the same fierceness she used to protect the short list of those she loved.

"I do trust her," I said. "She knows me better than I know myself."

"That's either good or bad," Jamie said dryly, "depending on how she uses the information." He walked around to the driver's side of his car. "Be careful, Katie. I don't want you to . . ." He put his hand on the car door and left it there. "Just be careful, okay?"

I felt sick and empty. This case had made enemies of all of us, spies and liars and cheaters.

Jamie leaned on the roof of his car. Wind moved through his hair and he shook it out of his face. "You didn't call me," he said.

"Call you when?" I said in a small voice. I knew when.

"Yesterday, after you talked to Matt," he said.

"Oh."

"Normally when you find something, you call me immediately, interrupt whatever I'm doing, I give you suggestions, you ignore all of them and do exactly the opposite." He gave me a quiet half smile. "I thought we had a system."

"I'm sorry," I said. "I guess I . . . didn't think you would want me talking to him." The tips of my ears blazed. He was leaving it vague on purpose, what exactly he had a problem with. I was making a lot of assumptions here. *Help me,* I wanted to tell him. *Tell me what you want to hear.*

"Look, Katie," he said. "If you want to catch up with an old friend, that is none of my business." Did he hesitate before he said friend, or did I imagine it? "I just figured when you find something relevant, I should probably know about it before . . ." He waved his hand. "Gina."

"What is that supposed to mean?"

He slowed down, as if to make sure I got every word. "It means that my goal here—my *only* goal—is to figure out the truth." Something acid crept into his voice. "I am, in fact, the only one here whose job it actually is."

A wave of shame hit me, threatened to pull me under. Jamie didn't care that I had had lunch with Matt. I should have been relieved, but instead I felt like he had punched me in the gut. All he cared about was solving the case, doing his job. Even colder: Was that all I cared about, too? Were we just addicts of a very particular drug who had confused the intensity of addiction for something more?

"You keep talking about having an outsider's perspective." He opened the driver's side door. "But for that to work, you need to actually stay outside of things."

He got in, slammed the door, and drove off. I watched the gray plume of exhaust rise into the air long after he was gone.

21

"The Wheel of Fortune." Rosie tapped the third card in the second row of the Major Arcana. "Or, as I like to call it, the Wheel of Shit Happens." The Wheel of Fortune lumbered through the sky, labeled with unreadable characters and surrounded by creepy winged creatures. "Some people think of it as the Wheel of Fuck Around and Find Out."

There was a soft but imperative throat clearing from the far side of the room. We had been so engrossed in Rosie's lesson, we hadn't heard my mom tiptoe down the stairs. She was staring at us with a sour expression on her face and had recovered her missing—now empty—box of crackers.

"Here's the find out part," Rosie side whispered.

"Anything else I can get you?" my mom said. "Some freshly torched crème brûlée? A bottle of our finest champagne?"

Rosie blinked. "Do you have all that?"

My mom rolled her eyes and was turning toward the stairs when the cards spread on the table caught her eye. "Is this some kind of game?" she said. "How do you play?"

"Whoa." Rosie's eyes went wide. "Some truly excellent questions."

My mom backed away and disappeared up the stairs.

In the space movie, things were starting to go wrong. Equipment was malfunctioning. The computer was being weird, its single red eye growing and shrinking.

"So yeah," Rosie said, staring at the screen. "You can't stop shit from happening is the deal. Whether you caused it or not, it'll knock you on your ass, every time."

"The question is, what are you going to do about it?"

"This is it?" I said.

We were parked behind a squat brick building with a dark blue awning over the front door reading SANDHILL LAKE POLICE DEPARTMENT in a utilitarian font. The building was the color of a box shoved in the back of a closet and forgotten. A baby blue water tower loomed over the empty back parking lot. Behind it, a field of electrical transmission towers splayed their arms into the gray night. "This is the police station?"

"This is where the magic happens." Gina killed the engine on the Public Works truck and set the brake. She wore a navy blue uniform belonging to someone named Skip and had netted up her long hair under a ball cap. The truck smelled like lemon and weed inside and had a set of fuzzy D&D dice hanging off the rearview and a chain of dancing skeletons across the dash.

"Do I want to know who Skip is?" I said.

"Skip refills the vending machine every Tuesday night. He owes me a favor." She patted her many pockets and pulled out a flat white rectangle. "And luckily, I hung on to this old floater key card." She pointed to the back door, where a keypad glowed a threatening red.

"You have a key card from when you worked here? There is no way that is still going to work."

"Oh, it'll work," she said. "You underestimate the laziness, cheapness, and overall inadequacy of the Sandhill Lake Police Department. They haven't changed the key codes since they installed the system. I don't think they know how." She pointed to the back door. "There aren't even any cameras back here."

A wave of jitters shook me. Something was off. I wasn't hallucinating—I really was seeing Public Works trucks everywhere. Every time I turned around, one was parked, or idling, or just leaving. And now, here was Gina bringing one to this extremely illegal excursion.

Gina checked her look in the rearview mirror. The idea of her beating the stuffing out of Officer Pete ate at me. Every time the images floated through my mind I shied away, clamped down on them.

"Hey, Gina." It came out in a whisper. I cleared my throat and tried again. "Have you ever killed someone?" I knew I would catch heat for this fuckwit question, but I couldn't ask her what I really wanted to know.

Gina checked her ball cap in the mirror, replaced a stray lock of hair. "What the hell is wrong with you?"

"I'm just asking," I muttered. A rose-shaped sticker was coming loose on the dashboard and I picked at its sticky edge. AMERICAN BEAUTY the sticker read.

She sighed. "Look, I know you feel weird leaving Jamie out of this but he can't be busted for something he doesn't know about, right? You're doing him a favor."

"I know."

"Then what's your problem? You're not in any danger. I'll go in, grab the laptop, and be out in five. You won't have to do anything at all. I'll handle everything myself."

"That's the problem," I said.

"What is?"

"You're doing everything yourself! I'm not doing anything."

"Not true. I told you, if things go south and you see me come out running, be ready to drive like hell." She punched me lightly on the arm. "Because you're the what? Come on. Say it."

"I'm the wheelman." I loved being the wheelman. It made me feel like I was in a movie full of cleavage and giant gas-guzzling cars. I grinned like an idiot before I realized she had just played me. "Knock it off. You're keeping me in the dark on purpose. You're supposed to be lying low. This isn't lying low."

"What can I say, delegating was never my strong suit. That's why I never got promoted at this place. Well, that and the tits." She cinched the front of her shirt to make said tits as invisible as possible.

I turned away and stared out the window at the lights ringing the base of the water tower. "That and that you turned a superior officer's bones into breakfast cereal."

Gina paused. I didn't want to turn around and see her face. "Technically I'd quit by then," she said. "So it was just a random asshole whose bones I turned to breakfast cereal."

I spun back to her. "When were you going to tell me you filed a complaint against him? What did he do that was so bad that you . . ." I stopped.

"That I what?" Gina folded her arms. "Killed him? Is that what you were going to say?" Her eyes went drippy and soft. "'Gina! Have you ever . . . killed someone?'" Her voice wavered with fake tears. "You think I killed that pathetic piece of shit? I wish. But since that privilege went to someone else, I don't feel like being on the hook for it."

She wasn't doing a whole lot to convince me she wasn't a killer right now.

"And the reason I don't want to *share*," she continued, "is that it's in the past. Where I would very much like to leave it. That is the whole entire point of this, so if you're not going to help me—"

A rusty squeak cut her off. Gina and I snapped forward, blinking through the windshield. The station's back door popped open, and out came a familiar stocky bald guy.

Oh, shit. It was Bald Jr. from the Olde Prairie Inn, the cop Gina had embarrassed. Bill. He was wearing a double-breasted pinstripe suit several sizes too big, with a red carnation in the lapel. He looked like a Build-A-Bear. The image of his bald head shoved in some woman's crotch rose before me and I stifled a bubble of horrified giggling. Gina palmed my head like a basketball and shoved. I found myself contorted, pretzel-like, under the passenger dash. The driver's side door opened and slammed.

"Hey, Skip," Bill's voice said. "How's tricks?"

A low, noncommittal grunt from Gina. Footsteps off toward the front of the lot. Bill was leaving. Was it possible Gina's stupid-ass disguise had worked? I began to climb out when:

"Hey, you know what?" Bill's voice came back loud again. I squeezed back into a ball. My gut howled. "Those Payday bars you've been putting in there lately? They're hell on my teeth. Can we have some Hershey's or something? Do an old man a favor."

"No problem," Gina said in a convincing male voice. It was one of her many creepy talents. "I'll pass it on."

I stopped breathing. There was no sound. What was happening? Was he leaving?

"You have got to be kidding me." Bill's voice was low and flat. "What the hell are you doing here, Gina?"

Fuck. How could I have let her convince me this was a good idea? We were both going to get arrested and I would have to call Jessie again. My life flashed before my eyes.

Short, sharp scuffle sounds. "Hey! Give me that." Gina's voice was normal now.

"Why do you still have this?"

"I don't know, Bill. Ask the IT manager. Oh wait, there isn't one."

"Resources were reallocated," Bill barked. "Are you alone? Who's with you?" I heard him stomp toward the truck. I slipped out the passenger side just before the driver's side door snapped open and dove behind a scrawny row of evergreen bushes at the side of the lot. From behind my prickly wall I watched Bill circumnavigate the truck. He actually kicked its tires. Then he huffed back to Gina.

She folded her arms. "I told you I was alone."

"What the fuck are you doing here?"

"What are *you* doing in that monkey suit?" Gina sniffed the air, wrinkled her nose. "What is that, Tommy Bahama? You're drowning in it. How about you give me my card back, and I don't tell your wife you've got a hot date."

Bill straightened his suit. "The hot date is *with* my wife."

"You bluff for shit, Bill. Give me that card." She fished her phone out of her pocket. "Patty and I did the torch run together, remember? I've still got her number. Give me the card, or I call her right now."

They faced off like an idle animation from the weirdest fighting game ever, Gina holding the weaponized phone, Bill drowning in his evening finery. Any second now, a deep voice would shout *Fight!* and they would launch at each other.

"It turns out Patty's had some adventures of her own." Bill ran his hand over his shining pate.

"Oh, ho!" Gina let loose a gibbering Woody Woodpecker cackle. "How the tables have turned."

"We role-play," Bill said. I had to strain to hear him. "She waits at the bar, I come in, we pretend we don't know each other." Bill started making sounds that were either choking or wheezing. "It's a . . . it's a therapy thing. You know what, get the hell out of here."

"Aw, Bill," Gina said. "I'm touched, man. Seriously."

Bill shoved his hands into his pockets. "We're working it out," he squeezed out.

"Yeah, you are," Gina said. "Bring it in, you big asshole."

Gina scooped Bill up in a hug, facing me. I inched my head up over the bush. Gina gave me a wild-eyed shrug. I watched her hand creep into Bill's pocket and fish out his key card. The white square shone in the moonlight.

"Go on, scram," Bill said hoarsely. "And maybe I won't tell anyone I saw you."

Gina gave me a look I would remember for a long time. *Are you in? Can I count on you?*

This was a sharp bend in the road we'd come to, a dizzy-fast spin indeed from the Wheel. This wasn't her asking me to nose around, talk to a few people. It wasn't even, as slimy as I felt about it, asking me to keep secrets from Jamie. It was full-on sneaking into a fucking police station to steal shit. I would be in serious trouble, for a very long time, if something went wrong. Or wronger.

Gina's eyes went blank. She was already writing me out of the equation if I failed her.

Something sharp clicked into place and I realized the question was not would I help Gina or did she deserve it. The question was, as always, will I keep going? Will I keep digging? Behind the rusty beat-up back door to the PD were more pieces of this puzzle. I needed them.

I gave Gina a wobbly thumbs-up.

A deft flick of Gina's wrist and the key card sailed out of her hand, landing outside the bush in front of me. I reached out silently and grabbed it.

I waited in the bushes for everyone to drive away. Then I crept to the door and held up the card with shaky hands. The red light turned green.

I slipped into a hallway stuffed with file cabinets. Someone had taken a stab at decorating with the occasional plaque or picture, then abruptly gave up. The place looked outgrown, like the exoskeleton of an animal about to burst out and crawl down the beach in search of more spacious digs. To my right was an alcove with a coffeepot and two predatory-looking chairs. To my left, a tiny broom closet. The place looked like a shrine to cutting corners.

I had no idea where this laptop was supposed to be. I hadn't super been paying attention when Jamie and Gina were talking about it because I didn't expect to be here. I wanted to do this on my own? Now I was doing it on my own.

Around the corner, someone was talking. I recognized Dan's horn-blast voice, cut through occasionally by others. I peered around and found myself looking through a large window into a bleak conference room where a group of near-comatose guys, Jamie among them, sat around a table, staring at Dan. He was gesturing to a whiteboard that had suffered years of writing and erasing. A message in Dan's clumsy block letters headed the board: KNOW YOU'RE VICTIM, FIND THE KILLER. It must have taken every ounce of Jamie's restraint not to get up and correct it.

I skipped back before anyone spotted me. What I didn't realize was that my reflection was clearly visible to someone looking at just the right angle. That someone was Jamie. His eyes went

wide. I leaped back again and toppled a set of files from a cabinet, which in turn upended a brass trophy, which tumbled headlong and clicked the button on the top drawer of the file cabinet.
The drawer sprang open with a triumphant clang.

Dan broke off. "What the hell?"

I hopped behind the cabinet, my heart whacking the inside of
my chest.

"I'll go see." Jamie's voice, the scrape of a chair.

Now he was standing in front of me, giving me his slow blink.

"I can explain," I whispered.

"I am not talking to you," Jamie whispered savagely. "Because
you are not here." He shoved a wad of papers back into place.

The conference room door squeaked open again. I screwed
my eyes shut like a toddler trying to be invisible.

"What the hell are you doing out here?" Dan's voice said.

"This file cabinet keeps popping open," Jamie said. "Just keeps
getting in the way." He pounded the cabinet door an inch from
my head. "I think we should take it out back and shoot it."

"That's between you and the file cabinet," Dan said. "You
want to hurry up? The sooner we hand out this batch of leads,
the sooner we can leave. Here's the next one." Paper rustled. "A
woman in Antioch says the ghost of Officer Pete appeared to her
on Fox News and revealed his killer."

"Be right there," Jamie said in a dead voice. The conference
room door clicked shut. Inside, Dan was talking again. I crept
out from behind the cabinet.

"Down this hall," Jamie whispered tightly. "Third door to your
left."

"You're the best, Jamie."

"Shut up." He slipped back into the conference room.

The chief's office was a two-desk space with four desks
crammed into it. It evoked a dorm room more than it did the seat

of a municipal police department. There was a banker's box on the desk full of files, pictures, odd bric-a-brac, and a decrepit Dell laptop, just like Gina had—

The laptop was open on the desk, lighting up the office in a cold white glow. A shiver shot through me. Someone had just been in here. I *knew* Gina was lying about those complicated boot-up rules. What were the chances someone else knew about them? My eyes flicked around the room, but I was alone.

On the laptop screen, the file tree was open to a folder titled simply "Explorers." The folder was empty.

Voices drifted in from the hallway, Dan's bray and Jamie's low, soft voice. I froze, listening to them get louder.

". . . if I really want to understand Lieutenant— If I really want to understand *Pete*, I should talk to someone he was close to. Like you." Jamie's voice was bright and friendly and edged with desperation.

"We were close, yeah." Dan sounded suspicious.

"And since you both grew up here, maybe I could learn a few things about the local community, too." Punching all the right buttons.

"I wouldn't want to *bore* you," Dan said. "Lake County is no California."

"Oh, but I bet you have some stories."

"I do. Some real doozies." Dan was warming to the subject. "Do you fish? Because some of these guys here don't know the difference between a float and a lure."

"Fishing is definitely something I have heard of."

"I'm on my way out, but catch me tomorrow. Just need to duck in here and get my stuff."

The doorknob rattled. I jammed my eyes shut.

"I'd love to hear about it right now," Jamie said quickly. "Let's go grab some coffee from the break room. In that direction."

"Eager beaver, huh? Oh! I've got just the thing. You need to see this picture. I always keep it on me when I'm working. Come in here, I'll show it to you."

The doorknob rattling intensified. Panicking, I tried to duck under the desk but the area was stuffed with boxes. The storage closet. I darted through its sliding door and slid it shut just as Dan and Jamie walked into the office. I cracked the closet door and peeked out.

An arm snaked around my neck, yanked me back from the door. A gloved hand slapped closed over my mouth.

22

I squirmed and made gargling noises but the hands held me fast.

"Be quiet," someone said in my ear.

Dan and Jamie looked up. "What was that?" Dan said.

The hands went slack and I wriggled myself loose enough to turn around.

Maureen.

She held a finger to her lips and let me go.

Jamie moved between Dan and the closet. Maureen and I glued our faces to the crack, shoving at each other.

"Foxes," Jamie said. Cool as ever, but he had his hands in his pockets. In Jamie code this meant either extreme irritation or terror. "They mate out there behind the station."

"It sounded like it was coming from the closet." Dan looked in my direction and I shrank back against Maureen.

"Foxes are mating in the closet?" The old *here's how stupid you sound* clincher. I had seen him deploy it dozens of times and had been its unfortunate recipient more often than I cared to remember.

Dan shrugged and rooted through his desk. "It has to be here somewhere," he muttered. Jamie cut his eyes toward the closet.

"Aha!" Dan excavated a wrinkly old-school photograph from the mountain of crap on the desk. "This is on Grass Lake. They've got lake trout there the size of a toddler. We'd been out there all day, not a bite, and then here's this motherfucker! Now, by that time we'd been drinking all day." He looked up wistfully. "Man, Pete could put it away." Dan stared wetly at the photo. "Look at that beauty. Here's the thing, though, these fuckers have teeth. See that?"

"Oh. Oh, God," Jamie said. "Yes. That is, that is really impressive."

"And not just in their mouth but in their gills. You don't watch where you're putting your hands, you could really cut yourself."

Jamie's face turned the color of ash. "This is a fish, right?" Jamie steered Dan toward the door. "Not a science experiment?" He flashed me a vicious look and shut the door.

I went limp. Maureen spun on me. "Did *he* put you up to this?" She nodded at the door.

"Jamie? He didn't even know I was coming."

"I smell Gina all over this," Maureen said. "Did she tell you about the laptop?" Maureen wore a military-looking black skinsuit. She'd come prepared.

"Is it that hard to believe I came up with this myself?"

"Do you *want* all the credit for breaking and entering a damn police station? What the hell are you doing here?"

"What are *you* doing here?"

"My job," Maureen shot back. "Pete owed me some files for my audit, and he didn't have a chance to turn them in before he died. So I'm getting them myself."

"At night? Wearing whatever the hell this is?" I pointed to her ninja garb. "Can't you just walk in and fill out some form in triplicate and get whatever you want?"

Maureen pursed her lips. "Let's just say Pete had an unconventional approach to organization."

"Sounds like he had an unconventional approach to a lot of things."

Maureen slid open the closet door. "Let me tell you something about Pete. He always thought he was the smartest person in the room, and he was rarely right." She inched out of the closet and I followed her. "He was a slob and a pack rat and he had very little imagination. I just happen to know all his little quirks and hiding places. I have one more place I can check."

I was still waiting to hear why this had to be done in the dark of night without anyone's knowledge. "What did you take out of that Explorers folder?"

"Nothing," Maureen said. "It was already empty." She folded her arms and raised her eyebrows. *Your turn.*

"I'm looking for the gag reels," I said.

Maureen blinked. "Pete's gag reels?" She stared at me. "Why?"

I tried to channel Jamie's official-speak. "I have reason to believe there's something on there someone doesn't want made public." Jamie did it better.

"Who, Dan?" Maureen gave a sharp laugh. "Why, because he and Pete hit the nog too hard and got stupid at the Christmas party?"

"So you saw it," I said.

"Everybody saw it. Big deal. They argued all the time."

I felt like a popped balloon. "I thought maybe this was about Dan running for sheriff."

"You think Dan killed Pete over some bullshit video of him

walking through a screen door?" She ran her hand slowly down her face. "Solid detective work there. Did your cards tell you that?"

She pulled out a flash drive. "Here." She clicked around on the computer and found a folder labeled Year's Funniest. She stuck the flash drive in the laptop. "Knock yourself out. Copy whatever you need," she said. "Just do it fast before this thing shuts down and we have to sacrifice a goat to start it up again."

Huh. So Gina had been telling the truth about the laptop.

I backed out of the folder. Maureen's flash drive had a ton of room on it. It would be very easy to copy over the whole computer, let Gina look for whatever she wanted.

I glanced at Maureen. Could I trust her? Probably not. But she knew Gina better than I did, and she was there when the roots of this tangled story were still exposed. I had a rare shot here to glimpse something usually hidden: Gina's past.

"There's something else I need," I said.

"Uh-huh." Maureen folded her arms. "Of course there is. What does she want you to look for?"

I hit copy on the whole drive. The blue bar crept across the screen. "Maybe the more important question is," Maureen said, "why isn't she here looking for it herself?"

"Because I'm helping her," I said. "Because she's my friend."

I thought Maureen would laugh but she looked drained, like I had punched her.

"What happened?" I said. "Why aren't you and Gina friends anymore?"

"Because Gina doesn't have friends," Maureen said. "She has people she keeps around until she gets what she needs from them." She squeezed her hands like she was trying to warm them. "It looks an awful lot like friendship. I don't blame you for being confused." The pity in her voice was terrifying.

"I know about the complaint she filed against him," I said. "What did he do to her?"

"Not my story to tell." Maureen turned toward the door, listening for noises. I thought of the Two of Wands, the nobleman staring at the distant horizon over his domain, holding the Earth in his open palm. People read power in the card, but to me it showed loneliness. What had Maureen had to do to claw her way to the top of this heap? I wondered if it was worth it.

On the screen, the copy bar inched forward.

"Pete could be a real pill when he didn't get his way." Maureen shrugged. "I loved the guy, but that's the truth. Things went sour between the two of them, and she wanted me to take sides."

She put her ear to the door, then turned and gave me a cool, appraising look. "You want my advice? Stay away from her. Whatever you think you are, you're not friends." She regarded me. "Did she ever tell you the story of how we met?"

The copy bar on the laptop was almost home.

"She said you busted her for running a bunch of cons and eventually she became a cop and you two got to be close."

"Very sweet story. She left a couple of things out. Did she tell you about the crew of kids she had working with her? Ringers, accomplices?"

A vein pulsed in my forehead. "She might have mentioned a few friends."

"Friends? They worshipped her. She was like a North Shore Charles Manson. They would have followed her off a cliff."

Ice crystals webbed across my skin.

"She turned them all in," Maureen went on. "It was part of the deal. To get the charges dropped. Wrote out every single name in her perfect little handwriting, didn't even bat an eyelash."

My heart did a rubbery bounce. It could have been a lie, but it made too much sense. The files had finished copying. I popped out the flash drive and put it in my pocket.

"She's a killer, Katie," Maureen said. "I knew it the minute I laid eyes on her, and I knew I had to keep her close. Keep her on my side. She's too dangerous to have as your enemy. Peterson learned that the hard way."

Images of Gina beating up Pete came flooding in again but this time I let them come and willed myself to look. Pete's blood spurting from his nose, the crunch of bone against bone.

Is it possible she could have gone a step further and . . .

Outside the office, a door slammed. People were leaving. "Come on," Maureen said. She shut the computer down and put it back in its box, then motioned for me to follow her. We crept out of the room, turned the corner, and came out the side door into the freezing night. The water tower loomed in front of us, blue against black.

"Your friend Jamie." Maureen's eyes were hard. "He must be hot shit to land this detail. I'm guessing he wants to keep it."

"Just like you want to keep your job," I said.

She smiled a hard, humorless smile. "Beat it, girl."

She slipped around the side of the building and disappeared.

Gina was parked a quarter mile away, on the road's thin shoulder. She paced outside her truck, smoking.

"There you are," she said, walking to meet me. She saw I was empty-handed. "Where's the laptop?"

"We don't need it." I held up the flash drive. "I've got the whole drive copied right here."

"You are the shit." Gina squeezed her ball cap down over her ears and bounced up and down. "You are the cat's goddamn pajamas."

She set up a high five but I left her hanging. "Maureen helped me." My throat hurt. I wanted to burst into tears.

"Maureen?" Gina said. We headed for the truck. "What the hell was she doing there?"

"She was looking for some documents for her audit. Something about the Explorers." The shoulder was tiny, just a strip of gravel. Every time a car passed, splashing us in light, I felt my heart pound, some evolutionary holdover in a hidden part of my mind screaming *danger, danger.* "Peterson owed her some files but I guess he never gave them to her."

"Did she find them?" She clicked the truck doors open, tossed her ball cap into the back seat.

"No." She was expecting me to get in but I was rooted to the spot. "She said they weren't there. What do you think it means?"

Gina didn't hear me. She was already starting the truck. She'd gotten what she needed.

23

"**A**m I supposed to be laughing?" I asked Gina.

The next morning we were at Out of the Blue, because it was the only place I had a computer that could read the flash drive. I sat in front of Jessie's turbocharged Mercedes of a laptop that she told me to use for documenting sale comps but that I mostly used for Google-stalking high school classmates and watching ASMR videos. "I don't even want to be around these idiots, much less ask one of them for help."

After watching the first two gag reels, I needed a shower. Two more and I considered retiring to the bathroom to puke. I had started out writing down anything Dan might have considered a threat to his election run but gave up after filling an entire sheet of paper after one video. And Dan was, by far, not the only Sandhill Lake cop guilty of felony-level racism, sexism, incompetence, and general dickishness. I was, in fact, struggling to find one who wasn't.

"How do we even know Dan is the one we should be watching?" I said. "Everyone here is an asshole."

"Dan's the only asshole running for office." Gina, already tired of the videos, sprawled on the low fainting couch, flicking a lighter on and off. She wanted a cigarette so badly she was about to burst. "And he knows how fucked he is if this gets out. The department will make him a scapegoat, give the press a bunch of blah-blah about how we don't tolerate this kind of crap, and then once he's gone, everything will go back to normal again."

I turned back to the screen but my eyes skittered away again like unruly kittens. When I looked up, Gina had a cigarette dangling out of the corner of her mouth. "What is wrong with you?" I said. "Jessie will have my ass."

Gina rolled her eyes, dragged herself off the couch and cracked the front door. A blast of air chilled the room.

"I don't know how you could stand working with these people."

"This is nothing, Buttercup. A highlight reel." She lit up, took a long drag, and blew out through the door. "You make your peace with it or you don't."

"That's what Matt said about being married to a cop," I grumbled.

"When did you two hook up?" Gina said.

"How do you even know that?"

"You get that look every time you talk about him," she said. "Like you're chewing on tinfoil but you kind of like it." She flicked the lighter open, then shut. "I'd stay away from him if I were you. Something about apples and trees springs to mind, for no reason at all."

"Yeah, yeah." Everybody was telling me to stay away from everybody else. Gina was loose now, relaxed, although she'd been springy and tight when we first came in. She'd made a beeline for the computer, stuffed the drive into it, sat down, and started clicking around. I turned away and let her do her thing. I wasn't supposed to ask. That was the deal, although I didn't have to like it. I wished I could rewind the previous night to before I met Maureen, before I knew the real origin of Gina's law enforcement career. *Who are you?* I thought, watching her look for whatever she didn't want me to see. Eventually she found it and vacated the computer so I could start sifting through the gag reels.

Now she stubbed out her cigarette on the pavement outside the door. "I need to get going. You good here?"

"I'm good," I said. "I'll show Jamie this gag reel stuff and see what he thinks."

I waited until her headlights receded on Milwaukee Avenue. Then I closed out of the gag reel video on my screen and clicked over to the computer's recycle bin.

It had just been emptied.

Of course.

Whatever Gina had found and watched, she'd trashed it to keep me, and anyone else, from seeing it. What she didn't know was that Jessie's battle-ax of a computer kept a ghost version of anything deleted in the last month, if you knew where to look. I had discovered this to my great relief after accidentally trashing Jessie's entire client database.

There it was: a single sound file in the deleted-today file tree section. I clicked restore and it sprang back into its home on the flash drive. I was about to hit play when my phone rang.

It was Jamie. Odd. He was supposed to be interviewing June, and there was no way he was done yet. Normally I'd be pinging his phone every thirty seconds for news, but yesterday's events still hung around me in a noxious fog.

"Are you done with the interview?" There was some sort of hollow banging in his background, and a confusion of voices.

"We haven't started." Jamie lowered his voice. "We have a bit of a situation." The banging intensified.

"What kind of situation?"

"June found something this morning while she was cleaning out Pete's stuff."

"What?"

"A photo album," he said. "Full of pictures of women. A sort of trophy case, if you will." He paused. "And Maureen is in it, too."

"Oh, God." I stood up.

"June is not taking it well. Matt's here. He's trying to calm her down, but it's . . ." There was a glassy, tinkling crash. ". . . not going well," he finished.

"She's not doing the interview?"

There was an interesting pause. "Not with me."

"Is that right?" I knew where he was going with this. *You slick dog*, I thought. *I'm going to make you beg*. He didn't need to know I was already standing up and putting my coat on.

"I thought since you have a relationship with her . . ."

"You mean the inappropriately close, harmfully subjective relationship I have with this top-of-the-list suspect?"

More silence. "Can you come up here?"

"You're breaking up," I said. "I didn't hear the part where you said either *I'm sorry* or *you were right*."

"It's 2188 Crane Drive." I could tell he was smiling. "Fox Lake."

I hung up, flipped the sign to CLOSED, locked the door, and ran for my car.

24

"This one's easy." I picked up Justice, another grim red-robed figure on a throne. According to the Major Arcana, life was full of them. This one was holding a sword and an old-fashioned scale. "You do something wrong, you get punished."

The space movie had inspired Rosie to build a rocket ship out of Cheetos, toothpicks, and shiny shreds from a granola bar wrapper. Rosie's medicated afternoons tended to follow an abbreviated daycare schedule. Snack time. Arts and crafts. Sensory time (i.e., wandering around the basement poking at stuff to see what it did). Sleepy time. Restless, cranky predinner hour.

"You're thinking of real-world justice." Rosie slid three Cheetos onto a toothpick in order of size. "The kind with courts and lawyers and judges."

"What else is there?" My mom used the words *consequences* and *responsibility* a lot, big words everybody learned early and forgot immediately. Words that settled into a low background hum behind the daily business of trying to get away with stuff.

"This isn't real-world justice, this is *psychic* justice," Rosie said. "And it's not blind. This justice sees your whole past."

Psychic Justice looked like she'd beat the crap out of you as soon as look at you. "I don't want some judge banging around in my brain with her little bangy thing," I said.

"You're the judge, you goof." Rosie connected tinier cheesy balls to the bottom of the assembly to make fins. "Judge, jury, and executioner. This is the point in your life where you understand your past and your role in it. Only then can you make good decisions about what to do next. Balanced decisions. Fair decisions."

She accented the rocket's fins with silver from the wrapper and got ready for takeoff. "And the people we're most unfair with are ourselves."

The Petersons lived in nearby Fox Lake, in a woodsy, hilly jumble of modest houses set off from the street on sloped, rambling lots. Many of the long dirt driveways had boats parked in them, and mud-spattered SUVs that looked like they'd actually been somewhere rougher than the mall.

The Petersons' house was a dark diagonal-wood-slatted place with tall windows slanting from the pitched asymmetrical roof. It had probably looked cutting-edge in the 1970s.

Jamie's car was parked on the curb. He paced beside it, on the phone, and gave me an absent-minded give-me-a-minute wave. I pulled up behind him. Matt's Beach Haven PD squad car stood in the driveway.

Matt, in uniform, sat on the porch, elbows on knees. He looked like he was trying to keep it together on a roller coaster. Surprise flickered over his face when he saw me.

"Hey, stranger," he said. "What are you doing here?"

"Jamie thought I might be able to help." I sat down next to

him. A mournful mechanical whine drifted from the house. It sounded like a machine grinding up human bones. "How is it"—an empty bottle of Jim Beam sailed through the window and landed between us—"going?" I finished.

Matt picked up the bottle and set it beside the porch. "She called me about an hour ago and yelled a bunch of nonsense into the phone."

"At least you two are talking," I said. "Did you know?"

"You mean, about Maureen?" Matt stared straight ahead. "Or about the rest?"

"Either."

"I knew some things." He looked down at his hands. "Suspected others."

A kid trundled by on a trike shaped like a shark. White teeth, blood-red wheels. A disheveled mom shuffled after him, death-gripping a travel mug of coffee. Matt watched them pass, the shark tooth wheels going *ka-chuka, ka-chuka, ka-chuka* all the way down the block.

"My dad had a way of confusing you sometimes. Making any idea sound great. Or making you think it was your idea all along." He watched the kid and the mom disappear around a corner. "He was always so sure he was right. No doubts, ever."

"I wish I was like that sometimes," I said.

"Me too," Matt said. "'I don't have a choice, Matty.'" It took me a second to realize Matt was imitating his dad. "'The things you see on this job? You got to find ways to stay happy, you know? Stay positive.'" He looked at me. "He always had reasons. *If you haven't served, you don't know.* That one was his favorite."

I felt sorry for him, having to clean up his dad's mess. "Listen, Matt." My butt was numb and I scooted around, trying to get comfortable on the cold stone porch. "I was at the PD last night. Visiting Jamie." I left out the less legal elements of the evening.

"And I bumped into Maureen. She was looking for some of your dad's paperwork."

"For the audit? Yeah, I know," he said. "She asked me, too, and I gave her what I had. Did she need more?"

"I'm not sure. She was checking some places that . . ." I didn't know the best way to say that Maureen was sneaking around and generally being weird. "It seemed like she didn't want anyone to know what she was doing."

Matt scratched his head. "Why?"

"I don't know," I said. "I was hoping maybe you did."

"Honestly, my dad's stuff is kind of a mess. I haven't had a chance to go through all of it yet, so there might be more of what she wanted," he said. "I was going to do some digging tonight, but there's that Future Builders thing. Are you going?"

"What Future Builders thing? Oh, shit." I kept forgetting I was supposed to work Jessie's stupid real estate thing. "I'll be there with bells on," I said. "I think the outfit my sister picked out for me has actual bells on it."

Jamie hung up the phone and headed up the driveway.

"I didn't know you were going to bring in the cavalry." Matt gave Jamie a jagged smile. I wondered what kind of weirdo small talk the two of them had been forced to make in my absence.

"I thought I would try the solution that didn't make any sense." Jamie raised an apologetic eyebrow at me. I smiled. We were okay.

"Right," Matt said, watching us.

"I promise I won't upset her," I said. "I'm just going to listen."

"Good luck with that, because she doesn't want to talk to—"

The door slammed open and June appeared in the doorway. I barely recognized her. Her hair stood in stiff sheets around her head. She wore flannel pajama pants and a faded blue T-shirt with a cactus on it reading JOSHUA TREE. She was covered head to toe in sawdust and clutched a tangle of bright paper shreds.

Matt stood up. Jamie put his hands in his pockets and nodded at the scrapbook guts in June's fist. "You might want to keep that scrapbook intact," he said, "in case we need it for—"

June growled and flung the shreds at him. They spiraled down to the porch in jagged streaks. Jamie closed his eyes and spat out a thin red paper curl.

"Just tell me one thing." June wheeled on Matt. "Did you know?"

Matt looked at his shoes. "I didn't know about the book," he said. "He wouldn't have shown me something like that."

"Well, how goddamn noble of him!" June was shouting now, hoarse and scratchy like a bird of prey. She pounced on Matt, punched him with her fists, rained blows on his face and shoulders. Matt didn't move, not even when June split his lip. Red spattered his uniform. Jamie stepped forward but I held him back.

June gave a strangled cry and collapsed against Matt's chest. He hugged her and she sobbed and sobbed, her cries echoing in the empty street.

"I'm sorry." Matt leaned close and whispered in her ear. "I'm . . ." The rest was silent.

June shoved him away. Her face was a raw pink wound. When she saw me, her hands flew to her hair, her stained clothing. "Oh." Seeing me woke her up, as if I were the only one who could see her. She treated me the opposite of how everyone else did. "What are you doing here, hon?"

I took out my deck and shuffled. "I thought you might need to talk to some friends," I said. "So I brought all of them. Can I come in?"

June's face shifted and flowed. She glanced at Matt, then twisted the hem of her T-shirt in her hands.

I gave her the cards in a wide fan. "Choose one," I said. *Please, please, please,* I begged the cards. *Be something pretty and nice and not the Tower or some shit.*

The Hermit. I could work with this. "Help is on the way." I dipped in a clumsy curtsy. "From your weirdo guide."

June gave a sharp surprised laugh. She dropped the hem of her shirt and turned to Matt and Jamie. "Get out of here," she said in a low voice. "Both of you." She put her hand on my shoulder and steered me toward the door. "Come on in, hon."

Jamie's lip lifted at the corner. For him, it was the equivalent of a fist pump.

Matt rubbed the back of his neck. "Is this a good—"

"Let's go, Matt," Jamie said. Matt shifted from foot to foot, then followed Jamie into the driveway. He turned to June one more time and a final high-voltage look zapped between them. Then he got in his squad car and rumbled off.

June's living room looked like a picture book in which a kind-hearted toddler invites a polite but clumsy elephant over for tea. A giant paper shredder occupied center stage in front of the couch. Someone had shoved an entire wooden model boat into its teeth and given up halfway. The lovingly painted hull was in scraps and chips. Pieces of mangled paper lay scattered over the floor like angry confetti: more of the offending scrapbook, I imagined. The evil twin of the one sitting on my parents' mantel like Glinda the Good Witch in her oblivious pink bubble.

"Want a drink?" June walked over to an ornate liquor cabinet.

A sooty grandfather clock told me it was 10:36 A.M. "How about I make us some coffee instead?" I said.

June shrugged. "The pot's still on in the kitchen." She opened a fancy beveled-glass decanter and tossed the stopper behind her. It shattered a mirror and rolled away.

I went in search of the coffeepot. The house was dark and old-fashioned, full of curlicued furniture and dim paintings of storm-tossed boats. It looked like an Elks lodge. Any interest in housekeeping or decoration, no matter how fleeting, had faded years ago. There was a trophy case full of shining figures and plaques. Pictures of Peterson and his Explorers. Pictures of Matt. Signs of June—the celestial freewheeler I thought of as the real June—were nowhere to be found.

I loaded a tray with two coffees, a sugar bowl, and a thing of creamer and found June in the den, a man cave festooned with model ships and books on nautical history. Antiques and vintage posters covered the walls. Racy wartime ladies dropped their bags of lettuce—oops!—and bent over to reveal frilly underpants, or saluted in saucy sailor caps and skimpy faux military uniforms.

"Twelve-year-old scotch." June sprawled on a dark leather couch, studying the glass in her hand. "From our trip to England. He was saving it for a special occasion. I'd say this qualifies." She plunked her shaggy blue slippers on the polished mahogany table.

I swept a pile of wood chips onto the floor and set out the cards. June watched me. I had no idea where to start, what questions to ask. I closed my eyes and cleared my mind, drew a card:

The Lovers.

June scoffed. "That ship sailed a long time ago." She picked up her glass and drank for a disturbingly long time.

"This card isn't what it looks like," I said. "It's about choices." Rosie, years ago, had put this card at the cusp of adulthood, when you start owning your choices and their consequences. I thought of Pete's smarmy excuses for his behavior: *I had no choice, Matty.*

"Matt told me," I said carefully, "how Officer Pete always found a way to justify his actions."

June watched the gold liquid in her glass. "You mean about Maureen?"

I shrugged. I meant whatever she thought I meant.

"Maureen was news to me," June said, "though I can't say I'm surprised." Her eyes glittered in the dim light. "She was his real wife. I was for show."

"Did she have any reason to want him out of the way?"

"Are you asking me if she killed him?" June snorted and picked up her coffee. "Why would she? She had everything she needed. Her job and her partner. Wouldn't it make more sense for her to kill me instead?"

She reached back to the window and lifted the shade. A ray of light stabbed the dark. June flinched and let the shade drop.

"Maureen wasn't the worst of it." June's face went dark. "There was a girl in there. One of his Explorers. She's of age now, but who knows when that picture was taken." She drank from her coffee and set the cup down. "That's a choice most people would have to work pretty hard to justify, don't you think?" She leveled a gaze at me. "Not him."

Gina had hinted as much at the Olde Prairie Inn, but I'd hoped she was exaggerating. I felt like I was descending a spiral staircase into a dank basement full of mold and rot and darkness. It seemed to have no bottom.

The Explorers, Maureen, Pete. They whirled around each other in my mind like a cyclone. I was missing something that tied them all together. The next card was the Page of Swords— youth, energy, enthusiasm. Yes. The Explorers. I was on the right track.

"The house you're buying," I said. "Matt said Officer Pete

wanted it for the Explorers. So they could have something he didn't have when he was a kid."

"Is that what Matt said?" A crooked smile. "That's a very nice story. I'm sure Matt believes it. I bet even Pete did." Her voice cracked with rage.

"My husband was very dedicated to *service*." June looked out the window again. "The idea of it anyway." She went still, like she was watching someone she used to know walk by. "When I met Pete, my brother had just been diagnosed with brain cancer. Doctors, treatments, medications. We thought we would lose him. It was a bad time.

"Pete let me talk about it. He let me cry. He listened. No one had ever listened to me like that before. The first night we met, we stayed up all night talking. We wanted to know everything about each other.

"And then we got married and it all stopped." Light slipped through the shades and set her wedding ring on fire. "I still hung on his every word. I still wanted to know everything about him. But he stopped listening. He stopped asking questions. It was like he forgot about me." She turned her hand slowly, watching the ring with quiet astonishment. "I'm a human being. I have universes inside me. They just didn't interest him."

She put her hand down. "But here's the thing. He never stopped asking about my brother. How's your brother? Is he doing okay? Dave had been in remission for years, but somehow that didn't stick with Pete the same way his illness did.

"My brother, you see, was the exception that proved the rule." An odd expression slipped across her face, more grimace than smile. "Caring, serving, sacrificing yourself. Those things interested Pete, because they made him who he wanted to be. Matt interested him because Matt was a child and children need care.

For a while, I interested him, too. I had something he wanted. After that thing was gone"—she shrugged—"he didn't need me anymore.

"My husband was the most self-obsessed, vainglorious person I have ever met. The worst kind, because he thought he was in it for others. He was the quintessential cop."

Those are the ones you have to watch out for, Gina had said days ago.

"And those kids." June was whispering now. "Those poor kids. They worshipped him, and he used them. He built his reputation on their backs and threw them away." Soft, wounded surprise crept through her voice. "He was bleeding those kids dry.

"That house wasn't for the kids. It was for him. So everyone could see he wasn't poor anymore. Even if he couldn't afford it."

I thought of Pete's boisterous social media posts, all those glitzy good times. "He couldn't afford it?"

"He kept talking about his pension. Couldn't wait to get it. I could tell he was worried about money, he just wouldn't admit it to me. He wouldn't even let me look at the bills. He'd just tell me not to worry my pretty little head, that that was his job."

Pentacles, coins, gold, silver, bronze. Everything always came down to money. "If he wouldn't talk to you, would he talk to other people about it?"

June thought about it. "I would hear him on the phone sometimes late at night when he thought I was asleep," she said. "He talked to some guy named Popeye a lot. It sounded like they were trying to get money lined up for something."

I blinked. "Popeye . . . the Sailor Man?"

"The only Popeye I know is Popeye Moran," June said. "He's got a place out on Grass Lake, but I didn't even know he and Pete knew each other. Let's just toss that on the pile of things I didn't know."

There were so many reasons not to ask what I was about to ask, not the least of which was that my sister would disembowel me. "Are you still going to buy the house?"

"I have to," June said. "It's too late to call it off. I'm stuck. He's dead but I'm still stuck with him." She traced the shining rim of her glass. "We all are."

I drew a card: Justice. A thin tone rose from June's glass, like a bell.

"You're not stuck, June, you only think you are," I said. "But you understand a lot more now about your life up to this point."

June moved the shade aside again and squinted like she was staring down a kaleidoscope tube, or one of those old binocular toys with the scene painted in miniature on the back of a little projector. A house on a hill, steps leading to clear water, a boat bobbing on the waves. A sweet mirage.

"I think you should start being more fair with yourself," I told her.

25

Stepping out of June's dark house into the weak sun was like plunging into the tropics. Jamie had moved his car politely down the street, to sit at an angle in the ditch that passed for the shoulder. He had paperwork scattered all over himself and the passenger seat, and when I knocked on the window I startled him.

"I thought you'd be gone by now." I slipped into the front seat. He shuffled papers out of the way.

"I had this time blocked off, so it's kind of nice to be unaccounted for," he said. "Nobody has to know the interview was a miserable failure."

I wondered what it was like to be wanted all the time, to have people depending on you. It sounded exhausting.

Jamie yawned and checked his watch. "Did she get you drunk?"

"I don't think there was any booze left over for me, the way she was going at it." I returned Jamie's yawn. "Man, does she hate him. I don't think the scrapbook changed anything. It just let loose everything she's been feeling for years." I closed my eyes and leaned back in the seat. "I didn't do much good in there, Jamie. I'm sorry. I forgot to even ask about her alibi."

"It's okay," Jamie said. "Did she say anything about Pete himself? Was he acting any different leading up to this week? Changes in mood, behavior, anything like that?"

I thought about it. "She said he was worried about money. She overheard him talking to some guy named Popeye on the phone, like either Pete owed him money, or the other way around, or something. I like to think they were going in on a boxcar of spinach."

Jamie sat up. "Did you say Popeye?" He clutched the steering wheel. "Popeye Moran?"

"Yeah, I think so," I said. "I wouldn't even have remembered the first name if—"

Jamie leaned over, grabbed my face, and planted a furious kiss on my forehead. I was still gaping at him when he started the car. The engine noise shattered the thick silence.

"We're going for a ride," he said.

The dirt parking lot of Moran's was tiny but full. Jamie and I parked across the bridge spanning the narrows between Grass and Sandhill Lakes and doubled back over the pedestrian walkway. A ferocious wind attacked us, tearing the breath out of me. I made the mistake of looking down when we were halfway across and had to squeeze my eyes shut. Jamie and I hung in a gray void, nothing to either side but colorless water and air, indistinguishable from each other. I grabbed for Jamie's hand but he was marching ahead, unbothered, unreachable.

The bar at the foot of the bridge was a shabby two-story house the color of dust, with a wraparound porch and a warehouse in the back. Behind it down the shore, a trailer park was marked off by a sign reading PRIVATE PROPERTY, VIOLATORS WILL BE . . . The rest was ominously swallowed up by a creeping rust stain. Little white trailer boxes stared balefully across the lake at the mansions on Baines Hill.

Jamie marched up the front porch, past signs reading BAR, GRILL, VIDEO GAMING. The sign at the edge of the road read, improbably, CHESS TOURNAMENT TODAY. I hurried up the steps after Jamie. He shoved open the door, a bell tinkled, and we plunged into a dim hall lit by TV screens blasting some manner of sportsball. A square bar dominated the room, glasses suspended overhead. The place smelled of onion rings and man sweat.

Two guys in a dark corner booth were engaged in an animated argument about whether or not the money you deposit in a bank is available right away. "How fast is a computer, motherfucker?" one of them shouted. No one paid any attention or had an answer. The chess tournament consisted of two snappily dressed old dudes hunched over a shabby wooden board with their wool overcoats and fedoras next to them on the table. An old-fashioned chess clock ticked away between them.

A big guy in a leather vest ran a filthy rag sleepily back and forth over the bar. He was well over six feet tall, edging toward his mid-fifties, although his receding hairline was combed into an improbably high jet-black pompadour. The silver chains choking his thick neck were etched with astrological symbols and one of those talk-to-the-hand evil eye deflectors. He looked like a retired vampire. One look at his mean fish-eyed stare made it clear he was Mr. Popeye Moran himself.

"Mr. Moran. A word, please," Jamie thundered. He hadn't

slowed down yet. The chess players didn't look up as he maneuvered deftly around their table. My blood reared up in my veins. Whatever this Popeye Moran did to summon don't-fuck-with-me Jamie, I hoped for his sake he had a good excuse for it. A young gum-chewing blonde in ripped jeans perched on a barstool next to Popeye reading *The Martian Chronicles*. She looked up, then went back to her book.

The rag slowed its dim-witted circuit around the bar. "Officer Roth," Popeye said. "To what do I owe the pleasure of this repeat visit? I thought we'd talked everything out when you were here last week."

"Evidently not everything," Jamie said.

Popeye narrowed his eyes and resumed wiping the bar. "It's not a good time, I'm afraid," he drawled. "Big chess tournament today." He nodded toward the chess-playing dandies. "Janusz here is poised to take back the regional title from Maury." Blondie smirked from between the pages of her book.

Before I could register what was happening Jamie blurred past me, grabbed Popeye by the towering crown of his hair, and slammed him face-first onto the bar. Popeye uttered a strangled quack and twisted his head to the side. His cheek hit the bar with a sickening squelch, sending up a fountain of dirty water. Jamie grabbed a nearby glass of murky drink melt and dumped it, ice and all, over Popeye's head. Ice chips skittered across the bar and cascaded onto the floor. The girl blinked and moved her book out of the path of the spray.

"Aha!" Janusz (or Maury) slammed the trigger on the clock. Ding! The banking technology enthusiasts in the corner went quiet.

"What the fuck are you doing?" Popeye squealed. He sputtered and wriggled but Jamie clamped him fast to the bar.

"I'd be happy to return at a more convenient time"—Jamie sounded like a receptionist flipping through an appointment book—"with my colleagues from the ATF. I'm sure they would be very interested to take a look at your warehouse." Popeye gulped like a fish.

"Or you can give me the information I need now." Jamie shoved his face into the water, eliciting another strangled squeal. "All of it, this time."

"Danica," Popeye wheezed, "take the bar for a minute, huh?"

Danica rolled her eyes, put down her book, and hopped off the stool, white sneakers flashing. Jamie surrendered Popeye's head. Popeye unglued himself from the bar, dripping, and led us through a grimy door labeled OFFICE. Inside was a closet-sized room with a card table shoved in the corner, a couple of folding chairs, and a rusty file cabinet. Every inch of wall was covered with nudie calendars featuring ladies whose hairstyles had come and gone from the fashion stage several times over. The smell of expired man intensified.

"Who the hell's this?" Popeye flashed me a surly look.

"This is my associate," Jamie said.

I gripped my knees to keep them from chattering together like teeth. "I've got the eye," I told Popeye, staring at his jewelry. "I'll know if you're lying, so how about you stick to the truth this time." I deadpanned it hard. Either he would buy in or he'd think I was fucking with him, which was just as good.

Popeye smirked and said nothing, but his fingers crept to his necklace. He turned to Jamie. "Well? Let's have it. What is this all about?"

"It appears, Mr. Moran, that when I asked you during our first meeting if you'd had any dealings with Lieutenant Matt Peterson you didn't tell me the truth."

Popeye gave Jamie a murky stare. "I did tell you the truth. Not a single business transaction took place." He swiped his arms, sweeping the air clean of business transactions. "None. Zero."

Jamie turned to me. My turn? Oh, okay. "You did, however, speak to Lieutenant Peterson on the phone repeatedly over the past few weeks."

"Yeah? So what if I did?" Popeye laced his hands over his gut and leaned back against the wall. His head pushed up against a wall calendar so it looked like his pompadour had sprouted a pair of large breasts. "Just some friendly chats. Between friends."

"So you're telling me," Jamie said, "that Lieutenant Peterson, decorated officer of the law and all-around pillar of the community, was friends with a twice-convicted felony black market arms dealer and occasional contract killer."

Popeye's lips twitched. "They didn't get the killer stuff to stick."

Jamie folded his arms and leaned against the wall. He was throwing off cold blue sparks. "Either you're punching far above your weight class, socially speaking," Jamie said, "or the lieutenant required your services."

Popeye's fishy eyes darted back and forth between us. I tried to look like I was staring into his soul.

"He wanted a hit," Popeye said quietly. Things went glassy and strange. The light streaming through the filthy blinds shifted and strips of white sprayed over Popeye's face. Glitter and dust and smoke.

"You said you were retired," Jamie said.

"I keep my options open," Popeye said. "If the money's right. Man's got to make a living."

"Who did he want dead?"

Popeye shifted. Dust swirled in the weak light streaming over his face. "I'm going to need your word, Officer, that this won't come back on me. Whatever that asshole was doing, I got no part of it, and I want no part of it. You got me?"

"Deal," Jamie said. "Who was the target?"

"The boss lady," Popeye said. "The manager, the one from the city."

"Maureen?" I said. My skin was trying to crawl in all directions at once. "Maureen Loeffler?" My voice went dead in the air.

"But you didn't go through with it," Jamie said.

"Is she dead?" Popeye's chair legs connected with the floor. "He couldn't pull the money together so I called it off."

"Why did he want her dead?" I said.

"She wouldn't come to his birthday party." Popeye didn't move but his eyes crept toward me. "How the fuck should I know? That's between the two of them."

"Why didn't you tell me this on Monday?" Jamie said. "You could've claimed the reward."

Popeye gave a wheezy bark of a laugh. "You must think I'm a fucking idiot. *Fifty grand for information leading to an arrest.*" He broke into a snooty mimic. "Oh! But it didn't lead to an arrest, so tough titties for you, we'll just keep the fifty thou." He shot Jamie a knowing look. "And we'll stick you with all the shit you just owned up to."

"Why wouldn't it lead to an arrest?" Jamie said.

"Because I know you guys got nothing." Popeye produced a comb from somewhere in his vest and began smoothing his greasy hair, now wet with bar ooze, back into shape. "You got the whole goddamn force, Andy Griffith *and* Barney Fife, plus the entire goddamn U.S. government on this, and not one person in the whole show knows anything." He let out a satisfied grunt. "This thing with what's her name, the village lady." He didn't even know her name. "This wasn't gonna help you guys."

"Is that right?" Jamie said.

"Yeah, that's right." Popeye's mean eyes flashed. "It doesn't surprise me you don't know who did it. But it surprises me that *I* don't know who did it. You sure he didn't off himself?"

"Impossible," Jamie said.

"Well." Popeye swung his feet off the desk and stood up. "In that case, good luck to you. Because either your killer is long gone, or he doesn't exist. You're looking for a ghost."

26

When Jamie pulled up in front of June's house, the street was darker but also warmer, less empty. People drifted home from work, tiny yellow house lights blooming to life between the skeletal trees. Cars edged around us on the narrow road. June's house was dark. I wondered if she was sleeping off the morning.

Jamie and I got out of his car, but neither of us made any move to leave. Streetlights flicked on against the indigo sky and now we could see each other. Jamie looked flushed and glowy and loose. Gold flecks shone in his hair.

"I don't condone violence or anything," I said, "but you were kind of awesome today."

Jamie smiled and something moved inside me, like a boulder had rolled away from a dark cave mouth. Jamie, as a rule, didn't take compliments well. They made him squirm and deflect, but today I didn't care, and he didn't seem to either. Whatever quirk or glitch had popped up between us over the past few days, we were both tired of it. We missed each other, snapped back together like a rubber band.

"Popeye is a guy who won't cooperate unless he believes you can kick his ass," Jamie said. "I figured that out about him right away."

"Could you have kicked his ass?"

"Absolutely not," Jamie said. "Did you see him? He would have killed me. I gambled and won."

I laughed, and Jamie watched me, still smiling. "The human lie detector thing was a nice touch," he said.

I shrugged. "Gambled and won."

Jamie kicked a rock. It skittered off into the blue dark. He started to say something and stopped. He cleared his throat and tried again. "Do you want to come over tonight?" he said, kind of rushed and awkward.

"I'd love to," I said. "My brain is full. I need to unload some of this stuff."

Jamie shook his head. "I was actually thinking we could . . . not talk about Pete for a change. Just order some food and hang out." He ran a hand through his hair. "I keep hearing there are other things to talk about besides work."

His breath plumed in the air in quick bursts. He was sweating. I was not aware this was something Jamie did. I wanted to hug him. I felt a fast, pleasant dizziness, like I was strapped to the front of a speeding train and it was scary, but also exciting. The train was going somewhere bright.

"I would love that." I locked eyes with him.

"Okay. Great." Jamie let out a breath. "Dan's going to some real estate cocktail party tonight, so he gave us the night off."

"Oh no." I smacked my forehead. "Shit, shit, shit! Jessie's party." I had forgotten all about the grand opening event. Again.

Why couldn't I get this thing to stick in my mind? "It starts in an hour." And I still needed to go back to the office and grab the suit Jessie wanted me to wear. I was so screwed.

"You're going, too?" Jamie tried to sound neutral.

"I have to." I sighed. "Remember the house my sister was going to sell the Petersons? It's in this new subdivision on Baines Hill and they're having this fancy-pants grand opening thing. The company is called Future Builders and Jessie got them to let me read cards because, you know, future."

"Clever," Jamie said.

I checked my phone. "In fact, I'm very, very late for it right now. My sister will kill me if I'm late. Everyone's going to be there, Matt, June, Dan, Maureen, everybody."

"Ah." Jamie's face closed off at the mention of Matt. "Okay."

"I'm so sorry, Jamie."

"Yeah, no, I didn't mean to—"

"No! No, I'm not— I'd love to— I mean, any other night—"

We shouted some more assurances at each other and then I turned toward my car, feeling like an asshole.

"Hey," Jamie said before I got in. "If I were you I'd keep quiet about what we found today. Until we figure out what it means."

"Yeah, of course," I said. We were talking about work again. It was a nice break while it lasted.

I hauled ass back to my office, screeched into the lot, and parked crooked between two spaces. Inside, Jessie's suit hung on a persnickety cloth hanger. I grabbed it and was halfway to the bathroom to change when I realized something was wrong.

The dark room was glowing. My computer, which was long past due to go black in the time I was gone, filled the room with blue-white light. On the screen, a document was open. In tiny letters off to the side it said:

YOU KNOW HE DESERVED IT.
LEAVE IT ALONE OR YOU'RE NEXT.

I looked around wildly. The flash drive with the gag reel footage—and Gina's recording, which I had saved from the trash—was gone. Someone had taken it. Had the lock been forced? No, it had been locked when I came in. I remembered locking it this morning when I left for June's.

I slammed the door open and ran outside. Cars blurred by. The parking lot flowed with people running one last post-work errand or getting takeout to bring home. I spun, looking for anyone, anything to see, but there was nothing.

At the traffic light leading out of the plaza, the red taillights of a Public Works truck disappeared onto Milwaukee Avenue.

27

"This one's upside down," I said, turning the Hanged Man around in his slot.

"Nope." Rosie flipped the card back around. "He's right where he needs to be."

In the movie, the spaceship was broken and one of the astronauts was on a space walk to repair it. He drifted around the giant metal latticework of the ship, a tiny speck on the back of limitless black space.

"He looks dead." The Hanged Man was upside down on a hunk of wood, a golden halo ringing his head like sunlight. "Is he dead?"

"Not dead." Rosie watched the screen serenely. "Suspended. Sometimes you have to let go and accept who you are and what you've been through."

She tracked a star-speckled midnight fingernail across the Wheel of Fortune, Justice, and the Hanged Man. "We're in the middle of the road now. This process—change and acceptance—is at the center of life."

On the screen, the astronaut let go of his space pod and floated toward the broken part of the ship. My heart stuttered. My dad said a body in free-fall will keep moving in the same direction unless something messes with it, but I didn't believe him. What was to stop the astronaut from drifting out into space?

"You just have to believe there's peace on the other side," Rosie said. Had I spoken aloud? "That's why they call it a leap of faith."

The astronaut's breathing filled the room, deep and regular and loud. He had to trust the laws of physics would take him where he needed to go.

"I don't like this," I said. "It's scary."

"You ain't seen nothing yet, little sister," Rosie said.

I missed the turnoff to Baines Hill twice. The GPS led me in circles up and down the bleak lightning-fast lanes of Route 12 until I picked a random unmarked turn and got lucky. The dark road led me up a slope so gradual I didn't know I was rising until the trees fell away and the black lake opened below, pinprick lights flashing on the far shore.

I white-knuckled the wheel, my mind swimming in a gray fog. Who knew I had the flash drive? Gina. Maureen definitely knew, because she was there when I copied the disk. Whoever took it must have wanted Gina's recording. The one she was hiding even from me.

But . . . if the same person had been driving the truck the whole time, even during Maureen's accident, Maureen was off the list. The list was down to one person:

Gina.

I had circled the Peterson case all week, pretending I could creep unnoticed past whatever dark beast slept at its heart. *I'm just trying to decide,* Jamie said, the first time he'd caught me doing something more stupid and dangerous than it was worth, *if you had no idea you could get hurt, or if you just didn't care.*

"Beats me," I said aloud. Jamie's deadly serious face faded away. He never asked me that anymore. He knew by now that the confusion was, whether I knew it or not, part of the point. I took a sharp curve and for a wild second imagined my eyes slipping shut, the car sailing serenely over the guardrail into the pin-lit blackness on the other side.

The houses out here were huge, tossed wide over asymmetrical lots, each hiding somewhere deep inside it, like a crown jewel, its precious lake view, the whole point of living here on Mt. Privilege. Riviera Heights was the newest neighborhood subsection, stone pillars marking it off with a curvy script evoking an elite gambling playground, the kind that serves as a backdrop for an international spy operation and not the kind where people piss their chairs because their dollar slot machine is about to pay off. I edged past the markers into a patchwork of empty lots interrupted by the occasional house, like an unpulled tooth. No trees, not yet. One of these houses was probably the Petersons' intended forever home. I couldn't tell in the dark which one it was.

I screeched up to the sales model at ten after seven, imagining one of Jessie's Italian-leather-clad toes tapping. The circular drive was lit up like an airport runway and lined with cars. I parked behind a Jeep with a blue-line bumper sticker and wobbled out of my car, straightening Jessie's suit, a fitted black thing with a soft sparkle to the fabric. Jessie's grudging nod to the evening's celestial theme. It actually kind of worked. I looked like a god, like I was made of stars. Except for my Converse sneakers. The gods' underpaid intern.

Inside, the vibe was catalog lived-in, all veined marble, egg-white walls, floor-to-ceiling windows dotted with flickering candles, curvy sculptures, and decorative bowls waiting to be filled with keys and homey bric-a-brac. The place had Jessie written all over it: warm and aloof at the same time, like a temple. *Welcome all*, it said, *but don't forget who's in charge.*

Jessie stood in a cluster of pale-gray-suited Vikings that looked like swords stashed in a cabinet, shiny and sharp and waiting for their moment. Her Future Builders overlords.

"Ah! Our entertainment for the evening." Jesse clicked over and grabbed me by the elbow, pulled me in. "Right on time!" Meaning, *Where the fuck have you been?* I shook hands with a tall reverse bob and an electrical pole topped with a ferret. They each bestowed upon me a sick smile and a fishy handshake. I forgot their names immediately.

Jessie dragged me toward a small rectangular table covered with black cloth that matched the sparkle of my suit. Everyone kept trying to make me blend into the background.

"Keep it light," Jessie said through clenched teeth. Her hair was blown and straightened within an inch of its life, which meant she was hanging on by her fingertips. "Fun. Positive. You're here to *entertain*." She straightened the banner lacing the front of the tablecloth: THE FUTURE LOOKS BRIGHT. Crescent-shaped tea lights glowed on the table above it. "And no drinking," she hissed as a parting shot.

Behind me was the centerpiece of the room, a spectacular panoramic window facing the lake. I thought I could see Birdie's, the bright center of a line of warm downtown lights. I felt an odd stab of homesickness, like I'd crossed a vast dead space in search of something I couldn't see and was alone on the other side.

I sat down and laid out my deck. People floated past, public service types I recognized from the funeral. I felt like I was at a masquerade ball where everyone wore masks that looked like their real faces. Everyone was drinking from actual wineglasses, not the plastic glass-shaped cups that come in batons of one hundred at Binny's.

A woman stood at one of the smaller side windows tracing the lip of her untouched wineglass. June. I hadn't recognized her. She wore a bright red caftan embroidered with gold streaks and a tiara sprinkled with tiny blossoms or stars. She looked like a sun about to go supernova and destroy a fledgling civilization. I waved but she didn't see me. She was watching, across the room, Maureen flip through glossy marketing flyers spread out across the kitchen bar. Maureen wore khakis and an unfortunate ruffled blouse that made her head look like a cabbage. Her clothes always seemed too loose or too tight, even when they fit. She looked up at June and the two locked eyes. June turned to the window. Maureen looked up, tossed me an unfriendly glare, and walked off.

Next to the makeshift bar on the kitchen island, Matt watched June while he pretended to listen to Dan. When Dan paused to drink, Matt extricated himself and headed toward me. He'd gone smart casual: clean dark jeans, tight-fitting gray shirt, black sport coat. I hadn't seen him out of uniform since we were kids.

"You look great," he said. "There's only one thing missing: a drink. Can I get you one?"

"I'd love one." I tossed a nod at Jessie, who was at the stove scrubbing off a spot that was probably visible only to her. "But I'm on the clock."

"Too bad." He pulled the spare chair around to my side and straddled it backward, facing me. I could smell him, a sharp scent like pine needles and snow.

"Here." He offered me his glass but when I took it, he held on, tipped it toward me. The warm wine spilled into my mouth and I gasped, swallowed quick to keep it from spilling. The bitter, heady taste shot through me. Matt smiled, took the glass away. Something tight and inevitable cinched me around the middle, like a leash.

I looked down before he saw my flushed face. "Has Jessie given you the hard sell yet?" I said, just to say something.

He swirled the wine and set the glass on the table. "I'm just here to keep an eye on my mom." June was still staring out the window. No one came near her. She was surrounded by some sort of hot, impenetrable force field. "I didn't think she'd make it out of the house. Whatever you did this afternoon must have worked."

"I just listened," I said. "She seems like she doesn't get that a lot."

Matt reached out for one of the moon-shaped lights. His hand made the shadows dance. "Did she say anything . . . you know, useful?" He rubbed the back of his head and looked around. "I feel bad saying this, but I had high hopes for Jamie's interview." His voice broke and he looked away. "I need something. Anything."

My throat went dry. Did he need to know his dad was trying to hire a hit man to kill his extramarital girlfriend? June was afraid of the day Matt found out his dad was human, and I didn't love hastening the arrival of that day. I had also promised Jamie I would shut the hell up about it. Still, Matt deserved the truth. I just wished I could have more wine before I gave it to him.

"Do you know who Popeye Moran is?" I said.

Matt watched the white dot of an airplane move across the sky behind me. "The guy who runs that bar out on Grass Lake?"

"Yes." I licked my lips. "And also kills people. For money. Your dad was talking to him."

Matt dragged his eyes off the window and stared at me. "I don't understand."

I reached over, grabbed his glass, and took a gulp. "Your dad tried to hire Popeye to kill someone." I thunked the glass back on the table and knocked one of the candles aside. I felt woozy and hot.

Matt watched the wine wobble in the glass. He didn't look at me and he didn't move for a long time. "*My* dad?" he said. "Tried to hire a hit man?" His eyes flickered around the room and found June. "My mom told you this?"

"She said she overheard your dad talking to Popeye on the phone, but she didn't know what they were talking about."

"My mom was drunk this morning," Matt said. The emotion had left his voice. "Drunk and upset. She could have said anything." He uncrossed his arms from the back of the chair, moved away from me. *Shit.* I knew the risks.

"Here's what I think." Matt was looking around now. He was preparing to exit this unpleasant conversation and rejoin the room. Wait, I wanted to shout, don't go. Part of me wanted to take it back, but how could I? He had said he wanted the truth, no matter how ugly. "I think you should let Jamie determine what's a real lead and what's not," Matt said.

I felt a twang of irritation, like a wrong note struck on a guitar. He only trusted me for the scoop when the scoop was something he wanted to hear.

"It's real, Matt," I said. "Jamie was the one who recognized the name. We talked to Popeye. He confirmed that your dad approached him to kill Maureen Loeffler."

Matt, already half out of the chair, stopped. He sat down again, heavily, and rubbed his face. "Maureen?" Both of us looked at her. "Why?" Matt lowered his voice. "Because of the affair? Was she about to expose it?"

"I don't know," I said. "Could it have something to do with those documents she was looking for?"

I wasn't sure Matt heard me. Finally, he said, "Why didn't he come talk to me?" He closed his eyes. "We told each other everything. We could have figured this out together. I could have helped him."

"Maybe he was trying to keep you out of it," I said. "Protect you." For all his faults, June had said, Pete was actually a pretty good dad.

Matt was still watching Maureen. "He didn't take the job, did he? Popeye, I mean. Maureen is safe?"

"She's fine." We watched Maureen refill her glass. "It sounds like your dad didn't come through with the money, so the deal was off."

Matt drained his glass and wobbled to his feet again. "Does Dan know? We need to tell him."

"About that." I looked over at Dan, getting drunker and louder and more red-faced. "I don't think we should tell him anything."

"Okay, okay." Matt held his forehead like he had a headache. "I need to think. Katie, excuse me, but I need to go drink a lot of wine right now." He gave me his goofy grin and for a second the little boy surfaced in his eyes again.

"Hey, Matt," I called after him, and he turned to me. "I'm going to figure this out. No matter what."

Matt's eyes blazed. He strode back toward me, took my hand, and kissed it. "You might be the only one who can."

An odd thought bubbled through me and before I could stop myself I blurted out, "Is there any chance your dad set this up?"

Matt frowned. "What do you mean, set it up?"

"Killed himself. Could it be a suicide?"

Matt shook his head. "I've seen the crime scene. It's not possible. And it's just not *him*. He was looking forward to retirement. He was checking into chief positions at other departments. He just . . ." He shook his head. "No. He didn't have a suicidal bone in his body." He gave me a wistful smile. "He was a survivor."

28

The light rippled. Dan was in front of me, blocking off the room. He was bigger in person than he looked on TV, a menace stuffed into a gray suit, orchid-colored shirt, dark tie. He was sweating, holding a very full glass of red wine. Wine marks in the corners of his lips. I could hear him breathing.

My heart raced, beats twining with the notes of the amorphous jazz drifting through the air. I had forgotten this asshole was still in play. Maybe he could make himself useful.

"Well, now." Dan leaned on the table, gripped the edge. A class ring, a wedding ring. A gold chain trailed into the top button of his shirt, heavy and bright. "Looks like we have another detective on the team."

I tightened my hands on the cards. "We do, don't we?" I slid the other chair back into place across the table. "Have a seat."

Was he a killer? Would I be able to tell? In the movies, when you killed someone, you paid for it forever in flashes of guilt, jump cuts to bloody walls, twisted hands, gun smoke curling against darkened windows. It stuck to you, like a stain, for everyone to see.

In real life it was probably more like an outfit in a kid's dress-up game, put on the doctor's outfit, the astronaut's. The murderer's. A role you played by day and slipped off at night, until the truth disappeared under the rollover of days, months, and years. A tree growing rings around a diseased heart.

"You going to tell me my future?" He looked around like he was about to ride a mechanical bull at a Western-themed bar. "I don't have to tip you, do I?" He sank into the chair with a sigh and put his glass on the table. The dark wine swished and went still.

"It'll be my pleasure." I drew a card. "Six of Wands." Dan leaned close, peering at the horseman on his white steed, laurel crown, bright wreath, his army taking him home from the field. "Success," I said. "Victory."

Dan's nose was scrunched up from squinting so hard. He probably needed glasses but would rather go blind than admit it. "That's my future, huh?"

"It's *a* future," I said. Behind me, wind howled over the lake. I knew where I was going; the cards were the stepping stones along the path. "The future you want. The one you're angling for."

"Here's what you need to know about me." Dan picked up his glass. Wine sloshed onto his pants. "I see something I want, I visualize it in my mind, and boom." A waft of booze and mint Life Savers washed over me. "Just, boom."

"Boom," I said. *Take them back to the beginning,* Jamie always said. *Make them forget why you're there.* Suddenly I missed Jamie so badly it hurt. I shuffled the cards.

"Before we get to your future"—I tapped the Six of Wands— "we need to look at your past." I drew another card. "The Page of Swords." A young man in motion, hair flying, body twisting in mid sword thrust. "Courage," I said. "Conviction. Ambition." I softened my voice. "Do you remember your first job, Commander? Your first assignment as a cop?"

Dan sniffled. I let him take the tiniest peek into the bright rooms of memory, just enough to get sappy. "You worked right here at Sandhill Lake, didn't you? Officer Pete was your . . ."

"My sergeant," he said. "Oh, man, what a hard-ass."

"I'll bet." I tossed him a chuckle. "He kept you sharp. Kept you on your toes." I dropped to a whisper and Dan leaned in. "Officer Pete made you who you are, didn't he? You owe him everything."

Dan's smile hitched at the corners. *That's it,* I coaxed in my mind. *Follow me.*

"Not *everything,*" he said. A note of petulance crept into his voice. I'd hooked him. He was a fishing guy, right? I owed Jamie big for making him endure Dan's nightmare fishing stories the other night. If this reading went the way it was going, Jamie would be repaid a hundred times over.

"I'd say I taught the old man a couple of things right back." Dan raised his arms and stretched. "There comes a time when the student becomes the teacher."

"So ironic, how that works!" Shuffle, cut, draw. "The Hierophant." Red, stiff, unyielding. "Now, this guy"—I tapped the card—"is the definition of old-school. The oldest. He's all rules and traditions. Even when they don't apply anymore. My-way-or-the-highway kind of stuff. Sound like anyone you know?"

Dan chuckled. "The old man was a little slow to change, I'll give you that."

"At some point, this guy is just in the way," I said. "Like old fishing bait. Time to clean out the old tackle box, huh?" I had no idea if you kept bait in a tackle box, or exactly what a tackle box was.

Dan was nodding along. "You fish?"

"I know a float from a lure," I said. "Here's what we got, Dan." I trailed a finger across the cards, pointed to each one. "Your future. Your past." My fingers stopped on the Hierophant. "Your obstacle."

"My obstacle?"

"You're running for office." Dan looked blank. "And Pete was in your way. He was trying to stop you."

Dan's cheeks ballooned out mid-swallow. A sharp gleam cut through the pleasant haze I'd woven around him. I had to work fast before it burned off.

"What are you talking about?" Dan said.

"The gag reel," I whispered. "The videos he was going to show everyone. He was trying to keep you from getting elected."

Dan looked like an ice-skater who'd collided with a rock and spun off, hurtling across the ice. "How do you even know about that?" His voice pierced the low buzz blanketing the room. "He was just goofing around. Yanking my chain."

Jessie's head popped up like a whale hearing an echo halfway across the world. Two steps and she was behind Dan, coiling her hands together. "Everything okay?" She smiled. Her teeth looked like they'd been filed.

"Fine," Dan snapped, watching me. He was squeezing the delicate stem of his glass with thick fingers. I shook my head at Jessie. She backed away and pumped her hands up and down in the air. *Take it down a notch.*

I drew another card and my eyes went dim. *Go*, the cards were saying. *Everybody out of the car. We're here.*

"The Devil." I traced the Devil's horns, circled his wide, mad eyes. "This is a very dark card, Dan. It's about feeling trapped, addicted."

Dan sat bolt upright.

"The Devil makes you do things you know are wrong," I said. "But you can't stop yourself. And why should you?" I leaned in. "When you see what you want, you visualize it, and then, *boom*."

Dan lurched like I had pulled out a gun. His eyes went dead and I could see the cold math running through them. He was calculating his escape, his survival. I closed in on him.

"The morning Officer Pete was killed," I said, "you weren't taking your son to soccer, were you?"

Dan leaped to his feet, hard and fast. His chair teetered and crashed backward. "Keep your voice down, goddamn it." He looked around. "How do you even . . ." He leaned in and bared his teeth. "Did my wife put you up to this?" he growled.

"Your wife?" The wine Matt gave me pounded through my head, clouding my vision. I couldn't understand what Dan was saying. "Was your wife in on it, too?"

Dan's glass tumbled, arced, flew, and fell. The smash sent shards of glass and gobbets of blood-red wine into the air. Dan's eyes were pools of black oil. He wobbled through the room toward a giraffy blonde in a salmon-colored sweatshirt reading #BLESSED in sequins. He spun her around by the shoulder and she squeaked.

"It's supposed to be anonymous," Dan bellowed in her face. "*Anonymous* is in the fucking name."

The room went dead. June, still watching the window from her stiff white armchair, looked up.

"What the hell is wrong with you?" Mrs. Dan shrieked, brushing wine off her #BLESSED.

"It's not enough you make me waste time with those goddamn hippies, now you have to tell everyone I'm a drunk?"

Titters rolled through the room, a couple of shocked sighs, a half-hearted "Whoo!"

The blonde snatched her shoulder out of Dan's grasp. "I didn't tell anyone, you dope," she said. "Maybe I should have. Maybe it would have done more good than the actual meetings."

I snapped my mouth shut. I didn't remember standing up, so I slid back into my chair. Dan wasn't in the swamp that morning. He'd lied about his alibi, but not because he was a killer; he was, however reluctantly, a friend of Bill W. I swept the cards back into their bag. I could see which way the wind was blowing, and it was definitely in the direction of the fuck out of here.

Dan lurched toward me. "Who the hell are you?" He looked around. "Who invited her?"

Jessie, struggling with a bottle opener, went still. The cork shot out of the bottle with a loud pop. Behind Jessie, the light pole ferret leaned over and whispered something to the frowning reverse bob.

Jessie collected herself, put down the bottle, and smiled. I could hear the calming mantra she was shouting at full volume in her head. "Commander," she said, "Katie's readings are for entertainment purposes only. For fun. They're not meant to upset you, or pry into your personal business, or discuss anything inappropriate." She turned her glassy smile toward me.

I shrank back and moved ever so slightly toward the exit. Oh, I was screwed for sure, and there would be consequences aplenty—and yet I burned with a loopy, white-hot righteousness. I had eliminated a suspect. I had gotten somewhere.

Dan, thick as a pissed-off bull, ignored Jessie and whirled on me. "Let me tell you something, little miss. You don't know anything about me. So go take your little cards and play Columbo somewhere else."

Across the room, I met Matt's eyes. He looked down quickly, and my heart sank. Next to him, Maureen stuffed her hands into her pockets.

"Leave her alone," a quiet voice said. June. She was standing now. She looked sober to a fault. "You're just mad because she got you to tell the truth for a change." She walked toward Dan. She was the only one in the room moving.

"You sucked up to Pete for years." She stood in front of him. Judgment, the angel blasting away illusion with her trumpet. "All of you." She looked around. "Because he was who he was. Because

you needed him. You would have let him get away with anything."
She turned and found Maureen. The other woman stepped
back, put her hand to her throat. "You *did* let him get away with
anything."

"Mom . . ." Matt stepped forward.

"No." She held him off. "I'm done. I'm not his wife anymore."
She set her glass down on the counter and turned to me. "Thank
you, Katie. Thank you for everything."

I looked slowly around the room. Every eye was on me. The
ferret, the light pole, the gang of cops, and most of all, Jessie.
"What did I . . . I didn't . . . Don't . . ."

"Thank you for telling the truth. For making me see the truth."
June strode over to Jessie, grabbed her by the shoulders, and
locked her in a fierce hug. Jessie's eyes goggled over June's
shoulder.

"I won't be buying the house." June released Jessie and took
her hand, cradled it. Jessie looked down at her own hand like she
didn't recognize it. "It's a lovely house. But I hated it. I'm sorry."
She let loose a bubbly stream of laughter. "Pete loved it. But he's
gone, isn't he?" She patted Jessie's cheek hard, just this side of a
slap. "He's gone!"

She turned and drifted from the room. Everyone stood aside
for her like she was a visiting monarch from an alien planet. "He's
gone," she repeated on her way out. "He's gone." We listened to
her move down the hall, the astonished echo of her voice — *he's
gone, he's gone* — trailing behind her.

29

A white blur swept past me down the hall. Jessie. I took off after her but she ducked into the tiny powder room off the hallway and slammed the door.

"Jessie?" I knocked.

Silence. Running water. I slid down the wall across from the door, propped my feet up on the wall, and promptly left a scuff mark. When I rubbed, it blurred into a full-on stain. All I did, wherever I went, was leave marks and then make them worse.

The water snapped off in the bathroom. In the living room the conversation was still heightened, bubbling like a pot left to boil over on the stove. "Jessie, come on," I said. "Let's talk about this."

The door opened and Jessie's pale face appeared in the crack. She had scrubbed it clean of makeup until it looked like a piece of raw chicken. Behind her, pomegranate-colored walls flared in another orgy of tea lights. Touch the wrong thing in there, and your soul would be trapped in the bathroom forever.

"Did you tell June not to buy the house?" Her voice sounded like dead leaves rustling.

"Not as such," I said. "I just told her she didn't have to live Pete's dream anymore now that . . . Yeah, okay, I see how she might have seen it that way." I closed my eyes and leaned against the wall. "I'm sorry."

"And the reading for Kaluza . . . ?" Jessie's voice was flat, calm.

"I might have accused him of killing Officer Pete." I couldn't look at Jessie so I looked down the hall at the picture window. Black lake, white lights. "But he didn't! Turns out he's not a murderer, just an alcoholic."

The door clicked shut. There were zipping noises, tiny porcelain clicks. Jessie was reapplying her makeup from the ground up.

"Look, Jessie, something very bad is going on here. Officer Pete was into some shady stuff. He . . ." I scrambled closer to the door so I could whisper. "He hired a hit man to kill Maureen Loeffler."

The door flew open again. Jessie was grinding new foundation into her face with the zeal of a construction worker filling a pothole. I could smell her acrid, fruity perfume. We'd bought it for my mom one Christmas after shopping all day and blowing out our collective sense of smell so badly we had no idea what we were buying. My mom thanked us graciously and never wore the stuff, so Jessie commandeered it. It always reminded me of the one time in a million we had fun together.

"Stop. Stop." Jessie put down her beauty blender. "Katie, just stop. I don't care."

"You don't care?" A wave of icy anger swept over me. Was it possible, after all these years of Jessie's eye-rolling and sighing, that I was the normal one and she was the freak? "How can you not care, Jess?"

"I mean, sure I *care*." Jessie twisted her mouth. "And once the cops figure it out, I'll read all about it on *BuzzFeed*. My point is, what does any of this have to do with you?" She tucked the beauty

blender away and produced a pale makeup stick she began rubbing all over her face. "A hit man," she mused. "Huh. Really?"

"Yes!" I jumped to my feet. "And Maureen is only alive because
Officer Pete couldn't afford to pay the guy."

Jessie snorted. Her mouth was distorted from the stick and
when she spoke her words were squished. "Officer Pete couldn't
afford a caramel macchiato. A hit man was right out of the
question."

"What do you mean?"

"The Petersons were broke," Jessie said. "Didn't you see their
files?"

"What files?"

"You didn't do it, did you?" Jessie said. "You didn't prepare my
checklist."

There was no way I was going to float to the top of this one, so
I shut my mouth and waited for the other Italian leather shoe to
drop.

An exasperated sigh. "I left a box of the Petersons' financial
documents in your office with a checklist of things I needed you
to find for the house sale. Loan and purchase documents, apprais-
als, home repair receipts, things like that. Did you even see it?"

"I . . . I've been busy?" Doing exactly the thing you told me not
to do, I didn't say. And trying not to get killed. "If they were broke,
how could they afford that big-ass house?"

"His pension." Clearly, I had been told this before. "They were
going to wait until he retired."

"But he's dead now, so . . ."

"Yes," she said in her best kindergarten teacher voice. "June
would have gotten his pension."

All of this pointed very much toward June again. Of course she
was going to get Peterson's pension. Why hadn't that occurred to
me before? Now that she'd made a big show of rejecting Pete's

poxy mansion, she was free to spend the money on whatever she wanted and no one would blame her. Much. I couldn't tell if it was disappointment I felt or relief at the guilt needle swinging off Gina.

More proof, also, that the life the Petersons lived on social media, the parties, the woo-hoo drinks-for-all-my-friends lifestyle they seemed so proud of, was fake. I felt a soft stirring on the back of my neck, like a breath. Money. The hit man. Maureen. The audit. A trail was forming; I could feel its swirls and patterns emerging from the shadows. Jesse's box of financial documents began to seem unexpectedly interesting.

"Look, Jessie, I'm sorry I screwed the sale for you. I really am. But it's just one house, right? There's a whole neighborhood out there for you to sell."

"For someone else to sell," Jessie said. "They took the exclusive away from me. Apparently, drunken chaos is not the image Future Builders wants to project to potential buyers." She closed her eyes, leaned against the mirror. "This was a test, Katie. And I failed it."

She gave me a dead look and closed the door. I put my cheek against it. At this point the words *I'm sorry* were just nonsense syllables belching out of me every few seconds. I bit them down and said nothing.

"I'm going to regret saying this," Jessie said, "but you might actually be better with people than I am." I looked up at the door. Compliments from Jessie? This was new. "I don't know how you do it, but sometimes you just know what people are thinking. I'm like, how did she know that?"

I stifled a chuckle. It amazed me sometimes, how mysterious listening and paying attention seemed to some people.

"I get it now. This thing you do with the cards. It works. It's amazing."

"Aw, thanks, Jess," I said, genuinely touched.

"And if you wanted to use it for, you know, something real, something useful, you'd be unstoppable."

Oh, well. It was a pleasant five seconds.

"You could be a part of the world, Katie. You don't always have to be on the outside. You don't always have to fight. This . . . this isn't you. This doesn't have to be you."

I leaned against the door for so long the paint grew warm against my cheek. "What if it *is* me?"

The silence lasted for seconds, or minutes, or years.

"I'll need you to clear out of my office," Jessie finally said. "By Saturday. Leave the Petersons' files inside."

"Bye, Jessie," I whispered to the closed door. "I'm sorry."

If she answered, I didn't hear her. I was down the hallway by then, moving away from the gold room where the party was already slipping back together around the hole I had punched in it. Moving on, the way power always did. I was out the front door by then, flashing through the humid night in my god suit.

I got in my car and started the engine. The lake faced me, black with white lights flashing on the far shore. Again I imagined closing my eyes and slipping free, tumbling headlong into the dark. This time it filled me with peace, as if the only way to get across that shore was to believe I could.

I found the box of financial documents perched unassumingly on a side table in my office, topped by a list of wordy bullet points in Jessie's serial killer handwriting. How I could have ignored it for the past few days was a stumper. Apparently I could ignore anything if I put my mind to it. I didn't relish any further visits from the Public Works doom squad, so I schlepped the box out to my car and drove home to do my deep dive into the Petersons' finances.

The dive ended up shallower than I expected. The first folder I spread out on my kitchen table—CREDIT CARDS—backed up what I'd seen on the Petersons' social media: tour-group-size charges at Rush Street and Mag Mile bars, concert tickets, sports events, airfare to shiny, sun- and beer-drenched destinations. A lot of OnlyFans and BangBros. I felt sticky and gross, like I was poking through bedside tables.

What you couldn't see on Facebook was that all the Petersons' credit cards—and even I, a financial dummy, could see they had way too many—were maxed out, dancing right up to crisis point every month, dipping a toe, and dancing back. Officer Pete knew how to have a good time. He just didn't know how to pay for it.

The next folder was the real kick in the teeth. This one, thick and unlabeled, was full of strongly worded collection agency missives, overdraft fee notices, and a disturbing note from the First National Bank, curtly warning the recipient that the loan he had secured was in danger of default. It was a whole folder of bald dudes in suits shouting and pounding their fists on their mahogany desks, upsetting their quirky crystal paperweights.

I was going cross-eyed chasing the parade of tiny numbers. When I blinked, white lines danced in front of my eyes. Surely June knew the depth of the financial shit Pete had landed them in and yet Pete's money woes didn't make the top ten in the litany of offenses she had poured out earlier today. Was she putting on the poor naive widow act? Playing the long game until Pete was lost in the past and no one cared anymore that his widow was living quite comfortably?

I whipped out my phone to dial Jamie, then put it down. He was the only person I wanted to talk to, but I felt weird shutting him down earlier then breezing back when I needed his help. Anyway, he couldn't help me now. There was only one person with any hope of tying these increasing loose ends into a knot that might actually hold.

Gina.

Gina was the only one who could connect Maureen and Peterson, who understood the dark underpinnings of his past well enough to fill in his final few months. She had had the answers all along. I couldn't put off confronting her any longer.

I picked my phone back up and dialed Gina's number with shaking fingers. The phone rang and rang. No answer. Of course. Music sputtered on at the neighbors' and shut off just as quickly: a sonorous cello playing two notes over and over: *What now? What now?*

I stuffed the loose paperwork back into the box, dragged it out to my car, and drove to Gina's.

30

"Number thirteen, baby." Rosie picked up the Death card. "The great equalizer. Divisible only by itself." Death's white horse stepped lightly through a doomed landscape.

In the space movie, one of the astronauts was dying. His air hose had snapped. He fought for air, his body an ugly grapple. The computer went berserk, killed the rest of the crew, blocked the surviving astronaut from coming back on board.

"I bet this card doesn't mean you're going to die, does it?" I was getting the hang of this. There was a way to sort of cross your brain and look beyond the card—not at the thing in the picture, but at the way people *thought* about the thing in the picture. At the stories they told about it. In a way I felt like I already knew how to read these cards. Maybe I had always known, or some other me who came before me did.

That white skeleton knight was still pretty creepy, though. "Whatever it means, it's got to be scary."

"Oh, it is," Rosie said. "Why are people scared of death?"

"Because it's the end?" I said. "And . . . because they don't know what comes next?"

"Bingo." Rosie traced the white flower on Death's black flag. "It's the same in life. People are afraid of any big change for the same reasons. This card is about change. Or the fear of change."

The dead astronaut went still. His body tumbled through space, loop over loop. His crewmate had tried to save him but in the end he had to let go. He had no choice now but to keep going, keep moving farther and farther into the void, alone.

"It's not easy to change," Rosie said. "Sometimes it can be a straight-up bitch." She sat back and watched the movie. "But that's life, isn't it? You don't change, you don't move forward."

Gina still lived in Pinewood, a shabby unincorporated enclave where her family had lived in government housing once her dad went to prison and dumped them. They eventually moved into their own house, but Gina had never left the neighborhood.

I had never been to Gina's house before. *Weird*, I thought, and then, *typical*. I inched along a patchwork of deserted streets with no sidewalks, just muddy ditches on either side of the road, filled with gravel and dirty snow. There was no grid I could discern. The houses were tossed together with empty lots between them, tiny boxes with dirt yards, patches of yellow grass. Some had aluminum siding, screened-in windows caked with grime. Others were big and outlandish, like they'd been airlifted and dropped from some ritzier town. The area was obviously *turning over*, in the middle of some painful transformation that was either just getting started or had stalled.

A chain-link fence cut Gina's street off from a strip of decrepit auto body shops and a brown hulking cube of a building that billed itself as a "security company," although what it secured was a mystery. The street ended in a playground with a sagging, cockeyed carousel, yellow paint peeling around rusty blotches. Gina's house was tiny and old, with dun-colored paint and old-fashioned shutters. It sat across from the mouth of the alley running along the edge of the playground. NO ENTRY, a sign read. Another sign detailed all the things that were not allowed at the playground.

I stopped at the lip of a small ravine in front of the house and edged the car back and forth, trying to avoid spinning it into the ditch. When I turned to check the back window there was a distant rumble, like thunder or a machine or a charging animal. The world exploded, slammed sideways, spun around, and now the sky was beneath me, a flash of broken glass, jagged edges. This is it, my mind shrieked. Time has looped, the road has come full circle. I'm back at the beginning, at the accident. My mom is bleeding in the front seat and Officer Pete is coming, any second now, to save me.

Dark. I was lying on something soft and lumpy. An oily taste filled my mouth. One by one, parts of my body came online, switches were thrown. When I opened my eyes a gray blob grew in front of me. There was a homey electrical buzz that sounded like aging kitchen appliances. Everything hurt. I wriggled like an overturned turtle and gave up on moving.

The gray blob shifted. It was a person sitting in a chair.

"Where am I?" I tried to say, but the sound didn't get past the rocky parched tunnel of my throat.

"Don't try to talk or move or anything," the blob said.

"What happened?" I croaked.

The Gina-shaped blob shifted in its chair. "I tried to kill you with my car," she said, "but you're tougher than you look so I brought you inside to finish you off."

I buried my face in the couch cushion. It had little red pilings that scratched my face like sandpaper. I wrestled the cushion out from under my head and tried to throw it but only succeeded in getting it to tumble softly off the couch and roll away.

"Oh, lighten up," Gina said. She picked up the pillow and stuffed it back under my pulsing head. A glass of water approached my lips. I sipped greedily.

"There was this god-awful crash, like a house caving in," she said. "Which, to be fair, is not unusual around here. I looked outside, and there you were, all busted up in your car. You're lucky you had that box of shit in your passenger seat. It saved your head from going through the windshield."

Jessie's paperwork. I tried to look at Gina, but it hurt to move my eyeballs. "Who . . . ? What . . . ? Did you see . . . ?"

"Some idiot came barreling out of the alley and took out the stop sign. Also not unusual. Anyway, I just caught the back of him. Big white truck."

A Public Works truck. Of course. I groaned and tried to sit up. I either needed to get Gina up to speed on what I knew or I needed to get the hell out of here as soon as possible. I hadn't decided yet which was the wiser option.

"Settle down, Lurch." Gina pushed me back down gently on the couch. "You have a concussion." There was a first aid kit on the heavy wooden coffee table, one of those old-fashioned metal boxes with the red cross on top. Band-Aid wrappers and red-stained wadded-up cotton balls covered the table. I touched my head and felt flexible plastic.

"Do I need to go to the hospital?"

"You're all right. I'm trained in first aid. Just take it easy and don't, you know, use your brain or eyes for a while. They'd tell you the same thing at the ER. For now, just shut up and rest."

"Someone did this," I said.

Gina got up and started picking up the first aid trash. "Nicely deduced, Sherlock."

"No, I mean, someone *meant* to do it." I touched the water glass to my head. It either burned or froze me. My sensations were twisted, scrambled, untrustworthy. An untrustworthy document—my body—read by an unreliable narrator—my brain.

Gina passed me a pill. I pushed it away. "What are you giving me?"

"It's poison hemlock I gathered at the height of the full moon and stuffed into a capsule marked Tylenol. What is the matter with you?"

"I can't swallow pills," I said. "I'm afraid to choke."

"Do it," Gina said, shoving the pill back at me. "You'll thank me later."

I managed to get the pill down, then buried my face in the pillow. "Do I want to know what state my car is in?"

"Don't worry about that. I'll take care of everything."

Why did this make me feel worse? I tried to close my eyes, but every time I did, the darkness spun around me like the carousel in the park, cockeyed, splotched with dust and bird droppings. You pushed with all your weight to get started but once it was moving nothing would stop it, so you just kept moving around in empty, pointless circles.

The note. The car. Someone wanted me out of the way, had tried to kill me. I drifted, spun. A sharp wind wandered the playground. A cool hand settled on my forehead. The phone rang. I had to get off the carousel, roll away, jump off. Someone was answering the phone.

What do you want? The voice was at the same time close and far away, like it was coming through a whisper tube. *What do you mean?* Sharper now. *Are you at home? I'll be right over.* The cool hand on my forehead again. The darkness took shape, stepped forward. *I have to go.* Gina had her coat on. *Stay put. Keep your eyes closed even if you're not sleeping. Here's water and more Tylenol. I'll be back soon.*

"Who was on the . . . Where are you . . ." I closed my eyes. The carousel started up again, spun me away. "Wait . . ."

I opened my eyes again. It was still dark and I was still on the couch. I stretched and realized the darkness was there to stay. It was night.

Faded off-white light poured in through the window. I couldn't see my car. Gina said she would take care of it. What did that mean?

I looked around Gina's house. It was modest and old-fashioned, like she had strolled into the neighborhood one day, said this one will do, and kicked out the gentle old lady who lived there. Mismatched secondhand furniture filled the room, and pictures in brown frames covered the walls. A rooster pecking at corn. A boy feeding ducks at sunrise. A man in a straw hat. On vacation or hard at work? The pictures were dusty and hopeful, like the world they wanted to show you was imaginary, had never existed.

Across from my couch was a stuffy recliner with worn arms. Gina perched on its edge, pitching forward like she was avoiding a whoopee cushion. She was either just sitting down or about to get up. I waited, but she didn't move. Her hands were claws, digging at the arms of the chair like she was still clutching at something that had made a narrow escape. Something she had wanted to save or destroy.

She lifted her eyes to me and I saw she had changed her

clothes, put on something bright, patterned with those cheerful 1980s paint splashes that kept cycling in and out of style. Then the light from the window caught her and I saw that she had not changed, she was still wearing the same faded white T-shirt but it was splashed in blood. Her arms were covered in blood. Her hands, fingers like talons. Everything was red and wet. A drop ballooned at the tip of her middle finger, arrested in midair.

The carousel ground to life again. My vision jittered and swayed. *No*, I thought wildly, *I need to get off. I need to stop.* The drop fell and disappeared in the carpeting. I opened my mouth to tell Gina I couldn't get up, I couldn't get off this thing. If I could just get up I could help her.

Pounding at the door. *It's open*, Gina said, or maybe *It's over*, and now the room was full of people. A dull hum prowled the edges of my hearing, bits of speech leaping out of it and fading back in. Someone was flashing a camera.

Flash: Gina's body twisting, someone was holding her, the flash of metal cuffs.

Flash: . . . *for the murder of Maureen Loeffler* . . .

Flashing lights, red and blue and white.

Flash: Gina's peaceful face, like she was watching fish flit through a tank.

Flash: Dan's face so close to my own I could feel his hot breath smelling like wet leaves and peppermint. He was shouting at me but the words kept fading in and out, soft and loud, spinning around me. And then Jamie was there. I couldn't see him, but I could feel him and hear his voice. *Are you? What happened?* And then off to the side, *She needs medical attention.* More chatter, more light. But nowhere in the flood of dark and light was I hearing Gina, where was she? Then Jamie, very close: *Katie, tell them the truth. Don't protect her. Just tell the truth, and you'll be fine. Promise me.*

Then someone was pulling him away and he was gone. *Officer Roth, you are out of line . . .*

I don't know the truth, I opened my mouth to say. *There is no truth.*

A dot on a screen, a howl, then nothing.

31

There were so many uniforms, and they were all different. The lady who examined me, was she a cop or an EMT? A young blonde with hair pulled back in a ponytail so tight I could see streaks of gel perforating its surface like the grooves of an old vinyl record. The shadows had moved off and now everything was too bright. I couldn't turn the dimmer switch down. I didn't know where the dimmer switch was.

"Lift your arms. Touch your toes."

I did what she told me to do. I could do everything. Was that good or bad?

"Close your eyes and touch your nose." She put out her arms and had me push against them.

"Where is Gina?" I said. "Where is Jamie?" The woman would not look at me. She was a mechanic running a maintenance protocol on a piece of machinery gone haywire.

"Wait here." She left and closed the door. A latch clicked shut. There was a chair and I sat in it although I couldn't stay upright and my head was starting to hurt again. Gina's Tylenol was wearing off. How long had I been here?

There was a glass of water in front of me on a small metal table. No windows in the room and no clock. I had no idea how long I had been sitting there when Dan finally came in. He was carrying a notepad and a laptop. He had cleaned himself up and stopped sweating, still wearing the gray suit and orchid-colored shirt. The only sign that he had been blotto earlier was a slight purple wine mustache. I figured he'd been honing his sober-switch skills for years, how to walk a straight line, touch his nose. Until he'd become a cop himself and didn't have to answer to anyone anymore.

"Where's Jamie?" I said.

"Officer Roth has been relieved of his assignment." Dan dragged out the chair across the table and the metal legs made a sick scraping sound on the floor. Somewhere, a rush of water moved through the wall, rounded a corner, and was gone. "His impartiality in this case was compromised." He held my gaze.

"Then what are you still doing here?" I said.

"I'm sorry, what did you say?" He darted toward me and put his face right up to mine, an awful zooming camera close-up. I flinched.

He made a tsk-tsk noise and sat back down. "Am I talking too loud?" He did not lower his voice. "They told me you have a mild concussion. You might be sensitive to loud noises right now. So, in order to avoid any potential discomfort, I suggest you leave the talking to me. Sound good?" He leaned back in his chair. "How well do you know Regina Dio?"

A black pit opened in my stomach. Hot, sudden tears leapt to my eyes. I willed them to freeze. Not now. "I know her a little."

"Did she ever talk about her relationship with Lieutenant Peterson?"

I closed my eyes and watched stars dance in the dark in front of me. *Tell the truth*, I heard Jamie say. "Yes." I would tell Dan the truth, but only the bare minimum. He didn't have a right to anything else.

"How did she describe their relationship?"

"They worked together. It was a coworker relationship."

"Did she tell you anything about the nature of that coworker relationship?"

Gina's fist breaking Officer Pete's nose. The spray of blood.

"I don't know," I said. "I don't remember."

"Then let me enlighten you." He shoved a stack of paperwork across the table. The typed script blurred in front of my eyes. "She filed a sexual misconduct grievance against him in 2016. It was heard fairly, and the conclusion was that no evidence of misconduct existed. Miss Dio, apparently dissatisfied with the ruling, followed Peterson one day when they were both off duty and gravely injured him. And because by this time she had already engaged in certain threatening behavior in the workplace, he had the forethought to record their encounter."

He went to the laptop. Its airplane-loud fan turned on, startling me. Dan tapped on a few keys. The sound was bright, metallic.

A voice sprang from the computer, mid-yell. "*. . . think I'll forget?*" a muffled voice said. "*Motherfucker, I will never forget, and one day when you've forgotten all about me, when you're going about your shitty little business and you find yourself in some secluded place I will be there, and I'm going to kill you. It is that simple. I will come up behind you and I will end your miserable fucking life, do you hear me?*"

The voice was a hoarse shriek, barely recognizable as human. And yet I knew it immediately as Gina's. *Is this my friend?* I thought. *Is this really her?* A cold sweat slid over me. I needed that noise to stop, stop, stop. I screwed my eyes shut.

Dan tapped a key and the screaming stopped. The water in the pipes ticked, gurgled, washed away into the lake.

"It's not a confession," Dan said flatly. "Not yet. But we'll get one."

"But why Maureen?" I said. "Why would she kill Maureen, too?"

"Because we found the recording on Maureen's desk." Dan unplugged a small storage disk from the computer and held it up. "Next to her body. She had been shot. We responded to a call from a neighbor who recognized Gina and saw her running from the scene covered in blood."

So Maureen must have found the recording that night at the police station after all. She must have called Gina to warn her, dragged up the last vestiges of their friendship to warn Gina she was in danger. *She's a killer, Katie.* Maureen had disregarded her own advice.

Dan shifted in the chair. "What were you doing at Miss Dio's residence?"

"I left the party," I said, "and I went to her house."

"Why?"

Because she was my friend. She was the only one who could help me. I trusted her. I loved her. The tears started again and this time I couldn't stop them. A hot, fat one trembled in my eyelashes, fell, and shattered on the table.

"I didn't have anywhere else to go," I whispered.

There were questions after that, a lot of questions. They were all different but they were all the same, like an axe biting over and over into the soft flesh of a tree, widening the wound until the tree has no choice but to teeter and fall: *Did you know, did you know, did you know?*

How could you not know?

32

I was dreaming about death. Not death, but Death, the dry Mad Max land this side of the sluggish blue river that circles the world. I knew everyone there. Hi, everyone! Peterson, the dead king, flat on his back. Dan, the arrogant asshole priest, trying to bargain his way out of the inevitable. Jessie, flower crowned, on her knees, turning away. And the kid, the only one with a lick of sense, offering flowers to the black knight on the slow white horse, because like it or not, that bitch was coming. Was I the kid? It didn't sound like me.

There was a soft knock at a faraway door. I was on the couch. I'd been there all night, losing consciousness every so often and jerking awake with my head pounding. I was still in the sparkly suit, or rather the suit was still glued to me. I was wearing a shoe. Just one. I didn't remember ending up in my apartment, though I remembered the ride from the station, kindly provided by a very young, very red-haired rookie who looked like he'd just popped in from a medieval Scottish battlefield. I remembered his animated ginger eyebrows, like small frisky fish leaping over his face. I had fixed my eyes on them to keep from getting dizzy and yakking all over his freshly deodorized squad car.

The parking lot of the sheriff's station, where Dan had harangued me until he was satisfied I knew nothing useful, was full of Public Works trucks. A whole sea of them, white with green and blue tree decals. I asked the rookie who had access to them, and the basic gist was everyone. Any Lake County government employee. Cops, admin people, park district landscapers, librarians, everyone. Also anyone who had any connections to law enforcement or public service or could lie and cheat and bribe into getting their way.

I flopped onto my stomach and buried my face in the scratchy couch. Scenes from the night before cycled past me like rooms behind doors off a spiral staircase I was slowly climbing. Matt in his smooth street clothes, his eyes wrinkling as he watched me make an ass of myself. Dan and me on opposite sides of a table. Jessie shutting the bathroom door. Maureen, a gap in the world where a human being used to be. All night, the same idiotic sequence, over and over, like a video on an endless mortifying loop. Up and up and up until the last door—the last door—

There was that knock again, almost a scratch, like an inquiry from a polite fairy-tale squirrel. I struggled up, staggered to the door, and jammed my face up to the peephole.

It was Jamie, holding a plastic Jewel bag. His hair was perfect. So, morning. He leaned against the door to listen. He looked like a curious raven. *The raven, with its comparatively large brain, is a uniquely intelligent bird. How will it solve this unusual problem?* He pulled out his phone, paused, put it away, and produced the tiny notepad he always carried. He scratched a few lines on it and set it on the floor on top of the grocery bag. I thought he would leave, but he didn't. I put my hand on the door, leaned in, closed my eyes. When I looked through the peephole again, the hallway was empty.

The crinkly white bag contained a six-pack of fancy bottled water aimed at dopes like me who fell for clever graphic design and outlandish flavors. Packages of frozen toddler food: chicken nuggets and dinosaur-shaped Tater Tots. Liquid Children's Tylenol. Jamie knew his target.

My eyes began to burn. I didn't deserve any of this. The dull ache in my head cranked up to a walloping pain. I sucked the tears back up, closed them off. I wanted to crumple the note, throw it away unread, but I wasn't convinced this was an actual thing people did outside of gothic novels set on moors.

Jamie's handwriting was absurdly readable, like a ten-year-old girl's:

> Didn't want to text in case you were sleeping.

A space, like a breath.

> Gina has been moved to the county facility in Waukegan. I hear it doesn't look good for her, at least not where Maureen is concerned.

More sudden pain, like a gunshot in my head. *I hear.* Jamie wasn't on the case anymore. He could only hear things now, not know them.

> Dan likes her for Peterson, too, and is working hard to close. Your car survived, but in spirit only. I had it towed here so you could say your goodbyes.

Another space, another breath.

> Katie, I know what you're doing. You're wondering what you could have done, or what you can still

*do. Don't. Just take care of yourself. Call me when
you feel better.*

Now I did crumple the paper, although I didn't toss it. Jamie
was wrong. I wasn't doing what he thought I was doing. I was
throwing my energy toward *not* doing those things, not looking at
the events of last night for any longer than it took to slam a door
on them and move up the spiral staircase. I sat down and opened
one of the bottled waters. Banana-pomegranate flavor. In what
universe did those two fruits belong together?

A shower seemed like too much work, but I managed to
change into a T-shirt and jeans, locate my missing shoe (it was
jammed in the toaster), and lumber outside into the damp gray
parking lot.

My car, or a modernist sculpture resembling my car, was nes-
tled in my parking space. Of course Jamie knew which one was
mine. The car's angles and contortions yawned at me like a howling face. I had been in there. I came that close to dying. The
corresponding door slammed shut in my mind. Nope. Not yet. I
wrestled the passenger-side door open, scooped as much of the
loose paperwork as I could find back into its scrunched, twisted
banker's box—the box that had saved my life—and schlepped it
back inside.

Then I slipped out the patio door and crossed the smelly loading alley into the parking lot of Chicago Asian Foods. This was
probably a terrible idea, but I needed to fill the galling emptiness
in my head.

Inside, I walked narrow aisles stocked with colorful snacks,
refrigerated bins full of bright slivers of fish, pristine white bricks
of tofu. Shelves of shiny makeup that looked like food, shiny food
that looked like makeup. In the nearly empty midafternoon food

court I nursed a green tea smoothie. Jasmine and honey. I imagined myself at the center of a bright bubble outside of time, sitting still while everything whirled around me in a soft red-gold wash.

What could I have done differently? What could I do now? Jamie's questions echoed in my mind as I floated up the spiral staircase with the doors. The higher I climbed, the harder it was to open each door, the worse the things behind it. Pressure mounted in my chest, like I was sinking into water.

Door #1: Dan. I had falsely accused him of murder (which I regretted) and embarrassed him in front of his cronies (which I regretted less). If history was any indication, no one would give a shit for very long. My only real regret was how badly I'd gotten things wrong.

Door #2: Jessie. I had singlehandedly erased a major career accomplishment that, no matter how silly and meaningless it seemed to me, she had worked her ass off for. Jessie and I were finally starting to act like adults around each other, and maybe this meant knowing when to stay out of each other's business— literally. Still, I had disappointed her, and whether or not these were growing pains, they hurt like a bitch.

Door #3: Matt. His warmth when he offered me wine, the smile that said *we both know what's going on here.* I wanted to be the person he'd told me I would grow up to be, when we were kids. I wanted him to see I was more than a speck of driftwood on the ocean of a colorless life. I wanted to help him figure out the truth behind his dad's lies, free him from their noxious spell, be there for him when he woke up. I was almost there; he had almost trusted me to help him. And the look on his face when I failed . . . I would never forget it.

Door #4: Jamie. I got him tossed off the best assignment he

was likely to have around here—not the first time my "help" had consequences for him. The part that hurt most was how quickly he had forgiven me. I couldn't face him. Not yet.

Door #5: Maureen. We were almost to the top now and I knew if I looked down I would lose my footing and fall forever. Should I have warned her? But of what? That her old friend, whom she trusted one last time, would betray her? Kill her?

My heart was sending painful, thudding echoes all over my body. We were here now, at the final door, the one that revealed all the others as a single nightmare. The stuff the staircase was made of—the interlocking nucleotides of its DNA—was illusion. *My* illusions. My stubborn insistence on seeing only what I wanted to see.

I wanted to see myself reflected in Gina's eyes. But if Gina was a liar, a selfish traitor, a murderer . . . what did that make me?

A fool.

Because after all of Gina's half-truths and all-out lies, after all the violence and rage and destruction she trailed in her wake, I still loved her.

No. Wrong. I loved the person I thought she was, a person who did not exist, a fantasy I created from a laundry list of my own needs.

I was no worse than the fools who elevate cops like Peterson to supermen when they're only human, or worse. Who watch them try to out-cruel each other for fun, look down on the people they serve, break the same rules they're supposed to uphold. I was no worse than the fools who refuse to believe, even when faced with daily evidence to the contrary, that their heroes are shit.

How I hated Gina right now for deceiving me, when the person who had deceived me, who had broken my heart, was me.

The food court was filling up and the noise was getting to me. My heart pounded and my head swelled and my vision blurred. The sweet flavor of the tea turned cloying and false. I should have known this place would be too much for me right now. I shouldn't have come. I was always in the wrong place.

33

A gunshot rang out behind me. I jumped off the porch and looked around. It was not a gunshot. It was not even close to a gunshot. It was the heavy front door to my apartment building slamming shut and Bear, the building manager, coming out twirling his car keys.

"What's shakin', bacon?" Bear bellowed on his way to his beloved midnight-blue Camaro, his forever restoration project. Today Bear was wearing a MARGARITAVILLE KEY WEST T-shirt with no coat, and a beanie cap stuffed over his yellow-blond-dyed hair. He looked like somebody's hot biker grandpa.

I sank back down on the porch and rubbed my face in my hands. An unpleasant layer of moisture coated the inside of my clothes. The slammed door was at least recognizable as a gunshot-like noise, unlike the dishwasher at my parents' house and the beep on the microwave. Gunfire followed me everywhere lately.

An LTPD squad car pulled into the lot, swished past Bear's outbound Camaro, and stopped at the porch. I opened the passenger door and got in. It was loud and bright in there, the dashboard full of buttons and the radio chattering away. A nice test for my senses. If I could survive Jamie's modified spaceship, I was, hallelujah, cured. Except for hearing gunshots everywhere.

It had been a few days since I had limped to Chicago Asian Foods. The only other time I had left my apartment was to see my parents, who wrung their hands at my vague description of my latest "fender bender" and asked if everything was going well working for Jessie. They were still, no matter how many times I corrected them, under the impression that Jessie had succeeded in her yearslong mission to set me on the path to a career in real estate and therefore legitimate adulthood.

Let's see, I thought, watching my mom dunk a tea bag in a tall white mug over and over, I was pukey and weak from getting my bean rattled, I was still peeking around corners for people trying to kill me, and I was racking up a list of balls I'd dropped, not the least of which was failing spectacularly to solve Officer Pete's murder. Also, my best friend, the one I'd been blind enough to elevate into some sort of life compass, had tried to kill me and was going to prison for killing two other people.

All good, I had told my parents. Never better.

Jamie signaled and turned out of the lot onto Route 60. "So . . ." I made myself as comfortable as possible in the tiny space between the passenger side door and the giant semiautomatic rifle wedged between the seats. "Which button activates the flux capacitor?"

Jamie grinned. Oh no. Normally he would never waste one of his rare smiles on a joke that stupid. He was handling me, being extra nice, like I was a sick kid. We had spent so long settling in with each other, and I had knocked us back to square one with one sweep of my reverse Midas touch. Each of Jamie's tiny, precious kindnesses felt like a punch in the gut.

Route 60 was in a midafternoon slumber, occasional cars

drifting through long lights. Anthropomorphic teeth did a saucy cancan on an orthodontist's marquee. FIX THAT SMILE. A dad held the door of a Dairy Queen open for his daughter, both of them struggling with identical gigantic poison-red cones. I felt like I was wearing distorting glasses that made everything look rotten and sad.

"How are you feeling?" Jamie said.

"I haven't barfed in days," I said. "But I can read minds now. Is that normal?"

Jamie sped down Butterfield and turned off on Greenleaf, toward the schools. "What am I thinking now?"

"You're thinking I can't believe this dipshit got me demoted again." I didn't feel like pretending everything was fine. I ran my fingers over the groove in a panel of lights and switches. Anything to keep my hands busy.

"I have not been demoted," Jamie said too lightly. "I'm simply not finishing out my *temporary* assignment to the Peterson investigation. Dan was looking for an excuse to can me anyway and believe it or not, I won't miss working with him." There was a back-off edge to his voice. Fair enough. I hit pause on the self-pity.

"Well, that's good," I said. "Because the uniform is really working for you. You ever consider a side gig jumping out of a large cake?"

"I don't like cake," Jamie said absently. There he was: the dork I needed right now.

We pulled up across the street from Lake Terrace Elementary North. A massive line of school buses wound around the building. The car line could generously be described as chaos. Jamie parked at the entrance to the townhouse complex across the street.

I drummed on my thighs and watched the line of cars inch past the school. "So what are you supposed to do? Just sit here?"

"Sit. Watch, make sure nothing goes wrong," Jamie said. "Sometimes I play this game where I try to figure out which prescription medication these parents are using recreationally."

Cars cycled through the line, replaced by other cars.

"So, where is she now?" I said.

Jamie didn't move his eyes from the snaking car line. "My info might be outdated, but last I heard, she was still in lockup," he said. "Dan's about to go live with an announcement. We can watch it on my phone." He checked his phone for the time. "I don't know what he thinks he's going to announce. They can't possibly have enough yet to charge her. He'll probably just make a big deal out of having a suspect in custody."

He was handling me again. The self-pity came roaring back. I sank into the seat, let my head droop on my chest. "I'm such an idiot," I whispered.

"You're not an idiot." Jamie's voice was tight and sharp. "You're not an idiot," he repeated evenly. "You knew who she was. Maybe you don't think you knew, but you knew.

"You cut her a lot of slack," Jamie said, "because she saw you the way you wanted to be seen. You thought you needed her, to be who you want to be." He watched a blue sedan with a set of robot family decals inch out of the lot and onto the street.

He turned to me. "But you don't need her for that. You are already that person."

I wish I remembered the few moments that came next, but the next thing I knew Jamie was holding me and it felt like glimpsing a faraway shore after floundering endlessly through murky water. My face was wet. The doors on the winding staircase flashed past me in a bright reverse, rewinding to the beginning. I could look at them now; I didn't have to pretend they didn't happen.

We separated and he held my chin so lightly, like he was holding a butterfly or a rare flower, something about to fade or disappear.

He ran his finger down my cheek and I closed my eyes, held my face against his hand.

Jamie's phone dinged. In the split second before he let me go there was a shivery indecision in the air, like a probability wave had passed through the car. *Did you hear that ding?* we were both thinking. *Was it real? Does it mean we have to stop?*

"The press conference is on," Jamie said.

Jamie and I huddled over his phone screen. The press conference was set up outside the Sandhill Lake PD, an empty podium on camera, with microphones sticking out into the air. Voiceovers were talking:

". . . a shocking development that could potentially signal the long-awaited end of this puzzling investigation." They were acting like it was already over.

"They are really milking this," Jamie said. "It's going to be a whole bunch of nothing, you'll see."

Dan took the podium, into a volley of camera flashes. "Ladies and gentlemen of the press, we would like to start by thanking you and the community of Sandhill Lake, and all of Lake County, still reeling from this shocking blow to our community. You, the community, deserve answers." He paused. "And today you will finally receive them."

"It's just an arrest, for God's sake," Jamie said. "They haven't even had time to—"

"The last twenty-four hours have seen significant progress in this investigation. We have obtained incontrovertible evidence pointing to Lieutenant Peterson's killer."

Jamie sat up. "Strong words."

"Yesterday evening, Mrs. June Peterson confessed fully and completely to the murder of her husband, Lieutenant Matthew Peterson, Sr., and to the subsequent murder of Sandhill Lake village manager Maureen Loeffler, in an attempt to conceal knowledge of the original crime."

The room exploded. Reporters shouted over each other, over Dan. His mouth moved but we couldn't hear what he was saying. I didn't hear the next question before Dan started answering it:

". . . presented the team with the murder weapon, a .40-caliber Smith & Wesson service pistol matching Lieutenant Peterson's in every way. She was also in possession of personal effects removed from the deceased, including a bloodstained personalized handkerchief and other items known to belong to the lieutenant. Mrs. Peterson was privy to crime scene details that had not been made available to the public. Laboratory analysis of the evidence is still pending, but we are confident it will uphold . . ."

I blanked out. I don't remember what came next. Just Jamie, lips a stiff white line, spinning through other news feeds, other stories, a blur of images, snapshots of the gun in a plastic bag, panicked voiceovers, off-the-cuff interviews. Everyone was saying the same thing: the wife did it, the wife did it, the wife did it. No one was saying her name.

"I don't understand." Matt's sharp, aquiline face looked washed-out under the lightning-colored camera lights. He looked like he'd been brought back from the dead. "I don't understand why she would do this."

34

Rosie picked up the next card: Temperance.

At first I thought the angel in the card was floating, but she was standing on water and land, one foot planted in each. She held magic cups, water flowing between them in firm defiance of gravity. She was peaceful but strange, unearthly.

"Doesn't Temperance mean like, not drinking?"

"Ugh." Rosie had her hand up to the elbow in a box of Cheerios. It was snack time again. She was grimacing and eating fast, like she was trying to finish them before she figured out she didn't like them. "That word's been ruined by people with sticks up their butts who want to limit just about anything that makes life fun. Eating. Drinking." She chewed dreamily with her hand still in the box. "Turtle racing." She looked at me. "Did you say something?"

"Temperance."

"Temperance! What the word actually means"—she stuffed a handful of Cheerios in her mouth and one popped out—"is moderation. You're more peaceful at this point in your life.

Balanced. You don't go too crazy over anything because you don't have to." She tapped her chest. "You have everything you need inside you already."

She pointed to Death. "Especially after getting through this big crisis here.

"Oh yeah." She looked down at the cards and remembered. "And we're at the end of the second row. You pulled back on some of the outside world stuff that shaped you"—she pointed to the first row—"and brought forward some of these cool inner things you've discovered.

"Now inner and outer are balanced," she said. "And you're ready for what's next."

From the porch, I could hear the doorbell ring inside Gina's house. No answer. A flick of the shades, then nothing.

Light, lazy snowflakes drifted down onto the porch. I felt like I was inside a snow globe the moment before it goes still. A pair of ceramic geese on the front porch were inappropriately dressed in sunglasses, Hawaiian shirts, and panama hats. I had the feeling no one had changed their clothes in years, trapping them in an eternal vacation.

Gina was not coming to the door. I rang again. "I have a six-pack of Red Dog and a pineapple-and-anchovy from Pizza Pandemonium," I called. "If you don't let me in, I'll eat and drink everything myself and pass out on your porch in a puddle of my own sick."

The door clicked open. I followed a flash of hair into the dark living room. The shades were drawn tight. Gina was wearing colorless sweats and had her hair pulled back in a messy bun. She sank back into the couch, like she'd used up all her strength opening the door. I took in the motley arrangement on the coffee table: food wrappers, empty bottles, silverware, cups, saucers, and a vicious-looking brass candelabra.

"They're just trying to cheer me up," she said when she saw me staring. "The Beast was so rude at dinner. I don't think he's ever gonna fall in love with me."

I ferried the flotsam to the kitchen, brought over the pizza and beer, found a couple of paper plates and napkins in the cabinets, and sat down across from Gina. We had switched places: Gina was on the couch where I lay in a stupor the other night, and I was in the armchair where Gina . . . where the drop of blood on her finger . . .

I stared straight ahead and willed my eyes not to go rogue and look at the carpet.

"When did they let you go?" I said.

"Yesterday morning, the day after June confessed." She reached for a beer, but it was too far away so she sank back again. I flipped open a Red Dog and passed it to her.

"Dan didn't want to let me go, but facts are facts." She smirked. "Not even that slick fucker could twist out of this one."

She took a few sips and set the can on the table. "You're doing better with the . . ." She pointed vaguely in the direction of my head. "You're feeling . . . ?" She trailed off and looked at the window, where the shades were still drawn and there was still nothing to see.

"I'm sorry," I said.

She didn't turn to me. "What are *you* sorry for?"

"I'm sorry I believed you killed Peterson," I said. "For a little while anyway. And Maureen." My heart was pounding. This was in the past now. I could say it out loud. "And maybe that you tried to kill me, too." I reached for a beer.

Gina turned to me. "It's a rite of passage, if you're going to hang with me. Mazel tov, today you are a woman."

The beer was shit. I loved it. A whisper of feathery light swept through the room, like a spray of snowflakes.

"You know, when I was sitting in the holding cell?" Gina said. "I actually started to believe I did kill him. I sure as hell imagined it enough." She piled a stray piece of pineapple on a slice of pizza and picked it up. "I started thinking I was in one of those shitty thrillers where there's all this unexplained blood dripping from the ceiling and people jumping out of mirrors and shit. And the big reveal is it was me all along. I was the killer, but I had blocked it out."

She gave a soft joyless laugh. "June, huh? That poor, sweet bitch." She lifted the slice to her mouth and the pineapple fell off again. "Did I call it, or what?"

"You really think she was trying to frame you with that dragon-fly pin?" I licked stray flour off my fingers.

"If she was," Gina said, "why reverse course at the finish line? She almost had me." She shrugged.

June was everywhere in the news now, in badly lit, unflattering candids from the dustbins of her life, pictures of her at peace rallies and animal rights protests. They made her look either frumpy and dour or like a drippy granola-eating doofus. The speculations as to her motive ran the gamut. She wanted his money. She was driven mad by suspicion of infidelity—though every foundation-caked news face rushed to point out that no evidence for said infidelity existed. (The trophy scrapbook, after all, was in shreds all over June's living room.) She was just a kook! A crazy bomb-throwing anti-cop kook who killed her hero husband for no reason. Same circus, different ring, mad calliope music and flashing lights. I x-ed out any pop-up news story that opened on my phone, which meant I pretty much didn't watch Peterson news anymore. No one was listening to June before, and no one was listening to her now. She was a plot twist.

"Why would she wait this long to come forward?" I said. "It doesn't make any sense." Nothing about June's confession made sense. I'd been rolling with the idea of her angling for Pete's pension, or wiping him out for treating her like shit, but the timing of the confession—and its existence at all—put the lie to those reasons. "Do you think she just didn't want an innocent person to go to prison?" June, the ethical murderer?

"That's me," Gina said stiffly. "Totally innocent."

"What did Maureen say when she called you that night?" I said.

Gina picked up a napkin and wiped her face and neck, like a swimmer emerging from a strenuous relay. "She said, 'I found something big. Can you come over?'"

"A copy of the recording." I sank down in my seat. The same copy that got stolen from my office? If so, who took it? June? Maureen? Neither of those made any sense either. I could not get a single pair of puzzle pieces to fit together. "Did you by any chance drop by my office on Wednesday after I was gone and steal my flash drive and leave a threatening message on my computer?"

Gina looked like she was trying to work up a joke, but the effort defeated her. "That sounds like a lot of work." She picked up her beer and slumped against the couch.

"So Maureen was trying to warn you," I said.

"I think so. June must have gotten there just before me, because Maureen was . . ." She closed her eyes and paused. "She was still alive, but barely. I did what I could, but she'd lost so much blood by then."

But why would June kill Maureen? Wouldn't the recording be exactly what June wanted: more evidence against Gina? Or did Maureen know something else that pointed to June's guilt?

"Lotus." Gina's voice pulled me out of my thoughts. She sounded like she was talking to herself.

"What?"

"Lotus," Gina said. "That's what she said right before she died. Just that one word."

Something flickered past in my memory.

"I heard someone coming," Gina said, "some nosy old broad started knocking on the door. Must have heard the gunshot. I panicked, I ran. I went out the back. I wasn't even being careful. I knew I should have stayed, but I wasn't thinking. I forgot you were here. If I'd remembered, I'd have gone somewhere else. I wouldn't have gotten you involved." She cringed. "How bad was it? Was Dan a prick to you?"

"He played bad cop for a bit," I said. "He wanted me to say I knew it was you all along. I really recommend being questioned when you have a concussion. Even the stuff you know, you can't remember." My slice of pizza suddenly looked gluey and tough, like a plastic toy. I put it down. "He played me the recording. And he told me what happened between you and Peterson."

Gina's eyes lightened. She looked like she was watching something move off into the distance. Time, maybe. She got up from the couch, fast, and went to the kitchen. She opened a cabinet, pawed through it, banged it shut, and stood there holding the knob.

"You know what tanked the whole thing?" she said. "Got the complaint thrown out, caused all the shit that came after? The retaliation, the fights with Maureen, me leaving? It was the 'no.' I said no to him. We took a call out in Grant Woods one day, just the two of us. And he said, You look tired, why don't you come over here and put your head in my lap."

She rubbed the brass cabinet knob, as if for good luck. When she turned to me she had this sort of triumphant smile on her face. "I thought I was doing the right thing. I was so pleased with myself. The look on his face. It wasn't anger or humiliation. It was shock. Just total shock that anyone, for the first time in his smug entitled fucking life, would dare say no to him.

"I thought I'd won. But that was only the beginning. He was my sergeant, so all of a sudden I got all the shit calls. He gave me desk duty. Filing. He wrote me up for every goddamn thing. Bounced me back and forth from days to nights so I could never get used to either one. I wasn't getting any sleep. I would find things in my locker. He would steal things to fuck with me." She let go of the cabinet and went to the window, lifted the shade. Pale yellow light poured in. Outside, the air whirled with chaotic flurries.

"That's how I lost those dragonflies," she said. "That must have been where June got them. I had a ball cap, too, this old torn-up green Kane County Cougars ball cap. My dad would take us when we were kids, anytime he felt guilty about being a shit dad. The only time I remember having any kind of fun with him."

I remembered the little cougar-face logo from a few of my own childhood games. The stadium had smelled like hot dogs and Coke syrup and summertime. More memories Peterson had stolen from Gina.

Gina shook her sweatshirt off and folded her arms. "It wasn't just him, either, it was everyone, all his dipshit friends. Forget about getting promoted. I just wanted to make it through a whole day without choking on a condom in my sandwich.

"So again, I tried to do the right thing. I filed the complaint. Filled out their thirty goddamn pages of paperwork. Talked to the union rep. Talked to the village. Dotted all the i's, crossed all the t's. And you know what they said? There was no sexual activity, so how could there be any coercion? Nothing happened, right? Of course, if something had happened, they would have just said there was no proof, because of course every blow job comes with a certificate of authenticity. Or he would have said it was consensual. My word against his. Or better yet, *Why didn't you just say no?* At every stage, I got punished for doing *the right thing.*"

"What did Maureen do?" I said.

"What she *didn't* do was fire him," Gina said. "Even though she could have. She was his superior. But she didn't. She put me on a different shift, moved us around so we didn't come in contact. She tried. But all I kept hearing was my mom's voice in my head whenever my dad took the belt to me: *Just stay away from him. Don't make him mad. You know how he gets.*"

Gina's messy black ponytail quivered. "God, I was furious with her. I yelled at her, called her names, told her she was a coward." She put her face in her hands. "I was so fucking selfish. I didn't understand that she was just as stuck as I was."

Flies struggling through the same jar of honey, I thought, or worse. Who was wrong here? Neither one. They'd both been screwed from the start.

"I kept thinking one of these days I should just put on my big-girl pants, pick up a six-pack, and go see her. Make it right. Even if we weren't working together, I thought maybe it could still be like it was before him. I kept thinking, at least I still have that in my back pocket. At least there is one thing he didn't take away.

"That's not even the worst part." Her voice thickened and slowed. "The worst part is, sometimes I wonder what would have happened if I'd just done what he wanted. If I hadn't done the 'right thing.' Would I still be a cop? Would Maureen still be alive? Maybe. Would I be better off? Maybe."

She was quiet for a long time.

"But would I still be the same person? I want to say no. But fuck, what do I know? Maybe I would. Maybe it wouldn't have mattered at all." She put her head against the window and watched a gust of wind spin the flakes in a slow spiral. "I have to wonder now, every day, who I am."

I put down my beer, crept to the couch, sat on the edge, and reached for her hand. She clasped it tight but didn't turn around.

"I guess that means you're just like the rest of us," I said. "I'm sorry you didn't think you could tell me."

Gina's shoulders gave a huffing little shake. "Would you have believed me?" She turned around and dropped the window shade pull string. "This was a guy who pulled babies out of car wrecks." She went back to the couch and picked up her beer.

Score another for Officer Pete's runaway mythology. I was feeling increasingly shitty about my own role in it. *I would have believed you*, I wanted to say, but I said nothing. How many people, while she had hacked away, alone, at doing *the right thing*, had said they believed her and still let her down?

"That fucking recording." She downed the beer, crushed the can, and reached for another. "I lost my mind a little after the whole thing went down, and Pete was ready for me. He made that recording, then held it over my head. Said if anything ever happened to him, I was going down for it. I knew it was only a matter of time before it popped up, and then I'd be screwed." She snapped the beer can open, then licked foam off her fingers. "Anyway, it wasn't my finest moment." She glanced at me. "I didn't want you hearing it."

Gina was worried that *I* was going to judge her? I wanted to laugh out loud, or throw something at her, but decided the moment called for mature adulthood.

"Let's make a deal," I said. "You stop worrying about disappointing me, and I'll stop freaking out when I find out you're a normal person who does things for complicated reasons that are sometimes stupid." I needed to start seeing Gina as a real person. Anything else was selfish.

Gina's eyes were purple around the edges. "Did Maureen tell you how I got to be a cop?" she said. "The whole story?"

"Yeah, she did." I felt a twist in my gut. "You gave up your friends."

"I gave up my friends," Gina said tartly. "Tanya's a teacher now. Miles is a state rep. Lives out in Saint Charles and sends me a citrus fruit box every year for setting him on the right path. Leslie's serving five to ten for carjacking." She rolled her eyes. "But he was already into that scene when I took him down, so that's on him, not me."

She picked up a crumpled pack of cigarettes and shook one out. "Do I feel great about it?" she said. "No. Was it wrong?" She gave me an exaggerated shrug. "The fuck should I know."

Outside, the last flurries drifted across the window and a patchy sunlight dappled the street.

"You really think June did it?" I said.

"She had his gun, K. It's tough to toss something like that out." Gina put the cigarette in her mouth, then took it out and put it back in the pack. "The truth is, I don't care anymore. I'm out. There's nothing here for me. It's over."

35

It's over. I drove and drove. Streets, trees, and buildings passed me in a colorless blur. Gina's words wound themselves through my mind. *There's nothing here for me. It's over.*

I moved down Waukegan Road between bony forests, car dealerships, and parking lots full of cars but empty of people. Today, I had decided, I would tie up loose ends. I had just gassed up the Camry of Death, the spare car that circulated throughout my family based on need (usually mine, whenever the Fiesta was under some form of duress). It had earned its name by bearing solemn witness to the army of suburban critters that had succumbed to it when my mom was at the wheel.

I was supposed to fill out this form the cops had given me when I filed the hit-and-run, detailing the damage to the Fiesta. The form sat blank and accusing next to me in the passenger seat. *Is "car looks like a pretzel" enough detail for you?*

I would miss the Fiesta. It was a pain in the ass, but it was mine. I kept losing things that were supposed to be mine. To that end, I was headed to my office—nope, Jessie's office—to clean up and leave the box of June's financial documents for Jessie to pick up.

Not that June would need them anytime soon. Where even was she? Counting wall cracks in a cell? At home, pacing around her living room, having tense phone calls with lawyers? I had no idea how things worked when you were accused of murder.

At the corner of 60 and Waukegan, a mom and a little boy waited to cross the street. The mom leaned down, her mouth close to her son's ear, pointing out the buttons, the lights, the street. *When you press the button,* I could almost hear her saying, *everything stops. You're the important one. You're the human being.*

June loved her son. If she believed in her heart, like Gina had believed about Maureen, that they could be together again, why would she do the only thing that would prevent that? I saw Matt's face in my mind after the press conference, the rage on it, the despair. She had lost him for good this time. Was I looking in vain for logic in what was essentially an explosion of raw emotion? Something not meant to be understood, only felt?

I walked through it in my mind. Here was June getting in her car, driving down to the white space on the map. Here she was lurking by the old cement factory, following Officer Pete. Here she was surprising him. This is where my mind went blank. How she got his gun away from him, how she shot him, how he ran, this I couldn't see. The movie had stopped. The old projector shut off, leaving a stuttering thread of loose film spinning over and over.

Maureen's murder scene was even muddier. Everyone, the news screamed, had watched June break down at the real estate event! She was unhinged, witnesses said, crazy! Except . . . she wasn't. She was calm for the first time that day, like she'd finally found some peace. If she had killed Peterson in a rage—

Wait a minute.

The signals changed. I watched the boy dance across the street, the mom rushing to catch up. June hadn't found Peterson's scrapbook until Wednesday, the day of her failed interview with Jamie—days after Pete was dead. Sure, she'd had plenty of reasons to want him dead before then, but they'd all been on a slow burner for years. Why now? Why that day?

I pulled the car into the shallow inlet of a forest preserve entrance. Voices clamored in my head. All the case details that didn't make sense from the start were shouting for airtime. Maureen's last word: *lotus*. What did it mean? Was there something she had found that June didn't want anyone to see? The recording pointed to Gina, not June. Wouldn't that work in June's favor?

A flash of blue out of the corner of my eye. Sitting on a fat arm-like tree branch in front of me was the brightest blue bird I had ever seen.

I crept out of my car, closing the door gently so as not to spook him. It was an indigo bunting. Izzy's little guy.

"What are you doing here?" I said. "You should be in Cuba playing golf." The bird chirped and whistled, buried his face in his shoulder. He looked like a scrap of blue silk. I peered into his brilliant feathers, tried to catch the trick the cold sunlight was playing on my eyes. All I could see was a deep, true blue.

"Don't you lie to me," I told the bird. "Anyway, it's over." The bird whipped his head up and fixed me with his tiny eye. *You don't really believe that, do you?* Then he sputtered to life and disappeared. The empty branch swayed behind him.

I got back in the car and headed toward Sandhill Lake.

By midafternoon, the lunch crowd at Birdie's was thin. A few old folks were scattered around the place, a lone waitress wandering between them. Izzy sat at the cash register, staring out the window at the turbulent lake, gray waves cresting white and disappearing. Baines Hill towered blue in the distance. The bird board was empty.

When Izzy saw me he bounced from behind the cash register and grabbed my elbow. "Did you hear about June?" He danced me across the floor and dumped me in a window booth. A coffee carafe had materialized in his grip and he was already pouring me a mug of coffee. (Red-winged blackbird.) "I've been watching the news all day." He looked around. "Is Jamie with you?"

"Just me today," I said. "Jamie's done. Now that, you know, it's over." Again, the words felt dry and chalky in my mouth.

Izzy gave me the same look the indigo bunting did. "You believe she did it?"

"Do you?" I said carefully.

He set the coffee down and sat across from me. "You have to be joking," he said. "June is not a murderer. Murder is a very complicated business. You have to think of all the details, every tiny thing that could go wrong. You have to think ten steps ahead. It is like running a business." He folded his arms and sat back. "And June, I love her very much, she is a wonderful, kind lady. But she is not a businesswoman."

"She is," I said. "She sells her artwork online."

"Oh." Izzy scratched his head. "I forgot about that."

We sat there, deflated at not having conjured the perfect evidence that would exonerate June.

"I saw you talking last Sunday," Izzy said. "What did she tell you? Did she seem guilty?" He peered at me as if he could see the playback from the conversation in my eyes. That day felt like it had happened a hundred years ago, and to someone else.

"She was pretty clear that she and Pete didn't get along," I said.

"They were married," Izzy scoffed. "Of course they didn't get along. That's why he came in every weekday morning and she came in on Sundays. So they didn't bump into each other."

"So she wasn't here the day he died?" We had never nailed down June's whereabouts on the morning of the murder. She said she was at home, but she was out.

"No," Izzy said. "It wasn't her day. But Pete was here, same as usual." He swirled the coffeepot, watched the dark liquid inside circle and slosh. "That's what I told Jamie and the guys. Showed them the video, too. They were trying to retrace his steps, you know. See if anything unusual happened to him right before." He scratched his head. "But no one ever asked about June."

"There's video?" My skin prickled. "Can I see it?"

Izzy's so-called security office was the tiny corner of a desk in an alcove behind the kitchen, next to a bursting file cabinet and a rust-stained utility sink. The tiny, ancient TV monitor had a slit in the bottom for chunky old VHS tapes.

"I got it years ago for the insurance discount," Izzy said. "But I've never had to use it."

I sat in a folding chair with a back that hung on by a single screw. Izzy rummaged through a cardboard box full of tapes, found the one he wanted, and popped it in. He turned on the screen and the front of the restaurant fuzzed into view: the register, the bird board with something red and white chalked on it. You could see out into the street through the big front window. The video quality was crap, but at least it was in color.

"It's at the end, I have to rewind it." The image shivered backward through time at double speed. "Here. This is him leaving." Officer Pete, in uniform, danced backward into the frame, spent some time at the register, then went backward into the restaurant to have his backward breakfast.

"And this is him coming in." Pete moved back through his arrival, piled into his squad car, and shot backward out of the frame. Izzy hit play and Peterson pulled in again, got out of the car. Something flashed white on the screen and my eye followed it: a truck parked in front of Pete's squad car, driving away.

My brain tingled. "Izzy, can you please rewind a little again?"

The truck moved back onto the screen and parked in front of Pete. The logo on its side leaped out at me: a semicircular canopy of trees under a sun, over a line of text: LAKE COUNTY PUBLIC WORKS.

My fingers went numb. Izzy hit play again and time moved forward. Pete got out of his squad car again, walked into Birdie's again. I stared at the driver of the Public Works truck, but I couldn't see his face, just a light spot in a gray wash. He was looking down at the passenger seat, digging through a white bag. He lifted something out and I leaned in to look. It was a baseball cap.

Now my toes were tingling, too. "Izzy, is there any way to zoom in?" I wished we were on TV and could hit the Make Everything Crystal Clear button. As it was, Izzy's system only had a few degrees of zoom, and the more you zoomed, the less you could see. The ball cap was green, I could see that. It had a round logo in its center that looked like a circle with a face inside.

My body went stiff. I knew that logo. The lettering around it was too small to read, but I already knew what it would say: KANE COUNTY COUGARS.

The driver shoved the bag away, took the wheel, and put the car in gear. Just before the truck drove off, the driver's pale, clear face flashed toward the window.

The counter moved forward, tick, tick, tick. The truck disappeared. I knew where it was going: to the white space on the map.

I sat in my car in the parking lot at the side of Birdie's, shaking.

No. No. No. It couldn't be. And yet, it made everything fall into place, every detail that was off, from that first day at Birdie's when Jamie laid it out for me in ketchup packets. The ghostly absence of chatter along the criminal grapevine. The single pair of footprints at the crime scene. The Public Works vehicles. Gina's missing belongings. The message on my computer. There was only one person who tied all these things together.

But why? And why both Peterson and Maureen?

My eyes stung and scratched. I closed them and put my head on the steering wheel. There was a connection between the two murders, a missing cog that, when slid into place, would set the whole machine into motion. And the missing piece, the reason for the murders, the dark connecting spur, was hidden in Maureen's last word: *lotus*. I needed more. I needed a reason and facts and proof. Without them, knowing who did it was worse than useless.

I pounded my head on the steering wheel. Think, Katie, think. Lotus, lotus. I had heard the word before, and I had seen it. I could see it now, unfurling in my mind in a curvy white script. But where?

Owen told me the story once of how the periodic table came to Dmitri Mendeleev in a dream. Just *bam*, fully formed and ready to insert into textbooks to be the bane of chemistry students everywhere. It was a great story, Owen said, but it was also nonsense, because for years before the dream Mendeleev researched, experimented, and discussed with other chemists the problem of periodicity. He worked on it with Brain One, and while Brain One rested, Brain Zero took up the slack and connected all of Brain One's work into a solution that seemed to come with great magical fanfare out of nowhere. And so the story was born, perpetuating the idea that scientists are all touched by divine madness and that you can get something out of nothing. The fact is, creativity is not magic. It's hard fucking work.

The answer was in my mind somewhere, hiding like Mendeleev's bright dream table. I needed a jolt of randomness to shut off Brain One, stop its idiotic chattering, so the answer could come to me.

I took out the cards, shuffled, and cut.

The Two of Pentacles. A dude balancing two pentacles, dancing around a gray plain while two ships, a large one and a small one, rode a dangerously wavy ocean behind him. Was it Peterson, trying to keep his finances afloat? Maybe. This was no help.

I put the Two of Pentacles aside and drew again. Ten of Cups, a happy family dancing in front of their happy domain—a farm, a house, a rainbow of cups in the sky. Why was everyone dancing? It had a bit of the same smarmy, self-congratulatory vibe, I thought, as a photo I saw on Facebook of Peterson in front of his boat, like some ancient king in front of his fortress. Look on my works, ye mighty, and despair.

Next card: Temperance. Yes, got it, I needed to be patient, hop off my dick already.

I drew faster and faster, tossing the cards on the passenger seat. Eight of Wands—disembodied sticks flying through the air. Confusion? No shit. The Chariot. The Queen of Cups. The Ace of Swords. I rubbed my eyes. This was getting me nowhere. The harder I looked, the less clearly I saw. I was panicking, overheating. I knew I had to let go of my brain and let it wander, but I couldn't relax, couldn't go blank the way I needed to. The Seven of Cups—a fever dream of riches and dangers, greed and . . . and . . .

I looked back at the first two cards: the smug family on their farm, the guy dancing in front of the boats . . .

I lurched up and banged my head on the car roof. The boats. I knew where I had seen the word *lotus* before. I sprang out of the car, dove into the trunk, and yanked the top off June's box of documents. There it was, the file I wanted: a boat storage contract from Sandhill Marine, on Route 12. "LESSEE NAME," it said: "Matthew Peterson, Sr."

"WATERCRAFT NAME: American Lotus."

36

Sandhill Marine was closed for the season, which made it easy to pace around the parking lot muttering to myself and checking the time as I waited for Owen.

If there was any place more depressing than a boatyard in the wintertime, I didn't know what it was. Sandhill Marine was a desolate harbor full of empty slips like the bones of a giant prehistoric fish. Boats in blue and white shrink-wrap were scattered among dingy blue barns with curved roofs. The office building / showroom was dark. There was a sign on the front window reading CLOSED FOR THE SEASON. SEE YOU IN MAY! with a little smiley face.

I got tired of waiting and went to building 3, where the rental contract said Peterson's boat was stored. The door was unlocked. I looked around and saw Owen's car parked ten feet from mine. I'd been too busy panicking to notice that he was already here.

Owen sat on a utility bench just inside the entrance, hands in pockets. "What are you doing in here?" I sat down next to him. "I thought we were meeting outside." The bench froze my butt.

"I was cold," he said. It was only slightly warmer in the storage building than it was outside. "I can't believe they would use a standard lock on this place." He handed me a little black foldout knife whose attachments were all picks for different kinds of locks. I stared at the malevolent blades spread out like a monster's hand. "One little twist, and I was in."

Owen stood up and moved into the building to explore. I shoved the tool into my pocket and followed him. The storage barn was a huge open cavern interrupted by support posts. Struts, wires, and dusty lights hung from the distant ceiling, and thin transom windows somehow made the place look even darker. It smelled like metal, machine oil, and damp. Rows of shrink-wrapped blue boats stretched off into an endless labyrinth, each slot labeled with a stenciled number.

"Did you figure out who killed Peterson?" Owen said. As always, no beating around the bush. It was a simple question but I was having trouble coming out with the equally simple answer. For the first time ever, I desperately wanted to be wrong.

"I need more information," I said. "I'm trying to get all the facts. Not jump to conclusions. All that crap Jamie is always going on about."

Owen eyed me suspiciously. I went on. "The night I bumped into Maureen at the PD, she was looking for something related to the Explorers, but it wasn't there. She said she had one other place she could look, because Peterson always used all the same hiding places. I think that place was the boat. The *American Lotus*. It was the last thing she said to Gina before she died. I think she found what she was looking for, and it has something to do with why Peterson died." I checked the crumpled storage contract I'd brought in from my car. "We need berth 89."

"Does Jamie know about this?" Owen said.

"I called him," I said. "His shift ends at six, so he should be on his way."

Jamie fell silent on the phone when I told him what I was thinking. "Are you sure that document says what you think it says?" His tone was faraway, like his mind had already moved on, sorting through the possibilities. "Otherwise, we can't legally get in there."

I took out the document and read it to him.

"All right," he said heavily. "Let me make some calls and set it up." The flatness in his voice scared me. "Katie, if you're right, this is very bad. Please, don't do anything until I get there."

We'd already blown right through that. I kind of hadn't told Jamie the part where I had invited Owen and his Hamburglar kit.

Berth 89 was the last in its row. A bright cherry red peeked out from under the standard blue shrink-wrap. I remembered the photograph: Peterson and Matt dwarfed by the boat, sun blind, like they were surprised to find themselves where they were. A warped snippet from an old song drifted through my mind. *This is not our beautiful boat!*

"Ooh, a Chris-Craft," Owen said. "I've never been inside one before." Owen had never gone through the obligatory train phase, but he'd gone through just about every other one. My parents' attic had a whole corner dedicated to a chronological accounting of Owen's extremely specific and intense interests. The boat shelf. The ancient Egypt shelf. The Great American Songbook shelf. His phases could be sparked by anything and would grow into a roaring fire that would consume his mind and emotions for weeks, months, or years at a time, each disappearing as suddenly as it came and leaving behind Owen's otherworldly storehouse of knowledge. I wondered sometimes how amazing it must be to experience everything in the world as a sort of first love.

"There should be a door." He went around the side of the boat and found a zippered curve.

I checked the time. "Jamie wants us to"—Owen unzipped the door and climbed into the boat—"wait for him."

I sighed and followed Owen. The boat smelled new inside, like lemons and bleach. Polished dark wood everywhere, a steering wheel, a central panel, everything shining and rich and spotless, even the floor. The shrink-wrap made the air dim and blue, like we were underwater.

"What are we looking for?" Owen said.

"I don't know." Again, I wished I had prepared more thoroughly. "Maybe there's a storage compartment or something?"

"There's a ski locker." Owen crouched down and located a long, skinny compartment built into the floor of the boat, perpendicular to the main console. I helped him pry it open. We pulled out skis, and boards, and other equipment I didn't recognize. Behind and underneath everything else was a banker's box, a twin of the one in my trunk.

The label read: EXPLORERS.

My head throbbed. Whatever Maureen had been looking for, officially at first, and then through increasingly secretive channels, was here. Every new cobblestone of information fit neatly into the road I had reluctantly started on. A road that led off a cliff.

I opened the box. There was a sheaf of bank statements from Sandhill Lake Community Bank dating back to the mid-teens, and a set of old checkbook registers. The sheer amount of information made my eyes scatter over the page.

"These must be from the Explorers' bank account. Maureen was looking for this stuff when I first met her. She said Peterson hadn't given her the records she needed." I leafed through the stacks of paper. "What the hell are we supposed to do with them?"

Panic spiked in my chest. "I'm not an accountant. I can't read this stuff."

Owen took the sheaf of statements from me. "I'll be Brain One," he said, and handed me a cheap, skinny kids' notebook with Pikachu on it. "You be Brain Zero. Don't look for anything in particular. Just look."

I opened the notebook. Someone had pencil-slashed each page into three columns: a minus column, a plus column, and a running total. It looked like a sort of reverse checkbook, with the total hovering as close to zero as possible. There was no indication what each transaction was for—only numbers and dates. I unfocused my eyes and the lines settled into a pattern. They came in pairs, at least at first. Two hundred dollars in the minus column, followed by that same two hundred dollars in the plus column. Total: back to zero.

"Licensing, tournament fees, equipment, supplies . . ." Owen leafed through the checkbook registers. "Some of these transactions don't have memos. They're just labeled 'cash.'"

"Give me some dates for those," I said. He read me one and I found it in the journal. "Two hundred dollars. Is there a matching deposit a month later?"

"Yep." Owen flipped through the bank statement pages. "They're scattered all over. They look like small loans. But for what?"

I knew for what. Restaurants. Vacations. Booze. Porn. All the stuff on the maxed-out credit cards. The Petersons were drowning in debt, and the Explorer account was their life raft. I leafed through the Pikachu notebook. The more time passed, the rarer the replacement deposits and the higher the total. It grew into the hundreds, the thousands, the tens of thousands, and then abruptly stopped.

"I don't think the loans were loans. Not later on anyway." I looked up, blinking. Ghostly numerical afterimages marched across my vision. "He was stealing. He was embezzling money from the Explorers."

Owen reached into the box and produced an old-fashioned off-brand flip phone. It came on with a fluty chime. No contacts, no names, only a single long series of text messages. Owen and I hunched over them, flipped to the beginning, and began to read:

> Hey can you front me 1500? The nat'l org fees are due this month and I'm short

> What happened to the 800 I gave you?

> Hawaii ate that up lol looks like it'll just have to hang for a while

> U sure it's ok? Maybe slow down a little before someone checks in?

> WHO??? Lol no one looks at the explorer stuff but me. Anyway all the shit I do for this town, nobodys going to care if I treat ma self every once in a while. Who do they go to when everything goes to shit? Me. Me and you. We will always be ok now quit being a ween

A few exchanges later, from last fall:

> Saw Maureen just got village mgr you gonna be ok?

Lol You really think MAUREEN of all people will give a rats ass. I'll slip her a little EXTRA and it's all good

Ew I don't need to hear this lol

Later, from earlier this year:

They got her doing this audit thing and she asked for the Explorer stuff. I put her off but she's being a real pain in my ass, trying to score brownie points with the board ugh

Um . . . hate to say ITYS but . . .

Fuck off this is serious she gets her hands on the checking acct I'm pretty well FUCKED. Any extra you got, start dumping into that account or you'll be visiting me in JAIL. Need to hang on until I retire and then this will all go away

The next few:

I'm not gonna make it. I need to do something NOW or I'm dead. Worse than dead. Dead would be better. I got a plan tho stay tuned . . .

P was a bust I think we need to go to plan b

P? Was that Popeye? And what was plan B? There were no messages for a long time, then a series from the same person, with no responses from the other one.

> Hey.

> Helloooooo. You there? Have you given any more thought to plan B

> Come on man I need you

The exchange started up again:

I already told you I am NOT doing it.

> Look I know its not ideal but this is the only thing left.

IDEAL? You have got to be kidding me. NO.

> You don't help me with this you are screwed too don't you understand? This is bigger than you or me. Do this and we both survive.

I can't do this dad. I love you.

> Are you OUT OF YOUR FUCKING MIND?? Don't you EVER identify yourself on here. Delete this shit now and destroy the phone.

A wall of black ice spread through my chest.

"Katie?" Jamie's voice called from outside the boat. "Are you in there?"

"I was right, Jamie." I scooted to the zippered door and backed carefully out of the boat. "It's all here."

Later, I realized I should have known something was off. I should have heard the edge in Jamie's voice, but I was too numb from what I had just found.

"Come on out and show us, Katie," said a second voice. I knew that voice, too.

I froze, half in the boat and half out. Owen stared at me, eyes wide. I put a finger to my lips and splayed my hand out to him silently. *Stay here.*

I hopped the rest of the way down to the concrete floor and turned around to face Matt.

37

"By the time you get to the third row," Rosie said, "you've figured a lot of things out. And that's when you start asking yourself, is there more?"

The TV screen came alive with color and speed. The astronaut was being sucked into some kind of portal, his astonished face twisting as lights swirled past him.

"More than what?" I said.

"The third row," Rosie said, "is when you try to go back here." She swept her fingers up, back to the Fool again. "Back to that pure nothing that contains everything."

Rosie sprawled on the couch looking exhausted, like she had personally walked the entire Road of Life in one afternoon. It was dark in the room now. What time was it? How long had we been here? The lights were off. The cards glowed in the light from the TV screen like little doorways.

"The Fool is the ideal. But you can't get there by going backward." Rosie zigzagged her fingers up the rows of cards. "By trying to get back what you've lost."

She pointed to the massive Devil, squatting behind a chained-up man and woman. There was a door behind them, but they didn't see it. They weren't even looking.

"You get stuck in your illusions. All the stuff that doesn't work for you anymore, but you can't break out of it. Look at these two dopes."

I looked at the prisoners. They didn't look upset, just exhausted. *Don't kid yourself,* my mom loved to say, usually about things no one had any intention of kidding themselves about. If I was kidding myself about something important, I would know, right?

She pointed to the naked pair. "They could slip those chains off in a heartbeat. But when the Devil's got you, you think you have no choice." She yawned and stretched. "Sometimes that illusion is so strong, only a crisis can shake it loose."

"I always wanted to show you the boat," Matt said. "Just not like this." He was holding a gun loose at his side, and there was another in his holster. The one he was holding was Jamie's.

Jamie was handcuffed, hands twisted around the back of a post. His face wore the blank expression I only saw when he was trying not to die or kill someone. I had hoped never to see it again. Survival Jamie was a lot scarier than don't-fuck-with-me-Jamie.

I took two quick steps and punched Matt in the face. It wasn't much of a punch, and I did it exactly how you're not supposed to if you don't want to hurt yourself. I would feel that later. For now, my senses had shut off. In the white desert of my mind, it was Pete I was hitting. Pete, Pete, Pete, who'd done all those horrible things.

But Pete wasn't here.

Matt lost his balance and stepped back, although the odd, stony serenity on his face didn't ripple.

"You lied to me," I said. "You manipulated me."

"I had to." He put his hand to his cheek. "I didn't have a choice."

"Just like your dad didn't have a choice?" Tongues of flame scorched the edge of my vision, as if I were seeing past the visible spectrum of light into heat. I punched Matt again, with the other fist this time.

"Katie," Jamie said.

Matt whipped his hand out and grabbed my wrist. His eyes flashed and through the blistering wall of my anger I realized, faintly, how much danger we were all in.

Matt twisted my arm and spun me around. A drop of blood from the gash I'd opened under his eye crawled down his face and disappeared on his black uniform. He whipped out a second pair of cuffs and snapped me in place next to Jamie.

"You knew, didn't you?" I said. "You knew about all of it. The women. The girls. The drinking. The accidents. The . . ." The words dried up in my mouth. There weren't enough to name every offense Pete had perpetrated on everyone who had loved and admired him. "You knew what he was."

Matt looked tired. "Everyone knew, Katie."

"And the money?" My scraped knuckles were starting to howl. "Did everyone know about that, too? Did your mom know?"

"No one knew but me," Matt said. "Not even my mom, not until after."

"But Maureen was about to find out, wasn't she? The paperwork she was looking for was here." I pointed to the boat. *Lotus.* Maureen's last word was a clue. "That's what . . . what I found in there." I had almost said *we found in there.* Matt didn't know what Owen's car looked like. He didn't know Owen was here, and I wanted to keep it that way. "Isn't it?"

"I didn't think she would get this far," Matt said. "Neither did my dad."

He always thought he was the smartest guy in the room, Maureen had said. *And he was rarely right*. She had outsmarted him, and paid for it.

"That's why your dad tried to hire Popeye," Jamie said quietly. "To get Maureen out of the way."

"But he didn't have the money," I said. "Guess all that booze and porn didn't leave much for murder. So you went with *plan B*."

Matt's eyes narrowed into slits.

"What was plan B, Matt? What was so terrible, after all your dad's other bullshit, that even you wouldn't go along with it? What did he ask you to do?"

"He asked me to kill him," Matt said.

I heard his words but they didn't make any sense. I gaped at Jamie to make sure he had heard the same thing, but he was still Survival Jamie, blank and impenetrable. An abyss opened beneath me.

"What are you talking about?" I said. "He wrote something about both of you surviving."

"He knew he was done. He could live down a lot of things, but stealing from kids? You don't steal from kids." Matt shook his head. "He was out of options. So he figured out how he could die a valiant death in the line of duty, go down fighting like a hero, keep his image clean, and have his pension go to my mom."

So she could buy a big stupid house she didn't want, in order to keep a corrupt, rotten replica of a beautiful dream alive.

"And someone else would go down for his murder," Jamie added. "A person everyone knew wanted him dead."

"So that's what he meant by 'survive.'" My voice cracked. It was more important to Peterson to be loved by strangers than it was to keep living. More important than the innocence of his son, who would be a murderer now forever. This was what survival meant to him, this disgusting, perverted lie. A deep stillness took me. I thought of the photograph of Peterson holding me, racing the clock against my death. It sifted to pieces, the past and all its illusions disappearing before my eyes, blown away by the inevitable wind.

"Your father was not a hero," I said. "Your father was a thief, a liar, a cheat, an abuser, and a hypocrite."

"Also a coward," Jamie said. "As are you."

"Did you do it, Matt?" I said. "Did you kill him?"

Matt's face crumpled and shook. Beads of sweat stood out on his forehead. *Please,* I thought. *Please let Matt have killed his dad in an act of righteous justice.* As messed up as that would be, at least it meant the delusions that had poisoned his dad would have bypassed Matt.

"I don't know," Matt whispered.

"You don't know if you killed him?" I said. "What does that mean?"

"I met him at the cement factory, like we agreed. I had Gina's things." I followed along in my mind, Izzy's security video playing on beyond what I saw, following Pete's squad car and Matt's Public Works truck out of the frame and toward the white space on the map.

"He called in the fake prowler." Matt's voice had a leaky edge to it, like it was melting away. "Then he kind of looked at me and got this smile on his face and said, 'Here we go, Matty. This is it. No turning back now.'

"He dropped his pepper spray, laid everything out. Made it look right." Of course he did. Pete had trained the Explorers in crime scene investigation. "Then he got in the right spot and he . . ." Matt stopped. His eyes shone. "He shot himself in the vest. Shattered his phone, his glasses. He put those out, too. All the little pieces. And Gina's pin that I'd brought for him from home.

"He was in a lot of pain by then. He was holding his side. He wasn't wounded, but it still had to hurt." Matt's face twisted.

"He gave me his gun and said, 'Okay, Matty, we're on the clock. If I don't check in soon, they'll send backup.' He seemed almost happy about it, excited. Like we were building a go-cart in the garage, or fixing the boat." His voice shattered. "That's when I couldn't . . . when I had to stop. It was like he didn't understand that he wasn't going to be here anymore." The last few words were swallowed up in a whisper. Matt was crying now. "Or maybe he did understand, and he just didn't care."

He swiped angrily at his face, leaving tracks. "I wouldn't take the gun. He got angry. He called me things. His face was . . . I didn't recognize him. He shoved the gun in my hand and said, 'Do you love me, Matty? Are you my son?'"

I reached for Jamie's hand but I couldn't find it.

"I don't remember what came next. I hated him so much at that moment. I went at him and he started to laugh. He laughed at me. We were fighting. I was choking him and he was making this sound. I didn't know anymore if I was trying to stop him or if I really was trying to kill him. And then the gun went off and I don't know who . . . I don't know which one of us . . .

"He fell. He was bleeding. The look on his face. The radio was dead and I'm sure they were trying to call him by now. I knew they would be on their way. I tried to help him and he pushed me away. He said, 'Run, you fool.' That was the last thing he said to me.

"I took his gun. I took this handkerchief I'd given him when I was a kid. It had his blood on it. I took a picture of me he always had with him. And I ran."

The air was so still it felt like we were trapped in ether—but instead of light the only thing moving across it was pain.

"And how about June?" I asked. "How about your mom?"

"She wasn't supposed to know. I was supposed to leave and let them find him, and Gina's pin, and let it unfold. But I panicked. I didn't think I could go through with it. I called my mom and she met me out by the back of the state park."

That was why June had lied about her alibi. She wasn't at the crime scene, but she was close by.

"She brought me a change of clothes. She took the gun. She took all his things so nothing could come back to me. She said she'd get rid of everything. I didn't know she would keep it. I didn't know she would take the blame. That wasn't the plan. That was not what I wanted."

I don't understand why she would do this, he had said on TV. June knew all along, from the moment her son came to her for help, what she would eventually need to do. *Do you think it's possible, truly*, she had asked me, *to do something for others?* I knew the answer now.

"There were two things you didn't count on," I said. "One, your mom loves you and would do anything to keep you safe. Two, she was smarter than your dad. She knew his stupid plan wouldn't work. How long did he think you could keep Maureen off his trail? Did he think she would just give up because he was dead?" A slow realization oozed up inside me. "Or did that miserable, selfish monster just not care, because it wouldn't be his problem anymore?"

Matt looked more like I had punched him than when I had actually punched him.

"That's why you tried to kill her with the truck," I said. "And when I got close, you tried to kill me, too." I should have realized Gina would never do something so sloppy and desperate. "But first you sneaked into my office and stole the recording of Gina threatening your dad."

"I had the recording all along." Matt had quieted now. "My dad gave it to me months ago. I was waiting for the right time to use it. When you told me Maureen was looking for the Explorer files, I knew I had to stop her fast."

A painful void opened in my chest. At every turn, I had given him what he needed. I had helped keep his dad's vile plan in play.

"I went to her house after your sister's party," Matt went on. "She had a copy of the Explorer files you found on the boat. I took them and left Gina's recording. Then Gina showed up and did the rest. I got lucky."

"But you didn't know your mom was going to interfere," Jamie said softly. His eyes were clear and dark. "How much did he steal, Matt?"

"He didn't *steal* anything." Matt leveled a glare at Jamie. "It was all going back eventually."

"Oh, God, Matt, stop lying to yourself," I said. "It's over."

"You don't get it." Matt wheeled on me. "It's not over. It was never going to be over for me, no matter what I did. I could either keep all this going and look over my shoulder for the rest of my life, or I could come out with it and be the guy who knew his dad was a disgrace to the badge and did nothing to stop him. We're the same. I am him, he is me. We are always going to be the same in everyone's eyes."

We're all stuck with him, June had said.

"At least you would have told the truth," I said.

"The truth." Matt smirked. "You think anyone gives a shit about the truth?" His voice went high and mocking. "*Your dad was your dad. We need people like him.*"

It took me a long second to realize he was imitating me.

"You were right," he said. "You helped me make up my mind that day at the crime scene. You showed me I had no choice. That I never had a choice."

I saw doors and windows banging shut in his eyes, battening against what was coming. He raised the gun. "Just like I never had a choice when I found you two trespassing on my boat. Attempting to remove private property."

You two. He still didn't know Owen was here. I prayed Owen would take my hint and stay put. Hint taking had never been Owen's strong suit.

"That would be true," Jamie said, "if this boat and everything on it belonged to you."

"My apologies for not inviting my estate lawyer to this party," Matt said. "In case you hadn't noticed, my dad's gone. It's mine now."

"The boat belongs to the First National Bank of Sandhill Lake. They repossessed it months ago."

Matt stiffened but the gun remained steady.

"And they were happy to comply with a search warrant on suspicion of evidence pertaining to the murder investigation of Lieutenant Matthew Peterson, Senior."

Matt smiled thinly. "You still don't get it, do you?" He checked Jamie's gun, tucked it into his belt. "There was no way for me to know that." He removed his own gun from his holster. "And when you failed to comply with my commands to stand down and leave the premises"—his face choked up with convincing emotion—"I truly believed my life was in danger."

A bolt of steel rooted me to the spot. He had almost convinced me there was still a drop of human being left in him—or maybe just enough of his mom to stop him. But in the slip of false emotion on his face, I saw only his dad. Survival at any cost. Even as that survival radiated destruction.

Matt firmed up the gun and took aim.

You think of the dumbest things when you're about to die. I wondered if Matt had forgotten by now that the seed of all his violence and deceit, the tiny red heart in this sea of blood, was love. It drove me mad with rage that I was about to die in the name of love's poisonous, polluted mirror image when there was real love in the world that went unrecognized, unappreciated, until it was too late. June's love for her son. My love for Owen, for Jessie, for . . .

Jamie's hand crept into mine. Time slowed to a stop.

A deafening roar split the air and for an instant I was convinced the sound was coming from me.

Behind Matt, behind the black muzzle of the gun, the *American Lotus* lurched to life.

38

"This is where the Tower comes in. Total and complete upheaval." The windows of the Tower were on fire. People with twisted faces were pitching out of it.

"Is it pleasant? Is it fun?" Rosie said. "No. It sucks balls. But you need it, if you're going to shake that illusion loose."

We had rounded the corner on the second row of the Major Arcana, and were starting the third. In the space movie, the astronaut was hurtling through a shapeless photo-negative void, all cosmic paint spills and inkblots. It was pulling him apart. His agonized face flashed on and off screen.

"Whoa," Rosie said. "That dude is really going through it."

"One time," I said, "Jessie and I kept asking Mom to take us roller-skating, and she kept saying *we'll see, we'll see*, until we finally figured out she was never going to take us roller-skating. She just wanted us to leave her alone." I scratched my head. "Like that? Is that an illusion?"

"That your mom would enjoy roller-skating?" Rosie said.

"Yeah, I'd say that qualifies. Classic mom move, though. How'd you feel when she did that?"

"Bad! Like she'd tricked us." I thought about it. "But then kind of good. Like, I'd figured out her trick and I wasn't falling for it again." I thought about it some more. "And now I didn't have to be disappointed."

"Yes!" Rosie reached over and gave me a sloppy high five. "And that, my friend, is the Tower. It sucks going through it, but you come out smarter, more realistic, and more balanced on the other side."

Now the space kaleidoscope was gone and the astronaut flew over the surface of a dark planet. Its midnight-colored peaks and valleys flew on and on, no end in sight.

"Illusion," Rosie said. "Wake up and let that shit go, or you can't move on."

Matt's gun snapped off of us and toward the boat. "Who the hell is that?" he roared over the engine noise. "Who's in there?"

"I'm Owen," said a tiny, muffled voice. "Nice to meet you."

"Turn off my boat and come out with your hands up," Matt shouted hoarsely.

"First of all, it's not your boat—"

"*Now*," Matt snapped.

I tripped and fell against the post. The noise was a thick wall of danger, like a herd of predators rumbling through a forest. I needed it to stop. My body constricted. I pressed myself against the post and something stabbed me, a rough spike in my back pocket.

Owen's lock-picking tool.

I went stiff. Was the sharpness real or a panic-induced tactile hallucination? I stretched and pulled my hand down into my pocket as far as the cuffs would allow, tearing at my already shredded knuckles. The cuffs bit into my skin. My fingers closed on the tool and I pulled it out, wrists pulsing.

"Jamie," I whispered in his ear. He shifted toward me. "Take this." I shoved the metal spike at him. His fingers closed on it. "For the cuffs." I shut my eyes against everything that could go wrong with this plan. It wasn't even a plan, just a stab in the dark.

The engine noise rose to a sick, coughing whine. A bitter, dangerous smell wound through the air.

"I'm going to count to three," Matt shouted. "And then I will shoot."

I could feel Jamie behind me, pushing, pulling, twisting. A few clicks and whirrs, and my cuffs sprang loose.

"Keep still," Jamie whispered. "Pretend you're still cuffed." He moved his hands toward me. "Now do mine."

An oily panic rolled through me. I had stupidly assumed my part in this was over. "I can't. I don't know how." My mind was clouding over, shutting down.

"You can," Jamie said. "Katie. You can."

I felt for the pick. Jamie moved his cuffs toward me and I scraped the tool across it, found an opening. The pick went in, clicked around uselessly.

"Keep it straight," Jamie whispered. "Feel for a little resistance. A little bounce. When you feel it, turn to the left. If you don't feel it, take it out and try again."

"One . . ." Matt shouted.

"He's going to shoot him, Jamie."

"He won't," Jamie said. "Katie. You've got this. Try it again."

"Two . . ."

Everything went black. I closed my eyes, shut off my shrieking mind, and felt with my fingers. There was the spring, the bounce, just like Jamie had described.

Turn. Click. Jamie's cuffs fell away.

"Get Owen and run," Jamie said. Then he was gone.

"Three!"

Jamie lunged at Matt, slammed him forward into the hull of the boat. Matt swung wildly, punching the air. They crashed to the floor and Matt's head snapped back. They grappled for the gun. Deafening shots echoed around the cavern and whined off the walls, rising like screams above the noise. The boat's blue shrink-wrap tore and buckled.

"Owen!" I couldn't hear my own voice over the engine and the ringing in my ears from the gunshots. Jamie and Matt wrestled on the concrete. I flew past them into the blue bubble of the boat.

The boat was empty. "Owen, where are you?" The smell in there was indescribable, an evil, poisonous plastic burning that smelled like the foyer of hell.

"Down here," a voice said. Owen had wedged himself into the ski locker. "I'm stuck." A foot popped up into the air. I dropped to the floor and pulled. Owen's body was jammed into the ski locker like a set of jumbled doll parts in a cardboard box. Wedging his weirdly flexible ferret body into tight spaces had always been one of Owen's special talents. Getting out of said spaces, less so. We would find him folded into human origami between banister poles, inside washing machines, around playground equipment, and, on one memorable occasion, in a parakeet cage in a PetSmart.

I had freed one leg and was working on the next when a shower of bullets ripped up the shrink-wrap inches above my head. I flattened myself over Owen. My lungs screamed.

"Owen, how the hell do I turn this thing off? It's going to blow up!" I lunged toward the controls but another shot knocked me down.

"It's not going to blow up. That only happens in movies," Owen said. "The impeller might burn out, which is probably what's happening right now." He tried to scratch his nose but his arm was still wedged in the locker. "Although if the engine heated up sufficiently and there was a direct hit on the gas tank, it might—"

Fwoom! Heat rolled through the boat from underneath.

"—catch fire," Owen finished. Crackles and pops rolled through the cabin, like a giant munching on cereal. The sharp chemical smell intensified. My face was burning from the inside.

I scrabbled at Owen—arms, legs, anything I could get my hands on. An oily fog darkened the blue air. I tried to shout and could produce only wet, oily hacks that shook my whole body. Owen was coughing, too, tiny kid-like barks. I tore off my sweatshirt and stuffed it over his face. "Breathe through this," I wheezed.

Everything was dimming, either in my eyes or in the cabin. I couldn't see Owen anymore, I could only feel him hanging on to me. Another yank and he was out. We rolled over each other toward the zippered door.

Hands grabbed me, pulled me out of the boat. I sucked in a breath, but the air wasn't much clearer here. I collapsed on the oily concrete, choking.

The hands pulled me up to my knees. I pushed Owen away. "Run!" Out of the corner of my eye I watched Owen stoop in the corner, pulling on a twisted body.

Matt stepped in front of me, shutting off the light. I could see only his face. I shoved at him but he knocked me to the floor. He was covered in oil, soot, blood, tears. He looked like a kid who had been ordered by the adults in charge to stay put, sit here on this rock by the path, don't go into the forest. But he had wandered off, like kids do, and now he was lost. And worse, he knew he was in trouble for disobeying, but he had to keep walking, keep moving farther into the dark because the path home was gone.

"Matt . . ." My throat was full of needles and the sound that came out was a whisper. "Stop. You don't want to . . ."

His face slipped away and re-formed, and now we were in my backyard playing cops and robbers. Time had looped on itself but it was a wrong, misshapen loop like a stuck record or a wounded animal biting its own back to stop the pain. The strength was leaving my body. It was so easy to lie down, stop fighting, watch him pick up the gun. When he put it to my head the hot metal woke me up and I thought, *no*, but the gun was so close I couldn't see it anymore. You never saw what was right in front of you, I thought. That's why we needed help. That's why we needed other people.

I squeezed my eyes shut.

"Let go of her, Matthew," a woman said. My eyes flew open. The burning gun slipped off me. Behind it, the silent room was aflame. A woman in crimson and white stepped down off a fiery throne. She wore a crown of stars.

The Empress.

I flipped over, scrabbled to my knees, crawled away, collapsed. The world crashed in on me. Voices shouted: *June, get back, get away from him.* And then, *Put down the gun, put it down, hands up. Matthew Peterson, Junior, you are under arrest . . .*

June knelt beside Matt and plucked the gun from his hands. He let it slide away, hands still curled around something that wasn't there.

"I tried to help him." His voice was thick. "I tried to save him."

"Matty." June closed her hands around his. "The man you wanted to save, that wonderful man we loved . . . he was gone years ago." She took his head in her hands and put it on her shoulder, wiped his face. "Let him go."

Matt said something but his voice was muffled by fabric and tears. "I just wanted to be . . ." I heard Matt say. His shoulders were shaking.

"I know you did," June said. "But you're *not* like him. You're better."

The last thing I saw before the world ended was the mother and her son locked around each other while everything around them burned.

The oxygen mask on my face smelled like plastic and wet dog. I was lying on the cold ground with my soot-stained coat draped over me. I shook it off and tried to sit up.

"Take it easy, now," a high voice said in a no-nonsense brogue. A miniature woman who looked to be in middle school adjusted my oxygen mask. "I'm Clodagh," she said. "Let's check the damage, eh?"

The Sandhill Marine parking lot drifted into focus. Figures moved in front of me like in an old-fashioned film, too fast. Everything had a sharp, bright halo around it. Cop cars, ambulances. A tow truck stood in the lot's exit lane, pulling behind it the blackened husk of the *American Lotus*. The polished red hull was riddled with bullet holes, the flowery script burned away to one word: *American*.

I tore the oxygen mask off my face and tried to scratch out my burning eyes until Clodagh told me to stop. Dizziness spun the world around me. Across the lot, Matt sat in the back of a police car with its door open. June, standing next to him, held his hand.

A cop in a Lake County Sheriff's uniform stood off to the side with his arms folded.

"Where's Jamie?" I said. All I could manage was a snaky hiss. "Where's Owen?" I tried to get up, regretted it immediately. My head spun. I sat back down and closed my eyes.

"He's fine," a familiar voice said. "Can't get rid of him that easy." Dan squatted down next to me.

"Pulse," Clodagh said. I offered my wrist like a limp fish and she took it with cool, businesslike fingers.

Across the lot I could see techs loading Jamie onto a stretcher. Owen loped along next to them, jabbering. Being trapped in the ski locker must have shielded him from the brunt of the smoke. He looked a hell of a lot better than I felt.

"Jamie called me," Dan said. "Explained everything. Told me to come with a team. And June."

"Let's go through your symptoms, kiddo," Clodagh said. *Kiddo?* I thought. *You're twelve.* "Just nod yes or no. Dizzy?" She was holding a clipboard.

I nodded.

"He said June's confession was false," Dan continued. "And that she was covering for Matt. Of course, I didn't believe him right away. Matt's a good cop." Dan wiped his face. He looked tired. "Talk about a bad apple."

I stumbled up, tripped over to a nearby oil drum garbage can, and yakked into it as neatly as I could.

"Nausea," Clodagh said briskly, scratching the clipboard with a pen. "Yes."

"Jamie's a good cop, too." Dan looked more disgusted at admitting this than at seeing the inside of my digestive tract. "Besides, he told me if he was wrong, he'd owe me an Orvis Superfine Glass rod."

He watched the cops close the car door on Matt. "They're

going to have to start the party without me." He sighed heavily and checked his watch. "If I don't make the evening AA meeting my wife will kill me." He grimaced. "Apparently I'm still struggling with step one: admitting I'm powerless."

A white van with the logo of the local ABC News affiliate pulled into the lot. A woman in a bright blue wool coat jumped out of it, followed by a cameraman.

"Aw, Christ," Dan said. "Who the fuck called these guys?" Finally, a glimpse of the real Dan underneath Commander Kaluza. I liked Real Dan a lot better.

"Hey! Hi!" Dan jogged toward the press team. "We're not taking questions right now, but communicating with the public, once we're ready, will be our first priority."

And there went Real Dan. Before he disappeared he turned back to me one last time, his TV grin already shellacked to his face. "This is going to be a PR nightmare," he said through his teeth.

I smiled. I was counting on it.

39

"I love this one." Rosie picked up the Star. "The nice thing is after the storm comes the rainbow, right? Peace." On the card, white diamond stars flashed in the sky around a yellow supernova. A woman poured sky-colored water into the earth. "This card says: for the moment, the road can wait."

On TV, the astronaut was in a glowing white room full of old-fashioned furniture, still as a museum.

"The Moon." Rosie squinted at the next card, looked at it from all sides like it was one of those lenticular stickers you get in goody bags at birthday parties. There were no people in the Moon card, only howling beasts and creepy-crawlies under the dreaming face in the sky.

"The Star's moment of stillness opens you up to the Moon's imagination. Creativity," Rosie said. "It can be weird and scary—I don't know about you, but lobsters creep me the hell out—but it's also fertile. That's why they named menstruation after it." She tapped the card. "You can't give birth unless you bleed for a week out of every month first, right?"

"Unless you do *what*?"

"Oh, shit. Ask your mom. Anyway," Rosie said, "you take the creativity the Moon gives you, and you act." The Sun was the brightest card I had ever seen, all triumphant yellow light. "You get back on that horse, just like this tiny naked weirdo." Rosie pointed to the flower-haired child on the card. "Back to the road, full speed ahead."

After the bright celestial sequence of the Moon, the Star, and the Sun, the zombie apocalypse on the Judgment card seemed like kind of a letdown.

"Aw," I said. "How many times am I going to have to die?"

"You're not dying here," Rosie said. "Just looking back on how far you came. Sometimes it's hard to see that when you're in the middle of the road. So you stop and turn around. This one looks gnarly, but it's actually kind of sweet. Like standing on a hill and seeing all the twists and turns you took behind you. Some of them had apple orchards you could sneak into and grab some free apples, and others were full of grouchy old cops who kept telling you to move along, you goddamn hippies. But they were all part of your road and you better accept all of them if you're going to get where you're going."

The astronaut was looking in a mirror. The face staring back at him was scarred with age.

"He's old." I sucked in my breath. "When did he get old?"

Rosie laughed her airy cascade of a laugh. "Ain't *that* the way it goes, kiddo."

Now the astronaut was a dapper old man in a long black suit. He turned to look behind him. Who was that? Where did he go? His younger self was gone. Now he was an old man, dying in a big bed, and then he was gone and in his place was a silvery orb, a luminous baby waiting to be born. The baby's face was smooth as starlight. It drifted back toward earth.

40

The poster of Peterson at the Sandhill Lake Metra station had big spidery black letters spray-painted across its face: LOSER.

"Fourth one so far," I said.

"You'd think after five months they'd start slowing down," Jamie said. "I think they're enjoying hating him more than they enjoyed—"

My phone went off for the third time in fifteen minutes. I checked the number and sent it to voicemail.

"Speaking of not slowing down," Jamie said. "Another new customer?"

"Probably." I put my phone away. Every time it rang, I wondered if it would be Jessie. It never was.

In my smoke-choked moment of trauma during Matt's arrest, a reporter had sneaked past Dan and got a video "interview" with me. I remembered very little of it. Apparently it consisted of my claims to have solved the entire case by myself, with my tarot cards and general psychicness. I may have also mentioned Peterson's ghost and the sudden miraculous appearance of the Empress. The video went viral. Needless to say, it was one of the many reasons I was currently not popular with Dan and the entire law enforcement establishment of Lake County, not to mention a host of national law enforcement agencies. On the upside, the video got me a rush of new customers who were either undeterred by the possibility that I might be a kook or actively encouraged by it. I didn't have a reading room anymore, but at least I was doing readings again—real ones. It felt good.

The victimology process had dragged on for months, grinding through emails, texts (some recovered from deletion through mysterious high-tech government means), and hours of interviews with anyone Peterson had ever talked to. Together with findings from forensics and pathology, the investigation concluded that Peterson, with Matt's knowledge and assistance, had embezzled close to twenty thousand dollars from the Sandhill Lake chapter of the Law Enforcement Explorers over the course of seven years, supported by the general laxness and incompetence of the Sandhill Lake Police Department. It proved that Pete, knowing Maureen was on to him, had tried to neutralize her and when that didn't work, convinced Matt to help him stage an honorable death in the line of duty that would guarantee his pension for June, wipe out all his debts, and assure his place in the pantheon of local heroes, world without end, amen. It proved that Matt, in his attempt to keep the cover-up going, had deleted the photo evidence Maureen had snapped on the *American Lotus* and replaced it with the incriminating voice recording of Gina.

Basically, it would have all come out eventually.

Still, I thought with a shiver, I had figured it out first.

"Did Pete really believe," I asked Jamie as we skirted Sandhill

Lake, "that no one would figure it out?" The lake streamed with boats and families enjoying the last weeks of the season.

"I think he figured even if he was found out, it wouldn't be for months. By then he would have had all the fanfare and the big fancy funeral, and that's all anyone would remember," Jamie said. "The rest would just be a footnote. Nobody reads the footnotes."

Jamie had escaped the scuffle at the marina with a dislocated shoulder and a bullet graze to the midsection. In other ways, he didn't get off so easy. He seemed softer, sadder. I would catch him brooding. Broody Jamie was not a Jamie I had ever met before.

June went through a wringer of interviews meant to determine exactly what she knew and when. She was cleared of any knowledge of Pete's financial tomfoolery or involvement in his murder, though there was no getting around her role in Matt's cover-up— a major legal no-no trailing all manner of terrible consequential strings.

And yet, as the rude messages and defacements of Pete's posters were popping up all over town, so were flowers outside June's house, heart-studded cards made by local schoolkids, gifts and tributes and messages of love and support. The media hopped on board and cranked up the volume on the story of the honest-to-a-fault, long-neglected wife and mother sacrificing everything for her son. THE REAL HERO, shouted the headline of a *Lake County News-Sun* feature, over a scrapbook-worthy shot of June staring wistfully at a Sandhill Lake sunrise. When the village, after months of debate, voted to award Peterson's pension to June after all, despite his death being in no way "honorable" or "in the line of duty," it was clear the court of public opinion would be the only one to hear June's case.

"The state's attorney won't touch her with a ten-foot pole now," Jamie had said, reading the article. "They won't bring it to trial if they know they can't win."

Now Jamie parked in front of a cheery salmon-colored house-style building across from Birdie's. Both sat at the end of the downtown street that ran into the lake, each with a deck and stairs leading to a pier. JUNE'S TREASURES, read the store sign. A GRAND OPENING banner trailed over the door. June had used Peterson's pension to open a brick-and-mortar shop in downtown Sandhill Lake, to sell her jewelry, decor, artwork, and clothing.

The store was a dark, cozy jumble of rooms full of overstuffed armchairs, jewelry trees, mannequins decked out in bright, flow-ery clothing. It smelled like spices and incense. A lively crowd checked out June's work and nibbled at a huge spread of pastries from Birdie's. I looked for Izzy but couldn't find him or June anywhere. Most of the guests were recognizable from Jessie's real estate event months before, except this time they were having fun.

I snagged a chocolate chip cookie, left Jamie talking to Dan, and went out onto a back deck lined with gold and silver hanging butterfly lights.

Gina sat alone in a sky blue Adirondack chair facing the lake. She wore a floppy, wide-brimmed hat and giant star-shaped sun-glasses that made her look like the fanciest-ever World War II bomber pilot. She sipped from one of the plastic cups June had put out, grimacing with every swallow.

"Have you tried this shit?" She lifted her sunglasses. "Kombu-cha. It is so freaking terrible I can't stop drinking it." She offered me the cup. "Want some?"

"Tempting, but no." I sat down in the chair next to her and offered half my cookie.

She let her sunglasses fall back into place. "Man, people have really turned on Pete." A speedboat raced past us. Gina watched the wake unfurl behind it. "I thought it would make me happy, but it just makes it worse." She took a disgusted sip. "Where were all you assholes before?"

The Sandhill Lake PD staff was fired nearly in its entirety after an investigation by an independent internal affairs commission. Dan had been right to expect a PR nightmare. We watched him shout down reporters during hot, loud press conferences under harsh lights in rooms with ugly curtains. He couldn't seem to do anything right. His people pushed the bad apple angle hard, but it was tougher to do with every new piece of slime that crawled out from under Peterson's crumbling reputation. Allegations of alcohol abuse on the job, suspensions for procedural sloppiness, countless accounts of sexual harassment. Everyone had some juicy story, in a dark reversal of the hysterical hero-worship that had so disturbed Jamie when the case began. *Oh yeah*, it became fashionable to say. *I knew all along he was a piece of shit.*

"I heard about those other women talking to the news," I told Gina.

"Yeah, they came to me, too." Gina put the cup down. "You know how I love to wallow in the fetid swamp of the past, but I had to pass." She gave a little headshake. "At least it's out there. Not that anything will change."

She got up and walked to the rail. "You know, I spent so much time being mad at Maureen for choosing Pete over the right thing." She shrugged. "I guess she chose the right thing after all. And it cost her."

Gina watched the speedboat go back the other way, then turned to me. "How about you? I hear you've got more business than you can handle."

"I just wish I had a better place to conduct it than the Star-bucks with the overflowing toilet on 60," I said. "At least they give me free coffee."

"You talk to Jessie yet?"

"She still hasn't called." I popped the remains of the cookie into my mouth. "I think I broke her this time. She sublet the Lake Terrace Estates place to, get this, a hobby shop. To Jessie, there is nothing lower or more shameful than a hobby shop. I think she did it as a fuck-you to me."

"You could call *her*," Gina said.

"Who do you think you're talking to, an emotionally mature adult?"

"Excuse me." A tall redhead had slid open the glass door to the deck. There was something familiar about her build and the way she moved. "I'm Renee Loeffler," the woman said. "Maureen's daughter. Are you Gina?"

"That's me." Gina stood up. Neither woman looked like they knew what to do next. Renee stepped toward Gina, and Gina stepped back. Renee moved forward and clasped Gina in a hug. Gina looked like someone had punched her. Renee whispered something in Gina's ear, and for the first time since I walked onto the dock I saw Gina's body relax, go still. She put her arms around Renee. A flash of light bounced off her star glasses.

"I know she did," Gina said to Renee. "I did, too."

I went back inside and found June in a workroom off the main space, bent over a table heaped with thread, colored silk, beads, sequins, ceramic, and glass. She had a magnifying glass strapped to her forehead and was using tiny forceps to glue emerald green feather flakes to the body of a hummingbird.

"You should be celebrating," I said.

June smiled without looking up. "I am celebrating." She lifted the half-finished bird to me. "I'm making this for Izzy."

"It's beautiful." I sat down across from her at the table. "Where is Izzy anyway?"

"He's around here somewhere." June slipped a feather into place and regarded the bird. "I think I like them better when they're not finished," she said. "I like seeing the in-between stages." The hummingbird's feathers shone a deep, true green. Even unfinished, it looked real, like any second it would raise its wings and disappear. "Anything worth doing takes time. Work. Change." The magnifying glass made June look owlish and celestial. "If it doesn't change," she said, "it's not beautiful."

"How have you been?" I said.

"I'm good," she said. "Matt moved back to the house while we wait for the *process*. We're getting along better than ever now, isn't that strange? We still have some making up to do, but that's okay. We have all the time in the world." I watched her knit something beautiful together, feather by jeweled feather, out of sheer patience and attention. I knew she and Matt would be okay.

The investigation had ruled Peterson's death a suicide. Forensics and pathology found inconsistencies in the crime scene and on Peterson's body, which, combined with Matt's cooperative account of his dad's final minutes, determined that the deadly shot was delivered by Peterson to himself. Matt was cleared of his father's murder.

He was, however, still on the hook for the murder of Maureen, as well as a myriad of other charges that were basically fancy names for criminally punishable stealing and lying. I hadn't seen Matt since that cold, windy day at the marina, and I didn't want to. As bad as the look on his face while he was trying to choke the life out of me was the reminder of all the things I didn't—or chose not to—see. I wondered if he had ever had feelings for me or if he just saw a convenient way to get what he wanted. I didn't know which option made me sicker.

"The lawyers say he'll definitely have to serve time, but they're trying to get it reduced." June scratched her head. "I can afford lawyers now." She giggled. "Pete is literally paying to get Matt out of the mess he put him in."

"Kind of looks like Pete is paying for everything." I looked around. "This place is great, by the way," I said. "It feels like home. I'm going to come up here to take naps."

"I might offer classes," June said. "Glassblowing, jewelry making. For kids, or maybe some of those cocktails-and-art evenings for the ladies. I have all kinds of ideas. You're not going to believe this, but the Explorers asked me if I wanted to lead them." She laughed. "Can you imagine? I told them thank you very much but I was done with all that. I did tell them they could use the store for meetings anytime, though."

After all that had happened, June was running the community center Pete had always envisioned. A real one, without all the stealing and lying and murder.

"I might even offer tarot readings," she said. "If I can find a good reader." She lifted an eyebrow at me.

"You're kidding," I said. "Really?"

She shrugged. "I can't do *everything* myself."

I excused myself and went looking for Izzy, but he was still MIA. Gina sidled up to me. Her hat had slipped off her head, making her look like a blowsy pharmaceutical heiress.

"Hey, so I was talking to Renee," Gina said. "She's very cool. But even better than that, she said Maureen had built up a pretty sizable nest egg and left it all to Renee. She has like, thirty children, and she wants to make the move up from the city. Get a bigger house. An upgrade, of sorts." Gina gave me a sordid wink. "Perhaps to Baines Hill."

"Okay," I said.

Gina shoved her hat back up on her head. "And she's going to need a good real estate agent. Someone local who really knows their stuff."

"Shouldn't be tough to find one around here."

"Jessie," Gina said. "I'm talking about Jessie, you dope. What is wrong with you?" She grabbed my phone out of my pocket and smacked me with it. "Call Jessie and tell her to get her Brazilian-waxed ass over here right now if she wants to make some god-damn money."

Jessie was cool and sniffy through my initial awkward greeting but warmed up quickly when I explained the situation. Thirty minutes later she was walking in the door, looking spectacularly overdressed in a strappy sundress with oddly shaped cutouts.

"Oh!" She looked around with a pasty smile. "Isn't this inter-esting!" She side-eyed the plastic cups of kombucha laid out on the refreshment table.

I opened my mouth to say I was sorry, but Jessie spoke first. "I owe you an apology," she said.

"You what?"

"I think that maybe I, um, haven't been a very good listener." Jessie moved a strand of hair out of her eye. When she was ner-vous, she played with her hair. "You know, because half the stuff you say is nonsense and I usually tune it out."

"I am really loving this apology," I said. "Please continue."

"That's it," Jessie said. "I don't have anything else. Except that maybe it's okay for us to be different from each other."

"I'm sorry, too," I said. "I think we've both learned something."

"Yeah," she said. "That we should never work together again."

"It's a deal." I hugged her. Jessie put her arms around me and I felt warm, like the sun was shining on my back even though we were inside.

"I saw your video," Jessie said. "You know, if you wanted to build a social media brand I could—"

"Don't even think about it," I said.

"Yep. Yep. I know." Jessie released me. "You're right."

I glanced over Jessie's shoulder through the front window. Across the street at Birdie's, the cash register was unmanned.

I excused myself and darted over. I found Izzy standing on a rickety stepladder next to his wall of fame, rearranging photos. The grease-spattered cardboard box on the rung below him was labeled DOORKNOBS AND FORKS. He was tossing photographs into it.

"Doing some redecorating?"

"Yes." Izzy scowled with concentration. "We need a little more color. And maybe a little less of this stealing, murdering cretin." Pictures of Officer Pete were, one by one, leaving the wall and going to live with the doorknobs and forks where they, apparently, belonged. They left behind a void shaped like a squished rhino.

"I'm sorry." I wished there was something less ordinary to say.

"Eh." Izzy shrugged. "How do my grandkids say it—disappointed, not surprised? I've seen a lot worse." He took down a picture and paused to look. For a brief second a smile flashed in his eyes, but then he tossed the picture aside. "I just hoped never to see it again."

Izzy put his hands on his hips and surveyed his work. "He was a crook," he said in a dreamy aside. He sounded like he was standing back and admiring a painting. "Worse than a crook. At least a crook who doesn't pretend he's not a crook is honest."

"As crooks tend to be," I said.

"He was pretending." Izzy shook an index finger at me. The ladder wobbled distressingly. "He took all these things people believed in—and I'm not saying they're all smart things—but he took all these nice, pretty, fancy ideas and used them against honest people."

He turned back to the wall and his lips squeezed shut. "You put up too many pictures and statues and things of one person, it never ends well." He yanked three pictures off the wall in a line. One tore. "Read some history books.

"Oh!" His face lit up. "This one's got you in it." He plucked a photo off the wall and handed it to me. It was the car accident picture. "I have to save this one, at least."

"Do you, really?" I groaned and handed the picture back. "I think that picture belongs with the doorknobs and forks."

"But you're a celebrity now." Izzy tacked the photo back up in the middle of the rhino void. "I was going to give you a whole section."

"Didn't we just decide too many pictures of one person is creepy?"

Izzy clapped his hands. "I know what we will do." He searched the wall and found a picture of a red-bellied woodpecker that looked like it had just robbed a bank. He took it down, folded it to size and shape, and tacked the woodpecker's head onto Officer Pete's. Now my infant life was being saved by a giant woodpecker.

"Now that," I said, "I can live with."

Back at June's, I found Jamie out on the dock where Gina had been. The sun was low and red in the west now, sharpening Baines Hill against the horizon. The playground below buzzed with the noise of kids playing, and down the shore, music and laughter drifted from a dockside bar.

"Excuse me, is this the brooding area?" I sat down next to Jamie. "I looked for it in the bathroom but I just found a bunch of people snorting coke."

"You know," Jamie said, "not to say I knew it all along, but something about this case hit me wrong from the very beginning."

"I can confirm you were extremely cranky about it." I handed him a cookie. He waited to start eating until I gave him a cocktail napkin.

"I thought maybe I was jealous," he said. "I could be a cop for a hundred years, and I would never achieve that level of adoration."

I took the cookie back from him and tore off a piece. "You don't strike me as the kind of person who thrives on adoration."

"That's the thing." He slapped crumbs off his hands. "Maybe he wasn't either. Maybe once you get a taste for it, you're done for." He turned to me. "I guess I just wonder if I would have been any different, given the same circumstances."

He looked genuinely upset and it made me feel not happy exactly, but special and trusted. I was the only one to whom Jamie would admit how much his job bothered him sometimes. I felt honored, satisfyingly responsible.

"I don't know," I said. "But if *you* wouldn't be any different, none of us would." I gave him the other cookie I was hiding in my pocket for later.

He accepted the cookie, broke it in two, and gave me half back. "People really loved this guy. Those kids, for example." He looked at me. "Even you, in your own weird way."

"That was a long time ago," I said. "Things change." *If it doesn't change, it's not beautiful,* June had said. "My aunt Rosie used to say something like that, too."

"She taught you to read the cards, right?" Jamie said. "What was she like?"

I thought about Rosie all the time, but I didn't talk about her much. When I did, most people dismissed her as a borderline-abusive weirdo, or said, Doesn't she sound interesting, and moved on. I had stopped years ago trying to explain that Rosie had created me.

I had wispy memories of a long afternoon where Rosie took

me through the whole Major Arcana, explained each card, tied them together into a long shining chain. At the end was the World, an air dancer wrapped in fluttering silk. There was a roundness to the card, a completeness. *Take every step*, Rosie had said. *If you fixate on the past, you get stuck there. The past is gone. Keep moving.* Then she had moved the cards into a wide circle, the World next to the Fool, round and round in an eternal loop, and for a split second I had felt the earth's spin, one tiny rotation in a universe of others, planets and stars and galaxies forever spinning around one another, forever in motion. *The road may be a circle*, she said, *but it only moves one way.*

Jamie was waiting for me to answer.

"Well." I took a breath and watched the sun sink into the lake. "She used to say that life was a road, and the cards, the major ones, were like road markers."

I felt a shiver of déjà vu. Jamie's mirror dream flashed around me, turning the air silvery and strange. Without thinking, I put up my palm.

"What is this?" Jamie held his palm up instinctively to mine. "Are we playing a game? Is this part of the lesson?"

I pushed gently against his palm, tested the boundary. His face softened, like he had just remembered something. I twined his fingers through mine.

"You start with the Fool," I said. We watched blue dark fall over the water. "The Fool is special."

AUTHOR'S NOTE

This is a work of fiction.

You've breezed past this line in the legal gobbledygook at the front of countless books, but it bears repeating when the work of fiction is inspired by true events, in this case, the death of police lieutenant Joseph "G.I. Joe" Gliniewicz in Fox Lake, Illinois, on September 1, 2015.

The idea of putting my sticky fingers all over real people's experiences in order to represent "the truth" has always made me a bit queasy. It's an impossible task: all writing is fabrication, even when—*especially* when—it claims to start with the truth. What is the truth, after all, if not a string of sensory information filtered through imagination and squeezed into pre-existing patterns? In other words, another story.

Katie's adventures have always been, for me, about the dazzling and dangerous tendency of the human mind to shape reality through storytelling. This time it seemed especially appropriate to embrace the inevitability of fiction and write this story from scratch, keeping only the emotions and ideas that the aftermath of Gliniewicz's death inspired in me. Peterson is not Gliniewicz, his family is not Gliniewicz's family, and his victims are not Gliniewicz's victims. Those stories belong only to the people involved. This one, on the other hand, is all mine. It would be easier to point out the few real-world details still rattling around in it than it would be to list everything I made up.

But why bother? You weren't there, and although I was closer than you, neither was I—not really. The facts, as Katie says, are gone. The stories are all that's left. I hope you enjoyed this one.

ACKNOWLEDGMENTS

To my family, near and far, thank you for your steadfast love and support. Brian, Leo, and Tammy, thank you for tolerating me as I hashed out plot points at the kitchen table.

Thank you to my agent, Joanna MacKenzie, who put me on this merry-go-round and keeps it spinning with kindness and grace. To my editor, Jenny Chen, and her team, thank you for shepherding this cranky, difficult book into its best shape. I remain grateful to you for continuing to teach me to write.

Thank you to George Filenko, retired commander of the Lake County Major Crime Task Force, and retired Vernon Hills Police Department commander Andy Jones, whose heartfelt accounts of investigating the death of Joe Gliniewicz were hugely instrumental in my connection to the story behind the story, even as I was busy tossing the facts out the window. Thank you to Crime Prevention Officer Jeff Hemesath at the VHPD for help filling in procedural details.

For tarot background, I leaned heavily on Rachel Pollack's *Seventy-Eight Degrees of Wisdom*, a fascinating resource for anyone interested in tarot, not just those pretending to know something about it. Pollack's insights into card interpretation, especially with respect to the sequential nature of the Major Arcana, often found themselves tumbling from Aunt Rosie's lips.

I owe the crew at Arrow Marine in Fox Lake, Illinois, a hearty thanks for their friendly, enthusiastic explanation of boating basics to this lifelong landlubber.

Thank you to the real Kate True, who was nothing like Katie, but indirectly inspired her by being one of the first people I knew to successfully blend an artistic life with everything else life demands. Consciously or not, this struggle bubbled away in my mind when I first started writing, and found its way onto the page as a tribute to Kate's kindness, peace, grace, and enormous creativity, now sadly gone from the world. She will be missed.

To my community of crime fiction oddballs: there are too many of you to name, but you astonish me every day with your kindness, brilliance, humor, honesty, and guts. Thank you for convincing me (finally) that writing does not have to be a solitary activity. I never thought I'd find you, but here you are.

To that end, thank you also to the readers who see themselves in Katie and reach out to tell me so. Writing for me has always come partially from a place of loneliness; thank you for the opportunity to create something that makes all of us a little less alone.

ABOUT THE AUTHOR

LINA CHERN's debut mystery novel, *Play the Fool*, won the 2024 Mary Higgins Clark Award and was nominated for the 2024 Lefty and Anthony Awards. Her shorter work has appeared in *Mystery Weekly*, *The Marlboro Review*, *The Bellingham Review*, *Black Fox Literary Magazine*, and *The Coil*. She lives in the Chicago area with her family.

linachern.com
Instagram: @linachernwrites
Bluesky: @linachern.bsky.social

ABOUT THE TYPE

This book was set in Electra, a typeface designed for Linotype by W. A. Dwiggins, the renowned type designer (1880–1956). Electra is a fluid typeface, avoiding the contrasts of thick and thin strokes that are prevalent in most modern typefaces.